Sleeping Sapphire

T J Gristwood

This book is dedicated to my husband, Darren, who has always pushed me to feel more and do more with this wonderful life.

Musical inspiration whilst writing this book:

'Hoopy Frood' – Psychonaut and Indigo
'Lights and Shadows' – Deep House
'Aura XV' – Fat Ken
'What I Might Do' – Ben Pearce
'Beautiful' – House Music
'Look Right Through' – Storm Queen
Teleportation into Outer Space
Asura
Vibrasphere
Disclosure
Rudimental
'Equinoxe' – Jean Michel Jarre
And many more!

Chapter One

Sapphire Whittaker lay on her back, head resting on soft feather pillows, her body cocooned comfortably under the duvet. She breathed calmly and evenly, making her hands – which were placed gently on her chest above the covers – rise and fall with each soft breath. The room was dark except for a sliver of moonlight that cast a silver-grey line across the end of her bed.

Her bedroom window was open just a fraction. She could never sleep within a closed room; fresh air was important for her mind to feel capable of rest. The night air was cool and a soft breeze caressed her face as it blew the curtains gently back and forth. The sound of the fabric touching the window ledge created a rhythmic sense of white noise. Despite the impression of sleep she was in fact quite awake; her mind was active but not anxious, her thoughts drifting across her mind with the same questions and patterns she had been experiencing frequently of late.

This night, the night of the summer solstice, she asked herself the same question again. "Will I see him again tonight? Will he be there in my dreams?" She smiled softly, her full pink lips lifting as if being teased slightly at the corners. "God, I hope so," she said. She took one last deep breath, allowed her mind to wander across the day's events ... tasks to do, places she would like to be ... until eventually, slowly, without being consciously aware, she slipped into a place where two worlds collided: a place of deep sleep and a place of dreaming.

And so it began, again.

Sapphire was now aware of being outside. It was cool, the same temperature it had been when she had closed her eyes in her bedroom. Dark surrounded her. She blinked twice, her big blue eyes growing accustomed to the darkness and her pupils dilating to help her see more clearly. Her senses began to kick in; her feet were naked and she was standing on wet grass. She could feel the cool strands between her toes and the sensation was deeply grounding. She could sense clothing, although she could not make out exactly what she was wearing; that really wasn't important right now.

In front of her was a large bush, dark in outline; she could just make out the leaves and small flowers. She was standing behind the bush at the bottom of a hill, where moonlight gave everything an eerie but magical outline. Now that she could see and sense where she was she needed to find out exactly why she was here. Cocking her head to one side Sapphire listened for a moment, aware of music in the distance. A drum beat, tribal and rhythmic, filled her ears; she was immediately drawn towards the unknown source. She started to climb up the hill, her naked feet digging into the earth as she strode with purpose and with her breath coming in short bursts at the exertion. As she reached the top of the hill more bushes and trees began to appear in her way, creating a screen that she could not clearly see through to find the source of the music. The music became louder, the beat building into a throbbing pulsing tempo. As she grew closer her curiosity became heightened, making her feel as if she were being seduced by the magic of the beat.

Time seemed to shift as she suddenly arrived on the other side of the trees which just a moment ago had obscured her view. Looking down on to the scene unfolded in front of her she stood still, the moonlight casting a wash of silver colouring on to the shapes below. Sapphire took a deep, shaking breath as her brain translated the picture before her.

Men and women were dancing below within a circle of bodies surrounding a fire; they were lost within the music, within the rhythm that vibrated from the drums that the men were pounding in rapturous joy to one side. They swayed and stamped, touching and swirling around each other, in a crazy but sensuous display of heavenly bliss. The flames of the fire grew with each pounding of the beat, with sparks shooting out from the top in bursts like a meteor shooting across the dark sky. The energy radiating outwards from the dancers was almost visibly thick with intensity; powerful, sensual and incredibly magical.

Sapphire crouched down on to her knees, partly because she was blown away by the energy and also from a deep sense of knowing that she should not be there; she was uninvited, a gatecrasher to something that right now she did not understand. As she watched the dancers she became aware that towards the centre of the circle, closest to the fire with his back to her, was a man who was familiar to her. Her heart began to thud quite loudly; her breathing became more rapid and she raised her hand to her mouth in excited realisation.

It was him. He was here. As if at that very moment he heard her thoughts he turned slowly, his dance a sexy, slow, rhythmic roll of his hips as he now faced her and opened his eyes. His eyes flashing with laughter he looked up directly at her, outlined in the moon's silver-blue haze. She caught his smile; he raised his hand and waved at her, gestured for her to come down to join him. She stared for a moment, realising her mouth was open like an idiot being caught doing something she shouldn't have been – red-handed, guilty.

His hair, a dark halo of braids, dreadlocks and glittering beads, moved around his face like she had seen him before: a strange, beautiful man; other-worldly, fascinating, compelling, dangerous. This had been the first time he had ever acknowledged her; he looked directly at her and motioned for her to come to him. Sapphire realised it was just daft to stand there with her mouth open, looking like she had lost a brain cell; even if this was a dream she was interacting with the man whom she had been praying would be here again, wishing that he would appear so that the fantasy could continue. She shut her mouth, licked her lips (which felt dry and cold), took one last big about-to-step-forward-and-do-something-crazy breath and started off down the hill towards him.

"Please don't let me wake up yet," Sapphire whispered to herself, her heart beating like a frightened bird. "I'm totally up for this."

Sapphire floated down the grassy slope towards the gathering. As she moved closer her eyes locked on to the man holding her gaze hypnotically; the warmth from the fire caressed her face and body. She began to smile. Every part of this dream was just as she had imagined, just as she had wanted; perfect for her to feel safe, excited and free. The man continued to sway to the music, his body a tall, muscular frame, with long legs and strong arms; his face was open and handsome with a wry, slightly dangerous edge. The smile never left his lips. His eyes locked on to hers; as she grew closer to the group of men and women he started towards her, still dancing, his body slipping between the crowds to get closer to her.

She stopped just on the edge of the gathering, the other people seemingly unaware of her arrival, and so wrapped up in the magic of the music they were oblivious to her presence. He stepped out of the circle and stopped in front of her, moving just slightly now, a tantalizing display of his body showing off the taught muscular frame to perfection. Sapphire held her breath; being this close to him for the first time seemed to start a slow hum within her own body, a vibration that touched her in a very intimate way in all the best places.

This was turning out to be one hell of a good dream. He stepped forward, closing the distance between them to just a fraction from touching. He was tall, much taller than her – although that wasn't difficult as she had always been a tiny woman, even in her dreams. His head bowed down so that he could look at her properly, arms held out and his fingertips just opening, as if he wished to touch her but did not know if he should.

Sapphire could not move, could not think. She was mesmerised by this man; this close she could now see his eyes clearly. They were a deep amber – a gold with the darkest pupils and a ring of black around the edge of the iris, creating an almost non-human appearance; they seemed to shimmer with a life of their own, the movement within them creating an hypnotic appeal. Sapphire was instantly lost within his gaze.

Then he touched her. Sapphire was suddenly on fire, a warmth that spread from his fingers instantly igniting a pathway along her nerve endings to the rest of her body. It pulsed in waves of explicitly, wonderfully tingling deliciousness. Her whole body was completely and utterly aroused, tuned into a new frequency she had no idea could even exist.

He smiled widely now, showing a row of perfectly white teeth. He licked his bottom lip and wrapped his fingers around her forearms.

"Hello, Sapphire. It's so nice to finally meet you."

Sapphire gulped at the sound of his voice, a smooth deep tone that slipped across her mind like a familiar blanket. Despite the continued beating of the drums around her his voice was crystal-clear in her ears; he was the only thing that mattered at that moment ... only his touch and his beautiful gaze were holding her in this heightened state of bliss.

He bent towards her and touched her cheek with the side of his face, his hair like warm silk as he whispered in her ear, "I have waited a long time for this moment." His lips brushed gently against her ear lobe, creating a shiver of anticipation throughout the rest of her body. She felt like a highly-tuned instrument which had just been struck, with the first chord vibrating outwards from her belly to her head and toes. He seemed to hum with the same intensity as he moved back: his hands were sliding down to hers, which he now grasped, their fingers intertwined as he pulled her towards him.

Walking backwards, he coaxed her into the circle of dancers. Bringing their hands up together above their heads he moved her body against his, their torsos touching, hips together. Still looking into her eyes he began to move again, dancing, swaying, leaning into her. "Let's dance," he said.

Sapphire felt like she had actually died and gone to heaven. She smiled, allowed her arms to float down with his to his waist where he placed them to hold on to him as he captured her within his embrace. She moved with him, looking up into those never-ending eyes which smiled down at her with a knowing that she could not quite understand. The beat picked up, the energy lifted; the group around her began to stamp, their bodies moving in a tribal, animalistic way. Sapphire was lost completely in the unity of it all, wrapped within the arms of this magical, beautiful man. She closed her eyes and surrendered completely to him.

With her eyes now shut Sapphire became acutely aware of her other senses, touching him, smelling him, listening to his heart beating next to her head as she leant against his chest. The drumbeat continued to captivate them; she could feel the other dancers around them, some of them laughing, chanting, gathering momentum as the beat grew faster and more intense. This strange man continued to move and sway with a delicate but insisting tension against her body, which now automatically followed his lead. Every part of her body was highly tuned to the sensations which enveloped her. His clothing touching her was soft leather; his arms were naked; his torso was covered with only a waistcoat and his trousers were made of the same soft leather as an American Indian would wear.

She smiled at this image in her head. Dancing with an Indian around a fire seemed very apt ... Somewhere in her mind it seemed very familiar. Perhaps she had done this before, maybe many lifetimes ago. His body was warm – hot, even to touch – radiating a comforting sexual energy that seemed safe but predatory at the same time. He smelt like a blend of patchouli and sandalwood; all male, intoxicating, subtle, and totally fuckable. Sapphire really was in dream heaven. She opened her eyes again and looked up at him as they moved. He was still smiling that knowing smile, his eyes shining bright like amber crystals. Sapphire tried for a moment to scramble her brain into some semblance of normality; she felt intoxicated – high, even – like she had smoked a big fat joint and was totally floating.

"Who are you?" Her question came as a whisper. She was finding it very hard to do anything other than stare and sway.

He lifted his hand and brushed her hair away from her face, touching her lightly and leaving a trail of sparks in his wake. "I am Fox. That is all you need to know."

Sapphire smiled a sleepy, happy smile. "You don't look like a fox."

He continued holding her tightly against him, rolling his hips just so into her now overly-stimulated body. "Looks can be deceiving."

At that moment he bent down and kissed her gently on the lips, a closed but sensuous kiss which promised so much more. The air around them seemed to crackle with intensity. Sapphire held him with a ferociousness she did not know she possessed. Opening her mouth slightly, tentatively, she prayed that he would follow her eager show of approval. He obliged, kissing her now with a fevered wanting, as if he had been waiting a long, long time to claim her.

Sapphire felt herself melt into him. This was unbelievable; by far the most erotic and fantastical dream she had had in ages. She let herself go completely, wanting more, wanting him, wanting this strange man called Fox. Her body was on fire; she believed that if she opened her eyes and looked down at her feet she would quite possibly see the flames licking up her legs into her groin and belly. Her head was swimming now; he held her so tightly that she could feel every goddam muscle – including the one that really mattered – hardening and rippling against her.

"OMFG, I'm going to self-combust," she thought, with glee. Sapphire felt the fire grow higher and higher up her body as he explored her mouth with his warm, very talented tongue. Just as he moved his hand to her lower back and pulled her even harder against him she felt a loud ping in her head. A sharp flash of white light overtook her senses and she became suddenly and completely limp with pleasure.

Chapter Two

Sapphire stirred, stretching her legs out beneath her, sensing soft bed linen and the warmth of her body inside her bedcovers. Her eyes were closed, but she could see through heavy lids the light of a new day shining through her bedroom window. She was awake again, in her own bed, in her own room. She felt heavy and peaceful, her body wrapped in the duvet. She wiggled her toes for a moment, allowing her senses to awaken and her body to feel real once more. Slowly she opened her eyes and blinked to regain full sight.

Her room was bathed in soft hues of yellow and gold from the morning sunlight which filtered through her curtains; everything was just as it had been when she had turned in for the night. Her toes felt slightly cooler than the rest of her body and – as she stretched them again – she felt a tickle, as if she had caught something on her feet. Moving very slowly, with a comfortable slide from the covers, she sat upright and rubbed her eyes for a moment. Lifting the duvet, she twisted round to place her feet on the floor. She looked down at them and frowned. Between her toes she could see something sticking out at random. It was long, thin and green in colour. She bent down to get a closer inspection. Grass. There was grass between her toes. Sapphire remained still on the edge of her bed, staring at her grassy toes. "Must have sleepwalked in the garden," she muttered to herself. "I've never sleepwalked."

Shaking her head in dismissal she stepped across her rug towards her dresser to find some clothes. As she reached the first drawer she heard a cry from outside the window. "Fuck. That fucking fox has had the chickens." The heated and distinct cry of her housemate and newly-acquired friend came up to her window from the garden. Grabbing whatever she could find quickly Sapphire dressed in jeans and t-shirt. Pulling her long dark blonde hair back into a hairband she left her room, dashed down the stairs of the cottage into the kitchen and headed out towards the back garden. Just as she reached for the door handle her friend pulled the door open and marched in, almost knocking Sapphire over as she pushed her way into the room.

"What's happened, Charlie?" Her friend sat on a kitchen bar stool and proceeded to pull off her wellies with gusto. "That big, fat fucking dog fox has killed all the chickens, every single one of them; taken Bess and left the rest for dead." Her eyes were stormy, a big frown across her forehead in angry declaration of what she had found. "The fox?"

Sapphire leant back against the door frame for a second, her dream suddenly crashing into her brain with vivid detail and a smile slowly creeping on to her lips. "Fox … mmmh, the fox." Charlie continued to scowl, looking at her with confusion. "Why on earth are you smiling at the fact that we have a chicken massacre in our garden, and now no goddam eggs?"

Sapphire snapped out of her dream memory and stopped smiling. "Oh, shit. Yeah. Sorry, Charlie. I'm gutted. I love those chickens … Just had a weird dream last night about a fox. Got confused then for a second." Charlie rubbed her foot, looking at Sapphire with confusion. "You mean you loved those chickens. They are well and truly dead now and you are going to help me clean it up in a minute after I've had a coffee and a fag and I've calmed down. Really didn't need this shit on my day off."

Sapphire nodded and moved across the tiny kitchen to the kettle. Busying herself with the task of making the coffee she sighed, and listened to Charlie rummaging in her bag for her tobacco. "How did he get in the pen? I thought we had secured it really well." Charlie let out a long, "Humph." "Obviously not well enough. They are wily little fuckers. Unless you dig the wire two feet under the ground they find a way in … although I actually can't see how, as there is no damage to the pen or the fence or anything. It's like he magically broke in with no sign of entry."

Sapphire waited for the kettle to boil. Leaning back against the counter, she listened to the water bubble inside. "That's really weird." Turning around to find cups, coffee, and milk, Sapphire reached for a spoon and suddenly felt a sick realisation in the pit of her stomach. "Charlie?" Her friend looked up at her, the cigarette she was rolling almost completed in her hand. "Yeah?"

"I know this might be the last thing that could have happened but, strangely, I found grass on my feet this morning and I might have sleepwalked last night and opened the chicken pen." Charlie licked the paper of her cigarette, rolling it with expert ease into the smoke she needed. "Nah. Don't be daft; the pen door was shut. You never sleepwalk, not that I'm aware of, anyway. He must have climbed the fence. I don't know. Don't worry about it; I'm just a bit pissed as it means clearing up and then sorting out another lot of girls for the pen."

Sapphire returned to her coffee-making now that the kettle had pinged off and steam was rising from the spout. "Yeah, I suppose so. I was just a bit confused, waking with grass on my feet. I had a shower before I went to bed." Charlie reached forward for the mug of steaming coffee Sapphire handed her. "You're just weird; we both know that." Charlie smiled again, heading for the back door – which she opened – and stood in the doorway. Placing her coffee on the window ledge after taking a big sip, she lit the cigarette and blew the smoke out into the garden. "Maybe your dream of a fox was a premonition. Shame he got to them before you could warn me."

Sapphire looked out of the door into the garden and saw a mess of feathers at the bottom of their little tidy haven. "It wasn't actually a real fox. It was a man called Fox." Charlie continued with her coffee and cigarette relay. "Sounds like one of your mad dreams." Sapphire laughed softly. "I have to say, without boring you with all the details, that it was a bloody brilliant dream. He is gorgeous." Charlie smiled at her. "Seen him in your dreams before, have ya?"

Sapphire sipped her own coffee, looking out on the garden, which was dappled in the morning sunshine. "Strangely … Yes, I have. Just never interacted with him before, and never knew who he was until last night." Charlie watched her face with interest. "Wow … dreams which have characters that reappear. You have a mental imagination. Either that or you've been reading too much again." Sapphire laughed. "Yes, I've always had a vivid imagination. My mum would always scold me for the stories I told." Charlie nodded, stubbed out the cigarette just outside the door and plopped it into the almost-full pot next to the drain. "Mmmh, well … Tell me the details later. Let's get this mess cleaned up and then we can get on with our Saturday." Sapphire nodded, gulping the last of her coffee and reached down by the door to grab her own wellies, ready for clear-up duty.

Clearing up a pile of massacred chickens turned out to be a grim job. Sapphire felt particularly sad as she lifted her favourite brown hen and placed her in the box they were using to gather up the feathers and bodies. They had five chickens to dispose of now, and not a particularly big garden to bury them in. You can't just put a bag of dead chickens in the dustbin.

Charlie finished clearing up a pile of feathers and looked up at Sapphire. "Thank God the ground's not too hard. We can bury them at the back by the compost heap, a kinda good place for recycling." Sapphire turned her nose up. "Eeww, Charlie, that's horrible. You are cruel." Charlie smiled half-heartedly. "We all get recycled eventually, hon. Good old Mother Earth takes us all back into her womb at some point. Whether it's as bones or as ashes she really doesn't mind." They lifted the box together and headed towards the back of the garden to start digging. "I've never thought of it like that. I suppose you're right."

After placing the box next to the compost heap Charlie headed off to the shed to get the spades. Sapphire looked up at the sky for a moment and watched the clouds above drift lazily across the pale blue horizon. June was always a mixed month for weather in England; they had a few days of sunshine and usually a lot of rain – who knew from one day to the next? She was glad summer was on the way. It was always good to feel the sun on her skin again after the cold, damp winter. Yesterday had been the summer solstice – the longest day – but to Sapphire it was the start of the summer season, a celebration of warm evenings and cold cider in the pub garden.

Her thoughts drifted back to her dream last night. She watched Charlie walk back towards her with two spades and, as her friend passed one to her, she reflected on her dream. "Charlie, do you know much about the summer solstice?" Charlie started to size up an area for the new recycling point. "What do you mean?" "Well, what is it all about? What are all those people at Stonehenge doing every year on the solstice? Is it like a big party, or what?" Charlie started to dig,

Sapphire joining in, lifting the turf with the tip of her spade as her friend was doing. "Oh, yeah, I know … It's a kind of celebration for the turning point of the year. The pagans celebrate certain points in the calendar, have a big party, get drunk, get off their heads on drugs, run around naked … all that kind of cool stuff." Sapphire laughed. "Sounds like fun; that was kind of what my dream was like last night."

Charlie was getting stuck in now; the hole she had started was getting pretty big. Sapphire's efforts were somewhat less enthusiastic but she continued to dig alongside her friend. "OK. Now I'm interested; give me the details." Sapphire could feel heat beginning to rise in her chest and throat as she relived the dream: the dancing, the people moving to the drum beat, bumping and grinding like crazed animals, Fox pressing against her, his eyes watching her. "Ugh … hello, Saf. Why so red-faced? Give it up; now I want to know what this dream was about. Sounds fun."

Sapphire stopped digging and looked up at her friend with some embarrassment. "It just felt so real, vivid, like I was actually there … all these people were dancing around a massive fire. It was amazing; the best rave I've ever been to. And this guy that I keep seeing in my dreams was there; he saw me, actually made me come down and join them. He danced with me, he knew my name. It was kind of weird, totally erotic; I think I actually would have exploded if I hadn't woken up." Charlie giggled, "Sounds like you had a wet dream, hon." They both stopped and looked at each other, bursting into laughter at the same time. "I thought only adolescent boys had those."

Charlie put the spade to one side, started to lift the chickens out of the box. "Well, them and frustrated thirty-year-old women, obviously." Sapphire laughed again, "Yep. It's time to get laid, I think." Charlie placed the first limp body in the hole and looked at Sapphire. "I cannot believe we are talking about sex while burying chickens. Are we fucked up, or what?" Sapphire helped her with the other bodies. "I know. I know. Let's be respectful for a moment." She laid the last brown chicken in the hole and they regained enough decorum to re-cover the girls, placing the grass turf Charlie had expertly cut out on top so that the area did not look quite so grave-like.

They stepped back after stamping lightly over the area, Sapphire collecting a few large stones to put at the top as a marker. "May you rest in peace, girls. Thank you for all the eggs. Have fun in chicken heaven." Sapphire actually felt slightly tearful as she placed a handful of daisies on top of the stones. "We will miss you, ladies."

Charlie put her arm around her friend's shoulder and leant her head to nestle into Sapphire. "Crikey. I feel well miserable now. Let's go out for a while and try to cheer ourselves up." Sapphire returned the hug. "Yep, defo need to be cheered up now. Methinks a big mug of hot chocolate with marshmallows is in order." Charlie nodded in agreement. "We need to get cleaned up – and let's pop down to the high street; I need to get a few bits, anyway." They walked back to the house, leaving the little grave site behind them, hoping that was the last time they would ever have to do that crappy job again.

Sapphire dipped her spoon into the whipped cream on top of her hot chocolate, lifting the sweet blob of niceness to her mouth in one quick swoop. Charlie sat opposite her, sipping her own mug of calories; her whipped cream was long gone, as she was an eager eater. "Are you meeting up with Nathan tonight?"

Nathan was Charlie's current boyfriend, a cute guy she had met down the local six months ago. Their romance had been blossoming nicely and Sapphire liked him. He was younger than Charlie by a few years and she would joke about her toy boy's enthusiasm regarding life in general; he made her laugh and was apparently pretty amazing in the sack. Sapphire could vouch for that by the sound of their very vocal get-togethers, usually on a Saturday night: her investment in earplugs had done little to mute the satisfied cries coming from Charlie's bedroom on said nights.

Charlie licked her lips with satisfaction, a smug smile on her lips. "Yep, we are having a few bevvies at The Swan and then going to a party at one of Nathan's friend's houses." She smiled across at Sapphire, who started on the hot chocolate with cautious sips. "Do you want to come with us? Meet a few new people. Let your hair down, honey. Might be good for you; it's been a while since you ventured out with me." Sapphire raised her eyebrows. "Mmmh ... Last time I came out with you I got shit-faced and ended up in the bush outside our front door, if I remember rightly." Charlie laughed. "Yeah, but it was fun. Come on ... Nathan won't mind. He likes you – it will be good to just kick back. The party's at his friend Simon's place; he lives in that really gorgeous pad at the end of the lane. Apparently he has his own decks; we can have a dance without having to drive miles to the next civilised town and pay door charges for the privilege of listening to some other DJ."

Sapphire contemplated for a moment; she hadn't actually socialised a great deal since moving to the area. Charlie was her only real friend apart from the people she now worked with at the cafe; it had been slow making friends in a new village. "OK, but if I start to feel like a gooseberry I'll walk home and leave you guys to it." Charlie reached into her bag for her iPhone. "I'll text Nathan now, let him know you will be coming tonight and that we will meet him in the pub. What time do you fancy meeting up?" Sapphire stirred the hot chocolate with the ultra-long spoon, watching the dark liquid swirl around in her mug. "Let's say 9 p.m.; gives us a chance to get ready, have a glass of wine before we go out." Charlie started texting, her fingers moving with lightning speed over the keys as she relayed the message to Nathan.

"That's more like it, honey pie. We need some fun after this morning. Let's finish these, get the bits I need in the corner shop and head back to decide what tantalising outfits we should wear." Sapphire laughed. "I don't think that will be necessary for me. I'm really not looking to tantalise anyone just yet." Charlie finished her text with a beep as it was sent across the ether. "Oh, shut up; it will be fun to dress up just a bit, and I never get the chance in this hick country village to glam up. I'll do your hair for you." Sapphire fished some change out of her purse to pay for the drinks, rummaging through the usual collection of unnecessary objects in her handbag to find the money. "All right, I'll submit to the hair-pampering, but it will be jeans and a cute top for me." Charlie plopped the phone back into her bag with a smile. "Cool. Let's go."

They smiled and waved goodbye to the girl behind the counter of the coffee shop, Sapphire opening the door into the high street.

Directly across the street was the only other coffee shop in the small village of Heckfield, the one where Sapphire had been working for over the last three months. She thought it mildly amusing that they were both really busy, despite being so close. The local community really liked their caffeine. "Nothing wrong with that," Sapphire thought. At least it was bringing her in some money now.

As they walked towards the corner shop Sapphire noted how neat and tidy everything was around her; the little village she had moved to only seven months previously was quintessentially British, with quaint eighteenth-century buildings which held various shops along its small but functional high street. It was a nice place to live; they were close to the countryside and it was not a long drive to the south coast – a far cry from where she had been living in a tiny flat in London with her mad ex-boyfriend.

As they entered the corner shop Charlie collected a basket, and Sapphire followed her around as she collected a few essentials. Charlie chatted to her about, "the price of this, and do we need that?" Her voice babbled quietly in the background as Sapphire's mind drifted. She felt blessed to be here, to have Charlie as a new friend and to have even found herself a little job so close to the house she now lived in.

Her life had changed overnight when her father had died unexpectedly from a heart attack, leaving her a rather large sum of money. It had given her the excuse and chance to escape a miserable existence in London, dump the crappy draining boyfriend she had tied herself to for the last three years and start a new life here in the countryside. She had found Charlie and her lovely little cottage on Gumtree, of all places. "Single lady looking for lodger in delightful house in the countryside," the ad had read. After looking at the house online and speaking to Charlie on the phone for an hour she had jumped at the chance to pack up and move down to the little village in the south east of England. It had been a huge change for her (her family and friends thinking at the time of her decision that she had gone slightly crazy) but now, seven months on, she was happy. Happy for the first time in a very long time.

It was around the same time that she had started to have the dreams; the vivid, crazy and strange dreams. Often they would mean nothing; sometimes they had been a collection of what she had been watching on TV, reading in her book, or people she had seen in the coffee shop. But in the last two months she had been seeing the same man appearing in the background, dark-haired, tattooed and deliciously sexy … the now mysteriously-named Fox.

Charlie nudged Sapphire hard. "Hey, you deaffo, I'm talking to you." Sapphire came back to reality. "Sorry, Charlie. What did you say?" The basket Charlie was carrying was now almost full; she held a bottle of wine in her hand up to Sapphire for inspection. "I said, 'Prosecco OK with you, darling?'" Sapphire laughed, grabbing the bottle. "Do you really have to ask that question?" Laughing, they headed for the checkout.

Many outfit changes and several glasses of said Prosecco consumed later, Sapphire and Charlie were in the last stages of getting ready for their night out. The afternoon had been spent doing some laundry, pottering around the cottage, reading, and then cooking a light supper, before they began the ritual of preparing the inner goddess. Charlie was exceptionally well-practised at the art of making herself look beautiful; she was a pretty willowy woman in her late twenties, with blonde curly hair that spiralled naturally, just as the models on TV were. She was much taller than Sapphire, who was petite and buxom. Sapphire's rack was one of her greatest assets, whereas Charlie had a certain chic, something which had heads turning.

Sapphire, with her long straight dark blonde hair, could be overlooked if you did not see her eyes. Her big dark blue eyes with long lashes were Sapphire's other winning feature. Sometimes her eyes looked almost purple in colour; her parents had named her Sapphire due to the striking colour of her eyes. Charlie stood behind her, teasing her hair up into a tumbled display of clips and curls, tongs in hand, as she created a funky but tasteful updo for Sapphire. "How many people are likely to be there tonight?" Sapphire looked into the mirror at her friend's reflection, asking the question as she blinked back at her. "Not sure. Could be just a few people or it could be a mad one – apparently it can be a surprise mix. Nathan has known Simon since school; he has good parties."

Sapphire bit her bottom lip, suddenly feeling a little nervous despite the warmth of the alcohol now spreading through her body. "Just don't leave me with some idiot, please, Charlie." Charlie laughed, finishing her masterpiece and spraying her with hairspray to hold it all in place. "Of course I won't. You'll be fine. It will be a lot of fun ... OK, you're done." Sapphire stared at the person looking back at her in the mirror; she looked mighty fine indeed. "Good job, Charlie. I actually look half-decent." Charlie smiled her sweet smile back at her. "You totally underestimate your gorgeousness, hon. Right. Shoes on; let's get going. It's already nine o'clock ... We're running late, as usual."

Chapter Three

The Swan pub was a cosy country haven, complete with inglenook fireplace and a smelly dog lying by the bar; and it was busy tonight. Nathan had saved them some seats at a table with two of his other friends. The girls had tumbled through the door at 9.20 p.m., Nathan pointing to his watch and shaking his head with a smile because they had come in late. Sapphire was now on her second drink; she was sticking to vodka and cranberry juice after the Prosecco, just to save any falling into bushes later. She was enjoying being out and about with her friend and Nathan had introduced her to Dave and Grace, who seemed like nice twenty-somethings.

Sapphire, at thirty-two, was the oldest at the table; she was lucky enough to have a young face and could get away without looking like the totally old spinster she was starting to feel she was. The pub was filled with the sound of chatter and laughter; music from a really outdated jukebox competed with the noise of happy, drunk people. Sapphire felt herself slowly relax. People-watching was her thing. When she lived in London it had been a fascinating pastime; she had a knack of being able to read people very quickly and almost guess their lives without even having met them.

She watched Dave and Grace opposite her; they sat comfortably, familiar with each other's presence. Sapphire guessed they were very much in love; each mirrored the other's body language and they often whispered into each other's ear or gave a soft kiss to remind the other they were still paying attention. Sapphire hoped that one day she would be doing exactly the same thing with some wonderful man she had yet to meet. Charlie was laughing loudly at some comment Nathan had made. They were also curled up against each other, Nathan brushing a curl away from Charlie's eye with a tenderness that made Sapphire realise he was very much falling for her friend.

Last orders was called and Sapphire realised how quickly the time had flown by; she had actually really enjoyed the company of the people at her table without feeling like the single odd girl out. Nathan started to tug on his jacket. "Right. Who's up for Simon's?" Charlie put her hand up, now slightly inebriated, and jumped up and down in her seat. "Me, me." The others laughed. "Course you are, my gorgeous girl. Let's go; it's not far to walk from here." Despite the sunshine that day the evening had a slight chill to it as they left the pub, somewhat noisily, to head down the lane to Simon's house. Sapphire was glad she had put her wrap on and opted for ankle boots instead of sandals.

They headed on up the lane towards the big house at the end, a place Sapphire had noticed a few times on her way into the high street but never walked past properly. The alcohol in her system made her feel warmer and slightly fuzzy. Dave and Grace walked ahead, obviously knowing where to go – their arms wrapped around each other as they stumbled slightly, laughing along the way. Sapphire tipped her head back and looked up at the clear sky; tiny stars twinkled down at her and a large moon smiled its silver hue down on to the group. She wondered absently what the rest of the night might bring, and smiled again to herself.

Ten minutes later they stood at the entrance of an impressively large house set back from the road, with a long gravel driveway. Sapphire admired the house, set in lush lawns and tidy landscaping. Music drifted from the house, a steady thump thump; windows were lit up randomly, giving the house an almost clown-like, grinning expression. She guessed it had at least five bedrooms and wondered what this Simon did for a living; obviously something that paid well.

Laughter mingled with the music, giving an appealing welcome call to their small group approaching the front door. Nathan was first to the front door and banged on the large knocker with enthusiasm, obviously hoping someone inside would hear them. Sapphire stepped back slightly from the couples, a little intimidated by the house and the fact that she did not know anyone inside. They stood for only a few moments before the door swung open and a tall slim guy with shaved head and goatee smiled at them in welcome. "Nathan. Good to see you, man. Come on in; the party's just getting started."

He stepped aside and Nathan moved forward, gripping his outstretched arm at the forearm in a gesture of brotherhood. Nathan looked back at his group of friends and nodded his head. "This is my lady, Charlie, her friend Sapphire – and you know Dave and Grace." Simon smiled back at them. "Cool, my friend. Welcome, beautiful people. Come, enjoy the music; *mi casa es tu casa*." They proceeded into the hallway, Sapphire bringing up the rear, her eyes widening at the paintings and artwork decorating the wide hallway.

Simon jigged a dance up the hallway to the muted music, then opened the doorway, which led into the kitchen. As he did so the music turned up a notch and the laughter and chattering voices did, too. The kitchen was bustling with bodies; Sapphire noticed that the counter was impressively covered in bottles of drink and hard liquor – the good stuff, too. "Help yourselves, guys. I'm on the decks, so catch you in a while." A young blonde grabbed him as he walked by, planting a large kiss on his cheek. "Simon, please can we have the hot tub lights on? I can't see properly out back." He laughed, holding her waist lightly as they slipped through the crowd.

Charlie smiled at Sapphire and mouthed "Wicked" silently at her. Dave and Grace were now engaged in a conversation with people at the makeshift bar; Sapphire felt the need to join them, just so she did not feel quite so awkward. Picking up on her sudden attack of nerves, Charlie grabbed her hand. "Come on; let's get a drink and check out the rest of the house." Sapphire nodded in agreement; they grabbed a plastic cup each and Charlie sifted through the bottles looking for something suitable for them both. "Bingo," she smiled, lifting a bottle of Moët up, and began pouring the sparkling liquid into the cheap cups. Sapphire took a healthy sip.

"What does Simon do? He is obviously not short of a few quid." Charlie joined her, sipping on her drink with a happy smile. "I think he's an architect … not sure, but he's got good taste, so let's enjoy." Nathan came up behind her and hugged her around the waist. "Got a drink for me, hon?" Charlie smiled back up at him, "Sure, honey. What's your poison tonight?" Nathan inspected the bar. "Think I'll stick to beer for now; it could be a long night." Sapphire leant back against the kitchen counter and looked out into the adjoining room, which appeared to be a large sitting room also full of people, some dancing, some standing and talking. The music was some kind of euphoric dance; it was uplifting and hypnotic. She could see Simon at the back of the room on the decks; he looked very at home and very happy. She smiled, allowed the music to melt into her mind, soothe her body with its vibration; the Moët was also helping unwind her from the inside out. Charlie and Nathan headed off into the main room, drinks in hand; her friend gestured for Sapphire to follow them.

An hour and much bubbly consumed later, all inhibitions had left Sapphire and she was lost to the music; eyes closed, body moving in rhythm with the pulsing vibe coming from the speakers all around the room. The bass was shaking the floor; it tingled up her legs into her groin, making her feel slightly aroused and totally pliable. Charlie suddenly caught her attention by shaking her shoulder and leaning into her ear to talk above the music. "Hey, babe. Having a good time?" Sapphire opened her eyes and smiled at her, nodding in agreement. "Ohh, yeah." Charlie hugged her. "Do you wanna feel even better?" Sapphire continued to dance as her friend held her. "What do you mean?"

Charlie pulled back slightly and opened her hand in front of Sapphire, uncovering a tiny white dot that looked like a screwed-up Rizla. Sapphire blinked, not quite registering what her friend was offering her. Charlie licked her lips and smiled sweetly. "It's good stuff, hon. Nathan and I dropped half an hour ago and I'm flying like a G6." She giggled and bumped her hip into Sapphire's. "It's up to you, hon. I won't hold it against you if you say no, but I'll take care of you if you wanna fly with us"

The penny dropped. Sapphire suddenly felt a little giddy. Her heart rate went up a notch at the thought of taking a drug. She had missed the drugs scene in her twenties, smoked some pot on the odd occasion. She had been afraid to try anything else and hadn't really mixed with people who were into the harder stuff ... but that had been some time ago and she was new to this place, did not really know these people. Charlie continued to dance next to her. Sapphire was now aware of her friend's newly-charged vibe; she seemed to hum slightly, her energy now totally different, soft and sweet. She was in tune with the music, at one with the beat. Sapphire suddenly

21

wanted to be right where her friend was. It had been a long time since she had let go completely; she had been holding everything together for such a long time now and she suddenly – almost irrationally – now wanted to let it all go, let her hair down. Completely down. She smiled at her friend. "Why the hell not?"

Charlie hugged her again and passed her the bomb and a paper cup filled with water to wash it down with. Sapphire took the little piece of as-yet-unknown heaven and paused for a moment. "I'm trusting you, Charlie. If I end up on the floor making a total prat of myself or worse, it's your fault." Charlie laughed. "You will be absolutely fine, hon. It's from a totally trustworthy source and good stuff. I will take care of you."

Sapphire held the paper cup. The music continued to throb around her; the room was now electrically charged with happy party people. She took the bomb quickly into her mouth and washed it down with two big gulps of water, her heart rate now a steady race of excitement. "See you on the other side," Charlie giggled into her ear, grabbing her hand and raising it in the air for a victory pump. Sapphire took a deep breath, not sure whether she had just made the biggest mistake of her life or not.

Forty or so minutes later Sapphire was on the other side. She had lost track of time; her body was not hers and she was observing everything from a different plane. One moment she would be within her physical body … the next she would be humming outside it, watching herself swaying and grinding to the beat with a satisfied smile on her face. It was weird, it was scary; it was fucking amazing. She felt sooo good. Her smile was permanently fixed to her face, everything felt warm and soft and erotic, the strangers she had been dancing next to now felt like long-lost friends … they danced with her, sometimes touching, sometimes alone in their world of niceness.

Sapphire wondered what the hell she had taken; whatever it was it was totally new to her body and mind and she was loving it. Charlie appeared again and gave her a big kiss on the lips. "Darling Sapphire, you are rolling now." Sapphire smiled back at her, holding her hands in an overly-zealous grip. "God, yes. I feel amazing. I had no idea how tightly fucking wound up I was. My body now feels like a jellyfish; surprised I'm still standing." Charlie threw her head back and closed her eyes, smiling like the cat who had got all the cream. "Welcome to the wonderful world of class A, my beautiful Sapphire." Sapphire gulped, "I need water; I'm proper dry." Charlie nodded in agreement. "Come on, let's get you a drink – get some fluid in ya, make sure you are not tooo high." She said the last few words at a squeal, making Sapphire laugh out loud. They headed back to the kitchen, everything moving in blurred lines for Sapphire, like she was in a video game. After downing a pint of water, Sapphire felt much better. She could not stop moving; her body just wanted to keep jumping and dancing. She gestured to Charlie, "I'm gonna dance some more." Charlie smiled at her, catching Nathan in a hug as he came closer to her. "Go ahead, hon. I'm watching out for ya." Sapphire headed back into the throng of bodies, not caring now that she did not know these people. Suddenly they were all her friends.

Sapphire was on a journey; she was travelling through a musical time adventure; all of her senses were heightened to the point of absolute pleasure. She swayed and spun and drifted in and out of the room – one minute consciously aware of where she was, the next floating in outer space, surrounded by stars and moons that sparkled and shone around her. Her mind raced with different scenarios, running through green woods, touching the ferns and feeling the grass between her toes as she did … everything rushing at fast speed, like she was a vampire with super-strength and ability. Next, her hands tingled with energy; she looked down at them and could see them shimmering with gold and silver sparks. As she waved them slowly in front of her face they flickered in and out of sight, giving the impression that they were transparent for moments at a time. Sapphire smiled. This was awesome. It felt like she was home again, complete within her mind and body, visiting her true self.

She slowly became aware of a body pressed against her back now, hands on her arms, gently holding her, moving with her as she continued to dance. She smiled and leant back into the warmth of this person. "Most likely a man," she thought, wickedly. She had been dancing and touching people all night and was totally OK with this new, sharing experience. As she allowed herself to relax into this person's touch she suddenly became aware of a new shift in her energy. Her body began to hum very gently. Her body temperature was warming up a notch, and her head felt lighter … it was an intense sensation and she opened her eyes for a moment to regroup. The man behind her tightened his grip on her arms and gently pushed his groin into her, which switched on Sapphire's inner goddess so that she was now sparkling like a star. As she turned her head to see who was causing this sensation, she caught a wave of patchouli scent which filled her nostrils; it was familiar, and sexy as hell.

Sapphire slowed her dancing slightly, blinking her eyes to try and focus; the man tipped his head down to rest his cheek against hers. She felt his soft hair fall across her shoulder, long hair that was braided and wild.

"Hello again, Sapphire. Fancy meeting you here." Sapphire turned now to take a look at this man, the man whose voice she recognised, whose touch felt so familiar and wanted. He continued to hold her as she looked, his hands now travelling softly up and down her forearms, creating sparks across her skin as they did so. She faced him, looked up into those deep amber eyes. It was him, Fox. He was here, holding her, dancing with her again.

Sapphire shook her head gently and smiled up at him. "Now I know I'm totally off my head. This isn't real."

Fox held her gaze. "You are a very naughty girl, Sapphire, treading on dangerous ground now. I'm here to keep you safe." Sapphire nodded, looking up at him, and giggled. She placed her hands around his waist and squeezed his buttocks, with a slow moan escaping her lips. "Oh … yes, yes, yes. Dangerous ground; I need to be taken care of." Although the whole experience of holding him, feeling his firm muscles under her hands, his smell, and the warmth radiating from his body all felt totally real, Sapphire knew there was no way in heaven it could be. She was flying so high that her dream man had become reality within her drug-induced bubble – but at this moment, with the music beating in her ears and surrounded by people dancing and laughing, she couldn't give a flying fuck. She was enjoying every damn second and she realised with a naughty smile that she didn't want it to end.

Smiling, Fox stared down at her, obviously enjoying her willingness to let go, and by the feel of the bulge in the front of his trousers he was very happy she was being so wanton.

"You left rather abruptly last time. We didn't get to finish our dance, but perhaps we can spend some more time together now." Sapphire watched his mouth as he spoke. He had wonderful lips, which could have belonged to a woman ... they were full and beautiful. She desperately wanted to touch them, kiss him again ... like she had the last time she had seen him in that wonderful dream. She knew this was not real; it was so not real, but it felt wonderful ... he was wonderful. His face was as handsome and beautiful as she had remembered; his eyes glittered in the lights which blinked on and off from across the room; his hair was crazy-wild, decorated with beads and leather braiding. He looked like a rock star, only better.

Sapphire lifted herself up on her tiptoes and whispered into his ear. "Please stay. I want you to stay."

He held her tighter to his body. They melted for a second into each other ... the sensation made Sapphire gasp slightly, it was so intensely good. "I'm not going anywhere; I'm taking care of you, my beautiful Sapphire. Flying this high, you need a hand to hold."

Sapphire laughed, and now placed her hands up to his face. She touched his cheek on one side and placed her other hand into his hair; the softness of his skin felt so amazing to her fingertips. She stroked lightly, watching the sparks fly outwards as she did so.

Fox laughed and took her hands in his own. Holding them to his lips he kissed them gently, his mouth opening just slightly as he took the very tip inside his mouth, touching the sensitive pads of her fingers with the tip of his tongue. Sapphire felt this lightest of touches in her groin. She shivered all over, another groan escaping her lips. What was it with this guy ... even in her dreams ... and now in her drug-induced state, having this so-not-real-trip ... that he could make her body sing like a canary? She was in trouble, she knew that; totally and utterly in trouble.

Fox continued to dance with her, watching her eyes, holding her hands, creating a protective bubble around them from the other party-goers. She was in his world with him, and no one else mattered right now. They danced like this for some time. She felt his warm breath on her face, his heart beating against her body as she melted into his embrace. At moments, while they moved, she felt the soft press of his lips against her skin – on her neck, her face, against her hair, as he worshipped her gently. She heard him whisper words in a language she did not understand, in tones that rose and fell against the sound of the music. She really was in heaven again, with him.

Time seemed to jump. They moved together as one, aware of the other people around them, but totally engrossed in their own world. Sapphire felt safe, safe and totally happy. The music held them, the bass pulsing through Sapphire's body. She held this wild, magical man and surrendered to him completely. They danced together, their bodies interlocked, moving in rhythm. Everything around her felt unreal. She was as light as a feather, and he held her the whole time.

Without warning, Sapphire felt a slight shift within her body. The air around her seemed to bend for a moment; the warmth of the living room disappeared and she was now cooler. The music faded behind her. She opened her eyes. Fox was now holding her in his arms like she was a damsel in distress. He watched her intently, a slight smile on the edge of his lips. His amber eyes swirled with sparks of black and gold, making him look other-worldly, not human.

They were outside. She pulled her eyes away from his stare and looked up at the dark sky above her; the moon was bright, surrounded by her ever-faithful stars, twinkly and glowing around her. She realised they were still at the house; she could hear the party continuing behind them and was aware of other people outside near to them, but far enough away to preserve the sense of being alone in the bubble they had created.

Fox was carrying her effortlessly; her limbs were limp and hanging languorously as he held her within his strong hold. He stopped next to a large tree. It was ghostly white in the moonlight – "A silver birch by the look of it," Sapphire thought, absently.

He crouched down and placed her on the grass. "Time to ground, my gorgeous." She felt the coolness of the grass beneath her, her hands touching the slightly damp earth creating super-sensitive surges travelling to the rest of her body. She smiled at him with a drunken, drug-happy smile. She was aware of him taking off her ankle boots, removing her socks and placing her feet on to the ground. He sat down next to her, crossing his legs, and for the first time leaning back slightly so that they were not touching.

Sapphire jolted slightly back into almost-reality. She blinked her eyes, his image still strong in front of her. He was tipping his head back, looking up at the sky with an air of contemplation, the wry smile still slightly edged upon his lips.

Sapphire swallowed. Suddenly her mouth felt very dry. "I'm still flying. Are you still here?"

He looked back at her, brushing a stray hair away from his eyes. "Yes, I'm still here, Sapphire." He blinked at her for a moment. The music from the party was still drifting from the house, though Sapphire noted that it had turned down in beat just a notch – more ambient now than the hard pumping house music it had been earlier. The mood was shifting slightly. She was more aware, in her body slightly more … it felt just as good as before, but now everything was becoming clearer. In fact Fox actually looked more real in front of her. She blinked again. That just couldn't be; no, no. He laughed, a soft, amused laugh.

"There is so much you must learn, Sapphire. So much I need to tell you. It's frustrating for me that our time is always limited." Sapphire was stroking the grass now. She had been subconsciously doing this as he talked to her; it was soothing.

"What kind of things do I need to learn?" He leant forward slightly. "Well, for one thing, that it is not really safe for you to take drugs. Travelling like this can be very dangerous for someone like you. If I had not seen you, someone else may have jumped in, and then God knows what could have happened." Sapphire rubbed her head, slightly confused. "I have no idea what you are talking about. In fact, I'm feeling a bit weird now. My buzz is going … You are making my head hurt."

Fox smiled, taking her hand in his, the warmth immediately travelling up her arm and easing the slight tension that had just started creeping in to her mind. "It's OK. Don't stress. I'm always here for you, watching you, but you must be careful, Sapphire. Your energy changes more than others when you take drugs." He paused for a second. "You can switch vibrations so much more quickly. You need to be aware of that now. Your power has grown immensely in the last few months, I'm not sure exactly why, but it has, and you are making my job very interesting." Sapphire shook her head again. "I'm really, really not sure what you are talking about. Can I just lie down for a second?"

He nodded, smiling at her. She leant back and stretched her body out on the damp cool grass, blinking slowly to clear her head. She became aware of Fox lying down next to her. He held her hand, which was now placed on his stomach, their bodies touching again slightly. It was immediately comforting. "I wish you were real. You feel so good; I feel so good when I'm around you." She felt his stomach jump a little as he laughed softly. "I am real, Sapphire. Real to you, anyway. Just trust for now; it will all make sense eventually." Sapphire sighed loudly. "Eventually. Right. I'll wait for eventually, then."

Sapphire closed her eyes for a moment, felt the thrum of the earth beneath her – the wonderful grounded feeling of lying on Mother Earth as she comforted her. Fox let go of her hand and was, in a swift elegant movement, on his side, his face hovering over hers. Even with her eyes closed she could feel how very close he was to her. "Just promise me. No more drugs. I can't always come here to take care of you like this. In your dreams it is easier for me." Sapphire nodded slowly, feeling like she really was going insane. "I promise." Fox leant closer, his hand now holding her head gently. "Good."

He kissed her then, softly at first, his warm lips coaxing her mouth open so that his tongue could slide inside with a slow wet caress that made her whole body tingle. The kiss deepened and Sapphire melted again, into the ground, into him, losing herself in the moment, his warm hard body now pressing on to her. Her breathing became rapid and her body responded to him eagerly. He murmured softly between kisses, "My beautiful Sapphire, always remember I am here for you, watching you, taking care of you." Sapphire was practically panting now. "Yes, yes; always there."

She didn't care if this was real or not; it felt wonderful again. She pressed herself into him and decided that she didn't give a shit if she was going mad or not; this was incredible. Fox moved his hands restlessly up and down her body, his breathing also becoming rapid and urgent. His fingers found an opening under her top and he touched her stomach, stroking softly across her navel, slowly moving down towards her groin. Sapphire was gasping with absolute passion now; she raised her hips, wanting more, wanting his touch. Her body was on fire. She felt amazing, his tongue still dancing in her mouth creating a pulsing tightness within her breasts and groin. As he deftly undid the buttons on her jeans and slid his hand inside her pants Sapphire felt herself tip backwards slightly. He was kissing her so hard now it almost hurt but she wanted it, wanted it so much. With a bitterly sharp sweetness she felt his hand push down inside her knickers, his fingers searching for her most intimate area. She was wet and warm, her hips lifting up for him so that he could find her easily.

"Oh, my fucking God," she gasped now, as his finger slid inside her. The sensation was exquisite; she felt like she might come right now. Fox pushed himself against her, kissing her again and again, his fingers now sliding in and out with a most wonderful rhythm. "My beautiful woman, you are mine. I will take care of you, always, always." Sapphire released her mouth from his, threw her head back in a moment of wild ecstasy. There was no way to stop it; she was going to come. Just from this slightest of touches this man had set her on fire. She screamed out in pleasure, her head spun, multicoloured lights were exploding in a mini-firework display behind her eyelids. She throbbed uncontrollably. Holy shit. Sapphire vibrated like a tuning fork; she could feel everything.

Fox was holding her tightly, his mouth now against her neck, sucking lightly on her skin, slow rhythmic sucking causing her orgasm to continue as his finger carried on with its unrelenting dance in and out as the sensitive tissue inside her pulsed around it. She became like water, fluid and viscous. Everything felt dreamlike again. She was floating on her orgasm ... slowly, slowly, the intensity calmed and she felt herself again, felt the grass beneath her fingers that she was now gripping less tightly. Fox murmured into her ear, his hand now released from inside her pants, stroking her hip gently. "That's right, my beautiful lady. Ground yourself again. Feel the ground beneath you."

Sapphire blinked and licked her lips, aware now of everything around her. His warm body held her gently, like she was a precious object. He continued to kiss her neck, slow licks up to her ear making her toes curl involuntarily. He sighed deeply. "Remember to ground, my goddess. This will help you in the future, stop you flying too high." Sapphire let her head fall to one side. Her body was like liquid lava. She focused on the sensation of his lips flickering across her skin, his hand stroking her body like a cat. She purred out loud. Fox shifted, slightly small animal-like noises of his own escaping from his lips. "I will remember."

"Saf, Saf. Is that you? What are you doing lying on the wet grass, honey?" Sapphire felt a gust of air blow across her face, felt a shift of energy against her side. Fox suddenly and inexplicably disappeared. She was alone on the grass again, lying with her back on the ground, barefoot and shamelessly post-orgasmically sated. Sapphire blinked, her hands moving to her chest to make sure she was still dressed, at least. She felt like she was a naughty schoolgirl who had just been caught making out behind the bike shed.

Charlie loomed over her, swaying slightly, holding a drink in one hand, a fag in the other. She looked down on her friend with a bemused smile on her face, took a long slow drag on the cigarette. "Are you OK, Saf?" "Sorry I left you for a while. You disappeared … thought you might be out here." Sapphire pushed herself up slightly, looking around her in confusion for Fox. "Yeah, I'm OK. I'm just hot. Came out here to cool down." Charlie crouched down beside her and offered her the drink in her hand. "Here – have some water. You look cooler now. Where are your boots?"

Sapphire took the drink and gulped down the water, suddenly very aware of how thirsty she was. "They're around here somewhere. I must have taken them off." Charlie continued smiling at her, taking another drag on the cigarette. She paused before offering it to Sapphire. "Do you want some of this? Might help you ground a bit … you have been rolling for a while now, honey." Sapphire realised the cigarette was a joint and shook her head. "No. I'm OK. No more drugs for me tonight, Charlie. What time is it?" Charlie looked up at the sky, which was now changing from black to a grey-blue. "I think it's about 4 a.m. Do you wanna head home soon?" Sapphire nodded.

"Christ, it's the morning. Yeah, I think I need to get home now. I'm kinda feeling a bit weird; I majorly went off on one."

Charlie laughed, starting to rise again. Her face was flushed, her hair now slightly damp from where she had been dancing. "OK, hon. Let's find your boots, get Nathan and stagger back. It's been wicked. Hope you've had as much fun as we've had." Sapphire pushed herself up, noticed her boots were sitting side by side next to the trunk of the silver birch. She reached over to them, took out her ankle socks and started to put them back on to her wet feet. Sliding her feet back into her boots she stood up.

The sky was rapidly changing now as dawn began to appear over the horizon. The hazy feeling she had was now just a gentle hum inside her belly. She shook her head, smiling a little. "Yes, I've had a great time." Charlie offered her free hand to help pull her up. The paper cup was still on the floor. She took one last drag on the joint and lifted the cup from the grass. "Let's find Nathan and go. Is your wrap inside?" Sapphire lifted her shoulders. "Must be. God, I've been in another world, Charlie. That stuff was strong."

Charlie laughed as they headed back over the lawn towards the house, where music was still drifting out. More chilled now, she could see a few people still inside. The party was slowing down, coming to an end at last. Charlie opened the patio door; Nathan was just inside, talking to Simon, who was cuddling the blonde girl he had been with earlier in the night. Nathan smiled as they entered the room. "Hey, sweet thing. Found her, then?" He eyed Sapphire with a wicked smile. "Where's the guy you were dancing with gone, Saf? Looked like you were into each other in a big way." Sapphire felt herself start to blush self-consciously, as if she had a big stamp on her head saying, "I've just had a mind-blowing orgasm with a stranger."

Charlie looked at her friend, frowning now. "What guy?" Sapphire bit her bottom lip shyly. "Oh, I'm not sure where he went." Simon raised an eyebrow "Yeah ... who was he? Never seen him before. I thought he came with you guys." Sapphire was suddenly aware that all eyes were on her, waiting for her to spill the beans. "Um, yeah ... I kinda bumped into him, dancing. You know how it is." They all stared at her for a second, Charlie giving her the "What the fuck?" look. "Well, he must have taken off, but you had a good time, by the looks of things." Nathan chuckled and picked up Sapphire's wrap, which had been hanging over the back of a chair next to him. "Here, put your wrap on. Let's head home, let these good people get some rest." He leant forward and gave Simon a manly hug. "Great party, man. Give us a shout tomorrow if you need help clearing up." Simon waved him away "No worries, Nat. I've got the cleaner scheduled for Monday. I'll be on the sofa all day; you guys should do the same." Charlie took Nathan's hand and pulled him to her, wrapping herself around him like a koala. "Oh, God, yes. TV and duvet day."

Sapphire kept her head down. Her mind was racing with confusion. Had they seen Fox? Had he actually been real? She felt so confused, a mixture of feelings crossing her mind. He had felt real, but he couldn't be, could he?" She shook her head and followed her friends out of the room, waving goodbye to the last few people hanging around in the kitchen. Dave and Grace smiled back, looking very happy with themselves. Sapphire realised that pretty much everyone had been in the same place she had been, a happy, shiny, spangly world. She also realised with a wry smile that she had been the only one in Fox World. Perhaps it was a side effect of the drug, or maybe she was just going crazy. Who cared? For now she allowed herself to just go with it.

The three of them headed back down the lane, arm in arm, Nathan in the middle holding the girls up. They giggled and laughed, still catching the last little buzz that fizzed between them. Sapphire watched the sun slowly start to come up from over the trees. She had felt alive tonight, for the first time in ages. It had felt so good, but the dreamlike state was now ending and she sighed a little sadly that it was now over. She could still taste Fox on her lips, smell the lingering scent of patchouli on her hair. She held the moment to her like it was the most precious thing in the world.

Chapter Four

Sunday

Sapphire did not dream that morning; she had literally fallen into her bed after stripping naked rather hurriedly, dropping her clothes next to her bed in a scramble. She had fallen into a deep, dark and undisturbed sleep. Waking later, feeling very dishevelled and a little rough, she eyed her bedside clock with dismay. It was 3 p.m. She had slept heavily for over ten hours; she had obviously needed it. Her mouth felt like someone had tipped a cup of birdseed into it. She tried to shake herself back into reality.

Slipping into her dressing gown, she crossed the hallway to the bathroom for a pee. As she sat on the toilet and held her head in her hands she wondered what the hell had happened. She could still remember everything from the party – the amazing feelings, the absolutely real sensations of Fox holding her, dancing with her, playing her body like it was a highly-tuned instrument. As she finished her pee she acknowledged the slightly tender feeling between her legs and felt a slow blush spread up from her neck to her face. She actually felt like she had been touched there. No, not touched; more like manhandled like a wanton woman. The last time she had felt like that she had been pleasured by her high school sweetheart during a mind-blowing night of very good sex.

Sapphire flushed the toilet, stood up on somewhat shaky legs and stood in front of the bathroom mirror, looking at herself for the first time since the said night of supposed passion. Her reflection looked back at her, a surprised and ruffled expression on its face. Her hair was a mess. The pins holding her updo were now missing – some still sticking out randomly – her make-up now just a black ring around her eyes, making her look like a panda. She lifted her hand to her lips and brushed them gently; they were slightly tender and weirdly looked puffy, like they had been kissed hard ... really hard. She frowned at herself. Her hand moved to her neck; she lifted the stray hair that had fallen to her shoulders and lifted the strands to inspect more closely.

A gasp left her lips as the unmistakable mark of a freshly-given hickey looked back at her. The skin on her neck just below her ear was a soft purple and blue. She felt a shiver travel down her body to her groin … the memory of Fox sucking on her neck as she had come with his finger inside her was flooding through her mind. Holy fuckin' moly. Sapphire looked at herself in the mirror. She truly looked like someone who had spent the night having wild sex. "How?" she whispered the question to herself. She must have got up close and personal with some stranger at the party and hallucinated it as Fox. That was the only explanation. She suddenly felt slightly sick, dirty even.

A knock on the bathroom door shook her from her thoughts. "You finished in there, Saf? I really need to go." Sapphire washed her hands quickly. "Yeah. I'm coming out." Sapphire opened the door to an equally dishevelled-looking Charlie, who smiled at her sleepily. "You OK, hon? Was just going to wake you; thought you were dead." Sapphire stepped aside for her friend, who quickly shut the door as she went about her business. "I'm OK; slept real heavy. How long have you guys been up?" Charlie coughed on the other side of the door. "Not long … about an hour. Do you want some tea? I've just made a pot." Sapphire hung around outside for a moment. "Yes, please. I'll just jump in the shower and brush my teeth; I'll be down in a sec." Charlie flushed, opening the door while pulling her PJ bottoms up. "Ok, hon. Water's hot. See you in a mo."

Sapphire stepped back into the bathroom, turned the shower on and disrobed again. Stepping under the hot water she allowed herself to let out a big sigh of relief, feeling that she was at least back on the planet again now her friend had reappeared. The hot water soothed her body; she washed her hair twice, picking out the few remaining pins as she did. She washed her body slowly, still finding her tender private parts somewhat of an embarrassment but allowing herself a sly smile at the thought of Fox. Fuck it. She had gone out to have a good time; she had taken a risk with the little white bundle of drug joy … now she just had to suck it up. Hopefully, whoever it was that she had got down and dirty with would not show up at the pub or coffee shop and remind her of her slut-like behaviour. She was a grown woman; she could get away with it, couldn't she?

After smothering her legs in body lotion, dusting her lady bits with talc, and spraying her underarms with deodorant she felt slightly more human. Brushing her teeth actually felt like heaven. She went back into her bedroom to find comfy clothes. Deciding on jogging bottoms and a loose jersey top, with no bra or pants for extra comfort, she brushed her hair out as she padded down the stairs to the kitchen. She found the kitchen empty, but a cup placed next to the teapot gave her a renewed sense of thirst and a little rumble in her stomach demanded food. She fancied nothing.

Opting for a biscuit and the cup of tea, she headed into the small lounge at the front of the cottage. She noted that the sun was shining again. It felt a little weird that it was so late in the afternoon, but at least she had caught some of the daylight. Charlie and Nathan were snuggled up on the sofa, some animal planet programme on the TV played quietly in the background and the voice of David Attenborough soothing them nicely. Nathan smiled across at Sapphire as she settled into the chair beside them, tucking her legs up beneath her she sipped the tea. "You're alive then, Saf."

Nathan absently stroked Charlie's leg, which was lying across his lap. He seemed to have fared better than the girls and actually looked reasonably fresh. Sapphire smiled sheepishly back at him. "Mmmh. I'm alive, but slightly rough around the edges." Nathan nodded in agreement. "Yeah. Comedown sucks, I'm afraid. Be prepared for Suicide Tuesday, eh?" Sapphire frowned at him as Charlie gave him a soft punch to the arm. "Don't scare her, you idiot. She'll be OK." Sapphire took a biscuit and dunked it into her tea. "Great. You mean that I'm gonna feel worse than this at work on Tuesday?" Charlie smiled across as her. "Nothing that a Vit C and B complex won't sort, my lovely. Look … it was worth it, wasn't it?" Sapphire nibbled on the biscuit and smiled back at her. "Yeah, I suppose so."

Charlie eyed her friend suspiciously, "Who was the guy, then? I didn't see him, but Nathan tells me you were up real close and personal with some tall guy with dreaded hair." Sapphire gulped her tea a little loudly. "Yeah. He wasn't anyone I recognised as Simon's friend. Good-looking fella by the looks of it. You landed a good one,

Saf." Nathan snuggled back down with Charlie, absently playing with her PJ top. "I know this sounds really bad, but I actually don't know who he was. It was kinda weird; I think whatever you gave me took me off on a real trip. I feel a bit embarrassed about the whole thing." Nathan laughed. "God, Saf. Really, don't worry. You had a good time with a stranger; we all do that occasionally." Charlie looked at her man with a frown. "Not any more, you don't." Sapphire regarded the pair of them silently, looking over the top of her cup, trying to hide her flushing cheeks "OK. That's good; just don't want you guys to think I'm a total whore."

Charlie smiled across at her friend. "Saf ... honestly, you worry too much. It was fun. You did not show yourself up – everyone else was just as fucked. It was a great night. Chill with it." Sapphire nodded slowly. "I know. It's just not like me to do that." Charlie reached across for her mug of tea. "There is absolutely nothing wrong with letting your hair down every now and then, honey. It's good for the soul. Anyway, it's not like you have been out partying every weekend since you moved here. One night out and you are beating yourself up."

The three of them settled into a comfortable silence for the moment, lounging in the little sitting room, watching the TV and drinking tea. Sapphire still felt slightly fuzzy, her feelings of guilt gradually slipping away as she absorbed her friend's words. It was true: in life generally, she had never really allowed herself to have a good time – and whenever she had, feelings of guilt had overridden the fun times.

Sapphire wondered if this had been learned behaviour. She had been raised by her mother and stepfather. Her real dad had left when she was five; she was an only child and somehow had convinced herself that it had been her fault he had left them. She had never really known him; he had moved abroad shortly after his departure from her and her mother. She had had her fair share of therapy over the years, but sometimes she wondered if this abandonment had left her with the guilt – if it had created a pattern of never really feeling good enough. Her mother was still happily remarried. She lived in Scotland now; Sapphire only ever saw her once or twice a year. She spoke to her once a week, but her life had been her own for the last ten years.

Her job in London and the last relationship she had given up on seemed strangely distant now. How had she become so reluctant to enjoy her life? Slowly, steadily, she was now beginning to feel alive again – moving to the countryside, finding Charlie and the cottage, her new job in the cafe. It was all starting to feel easier; she was beginning to live life ... the last few months, the dreaming, letting her hair down at the party last night, her new imaginary man. It was all OK. She was doing OK.

Sapphire shook herself slightly, pushing her thoughts to one side. Her hangover was making her feel sleepy again. She decided to go out for a walk to clear her head. Charlie and Nathan looked like happy puppies bundled on the sofa; Nathan was sleeping now, Charlie playing with his hair. Sapphire finished her tea and stood up, stretching her body leisurely. "I'm going out for a bit, Charlie ... fancy some fresh air." Charlie smiled at her sleepily. "Good idea, hon. Don't go too far, though." Sapphire smiled at her caring nature. "I'll just go across to the woods for a while. I won't go off the path."

Sapphire dressed for the outdoors, changing into undies and fresh jeans and top. It looked warm outside but she took a light jacket just in case. She left the cottage fifteen minutes later, heading up the lane towards the woods just across from the cottage; she had often walked there since moving to the area. Charlie had showed her some of the pathways that linked the lane they lived in to the small village. Sometimes she would cut across the woodland path to get to work, but only sometimes. Coming from London, she still felt a little scared walking on her own. As she headed into the woods she took deep, soothing breaths of fresh air into her lungs, her body starting to feel better by the minute.

The sunlight filtered through the tree canopy above her. The path was fairly wide and well-trodden; she could hear birdsong around her and it made her relax just that little bit more. The green grass and ferns around her swayed gently in the light breeze, the sound of her footsteps slow and soothing against the earth. She walked for some time, taking in the scenery around her, the different trees catching

37

her eye, the subtle variations of greenery around her calming her mind.

She paused for a moment as she heard a rustling in the undergrowth beside her. A rabbit appeared just in front of her. It froze suddenly, sensing her presence. It stood up on its hind legs, nose twitching furiously, its ears moving around, listening for danger. Sapphire held her breath, afraid to scare him. The rabbit spotted her and took off quickly into the safety of the ferns; she watched its white tail bounce off into the greenery. Sapphire followed, deciding to check out this part of the woods.

After several near misses over tree roots she found herself staring up at the biggest tree she had seen in a long time. "It must be a beech tree," she thought to herself, looking up at the wide canopy. The trunk was huge, twisting and turning in a pattern of moss and vines. All around her was still – the rabbit long gone, the birds for that moment quiet. Sapphire looked up at the tree as she held out her hand and placed it on the trunk. She closed her eyes and breathed deeply for a moment, running her fingers over the trunk, sensing the deepness of its roots, the soft cool sensation of the moss covering its girth. "What a beautiful tree," she thought to herself. Keeping her eyes closed, she leant towards it for a moment and placed her cheek against the trunk. Sapphire felt a tingle in her hand, against her cheek – a soft hum not unlike the feeling she had had last night when she had taken the drug. She jumped back quickly, a little startled by the feeling.

The hum stopped. She held her hand out again … placed it back on to the tree trunk. It started again. This time Sapphire kept her eyes open. She could see a haze appear from the tree trunk. It covered her hand like the wave of heat on a car roof in the summer. She laughed out loud. "God … now I'm seeing things."

The crack of a branch made her spin round. An older woman was standing behind her, carrying a basket full of what looked like grass and twigs. She smiled at Sapphire kindly. "Lovely tree, that one. Old energy. Has a lot to say if you listen hard enough." Sapphire stepped away from the tree trunk now, a little conscious of her tree hugging. "Yeah … it's beautiful. I've not seen a tree this big before." Still smiling, the woman put her basket down on to the ground and looked up into the branches. "It's been here a long time."

She stepped forward towards Sapphire, her hand out in front of her in a friendly gesture. "Didn't mean to startle you. I'm Pearl; I live just the other side of the woods." Sapphire took her hand and shook it, surprised by how soft her skin felt. "Sapphire ... I'm fairly new to the area." Pearl regarded her, a soft smile on her lips. "What a lovely name, my dear. You have lovely energy, too." Sapphire looked down at the ground, smiling shyly. "Well, I don't really know much about that kind of thing." Pearl chuckled. "You will, my dear. You will." Sapphire frowned, not really understanding what she was talking about. Perhaps the old dear was a bit crazy.

Pearl took a step towards the tree and reached out to touch it herself. "I could teach you – if you like – how to link in with the energy in these woods. They are special woods, you know. This tree is actually the centre of the energy here ... not many people know that, but I was born in this area, grew up with the woodland ... my mother taught me how to live with the land." Sapphire nodded, trying to look polite. "That sounds lovely. Maybe some other time; I should really be getting back."

Pearl did not seem offended. She stroked the tree lovingly. "Of course, dear. You must be tired. After all, you had a heavy night." Sapphire stepped away slowly, slightly confused. "Yes ... yes, I did have a bit of a heavy one." "Well, it was nice to meet you." Sapphire stepped away cautiously, a little freaked out by the old dear. Pearl smiled at her kindly. "It was certainly nice to meet you, Sapphire. Until next time, then."

Sapphire walked a little more quickly now, wanting to get back on to the path. She left the old woman standing by the tree and as she moved back down the path she could hear the woman talking to herself, or maybe the tree. Either way, Sapphire wanted to get going now. The last twenty-four hours were going from strange to proper odd. She headed back to the cottage, rethinking what Pearl had said. Did she really have lovely energy? Why could she suddenly feel things she could not feel before? It felt like something was changing inside her. A slight tingle of fear spread across her chest. Or was it excitement?

Chapter Five

The next day Sapphire had risen early for her morning shift at the coffee shop. She had heard Charlie just getting up as she was leaving. Charlie worked for herself. A business lady in her own right, she designed and made her own unique style of jewellery. Her workshop was at the side of the cottage; sometimes she would head up to London herself to meet buyers and attend exhibitions. She was a talented girl: made good money, too.

Sapphire walked to the coffee shop. It was 7.30 a.m. when she arrived for her shift. Linda was already setting up; they opened at 7 a.m. every weekday for the morning coffee punters. She smiled at Sapphire as she made her way to the back of the shop to start work. "Morning, Sapphire. Did you have a good weekend?" Linda was wiping the counter top; she had already turned on the coffee machines and the smell of freshly-ground coffee lingered in the air. There were a few customers already enjoying their morning brew. It was reasonably quiet for a Monday morning, Sapphire noted gladly.

"Yes, I did. How about you?" Linda carried a tray of cakes over to the counter to be placed under transparent domes for clients to be tempted by during the day. Linda baked exceedingly good cakes. "Why, yes; I did, my dear. My daughter came to visit for the weekend. We went shopping on Saturday and had a lovely meal in the evening; it was very pleasant." Sapphire smiled as she started her routine of tidying and preparing for the next customer, a naughty thought of her decadent dancing on Saturday night flickering through her mind. "Good. I'm glad."

The rest of the day passed quickly. Sapphire was kept busy from 8 a.m. until 3 p.m., when her shift finished. She quite liked the morning shift – giving her the rest of the day free – a steady flow of latte demands and sandwich orders giving her no time to reflect on the strange events of the weekend. She still felt slightly hungover and was glad to hang up her apron after her shift. Linda had packed her a couple of chocolate muffins for her to take home. She was a good boss and Sapphire was grateful that she at least would have no idea that she had been off her head at the weekend, rolling around on some stranger's lawn at four in the morning.

Heading back home again, Sapphire noticed the old lady she had seen yesterday standing outside the local post office. She looked up as Sapphire glanced across the road at her and waved with a smile. Sapphire waved back slightly awkwardly, feeling a little strange that the woman had now befriended her.

The cottage was empty and quiet when she entered later. Charlie was obviously in her workshop. She flicked the kettle on and opened the bag Linda had given her to inspect the chocolate muffins; they looked back up at her wickedly, inviting her to indulge. She made two cups of tea, placed the muffins on a plate and headed outside to the workshop to find Charlie. Her friend was on the computer at the back of the little workshop. The desk pushed against the window gave Charlie a view out over the garden; beside her was an unfinished piece she was working on.

Charlie was oblivious to her entry until the door clicked behind her. She jumped a little and turned around to face Sapphire, tea and muffins in hand. "Crap, Saf. You scared me." Sapphire placed the cups down on the desk. "Sorry, Charlie. Thought you might like a break. What are you working on?" Charlie eyed the muffins with appreciation. "God, is it that time already? I've been trying to redesign this piece for some lawyer in London; he's planning on surprising his wife with a necklace and earring set. He has some ideas that I just can't seem to get right for him. I'm doing some research ... a sugar fix should help."

Sapphire handed her a muffin, helping herself to the other mound of chocolate as she looked over Charlie's shoulder at the screen in front of her. "Looks good to me, but then what do I know about the world of jewellery design?" Charlie stuffed the muffin into her mouth, licking her lips with approval. "I'm still a little rough from Saturday night. How are you faring, hon?" Sapphire smiled. "Same. Work was busy. I think I might take a nap, actually." Charlie raised her eyebrows in envy. "Lucky you." Sapphire chuckled, finishing the last tasty chocolate morsel. "Yeah, lucky me … but then I don't earn the big bucks like you." Charlie smiled at her amiably. "I'll see you later, then. Enjoy your nap." Sapphire left her friend to it and headed back into the house, looking forward to getting horizontal.

Sapphire decided to lie on top of her bed with the blanket she had for extra warmth laid across her legs. She had changed from her work uniform of t-shirt and black trousers into her joggers and jersey top; she was too tired to shower just now. The curtains were still open, her window slightly ajar, so that the light breeze of the afternoon could flow into the room. She nestled into her pillow and closed her eyes, allowing herself a little time for a short catnap before dinner. It wasn't long before she drifted off, the weekend's overexertion still weighing heavily on her body. Sapphire drifted into a heavy sleep. Feeling comfortable and safe, she started to dream.

Sapphire could feel soft feathers beneath her fingers. She was gripping on to a bird … an eagle the size of a horse. She was flying high above the clouds. Her hair whipped in the wind behind her, away from her face, as the eagle swooped and glided through a clear blue sky dotted with patches of cool, soft clouds. The sensation of flying so high was exhilarating. She felt free and happy. The eagle was calling to her as he flew; a cry of friendly familiarity. They were in synch with each other, twisting and turning through the air. Sapphire smiled. She felt light as a feather, as free as the bird she hitched a ride with.

Without warning the eagle began to dive towards the ground at breakneck speed. Sapphire let out a whoop of excitement. Her head down, she gripped tightly as they plummeted to the ground. The long eerie cry of the eagle rang in her ears, the ground looming up quicker and quicker until she could bear it no more and closed her eyes ready for impact. With a jolt Sapphire suddenly landed back on her bed. Her breathing was rapid and she felt disorientated for a second. She was in her room again under her blanket, lying on her side, as she had been when she had lain down. She blinked, her eyes still feeling heavy. A strange tingle began in her chest. It grew as she stretched lazily … she suddenly recognised this feeling. It was unpleasant; it was instinctual: it was fear.

Sapphire was now aware, without seeing, that someone was standing in her room with her. Her heart began to beat faster. She held her breath. A dark shadow was next to her bed. It moved towards her ... she could just make out its shape in her peripheral vision. She opened her eyes, paralysed now by the fear that was gripping her chest. She could not move, could only hear her breathing that was coming in short, fast bursts from her lips. The shadow was right next to her now, tall and forbidding. It was a man, a man in a dark cloak. She could not see his face. The urge to scream was fierce in her chest, but she could not scream. Without warning the figure seemed to bend down and a hand shot out from the cloak and grabbed her ankle. It pulled her hard across the bed towards it. Sapphire screamed.

Charlie was standing next to her, a worried expression on her sweet face. "Saf, sweetie. It's OK. You were dreaming. It's only me – it's OK." Sapphire opened tearful eyes and sat up quickly. She was panting with fright. "Oh, my God. Oh, Charlie ... that was horrible. I had the most horrible dream." Charlie sat on the bed next to her and stroked her forehead gently. "I can tell. Are you OK now?"

Sapphire looked around the room. It was still light, although the dusk was rapidly drawing in. There was no one in the room except her and Charlie. She could still feel the lingering fear of having the man in her room, his grip on her ankle ... she was shifted across the bed as if it had been real. The blanket that had been on her legs was now on the floor.

Charlie continued to watch her cautiously. "What did you dream?" Sapphire shook her head slowly, pulling her legs up to her chin and hugging herself protectively. "It started OK. I was flying on an eagle, really fast, really high. Then I thought I'd woken up. I was here back on the bed again, then ..." She paused, remembering the last part of the dream, almost afraid to speak the words in case he came back. "Then there was this man standing by my bed in a cloak. He grabbed my leg and pulled me towards him off the bed. It was awful." Charlie sighed deeply. "Oh, honey. That's not nice. It was just a dream, though maybe just a bit of the comedown still hanging around. Shall I make us a cuppa?"

Sapphire smiled up at Charlie weakly. "Yes that would be nice. I'll come down with you." Charlie stood up, the bed shifting slightly. As she walked toward the bedroom door she looked back at Sapphire. "It was just a dream, Saf." Sapphire nodded and started to follow her, suddenly wanting to leave the room quickly.

They sat in the kitchen sipping the tea Charlie had made. Charlie had put the radio on quietly, almost sensing that Sapphire needed some distraction to bring her back to reality. "What do you fancy for dinner, hon?" She looked across at Sapphire, who still looked slightly shell-shocked. "I could do some chilli." Sapphire shook her head. "I'm actually not that hungry. I think I'll just have a sandwich... I think that muffin filled me up earlier." Charlie nodded. "OK. I'll grab something from the freezer." She wandered off, leaving Sapphire alone in the kitchen for a moment. The freezer was out in their utility room. Sapphire could hear her rummaging through its contents.

"Do you ever dream, Charlie?" she called out to her friend, who reappeared with a ready-made pasta dish. "Yeah, sometimes. Mostly a load of rubbish ... you know, people on the TV and weird shit sometimes. Nothing major." Sapphire blew on her tea, her fingers wrapped around the mug, finding comfort from the warmth. "My dreams feel so real. Sometimes they are so vivid ... it's kinda strange... they have been getting stronger since I moved here."

Charlie inspected the ready-meal box. Pulling out a sharp knife she began punching holes in the plastic covering, before popping it in the microwave. "Really? Must be all the changes in your life. It can't have been easy uprooting ... and, obviously, losing your dad and all that." She smiled kindly at Sapphire. "Change can mess your head up for a while, and grieving can be worse." Sapphire raised her eyebrow in contemplation. "Oh, I haven't really grieved. I didn't really know my dad. It's not that. Must just be the energy round here. I met an old lady in the woods yesterday – Pearl – she told me that the woods out back are really old and the energy is strong there."

She paused, watching Charlie's expression, which now seemed confused. "Not that I know anything about that sort of stuff...actually, she was a bit weird." Charlie turned the microwave dial to ten minutes and pressed the on button. She looked back at

Sapphire and chuckled a little. "Ah, Pearl … yes … she's the local witch. Harmless, but I would take what she says with a pinch of salt." Sapphire nodded, suddenly feeling a little silly. "I suppose it must just be the changes in my life recently. Anyway, I'm sure it's nothing." Charlie leant across the kitchen table and patted Sapphire's arm. "I think you just flew a bit too high on Saturday night, hon. Now you're coming back down. Look … I'll get you some vitamins and you'll be fine tomorrow." Sapphire watched her friend with hope. She was starting to feel like she was going a little bit crazy.

The rest of the evening passed without incident and, as time went by, they watched some TV and chatted. The dream faded into the back of her mind. She went up to bed at her usual time of 11 p.m., read for a while, listened to Charlie chatting on the phone to Nathan, put her book to one side … then hesitated as she went to turn her bedside light out. Just for one night she would leave it on. Just for tonight.

Chapter Six

Tuesday

Sapphire woke from a dreamless night to a darker sky. It was raining. She showered and dressed for the weather, heading out for another early shift at the cafe. She took the long route to the cafe, avoiding the woods. Linda was there as usual, bustling around her morning clients with a happy smile. Sapphire was glad for the normality. She was feeling slightly shit today, just as Nathan had predicted. It was not only raining outside; she felt like her own individual rain cloud was hanging over her head and covering her in a gloomy mist of crapness. She got stuck into her daily routine of coffee and cake, happy for the distraction of the customers.

Sapphire was wiping down the tables. It was 2.30 p.m.; nearly time for her to finish her shift. The cafe was quiet now. As she lifted a menu to wipe away a smudge of spilt sugar she felt a presence next to her. She jumped, still a little edgy. Her personal rain cloud was still happily pouring a sheen of rain on her head.

Pearl was settling into the chair at the table she was cleaning. She smiled at Sapphire warmly. She was wearing one of those old-lady see-through rain caps; she looked quite chirpy, despite being more than a little wet.

"Hello, my dear. It's so nice to see you again."

Sapphire regarded her cautiously, backing off a little. "Hello, Pearl." Pearl started to undo her rain cap, a cup of tea in front of her. Sapphire had not even heard her come in, let alone go to the counter.

"Oh, my dear. You look a little rough around the edges today. Bad night?"

Sapphire smiled tentatively "You could say that."

Pearl tipped her head to one side, sizing Sapphire up with X-ray eyes. "Mmmh ... not sleeping well, are you? I have something for you that could help with that."

Sapphire watched as she reached down into an oversized cloth bag. She rummaged for a moment, mumbling under her breath. "Ah, here it is." Sapphire watched as she pulled out a large sprig of herbs. "Put this on your headboard; it will help you sleep." She pushed the herbs across the table towards Sapphire. "It's lavender, my dear. Good for sleep." She paused for a moment. "Oh, and you could try putting some salt around your bed. It will keep the nasties away." Sapphire touched the lavender gently with her fingertips, frowning slightly. "The good stuff, mind you ... not that table salt stuff. You need proper rock salt." Sapphire nodded, her mouth slightly open in mild confusion. "OK. Yeah, the proper stuff."

Pearl smiled up at her and took a big gulp of tea. "People like us need protection, you know. Otherwise we don't get a minute's peace." Sapphire took the lavender and moved away, slowly nodding at the old woman, trying not to appear rude. "Mmmh ... well, thanks very much. I'll think about that." "You do that, my dear," Pearl continued, smiling, looking slightly vacant.

Sapphire made a swift turn out of the back of the cafe to the rest area and raised her eyebrows in dismay. "What the fuck?" The old woman was clearly nuts. She eyed the lavender suspiciously but decided to bag it anyway, just in case. Linda passed her in the corridor. "You OK, Sapphire?" Sapphire nodded. "Oh, yeah ... I'm fine. Just finishing up; I'll be off in a minute, if that's OK, Linda." Linda smiled sweetly at her. "Of course, my dear. You go; it's quiet now. I'll see you tomorrow." Sapphire found her raincoat and grabbed her bag, noticing with surprise as she walked back into the cafe that Pearl had gone. She left, shaking her head in confusion. How had the old woman drunk her tea so quickly?

Sapphire stopped by the corner shop on the way home and browsed the aisles for salt. She found some Cornish rock salt, paid at the counter and left, feeling slightly stupid. For some unknown reason she felt compelled to do as the old woman had said, "Buy the good stuff." With the lavender and the rock salt tucked into her bag she walked home. The rain had at last stopped and she noticed her own personal cloud had also given up on its relentless onslaught. She did feel slightly better.

She peeled off her raincoat and kicked off her shoes when she got back to the cottage, dumping her bag on the kitchen counter. She shouted out for her friend. "Charlie, are you home?" Charlie emerged from the living room. She was wrapped up in her cardigan, a frown on her face. "Yeah, I'm here." Sapphire laughed. "Are you feeling as crap as me today?" Charlie continued to frown. "God, yeah. Suicide Tuesday. Nathan jinxed us."

Sapphire ran her hand through her slightly damp hair. "Have you finished work for the day?" Charlie nodded. "I've given up. Managed to finish the necklace and earrings eventually ... didn't feel like starting anything else." Sapphire watched her friend, slightly amused by her disgruntled expression. "Let's watch a movie. You can skive off for the afternoon with me." Charlie allowed a small smile to cross her lips. "OK. As long as it's got someone nice to look at in it." They settled for *Pirates of the Caribbean*. Something fun with Johnny and Orlando in it would help them both pull out of the downer they were on. They snuggled up together on the sofa. Despite the fact that it was nearly summer, the damp day and their comedown had made them resort to finding warmth in each other.

Two hours and much tea consumed later they both felt better. Sapphire cooked them egg and chips for tea – comfort food. By ten o'clock Sapphire was ready for bed. It had been a weird and tiring couple of days. She hoped that she would feel better tomorrow; paying back for the weekend was now becoming a little draining. Charlie had agreed an early night would do them both good.

Sapphire took her bag upstairs and, feeling a little stupid, unloaded the lavender and rock salt. She had lit an incense stick and looked around the room a little hesitantly before finding some ribbon in one of her drawers to hang the lavender from. Her bed frame had an ornate iron headboard – perfect for tying the lavender to. Sapphire noticed with pleasure the smell of the lavender as it crushed slightly under her hands when she tied it to the centre of her headboard.

After undressing and brushing her teeth in the bathroom she put on an oversized t-shirt with a picture of a large rabbit on the front. It was her favourite. With a slightly crazy chuckle she took the box of rock salt out of her bag and contemplated the packet for a moment, wondering how exactly she was supposed to do this. With the scent of the incense (Nag Champa – more good stuff) and the lavender her room did feel lighter and safer. She decided to sprinkle the salt all the way around her bed, from one side of the wall to the other, so that a neat square of salt surrounded her bed. She laughed at herself, hoping Charlie would not come in and have a fit that she was throwing stuff on the carpet.

Standing back to admire her work, she wondered just how she had ended up carrying out this strange little ritual. It was just a precaution; she did not want to have another bad dream and she really did need a good sleep. She nodded with satisfaction, lifted the covers and slipped into her cool bed. It felt good to feel so comfortable at last. She picked up her book and started to read. Before long Sapphire could feel her eyelids becoming heavy, dropping every so often as she read her Charlaine Harris book – she loved a bit of *True Blood*. It was 10.45 p.m. before she put her book down. Feeling sleepy and comfortable, she settled into the pillows. She turned the light out tonight, drifting off with the scent of lavender and Nag Champa soothing her mind.

Sapphire could sense she was dreaming again. Her body was light, her mind was alert, but she felt safe. She was lying down on grass again. It was dark; the sky was obscured by the branches of the tree she was underneath. She noticed with surprise that the branches were lit up with tiny sparkles of light; they twinkled and shone down on her, making her body glow in the dark. She sat up slowly and took in her surroundings. She was in a forest, but it was unlike any she had seen before: the grass also glowed with a throbbing network of lights. As she touched the blades beneath her they lit up brightly and a sharp tinging sound echoed in her ears. The plants and flowers surrounding the tree were brightly-coloured ... fluorescent in pinks, blues and purples, like something on Pandora.

A low humming noise was coming from in front of her. She shifted position so that she was sitting up properly, her back now against the tree trunk. As her eyes began to focus she watched in awe as a ball of white light grew closer and closer ... growing in size, its brilliance was making her squint. Within the centre of the light she could see the outline of a person. It became clearer and the light slowly began to dim.

It was a man. He walked towards her. Sapphire raised her hand to her mouth and gasped. He was back. Fox was back. He stood over her, looking down, his amber eyes swirling with gold and black specks. He was magnificent. For a moment she could not breathe. His beauty was breathtaking, and she was so utterly and completely overwhelmed by his return. "Fox." He bent down, his hair falling across his shoulders, his hands placed on his knees as he crouched. He had a flower in his hand. It was a white calla lily.

"Hello again, Sapphire." Sapphire licked her lips and breathed again. "Where have you been?" He smiled, his handsome face open and warm, so very pleased to see her. "I've been right here, my beautiful lady." Sapphire reached up to take the flower from him. As he leant forward to place it in her hands it changed from white to red as she touched it. "Are you OK, Sapphire? You look worn out."

Sapphire looked into his eyes, knowing that at any minute she could wake up and he would be gone. "It's been a weird few days." He sat next to her, brushing his hand across her cheek, leaving the signature tingle as he did so. "Yes, I know it has, gorgeous." Sapphire placed the lily on the grass. It changed back to white again. "What's happening to me, Fox? This can't keep happening. You can't keep appearing in my dreams ... I'm so confused."

He slipped his arm around her shoulder and pulled her into his chest. She was immediately engulfed in the sweet smell of patchouli and sandalwood. "It's OK, Sapphire. I'm here again. I'm always here to protect you." Sapphire snuggled into him, pushing her hands into the warmth of his clothing, his soft loose shirt and the heat of his body calming her. "You keep saying that, but this is getting crazy. I need to understand what's going on." Fox kissed the top of her head.

"They have been watching you. I have been trying to hide you but they are noticing now. It's getting harder for me to keep you a secret; it's not so safe any more. But don't worry. I won't let anything happen to you." Sapphire looked up at him. Now the dream was making her feel woozy, almost like she was drugged or drunk again. "Who are they? And who are you?" The air around them smelled sweet and a light breeze played with Fox's hair, making it rise and fall gently. "They are the gatekeepers. You have been travelling in and out often now and it's getting more difficult to keep track of you."

He sighed, his eyes still flashing gold and black, "I know this is hard for you to understand, but you have to trust me. I am here to help you; I have always been here for you." Sapphire lifted her hand and touched his mouth softly, revelling in how warm he felt. "You talk in riddles." He laughed and kissed her fingers gently. Sapphire felt a surge of arousal in her groin as his lips caressed her fingertips. "You will remember in time, my lady."

Sapphire leant back into his arms, wanting to remember this feeling – the feeling of being safe and cherished again. "I am glad you have met the wise woman. She will help you on the other side. She has put protection in place for you already. She is a strong soul." Sapphire smiled. "Oh, yeah – you mean Pearl, the crazy lady." Fox stroked her arm, sending shivers along her spine. "It is no coincidence you have met, Sapphire. She understands our world. She is one of us; her job is to protect the balance."

Sapphire felt her mind swim with confusion. The dream was becoming hard work. She really did not understand what the hell was going on. She just wanted to touch him, be with him, enjoy the naughty side of the dreams she was so happily now having with this imaginary man. "Can we talk about that later? I'd very much like to begin where we left off last time." Fox slid her down in one graceful movement and hovered above her again. "As you wish, beautiful."

Once more Fox was kissing her, devouring her, and she was up for it like a dog on heat. Sapphire closed her eyes and wrapped her legs around him. His body was now pressed to hers and she felt every inch of his hard muscular form. His hands were everywhere and, in a blur of movement so fast she could not keep up, he had removed whatever clothing she had been wearing and she was now blissfully and very thankfully naked. He caressed her breasts, making her moan with pleasure. Taking her nipple into his mouth he sucked slowly, his hands sliding up and down the rest of her body in a slow, tortuous dance. She noted hazily that he was also naked from the waist up. The lower part of his body was still frustratingly covered in leather trousers; the leather was so thin that he bulged against the fabric.

51

As his fingers danced across her skin she reached down greedily to touch him. He growled, releasing her nipple, as she found what she was looking for and squeezed slowly. This was a most excellent dream; he was nicely well-endowed, of course. Sapphire was reliving the moment they had lain on the lawn in Simon's garden. She was quivering like a bow, heat coming off her body in waves. Fox claimed her once more, his fingers now inside her, as she rode the waves of pleasure. He was so fucking good at this.

Sapphire came up for air. Fox looked into her eyes and smiled. "You are mine." Sapphire squeezed again and he closed his eyes for a moment, the smile turning into a look of absolute surrender. With a swiftness that Sapphire did not know she was capable of she undid his trousers and released Fox from his restriction. Without having to look she knew without a shadow of doubt that she was in trouble again – big, big trouble. Fox slid himself free and, like her, was now absolutely and most magnificently naked. Sapphire felt like time had suddenly stopped. Fox was suspended above her, his hair flying around his head, his eyes flashing with a raw need that almost frightened her. She could feel his whole body grow tight above her as he paused for a moment, his fingers sliding out so very slowly as he eased himself over her. She bit her lip, grasping his back now … waiting, waiting in anticipation for him to take her, for him to claim her completely.

She wanted this so badly it hurt. Fox slid down, his lips taking her own, his cock rubbing the outside of her now overly-wet pussy. She thought she would explode any second. As he pushed himself inside her the feeling of intense pleasure took over, and she shook with a need that was so great it consumed her. Sapphire let her body go. She was floating on an erotic roller coaster, riding this man with an enthusiasm she did not know existed inside her. The air around them crackled and Sapphire felt herself spin out. She was falling, spiralling out of control. She could feel his hard body moving above her; she gripped him tightly with her legs as he pushed himself rhythmically inside her.

Each time he pushed inside her body she melted a little more. His pace was slow at first, an exquisite form of torture that she did not want to end. As he kissed her harder his pace began to quicken. She could feel his whole body start to tremble … the tension between them was intensely sweet. She could feel his heartbeat grow faster and louder. Fox was becoming the animal she had seen within his eyes. He paused between kisses and whispered low guttural words of pleasure in a language she did not understand. The heat from their bodies caused a halo of light around them. They were lit up like a Christmas tree … the very ground beneath them seemed to be scorched with the heat they were creating. She could sense his need to possess her, to devour her. The thought of this possession only made her grip him tighter. She could hear Fox now calling out her name – a wild, desperate call, as if he was losing his ability to hold back, his need to release inside her overwhelming him. Her body was almost numb with pleasure. She threw her head back in ecstasy, riding, riding, until something broke inside her and she was lost completely. White light engulfed her; her body shook like a volcano about to erupt. The light was so blinding she felt like she would never be able to see clearly again. Abruptly and without warning, just as she felt Fox lift his head to howl up at the moon above them in primal release, the man she held between her legs shattered into a million tiny pieces.

Chapter Seven

Wednesday

Sapphire sat bolt upright in her bed; it was still dark. She was hot and panting. She instinctively turned on her bedside light and looked at her alarm clock. It was 4 a.m. The room was still and silent around her. Beside her on the pillow was a flower. It was a red calla lily. Sapphire blinked, blinked again. It was still there, sitting on the pillow. Sapphire touched her face; sweat was covering her skin in a fine film. Her body was shaking slightly and she noticed that she was naked; the rabbit t-shirt she had been wearing earlier was nowhere to be seen; the covers were pushed to the end of the bed. Her hand moved tentatively down to her groin; she was wet and sticky, the tender flesh swollen and tingling. Sapphire felt a hot blush rise up from her belly to her cheeks. "Fuck me."

She lay back down on the bed, allowing her body to calm her mind, which was racing from the dream she had just awoken from. It had felt so real; she could still feel him inside her, his mouth claiming her, his body pounding her ... "Oh-my-fuckin-crazy-losing-my-mind-God." Sapphire closed her eyes. Her body was starting to cool now; the trembling inside her belly was calming down. She felt utterly spent, totally wonderful, in awe of the fact that she had created this fantasy that felt so real. Sapphire reached out and touched the calla lily, her heartbeat jumping a little ... but this was real – it was actually here in her room, an organic object. How could that be? She found herself giggling a little uncontrollably. Suddenly this all seemed so completely crazy. She had to get a grip; she was losing her mind. A smile crept on to her overly-sensitive just-been-kissed-to-death lips, but it felt so fucking good.

Sapphire left for work as usual for her early shift. She had fallen back to sleep for a few hours, a deep, wonderfully satisfying sleep. After showering and smiling at herself in the bathroom mirror, admiring the hickey that was still blossoming in a nice shade of blue and yellow on her neck, she dressed and headed out the door.

The sun had decided to appear again. She was feeling extremely smug and happy with herself, despite the fact that she might actually be carted off to the funny farm very soon. Her body and mind was singing like she had just won the lottery. Her night with Fox, even if it had been a dream, was making her feel on top of the world. Her comedown was well and truly gone; the day couldn't be more different from the previous two she had trudged through after the weekend.

She pushed the door to the cafe open with a spring in her step. Linda eyed her suspiciously, but made no comment on the extreme change in Sapphire's mood from the day before. Sapphire worked like a woman on a mission; she was overly enthusiastic and smiled to herself all morning. She almost fell over laughing when at 1 p.m. on the dot Pearl walked through the door.

Pearl, on the other hand, took it all in her stride and smiled at Sapphire like she already knew she had gone bat shit crazy. "Oh, Sapphire; it is so good to see you back in good spirits. I take it you had a much better night's sleep." Sapphire laughed, almost a little too loudly. "Oh, God. Yes, thank you, Pearl. The lavender and salt really helped me sleep." Pearl nodded, a big knowing smile creeping on to her lips. "Ah, yes. They did, didn't they? I'll have a peppermint tea, my dear. If you have a minute come sit with me."

Sapphire continued to smile at her like the Cheshire Cat on acid. "I'll see if I can take ten minutes. I haven't actually had a break today yet." Pearl had settled into the window seat. Linda had no objection to Sapphire taking a break; she had watched her whizz round all morning and was rather worried she was overdoing it (or had taken speed that morning, not that she would say that). Sapphire had made herself a tea; coffee might be pushing it with the high she was already on.

Pearl smiled at her sweetly as she placed the drinks in front of them. "Well, my dear, you must be feeling the after-effects today of holding the lantern just a little bit too long." Sapphire sipped her tea, feeling a strange little buzz in her chest as Pearl held her gaze. "Sorry, Pearl. I have no idea what you are talking about. Don't you mean burning the candle at both ends?" She let out a little giggle as if she was drunk, and put her hand over her mouth. "Ooops, sorry. I don't know where that came from." Pearl gave her own little chuckle as if she was in on the joke. "Oooh, dear. My, my; he has been naughty, hasn't he? You are shining like a beautiful star today, my dear. We will have to dampen that down a bit or the whole town will be thinking you are drunk."

Sapphire noticed the buzz getting stronger and she did indeed feel a little drunk. She looked down into her tea, wondering if someone had slipped something into it. She laughed again. Pearl reached down into her bag and pulled out a packet with some crushed substance in it. It looked suspiciously like weed. Sapphire put up her hand in mock horror, "Oh, God. No, Pearl. I really don't need any drugs. I'm fine, just really, really happy today."

Pearl continued to nod. Smiling, she took a teaspoon of the herb from the packet and slipped it into Sapphire's tea. "Believe me, dear, you need this. His essence is still on you; it's like a beacon shining in the harbour for all to see. We need to dull the signal a bit, otherwise 'they' will get a whiff and be knocking on your door. We really don't want that, do we?" Sapphire shrugged her shoulders and sniffed the tea. With all the crazy events that had been happening over the last week she actually didn't care that the old woman was adding to the World's Craziest Week award.

Sapphire sipped her newly-spiced tea. It actually tasted amazing, liked cinnamon and vanilla. As the warm liquid filled her belly the buzz started to fade and she did feel slightly less mad. Pearl looked at Sapphire, her eyes wandering around her head, as if she was admiring something on top of her hair. "Oh, yes. That's better, Gosh, you do respond very quickly, don't you?" Sapphire leant forward slightly and whispered, "Pearl … really, I do not have any idea what you are talking about." Pearl laughed. "Of course you don't, my dear … not yet, anyway … but everything will become clear eventually." Sapphire raised her eyebrows. "Oh, God. You are the second person to tell me that in less than a week." Pearl nodded again. "You and I need to talk properly, my dear … not here. Come and see me at my house; it will be safe and much easier there. Are you free at the weekend?"

Sapphire smiled at the old lady. Despite the fact she was proper Looney Tune, she had actually warmed to the woman. "Actually, I am working all weekend, but I could meet up with you in the evening on Sunday. I don't have any plans, but then again I never do." Pearl patted her hand affectionately. "That would be lovely, dear. In the meantime, take some of this with your tea each day. Just a spoonful, mind; don't want you fading out on us completely. Here is my address – I'm not far. Shall we say 7 p.m.?" Sapphire took the packet of weed and the slip of paper Pearl had scribbled her address on. She noticed that Pearl's house was ironically called Foxglove. "OK, I'll see you Sunday. Shall I bring anything?" Pearl chuckled as she finished her tea. "Just yourself, dear. I will provide the tea and nibbles."

Sapphire watched the old woman push her chair back and stand to leave, with some disappointment that she was leaving. Her happy buzz was still there but she did feel less twitchy. Pearl looked back as she was about to leave and smiled again. "Be safe, my dear Sapphire. Try not to encourage him too much." Sapphire felt her mouth open slightly as Pearl left the cafe, the bell ringing as the door closed behind her. Encourage who?

That afternoon Sapphire returned to the cottage to find Charlie busy in her workshop; she, too, seemed to be back on track after the weekend. The necklace and earrings she had designed and made for the London lawyer were finished and sat in a satin gift box. The chain was made from white gold; the design was a beautiful flower with diamonds set into its petals. The earrings were a matching set of delicate flowers; it was beautiful and unique.

Charlie had started on her next commission: a set of wedding rings that were due to be completed within a month. She was working on the design with a new enthusiasm. The couple had a large budget (this seemed the norm with Charlie's clients) and she had been given free rein with the design, the couple asking for something that would reflect their personalities – which seemed to encompass a theme of intertwined vine-like patterns and which on screen looked very *The Lord of the Rings* in its intricacy.

Sapphire admired her friend's work. She had brought tea out to the workshop and they chatted for a while before she left her friend to it to return inside for some time on her own before dinner. As she felt much more like her old self this afternoon she set about with mundane chores – putting a load of washing on, cleaning the bathroom, tidying the kitchen for a while. She was happy in her work and glad to feel some normality returning to her life. Her mind drifted over the past few days and the events that had happened; seeing Pearl again today and their date for Sunday made Sapphire feel quite excited. She was actually looking forward to seeing the old lady again, plus it might help her understand just exactly what was going on with her newly-muddled brain.

She had prepared some fish and vegetables for their dinner and had a little time on her hands before Charlie would come in to eat with her. Sapphire fired up her laptop and decided to do a little internet searching and catching up on her Facebook page. She hardly used the social networking scene but it had been a while, and sometimes her mum sent her messages and pictures. She noticed that some of her old work colleagues in London had sent her a "Hi, how are you doing?" message, and was glad once more that she had left that world behind her. Despite the fact that everything had seemed a little crazy here lately, she was so much happier now in her new life.

After checking her messages and sending her mum an update on how she was – totally missing out, of course, the fact that she had been partying at the weekend, taking drugs and having (sexually) mad dreams with a hot stranger (mums really didn't need to know that kind of thing) – she found herself surfing the net looking for information regarding dreams. Sapphire was amused to see that there was a minefield of information – what dreams meant, how we can lucid dream, how our brainwaves change in our sleep patterns, etc., etc.. She was intrigued to learn that dreaming was a way of releasing trauma from our bodies; that sometimes a bad dream was good – it was a form of mind therapy. She came across some Freudian stuff that basically said – from the dreams she had been having regarding Fox – that she was a sexual deviant. It all became a little deep and dark and she decided not to look too much into that page.

She was unaware of Charlie returning to the cottage and jumped as she realised her friend had been looking over her shoulder at the page she was studying. "Mmmh … dream interpretation, Saf. Are you working out what your naughty dreams mean?" Sapphire blushed a little, quickly reduced the page on the screen. "Just curious, you know. I've been dreaming a lot recently; I just wanted to see whether there is something behind it." Charlie walked over to the oven and checked out the food inside; she pulled back a little as the heat hit her face. "Is this nearly ready? I'm starving." Sapphire pushed back the kitchen chair. "Yep. I'll dish up; you set the table."

Charlie busied herself, grabbing cutlery and some water for them each, setting the little kitchen table for them to eat their dinner on. Sapphire dished up the poached fish and roasted vegetables; she, too, was pretty damn hungry. They munched silently for a moment, both tucking into the food. Sapphire watched her friend, a little cautious to tell her about Pearl, but wanting to share what the old woman had said to her. "Charlie ... you know that old lady, Pearl, I bumped into in the woods?" Charlie tackled a piece of carrot; she was food-focused. "Yes, hon. What about her?" "Well, I've seen her a couple of times in the coffee shop. She invited me to her house on Sunday evening for tea. She seems to be quite sweet, but I'm not entirely sure she is all there."

Charlie laughed, taking a sip of her water. "Really? I don't really know her, just know of her. She's apparently harmless; lived here all her life. I think she's a little eccentric, but you should be OK. It would actually be quite interesting to see where she lives." She paused for a moment. "I mean, I don't think she's a serial killer or anything. You should be safe." Sapphire laughed. "Well, that's good, then." Charlie licked her lips. She had devoured the dinner in double quick time. Sapphire wondered how she stayed so slim; she always ate with such gusto, and always ate so much. "How come she has been talking to you? She normally keeps herself to herself ... bit of a hermit ... weird that she's suddenly reaching out to you." Sapphire nodded. This thought had also crossed her mind. "I don't know. It's kind of strange. We've only chatted briefly a couple of times, and most of the conversation hasn't made a lot of sense to me, but do you know what? She seems very familiar to me. Maybe it's because my mum is all the way up in Scotland and she's kind of mumsyish." Charlie nodded, smiling at Sapphire, "Aw, bless. That's cute. Well, go for it, hon. You are making new friends, after all."

They finished dinner, Charlie including a slice of cheesecake at the end of her meal – Sapphire wishing she could do the same but knowing her butt would possibly grow another inch if she did. Nathan was supposed to be popping round and staying the night, so Sapphire knew it was time to make herself scarce and leave the lovebirds to their making-out session. She headed up to her bedroom at 9.30 p.m. and settled into her book. She had lit her incense stick and inspected the salt barrier before making herself comfy under the covers. She suddenly remembered that she had forgotten to have another spoonful of the herbs Pearl had given her with her tea, but what the heck? It was late now; she actually didn't really know what they were for, anyway.

Sapphire read for over an hour. She had heard Nathan coming in around 10 p.m. Charlie was very happy to see him; luckily they were downstairs in the living room, which helped muffle the noises of their get-together. Tomorrow was Thursday; the week was actually flying by pretty quickly. Sapphire placed her book on to her bedside table and turned her light out. She had set her alarm for her next early shift, thankful that on Friday she was working the afternoon and could have a lie-in. As she slipped down under the duvet and nestled into her pillows she absently wondered what tonight would bring. She actually hoped for a night off; all this virtual sex was taking its toll on her.

Chapter Eight

Sapphire actually got her wish. She slept the whole night without dreaming, or if she did dream she did not remember it. She worked her shift at the cafe and did not see Pearl again. Life had returned to normal, for now, anyway. That evening Charlie had gone out with Nathan to The Swan for a pint. They had invited her to join them but she wasn't up for socialising and was quite happy to have the cottage to herself. She had decided on catching up with some no-brain-required TV and was happily munching some tortilla chips, when at 8.30 p.m. there was a knock at the door. She looked up warily, pausing the TV box, her ears pricking up. She wasn't expecting anyone ... she didn't know anyone here. Whoever was at the door knocked again, somewhat loudly.

Sapphire got up a little hesitantly; it was a bit late for some random person to be knocking on the door. The outside light had come on; she could see through the side window that a tall, dark shape was standing at the door. Her heart fluttered a little with anxiety, her inner sense of caution pressing a big alert button. The person at the door knocked again, twice, just as loudly as before. "Hang on. I'm coming." Sapphire put the chain on and opened the door slightly with a somewhat shaky hand.

The dark figure stepped forward. She stepped back instinctively. "Sapphire Whittaker?" His voice was deep and gruff. "Yes." He seemed a little miffed that she had put the chain on. Despite the outside light shining down she could not see his face clearly; he had a hoody on and his face was tilted downwards. "I have a message for you." Sapphire could hear her heart start to thump a little wildly; her mouth suddenly became very dry. "Yes. Who from?" The man stepped forward and placed a hand on the door frame. She noticed his nails were just a bit too long and were particularly nasty in colour; he obviously hadn't washed properly for a while. "We are watching you. You have been marked. Your friend cannot protect you all the time. You have been warned."

Sapphire slammed the door shut. "Fuck off, whoever you are," she shouted at the closed door. Her adrenalin was rushing now. She stepped back into the corridor, hiding in the shadow of the hallway. Her heart thumped loudly in her chest as she held her breath, waiting for something to happen. Everything became still for a moment; the light outside clicked off as if the man who had been standing there had suddenly disappeared. Sapphire stumbled backwards, clutching her chest. "What the fuck? That was bloody scary. Who the fuck was that?"

She grabbed the landline phone and quickly dialled Charlie's number. Listening to the phone ring, she whispered, "Please pick up." It rang for longer than she wanted before Charlie finally picked up the call; she could hear the sounds of voices and music in the background from the pub. "Hey, Saf. What's up?" Sapphire let her breath go, not realising she had been holding it for so long. "Oh, God, Charlie. Thank God. Some crazy bloke just knocked on the door and scared the shit out of me. Are you guys coming home soon? It's kinda freaked me out a bit." Charlie muffled out for a moment. "What? Yeah. Oh God. Are you OK? Don't worry, we will head back now ... Don't worry, hon. Put the lock on the door. I'll call you when we get there so you can let us in."

Sapphire nodded and hung up. She hurried to the front door and put the lock on, ran back into the lounge and closed the curtains quickly. Not wanting to look outside, she sat down on the sofa. The TV was still on pause. She grabbed a cushion and held it protectively to her chest, curling herself up into a ball. Who the fuck was that? What did he mean by "We are watching you"? Chills ran up her spine. She suddenly remembered her dream of the man standing in her room, grabbing her legs. She began to shake suddenly, feeling very sick.

The phone rang, making her jump out of her skin. She jumped up and grabbed the handset. "Yes?" "Saf, it's me. We are literally two minutes away; I'll be there any second." Sapphire sighed in relief. "OK, Charlie. Thank you." Minutes later she heard hurried steps coming to the cottage door. Charlie called out to her, "It's me, Saf.

You can unlock the door, hon." Sapphire ran to the door and unlocked it, stepping back to let Charlie and Nathan inside. They tumbled in, worried expressions on their faces. Charlie hugged her; she was cold from the night air. Sapphire held her for a moment, glad to see her friend. Nathan shut the door behind them. "Hey, honey, you are shaking. What happened?"

Sapphire released her reluctantly and held on to her friend's hands. "It was weird. This guy was standing at the door, knocking really loudly. I had put the chain on, thankfully. He said they were watching me and I'd been marked. Fucking freaked me right out." Charlie shook her head in bewilderment, looked across at Nathan, who looked equally confused. "Shit. That does sound scary. Must be some local nut job; maybe he'd had too much to drink, decided to knock on a random door and scare you. Shall we call the police?"

Sapphire let go of her friend's hands and rubbed her forehead, feeling a little dizzy. "No, no. It's OK. It was probably nothing; I'm just glad you came back. Thank you, guys." Nathan was at the window, looking out of the curtains. "I don't mind scoping outside, just to check he's gone. Don't worry, Saf. I won't let some twit scare you again." Charlie nodded. "OK, sweetie; just be careful." "Saf, come and sit down. You look as white as a sheet."

Nathan disappeared out the door; he grabbed the poker from the fireplace on the way out. Sapphire sat down on the sofa; Charlie hugged her protectively. "Don't worry, Saf. Nathan will sort him out if he's still hanging around. He can take care of himself." Sapphire nodded, feeling majorly unsettled. "He just scared me; I'll be OK."

There was a knock at the door again, making both girls jump. "Charlie ... it's me, Nat. Let me in; there's no one around." Charlie left Sapphire on the sofa, letting Nathan in. He put the poker back into the stand by the fireplace. "No trace of anyone; it's as quiet as a mouse out there. Whoever it was is long gone. Look, I don't mind staying here tonight, if you want." Sapphire nodded. Charlie agreed, always happy to have her man around.

They rallied around and grabbed Sapphire a whiskey, telling her she looked like she needed one. They watched TV together for a while until the unsettled feeling of earlier had started to disappear. Charlie and Nathan were overly protective for the rest of the evening, making sure Sapphire was safely tucked up in bed after she had taken a hot bath to calm herself down. She left her bedside light on that night and doubled the salt barrier around her bed. She lay for a long time staring up at the ceiling before finally succumbing to a restless but uneventful night's sleep.

Chapter Nine

Friday flew by. Sapphire was glad it did; she was starting to feel a little ragged around the edges. She did not see Pearl again that day and the evening was spent quietly, with both Charlie and Nathan watching her like a hawk. They had decided to grab a takeaway and were watching *Avatar* on DVD. Sapphire remembered her dream in the woods, where the plants and trees were so similar to those on Pandora; perhaps that was where Fox lived, she thought with some amusement. A faraway parallel universe, where people danced around fires and made love under big shiny trees: she almost smiled at her own sense of humour about the whole thing.

Nathan had said it would be best if he stayed the night again, considering the night before had been so eventful. Charlie was more than happy to accommodate him and Sapphire had retired early again, so that she did not have to hear the lovebirds at their nightly coupling. She was feeling extremely tired that night and was glad she did not have to get up too early for her next shift at the cafe. After showering and brushing her teeth she picked up one of her favourite books by Laurel Hamilton. Dark fantasy was her thing; it would take her mind off her own life for a moment. Burning the incense had become a nightly ritual now, and she found it cleared her head a little and soothed her jittery mind. It was 11 p.m. before she turned her bedside light out; she could just make out the sounds of Charlie laughing from her bedroom across the hall and reached for her earplugs, just in case their headboard started banging. She fell asleep quickly, feeling heavy and a little sore in her body. She had been on her feet all day; the cafe had been particularly busy that day. Her mind drifted as she started to fall asleep; she prayed for a peaceful night.

Sapphire could hear music. It was a gentle and soothing tune, perhaps a flute or pan pipes. Her eyes were closed; she wondered if she was dreaming again, or if Charlie was playing music from her bedroom. No, it wasn't from Charlie's room: there was no way she would be playing something so New Age. Sapphire opened her eyes reluctantly. She was lying on a bed, but it was not her own. The sheets were white cotton, the expensive kind, and it was a four-poster. A film of white lace hung around the bed frame and above her head in an elaborate canopy. A gentle breeze touched the material and lifted it softly, creating a scene from a romantic movie.

It was just light. She sat herself up and looked down to see, with some amusement, that she was dressed in a long white gown like something from Roman times – a toga, she thought to herself. As she scanned the room she could see more detail through the white lace canopy. The room was sparse, with a few pieces of wooden furniture and a balcony in front of her. The windows were wide open and she could see a view that would take anyone's breath away; a vista of trees spanned out below her. She realised that she must be several floors up in a building she did not know. She was dreaming, for sure.

The temperature was warm and pleasant and the air smelt of herbs and freshly-cut grass. She pushed the canopy to one side and looked down at her feet and wiggled her toes, just to see if she could. The floor was tiled and as she placed her feet on to them the sensation of cool marble gave her a pleasant tingle. She walked with a slow floating sense of weightlessness to the balcony and looked out across the landscape before her. She could have been in Tuscany; it was beautiful.

But Tuscany did not have elephants and wolves roaming its lands. This was going to be one of those types of dreams: the ones where totally weird shit happened. The elephants were feeding from the trees and the wolves lounged sleepily under the branches enjoying the shade from the sun, which had now suddenly risen to full height. Sapphire noticed that the sky had not only a very large sun but two moons and a planet in the distance, haloed by rings, like Saturn. She giggled out loud, "I'm on Pandora." A noise behind her made her jump around quickly. "Not Pandora, my beautiful Sapphire. You are on Shaka now."

Sapphire smiled at the man before her. Fox stood in white linen clothing, making his skin appear more tanned than usual and his wild eyes deeper and darker than she was used to. "Fox." He came to her as she reached for him, hungry for his touch, wanting the comfort of holding him again. He grabbed her greedily and squeezed her tightly. Breathing in the scent of him, Sapphire sighed in relief. "I know this is not real, but I'm glad you came. My life is getting weirder and this dreaming is making me go crazy." He kissed the top of her head, stroking her face with the side of his hand. "I know, my darling. We need to talk. I need to explain some things to you; things have changed somewhat since we last met."

Sapphire looked up at him, drowning in his beautiful amber eyes. The black circle around the iris was glowing now. He looked so beautiful in this light; every contour of his face was crystal clear; he seemed to glow slightly. "I had a bad dream the other day, and then this crazy man turned up at my door the other night and scared me. I wish you had been there." Fox nodded with understanding. He dropped his hands from her waist and pulled her hands into his, wrapping his fingers between hers. "Come with me. Let's sit and talk for a while."

Without warning they were suddenly outside, sitting against a wall facing a fountain that threw purple and silver water into the air; it shimmered and twinkled in the sunlight. Sapphire was sitting beside Fox; he had his arm around her and was looking at her with a slight frown on his perfect forehead. She did not like to see this expression on his face. Fox leant forward and kissed her gently on the lips; it was a sweet kiss without the usual passion she felt when they connected. But it was perfect at that moment, reassuring and comforting.

He leant back, releasing her lips slowly. "I wish I had been there, but I have been kept busy here. They have been causing diversions to keep me away from you, but I will never let them harm you, Sapphire; you have to believe me." Sapphire shook her head slowly, confusion filling her already-addled brain. "Who are they? Why is this happening to me?" Fox took a deep breath and caught a stray hair from Sapphire's shoulder, playing with it absently, as if deciding which words he should say.

"Sapphire, you are special. You have been travelling between dimensions while sleeping; it is something only a few beings can do and when it happens bad things often come of it." Sapphire blinked at him. "But I'm dreaming now. This isn't real; none of its real. I must be going crazy." Fox released the strand of hair, slowly allowing it to slip back across her shoulder. "You must start to believe that some things in life cannot be explained, but they are real. This is real, we are real … you and me, this place, where you come from … they all exist."

Sapphire was lost for a moment, her mind spinning with this piece of information. "OK … so you are telling me that the last few times I have dreamt of you I have 'travelled'? What about the time I saw you at the party? What was that all about, then?" He smiled again, the frown now removed. "I can travel to be with you sometimes. If your energy is altered I can reach through the veil and step into your world, as can the others."

Sapphire reached out and touched his face, the skin warm and smooth. "Yes, the others … the mysterious others … Please explain." Fox took her hand and kissed her fingertips again, sending little shocks down into her belly. "The gatekeepers: they hold the balance, keep things under control. They don't like it when people slip through. It causes them problems."

Sapphire sighed, wanting to feel his lips on her mouth again. His body being so close to hers was causing her libido to hop up and down like a March hare. "But I have no idea how I'm doing it. I don't mean to do this; it just started happening a while ago. I seriously just want to be normal, not some strange 'jumper'." Fox laughed, his tone deep and silky; she felt it in her toes. "I've been watching you a long time. It's my job to make sure you understand everything, although – to be honest – I have become slightly obsessed with you. You are the most interesting person I have had to take care of for a very long time."

Sapphire switched into jealous mode. "There have been others like me?" Fox leant forward and kissed her again, this time with a deeper intensity, and she could do nothing but fall into it without caution. As he pulled away gently Sapphire held him tightly, not wanting him to stop. "Not like you, my Sapphire. Not like you." Sapphire wanted to climb on to his lap and kiss him until she burst into flames. All the other stuff could wait. Fox smiled widely at her as if he could hear her thoughts. Maybe he could. "I can teach you how to control it, but now that you have opened the door there is no turning back, my beautiful Sapphire. You are a dream traveller now. It is a gift in some ways, but as with all gifts there is often a price to pay."

Sapphire wiggled a little closer to him. She just wanted to hold him now, before the dream ended again and she woke up to reality. "Teach me later. I want you to kiss me now." Fox shook his head. As she lifted her leg to sit astride him, he placed his hands on her arms and held her away gently. "As much as I would really, really love to do so much more than kiss you, I have been given a rather harsh telling off by the powers above that I am not to saturate you too much with my essence. Apparently it makes you act strangely." Sapphire pushed against him, pouting somewhat sulkily. "This is my dream; I can have what I want. That's not fair."

Fox laughed loudly, his whole face lighting up as he did. "I totally agree, my horny woman ... but for now I have to restrain myself, at least until the old woman has given you some more protection so that our meetings can go undetected." Sapphire could feel her body temperature start to go up. She was turned on just sitting on his lap and she wanted release. She moved her groin around in little circles to get his attention. It worked. She could feel him start to grow hard beneath her and he moaned slightly, his eyes flashing. "Sapphire, you are making this very difficult for me."

Sapphire smiled and continued with her lap dance. She leant back and pushed her breasts into his face, sighing loudly as she did. "Well, if you really don't want to help me out I suppose I will just have to do it myself." He held her around her waist, a low groan escaping his lips. "You are so bad, my little Sapphire." She did not care one little bit. This dream was going to end as she wanted it to, with her being satisfied. Elephants and wolves could roam around behind them for all she cared, she wanted to get off on him and that's what she was going to do.

Fox's willpower caved in. With a growl he leant forward and seized her neck with his mouth, kissing her with a fevered passion. Sapphire continued to work out on his groin. She was really enjoying herself: the added sensation of Fox licking her and kissing her was just adding to the buzz now radiating from her charged and pulsing pussy. Fox had managed to release her breasts from the toga and was now continuing his tongue dance across her very erect nipples, moving from one breast to the other. Sapphire could feel every little lick and suck in her groin. She moaned loudly. Fox was gripping her tightly now, whispering to her again in the musical language she had heard him speak before. It turned her on even more. "Oh, my God, Fox. You are making me feel sooo good."

He let go of her breast, making her jump for a second. He seized her mouth again and kissed her hard. They melted into each other. Sapphire felt herself rising upwards; they were literally above the ground, and – most satisfyingly – they were totally naked. Fox was twisted around her, his legs imprisoning her within their grip. She could feel his very hard cock pushing against her stomach. In her mind Sapphire pictured them back on the four-poster bed, and – pop – just like that, they were. She smiled to herself smugly. Now she was getting the hang of this. Of course, it was her dream: she could make this happen just as she wanted it.

Fox rolled on top of her and lifted his head up. His hair was as wild as ever and his eyes were dark and hooded with passion. He smiled a wicked smile at her before pushing himself without any warm-up or warning into her wet and waiting pussy. Sapphire shuddered with glee. He felt so good, filling her completely. This time, without any holding back, he took her. Pounding her hard, his eyes flashed dark and light; she gripped him tightly, holding him closer, pushing her hips up to meet him. They were like animals, clawing and grasping at each other. They rolled across the cool cotton sheets, tearing at each other.

Sapphire could not get enough; she could sense the warm build of climax start to flicker in her body, growing hotter and hotter. She sensed Fox's own need to release. He kissed her again and again, taking her so close to the edge. She ended up on top of him, riding him like she was breaking a stallion in for the first time. He held her waist and stared into her eyes, licking his lips with greed. Sapphire pushed down on to him, took every inch of him inside her. Fox groaned loudly, his grip tightening on her hips. She bucked and rode like a bad, bad woman and felt her orgasm start to break. Like a wave hitting her full pelt with maximum power she cried out in pleasure as her body began to spasm uncontrollably. Fox gripped on to her, waiting for her climax to end. He pushed up with one last hard thrust and came full spurt into her, letting out a howl of victory.

Sapphire collapsed on to his chest. He was still there; he had not shattered into tiny, tiny pieces like he had before. She could hear his heart beating so very quickly, a film of sweat covering his perfect chest. She held him to her and breathed in patchouli, sandalwood and the undeniable scent of raw sex. She was in heaven. Fox stroked her back softly, little circles across her hips ... she lifted slowly and released him. He slid out heavily; she noticed with satisfaction that he was well and truly sated. Fox chuckled softly. "Now I'm in real trouble."

Sapphire lifted her head and smiled up at him lazily. "They can answer to me, whoever they are. Now kiss me again, you amazing man." Fox pulled her up and kissed her softly; his tongue was so very clever at making her tremble all over. As she slipped into his rhythm, she became aware of someone calling her name from far away. "Saf, Saf. Wake up, wake up." She tried to push the annoying voice out of her mind and concentrate on Fox kissing her, his warm body stuck to hers, his hands touching her. "Saf, come on. Wake up. You are seriously late for work."

Chapter Ten

Saturday

Sapphire woke up to Charlie literally shaking her. "OK, OK. I'm awake." She shook her head. Charlie let go of her, stepping back with an amused smile on her face. "Christ. Talk about heavy sleeper – your alarm has been going off for ages. I didn't hear it at first. I was out in the workshop, then realised you must still be in bed."

Sapphire pushed her hair out of her eyes, glad she was actually in her own bed, still dressed in her t-shirt. "What time is it?" Charlie was still smiling at her. "Some dream you were having, hon. You were panting like a dog." Sapphire could feel a blush begin to spread warmly across her cheeks. She lowered her eyes, checking that the duvet still covered her "Really? I can't remember. I must have been really tired. Shit – it's 12 o'clock. I was supposed to start my shift at 12."

Charlie stepped back as Sapphire launched herself from the bed. "Fuck, fuck, fuck." Charlie laughed as Sapphire ran towards the shower. She called out to her friend as she heard the shower start, "Do you want me to call work for you, let them know you are running late?" "Yes, please," Sapphire shouted out, before jumping under the hot water. In double quick time she showered, dressed and rushed out the door. She literally ran to work, feeling super-guilty that she had overslept. Linda smiled at her as she stumbled, gasping from the run, into the cafe. "It's OK, Sapphire. Slow down. We were quiet today; no harm done." Sapphire smiled sheepishly at her, going out to the back room to find her apron. "I'm really sorry, Linda. I never oversleep. I must have been really tired last night." Linda handed her a cloth. "Really, Sapphire, don't stress. If you could just check the tables are clear and give them a wipe … settle in."

Sapphire took the cloth and nodded, feeling like the kid who was late for class. Her heart was still beating fast from the run to work. She took a deep breath and got to work. She noticed that her hands were shaking slightly; adrenalin was still coursing through her body. She had not even had chance to reflect on her dream with Fox – the reason she had overslept. As his face appeared in her mind, those gorgeous amber eyes and full tempting lips slipping over her body, she grew hot and tingly all over. She felt the crazy bubble rise in her throat again and she let out an involuntary giggle. Oh, God, she was punch-drunk on essence of Fox again.

A customer came in and shot her a look of concern before heading to the counter. Sapphire stifled the next giggle with her hand and continued with her table-wiping. She needed to drink some more of the herb tea Pearl had given her; hell, she might even have to bath in it. If what Fox had told her in the dream was true then she had entered a world she had better understand fully pretty damn quick. Her meeting with Pearl tomorrow couldn't come more quickly. She worked hard to make up for her lateness and finished her shift at 6.30 p.m., Linda insisting she leave on time despite her late arrival.

She walked home at a slow pace. The evening was cool and calm, a pre-summer feel to the air. She entered the cottage to laughter and heard voices coming from the kitchen. She kicked off her shoes and deposited her bag in the hallway, curious to find out who was creating the laughter. Heading into the kitchen she was greeted by the smell of food cooking on the hob and found Nathan, Dave and Grace seated at the kitchen table, while Charlie stirred a big pot of brown stuff. She looked up and grinned at Sapphire. "Hi, Saf. We are having chilli. Get yourself out of your uniform and join us." Nathan was opening a bottle of red wine; Dave and Grace smiled up at her. "OK, thanks. I won't be long." She left them to their conversation and went to her room to change. It would be nice to have some normal company for the evening; it was only early and she had a feeling the night would most likely be a long one.

Dave and Grace were great company, funny and full of good stories. Sapphire did not feel like the odd one out with this little group; they included her in the conversations and the wine was going down very well. She had started to relax again. The wine was helping her to unwind and her belly was comfortably full from dinner. "You guys go get comfy in the living room. I'm just going out for a ciggy;

help yourselves to more wine." Charlie left the kitchen, her mission for a nicotine fix high on her priority list.

Dave and Grace followed Nathan out into the living room. Sapphire stayed to tidy up; her need to clean up spilling over from work into home life was quite a bonus at times. She was happily filling the dishwasher and wiping down the kitchen tops when she heard a squeal of alarm come from the back garden. "Nathan." Charlie pushed the back door open, stumbling inside with a look of fear on her face. Nathan ran in from the living room. "Nathan, some bloke is standing at the back of the garden." Nathan's expression grew dark; he shot out the back door.

Sapphire felt her heart start to race; instinctively she knew something was very wrong. "Charlie, are you OK? Who's out there?" Charlie placed her hand to her chest, calming herself. "I didn't see him at first – was just standing there having a smoke, when I noticed a shadow at the end of the garden. Then I realised it was a person. Really freaked me … maybe it's the same guy who knocked on the door the other night. Oh, God. I hope Nathan's OK." They both rushed to the back door.

Dave and Grace had appeared in the kitchen, worried looks on their faces. "What's going on?" Nathan appeared at the back door again, a frown etched on his forehead. "I saw him. He jumped over the fence when he clocked me but by the time I reached the end of the garden and looked over he was gone." He paused, scratching his head. "I really think we should report this. It's a bit strange, especially after Saf getting that crank door call the other night."

Sapphire could feel a cold spot growing in the pit of her stomach. This was all her fault; this shouldn't be happening. "I agree. This is getting silly now." Charlie hugged her man. "I'll make the call." Nathan grabbed the landline phone, Charlie turning around to face the others. "Come on; let's go back to the living room. I need another glass of wine." Nathan joined them again after finishing the call. "I've reported the guy. The police will send a car around to check the area; apparently there have been some break-ins recently so they have advised us to be doubly careful when locking up."

Sapphire wanted to cry. She knew this had nothing to do with burglars in the area. It was one of them; one of the mystery men Fox had warned her of. It was her fault. She was probably shining like a strobe light after her wild night of sex with Fox. She knew if they met again it would have to be purely for talking. No more rampant fucking in her dreams any more. She felt mildly annoyed that this bothered her so much. But the thought of some strange man with long fingernails outside in her garden made her stomach turn slightly.

Gradually the party started up again, Dave and Grace finding it all very exciting. Charlie did not go out for another cigarette the rest of the evening. After playing music for a while, Charlie dancing in the living room on rather wobbly legs with Nathan watching her and laughing, Dave and Grace admitted they were calling it a night and headed out. Apparently they did not have far to walk. Being residents of the village themselves, Nathan did not seem too worried about them finding their way home alone. Sapphire was not so confident, but then realised it wasn't them the strange man in the back garden was looking out for. As long as she stayed in the house tonight with Charlie and Nathan and they locked all the windows and doors they should be OK, shouldn't they?

Despite having drunk just as much as the others, Sapphire felt quite sober when she went up to bed later that night. She felt nervous and the cold spot that had appeared in her stomach earlier was still persistently throbbing in her centre. They had double-locked everything before retiring but Sapphire could not shift the feeling of being watched. It was unnerving. The only comfort she held was that she was seeing Pearl tomorrow after her shift at the cafe. Maybe she would have the answers, and the means to protect herself from the gatekeepers.

Closing her curtains quickly and lighting a candle and incense, Sapphire felt the need to say a little prayer before she got into bed. The thought made her laugh out loud; praying was not something she was accustomed to, ever. Finding herself on her knees like a little child beside her bed, she placed her hands together and looked up at the ceiling. "If anyone is listening up there, could you please help me? I really need some help, you know, with all this weird shit that's happening to me." She paused, realising just how crazy she sounded, and shook her head, smiling at herself. "Oh, never mind."

She got off her knees and climbed into bed, hugging her pillows to her body tightly. "Fox, if you can hear me, please just watch over me tonight. I don't think we should meet up – it's too risky, but I'm thinking of you." She whispered into the darkness, hoping he would hear her words and chase away the unsettled feeling in her belly.

Chapter Eleven

Sunday

Sapphire left the house at 9 a.m. the next morning. Charlie and Nathan were still sleeping and the cottage was quiet and still. Any evidence of the party the night before and the strange man in the garden were no longer visible. Sapphire was glad she only had a few hours scheduled at the cafe today. She was itching to meet up with Pearl; she had a thousand questions buzzing around in her head. Sundays were often busy at the little cafe and Sapphire was glad for the distraction; she even helped out with the sandwich-making and was kept busy with coffees, teas and fruit juices all morning until her shift ended at 1 p.m. She felt physically drained by the time she hung up her apron.

The other lady who helped out on Sundays had come in a little earlier today and she took over from Sapphire with a smile. Linda was out back making more sandwiches and placing handmade cupcakes under a transparent dome as she picked up her bag to leave. "Any plans for tonight, Sapphire?" Sapphire paused for a moment before replying, hardly believing it was only a week ago that the strange events of her life had started taking a massively weird turn into *Alice in Wonderland* World. "No, not really. I'm just visiting Pearl for a while. Do you know her? The old lady who came in the other day who was talking to me."

Linda raised her eyebrows "Why, yes. I know of her; she has never been into the cafe before. Funny, that. I've lived here all my life and have only seen her out in the village on the odd occasion before. Until she came in the other day I'd not really seen her any further than the post office." She finished placing the last chocolate cupcake with gold glitter on the top on to the cake display and looked at Sapphire curiously. "When did you get to know her?" Sapphire fiddled with the strap on her bag, suddenly feeling a little self-conscious. "Well, I bumped into her in the woods last weekend and then I just kept seeing her. She seems very friendly and, well, she just invited me over to join her tonight for some tea." Linda smiled. "Well that's very nice, my dear. She is an interesting character. Apparently some say she is a witch, but I think that's just village talk. Tell me all about it when I see you next." Sapphire smiled back, nodding sweetly. "Yes, yes I will. I'm quite intrigued myself. Well, I'll be off then. Have a good evening."

Sapphire was glad the weather had turned fair again as she walked home at a brisk pace. She wondered how she would pass the time before she could walk over to Pearl's cottage. She knew it wasn't far from where she lived with Charlie; nothing was very far away in this little corner of the countryside. Entering the cottage she could hear Nathan and Charlie in the living room, having what sounded like a pillow fight. There was much yelling and screaming coming from Charlie; Nathan was laughing his head off as a thump, thump, sound echoed off the walls.

Sapphire poked her head around the living room door and found the pair of them on the floor tangled up in pillows and throws. She smiled and left them to it. "I'm home, guys. Just going up for a shower." Sapphire heard one last shriek as she closed the bathroom door behind her and switched on the shower. It felt good to wash away the day's work. She spent time washing her hair, shaving her legs and washing her face with scrub to remove any trace of the coffee and cake smell. As much as she loved that just-baked smell and fresh coffee, which was always yummy, it started to get a bit overpowering after each shift.

Stepping out of the shower, she wrapped herself in a fluffy fresh towel and breathed in her new scent of apples and freesia. Brushing her teeth finished off the polishing process and she padded back into her room, listening out for Nathan and Charlie, who were now quiet downstairs. She assumed the pillow fight was foreplay and they were now getting down to some serious heavy petting. As it was still relatively early Sapphire decided to read for a while before getting ready for tea with the local witch. She wondered what would be a suitable outfit for such an occasion and giggled. She was engrossed in reading about Sookie and Eric in her latest *True Blood* book.

They were just getting to a really good bit when Charlie knocked on her door. She opened it straight after knocking, obviously assuming Sapphire wouldn't be doing anything that required a two-minute wait before entering. "Hey, hon; just letting you know that we are going out to the cinema tonight. I know you are over at Pearl's, but if you need us to pick you up on the way back we should be out by about 10 p.m." She was still a little worried after the man in the garden incident, it seemed. Sapphire looked up from her book. "No worries. I'll be fine walking back. It's not far, by the sounds of the directions you have given me, but if I get stuck I'll give you a call. Seeing anything good?"

Charlie wrinkled her nose. "Some action film. You know Nathan. He likes a bit of car chasing, gun shooting and all that. Hopefully there will be someone worth looking at in it." Sapphire laughed. "Well, enjoy. Don't eat too much popcorn." Charlie blew her a kiss as she shut the door behind her. Sapphire looked at the bedside clock and realised it was time to get dressed and get going; she felt a tingle of nerves as she pushed herself off the bed and headed to the wardrobe to find her best having-tea-with-a-witch outfit.

It was still light as Sapphire walked down her lane towards the edge of the village. Pearl's cottage was on the edge of the woods, according to Charlie's directions. She had decided to pick some flowers from the garden to take with her; she felt it would be rude to turn up empty-handed. The posy of geraniums she had picked was wrapped in a sheet of pink paper and tied with some raffia that she had found in their stationery bits drawer. The flowers bobbed their heads as she walked.

Turning the corner at the end of the lane, the houses that had dotted the village ended and the path became narrower and slightly less cared-for. As Sapphire continued the path turned into gravel and the wood seemed to close in on both sides. She wondered if she had taken a wrong turn. As she began to doubt Charlie's directions she caught site of a gateway ahead of her. It was overgrown with roses and other greenery and gave the appearance of a living portal; as she grew closer she could see a wooden sign carved with the words Foxglove. She had found Pearl's cottage.

The air around her seemed to grow thicker and Sapphire felt a strange tingling sensation begin to tickle the nape of her neck. As she reached out to push the gate open she realised with some hesitation that all around her was suddenly very quiet. No birdsong, no movement of tree branches in the wind ... it was as if this little bubble around her was holding its breath as she entered. Sapphire pushed the gate open and the bubble let out a sigh. The wildlife began its song again; she could hear a blackbird singing in the tree above her. Weird.

The garden laid out in front of her was a rambling mess of beautifully-established flower beds, with herbs and vegetables growing to one side in a tidy and well-kept vegetable garden. The scent of jasmine and honeysuckle filled her nose and Sapphire inhaled deeply, allowing the sweet, sickly tones to slip across her senses. It was the most beautiful, wild and chaotic garden she had ever seen. So intent on taking in the whole garden around her, Sapphire almost missed the *pièce de résistance* standing in front of her.

Foxglove cottage was straight out of a fairy tale. It was a golden oak colour in the evening sun. Made from what appeared to be wood and flint, it looked like it belonged in medieval times; it was tiny but intricate, with carvings over the doorway of vines and roses, stunning in detail. A chimney rose precariously, leaning to one side of the cottage. Smoke rose lazily from the top, creating a picture of idyllic peacefulness.

Sapphire hesitated for a moment, staring up at the cottage in awe. As she lifted her hand to knock the door opened and Pearl faced her, a beaming smile on her face. "Well, good evening, young Sapphire. Welcome to my humble abode. Come in, come in." Sapphire smiled back at her, feeling immediately at ease. As she entered the cottage she was overwhelmed with the smell of lavender and roses.

It was darker in the cottage; the hallway was lit dimly by large church candles in tall glass holders casting shadows up the walls, which flickered as she walked through. "I was wondering whether you would actually turn up, my dear." Sapphire followed her into a tiny kitchen that was warm and inviting. A range in the corner held a large copper kettle which had obviously just boiled, steam rising from the spout. "Oh, of course I was going to turn up. I wanted to come; I've been looking forward to seeing you."

Pearl turned to face her again, pulling out a chair from the wooden table. Her smile was fixed warmly to her face, her eyes sparkling slightly. "Oh, that's lovely, my dear; I've been looking forward to you coming. I know we have a lot to discuss. What kind of tea would you like? I have peppermint, ginger, chamomile … oh, and of course some Tetley, if you prefer." Sapphire laughed. Sitting down and placing her posy on the table, she noticed the lace tablecloth and crockery set out for two. "I'll have some chamomile, thank you. These are for you." Pearl noticed the geraniums and clasped her hands in glee. "Wonderful. I do so love geraniums. The oil is good for balancing … such a lovely plant, very calming. How very thoughtful of you, my dear."

Sapphire looked around her shyly, trying not to appear like she was gawping at her surroundings. There was so much to take in; every nook and cranny was filled with some object, utensils, pottery, ornaments, and glass jars filled with various pickled and dried fruits and vegetables. It was an Aladdin's cave. The little kitchen window allowed some of the last light to filter in, giving the room a soft haze, making everything appear slightly unreal. Pearl began to fill two cups with water, adding the tea, which was loose-strained through an old-fashioned tea strainer. Sapphire watched her, mesmerised by the old woman, who moved around the kitchen placing sugar and spoons on to the table with a grace and ease that seemed to belong to someone much younger.

"Would you like a flapjack, Sapphire? I baked them this morning. They have a little chilli and spice in them; you know, give them a bit of a kick." Sapphire nodded, smiling. "Yes, please. I would love one." After Pearl seemed satisfied that the table was laid to her liking and the geraniums were placed in a vase made of clay on the side of the table, she settled herself into a chair opposite Sapphire and picked up a flapjack, nibbling the edge. Sapphire copied her and found the sensation of heat tickling her tongue quite unexpected. She almost coughed, thought it would be rude, and swallowed, before taking a sip of her tea. Pearl smiled at her. "They do have quite a kick, don't they?" Sapphire smiled, not quite sure what to say now she was actually sitting at the old lady's table, eating firecracker flapjacks.

"Well, I'm sure you have a lot of questions for me, young Sapphire. I can see you are lit up again like the fourth of July. Did you forget to drink the herbal tea I gave you?" Sapphire fidgeted in her chair, a blush rising in her cheeks. "Erm, well, actually … yes, I did forget one or two days. It's been quite an eventful week." Pearl raised her eyebrows, still nibbling; she seemed unaffected by the chilli. "Do tell me."

Sapphire sighed, taking a deep breath before she began. "To be honest, Pearl, I don't really know where to begin. For the last week I feel like I've gone to Crazy Land and back, and I'm still up to my neck in it." Pearl nodded in sympathy. "Mmmh … what exactly has been going on? Well, except the obvious, that is."

Sapphire felt the blush grow deeper. Could this woman actually mind read? "I'm dreaming these crazy lifelike dreams, and they feel so real. In fact, it feels like reality and the dream world are getting mixed up, and, well …" She paused, looking at Pearl, in the hope the old woman wouldn't call for an ambulance. "People are showing up at my cottage who seem to be real – scary people that this other guy I keep dreaming about has told me are watching me." Pearl blinked slowly; Sapphire held her breath. "That's it. I've done it now; time to call the men in the white coats."

"Well, that must be very concerning, my dear. It's all happening rather fast for you, isn't it? This dream travelling – and, of course, all the hot action with your man rattling your hormones – doesn't help. He is such a very bad influence. Really, in all my years, I have never known such a reckless guardian as Fox." Sapphire choked on her tea, sending a spray of chamomile across the table. Pearl jumped back and laughed.

"You know him? I mean you don't think I'm going crazy?" Pearl lifted a napkin and patted her slightly wet chest. Sapphire was mortified she'd sprayed the old lady with her tea. "Of course not, my dear. It's all real; it's just a lot to take in over such a short space of time, that's all." Sapphire stared across the table at Pearl, her mind suddenly on stop. "Then you believe me?" Pearl leant across and patted her hand kindly. "Yes, my dear; I do believe you." Sapphire leant back in her chair and sighed in relief. "Now let me try to explain to you, young Sapphire, so that lovely brain of yours doesn't pop." Sapphire smiled weakly. "That would be good. That would be very good."

Pearl took another sip of her tea and held Sapphire's gaze; her eyes seemed suddenly very old and very, very wise. "There have always been dream travellers, throughout the ages. For as long as man has existed it has been possible for certain people to move across space, time and dimension." Sapphire felt her body become very still. "But there have not been many. It is a rare gift and it has not happened for a long, long time. The reason for this is quite simple: it can be very dangerous for the traveller and for the people they interact with. As you can imagine, bouncing around the ether and tipping the balance here, there and everywhere can create quite a stir."

Sapphire realised her mouth was slightly open and she was gawking stupidly at Pearl. "There is a balance to everything in life, you know, an order, if you like … and dream travellers can mess with this balance. They can change things unknowingly as they move around. It's often done quite harmlessly, without malice, but of course there are those who believe all action has a reaction and that these actions are deliberate and planned." Sapphire blinked, closing her mouth. "You've lost me now, Pearl."

Pearl smiled, taking another sip of tea. The room had become dark now; candles lit the room with a soft glow. Sapphire noticed that everything seemed to shine and twinkle around her; it was almost as if they were being watched by tiny little sprites which kept flitting in and out of her peripheral vision. "The balance, Sapphire. The balance is all that matters between light and dark, good and evil. Glitches in the dimensions become a problem; you have already left a few little glitches in the last week, you know." Sapphire sat up a little straighter, feeling confused by the accusation. "What do you mean?"

Pearl smiled again. "Every time you travel in your dreams you touch that world, causing a ripple effect, and every time you touch someone in another dimension you leave your presence. You've been doing a lot of touching this week." She nodded a knowing nod and winked. Sapphire wanted the ground to open up so she could disappear into it: the embarrassment burnt her cheeks a bright red, "But I thought I was just dreaming," she mumbled, eyelids turned down. Pearl chuckled. "And you were, my dear, you were; but because you have the gift of dream travel you can touch the other side. You can change the balance and you are causing quite a stir."

Sapphire suddenly felt a little cold and rubbed her arms protectively. "But I don't want to cause a stir; I just want to be normal." Pearl smiled at her. Pushing her chair back, she got up and walked the short distance to a large dresser. Opening one of the drawers, she rummaged around for a moment with her back to Sapphire. "Of course you do, my dear, but what's done is done. This gift has been given to you for a reason and I'm afraid you will have to deal with it." She turned around while rummaging and smiled apologetically at her. "I mean that in the nicest way possible, of course, my dear. I will help you; that's my job, to help you."

Sapphire was warming up a little now, but she was feeling positively weary from the conversation. Perhaps her brain was actually about to pop. "Ah, here it is." Pearl came back to the table with something in her hand. Holding her palm out for Sapphire to see, she placed a large dark crystal on the table. "It's my scrying stone. Haven't needed to use it in a while, but let's have a look and see who it is who's been pestering you." Sapphire peered down into the stone; it was pitch black and looked like it weighed a ton. "What does that do?"

Pearl had her eyes closed and seemed to have zoned out for a moment. Sapphire waited in silence for her to come back into the room. Maybe she had fallen asleep; could it be narcolepsy? Pearl jerked back, making Sapphire jump in surprise. "Right. Let's have a look, then." Sapphire raised her eyebrows; she was definitely in Wonderland now. Pearl placed her hands around the crystal and looked down into the seemingly black abyss. Sapphire watched her with morbid curiosity. She noticed that the stone seemed to shimmer slightly as Pearl gazed down into its mirror-like reflection; her eyes, fixed on the stone, were seemingly lifeless for a moment.

Pearl snapped back again after a second, a little gasp escaping her lips. "Oh, goodness. Oh, well; that really does up the ante." Sapphire leant forward, feeling a little anxious. "What? What did you see?" Pearl leant back and licked her lips as if they were suddenly very dry. "A particularly unpleasant gatekeeper – goes by the name of Hecta, he's not a very nice character – also has the ability, like you, to jump in and out of dimensions. Seems he's hanging around, waiting to see what you are going to do next … in between giving Fox a run for his money." Sapphire peered into the stone, looking for anything untoward. It stared back at her with a blank expression. "So what can I do about that? And please, for the love of God, explain to me what Fox has to do with all of this."

Pearl lifted one of her lacy napkins and placed it over the stone. "Well, there are actually lots of things we can do to keep him at bay. Yes, lots of things … but as for Fox, my dear … he needs to do some explaining himself, I think." Sapphire crossed her arms in front of her chest, feeling a little pissed now. "I'd rather you explain to me." Pearl chuckled again. "Well, he is your guardian. All travellers have one. He was assigned to you before you were even born. He has been waiting for you to become of an age when your awareness begins, so that he can protect you if you start to travel unknowingly – which of course you have." She paused pursing her lips a little in disapproval.

"But the role of a guardian is to protect, not to interact. He seems to have become somewhat obsessed with you and, well, we know the rest of the story there." Sapphire refused to blush again; she felt a little miffed by the whole situation which had been playing out around her. "OK, so he is my guardian; but he has stepped over the line while I've been thinking I'm in the dream world. Right?"

Pearl nodded. "Yes, that's right. Taking a little taste of the cake without permission. Very naughty, although I'm sure he has been well reprimanded for that." Sapphire could feel her backside becoming slightly numb; she realised time had flown by, although she had no idea what the time was now. "Will he always come to me in my dreams?" Pearl regarded the question thoughtfully. "Only if you want him to. You do have a certain amount of control over this, you know, and with guidance you can learn how to manage your travelling. I believe that is one of his roles – to teach you."

Sapphire grew excited at this thought. "Yes. He did say that the last time I saw him – that he could teach me. Is it safe to do that now, what with this Hecta hanging around?" Pearl nodded. "You do need to contact Fox again. He can come to you much more easily in your dream state but, as you know, he is also able to cross the void when your vibration changes in this world." Sapphire could feel the guilt trip start again, remembering her drug-fuelled experience last weekend. "Well, I will make sure that doesn't happen again. It's pretty hard trying to explain to my friends who this wild-haired sexy man is who just suddenly appears and disappears again in my life." Pearl laughed softly. "Yes, of course. You will have to be guarded as to who knows about your little ability. Caution is the key, my young Sapphire; caution and mindfulness."

She stood again, heading back over to the dresser. "Now, let's get you sorted before you go home tonight. We need some stronger protection and some more herbs to dampen that glow you seem to have permanently fixed to your aura. Fox has a particularly strong essence, you know ... well, of course you know that." Sapphire really wanted to go and lie down in a darkened room, take a sedative and wake up not remembering anything.

Pearl returned to the table with a new collection of oddities, including another dark stone which was encased in a silver cage attached to a chain, another bag of weed-resembling substance and a bunch of sticks. "You need to wear this now at all times. Never take it off. The only time you should is when you are with me at this cottage so that I can clean it, say, once a month. It's an obsidian, a particularly special one. My mother placed a very strong protection spell on it. I've been keeping it safe, not really knowing who it was for, until now, of course. You will need to drink the herbs every day. I mean every day. And this is sage. You need to smudge yourself in the morning and in the evening before you go to bed. Keep up with the salt and lavender: that will protect you when you are sleeping."

She stepped around the table and stood next to Sapphire, who looked up at her with wide eyes as she placed the chain over her head. As the crystal touched her skin in the dip of her cleavage a crackle of electricity travelled across her chest and up her neck, making her shiver. Pearl nodded. "It is done. The spell has linked with you; it was meant for you. Good. Now I feel much better, knowing you will be safe." Sapphire touched the caged crystal tentatively. It was warm and seemed to pulse gently between her fingers; it was instantly soothing to her frazzled brain. "Well, yes. I feel much better knowing that, too."

Pearl stepped back and regarded Sapphire solemnly. "Don't worry, young Sapphire. You will be OK. If you need me you know where to find me. It is absolutely no coincidence that you came here to this part of the world. It was your destiny." Sapphire laughed, feeling slightly drunk. "Sounds like something out of *Star Wars*." Pearl frowned. "And what is that, my dear?" Sapphire shook her head, seeing the funny side of all of this now. The old woman had probably never even seen a TV, let alone watched any films. "You have had a long night, my dear. I think you should call your friend to come pick you up now. Take yourself home and get a good night's sleep. I would advise you to not encourage Fox too much. Let all this soak in for a minute before you invite him back into your bed."

Sapphire nodded. She did in fact agree that that would be a very good idea indeed. "What time is it?" Pearl looked up at the ceiling as if some imaginary clock were placed above her head. "It's 10.30 p.m. Your friends will be coming home now, just in time to collect you at the gate as they pass by. Go on; give Charlie a call." Sapphire nodded like a stuffed zombie. This was all too much. "I'll do that."

She pushed herself up on shaky legs and took her phone out from her bag, walking into the dark hallway to call Charlie. She answered on the second ring. "Saf. You OK? We are just coming down the lane – do you want us to stop and pick you up?" Sapphire nodded, holding the phone to her ear. "Yes, please, Charlie. I'll stand outside so you can see me." She clicked the phone off and stepped back into the kitchen. Pearl had placed her bag of protective, get-me-out-of-trouble goodies into a paper bag and stood smiling at her sweetly. Sapphire took the bag, feeling a little like she was floating.

Pearl stepped forward and placed a hand on her shoulder. Sapphire immediately felt the ground beneath her feet again. "Oh, and I really must teach you how to ground yourself properly next time we meet, Sapphire. You are so terribly flighty." She leant forward and hugged Sapphire warmly. For a moment Sapphire was enveloped in the scent of sweet roses and she felt the urge to cry again.

87

In the next moment she was standing at the doorway. Pearl was behind her, waving. The cottage glittered with candles in the darkness like a hobbit house. "Be good, be safe, Sapphire. I'm here if you need me. Come visit me again soon." Sapphire raised her hand and waved back, still in zombie mode. She walked in a daze to the gate and opened it. Turning around to see Pearl still standing in the doorway, a halo of light around her head, she swore she could see lights buzzing around her.

Car lights swept the pathway outside the cottage gate and she heard Charlie and Nathan pull up at the very moment she stepped out of the enchanted garden. She walked to the car. Charlie had wound down her window and smiled out at Sapphire. "You OK, Saf? You look like you've seen a ghost." Sapphire nodded, a weird, slightly crazy smile on her lips. "I'm fine. Thanks for picking me up." She slipped into the back seat of the car, Nathan turned them around and they headed back down the lane. Charlie began chattering nonstop about the film, which apparently was pretty good. Sapphire leant back into the car seat and took a deep breath. This had to be the weirdest, most mind-blowing spangly night she had had in a very long time.

They were back home in minutes. The night sky was clear and the stars twinkled down on them like a scattering of diamonds across a sheet of black silk. Sapphire followed her friends back to their own cottage, finding everything slightly surreal. Charlie was illuminated by the porch light as she searched for her keys, Nathan holding her waist from behind and cuddling up to her as she rummaged through her oversized bag. "Come on, Charlie. I need a pee." Sapphire laughed, slowly coming back to reality as she watched the familiar scene of her friend getting flustered. "Here, I have my keys; I'll let us in." Nathan pulled Charlie to one side, allowing Sapphire to step up, "Hurrah for Sapphire." Charlie wiggled against him, complaining it was not her fault she had so much stuff in her bag.

They tumbled into the cottage, Nathan running upstairs to use the loo. Charlie eyed Sapphire with a wry smile on her face as they took off their shoes. "So, how was it? Did the mad old lady show you her collection of frogs and bats?"

Sapphire smiled at the joke. "It wasn't like that. She's actually a really nice lady, really interesting. Her place is amazing."

Charlie headed to the kitchen. "Fancy a cuppa, or something stronger?" Sapphire followed her slowly, contemplating the offer of a proper drink; she felt like her teaometer was definitely full.

"I'll have a whiskey. I think I could do with one."

Charlie reached for the bottle of Jack Daniels on the top shelf. "That good a night, eh?"

Sapphire hopped up on to the kitchen counter, letting her legs dangle down. She watched Charlie reach into the cupboard for three tumblers.

"She just gave me a lot of things to think about." Charlie poured the dark liquid equally into the glasses.

"The mind boggles."

Sapphire laughed. "Can I have some ice in that, hon?" Charlie nodded and opened the freezer compartment to the fridge. "Lightweight."

Nathan appeared at the kitchen door. "Are we celebrating again? Cool." Charlie passed him a drink. "Sapphire spent the evening with the local witch. Now her head's been zapped so she needs something to take the edge off. Anyone fancy something to eat?" Nathan, of course, wanted food of any description. He was a walking garbage disposal unit at the best of times. They settled on cheese and ham toasties and some tortilla chips (Sapphire's favourite) and retired to the living room to listen to some music to finish the night off.

Sapphire was glad Charlie did not continue to quiz her about her evening. She listened to them chat about the film and sipped the Jack Daniels, enjoying the warmth it spread down into her belly as she started to process the evening with Pearl.

She felt like she had suddenly acquired a very weird and wonderful secret, a secret that she could not even share with her best friend. It made her feel slightly uncomfortable and a little worried that if she let something slip she might be seen as a nut job.

Charlie had poured them another Jack Daniels and Sapphire went with the flow. She wanted to lie down and sleep but part of her was now suddenly afraid. The obsidian was nestled between her breasts; she could feel its warmth and the slight pulse of energy it gave off in waves around her chest. She realised that nothing would ever be the same again. The thought was fascinating and horrifying at the same time.

Chapter Twelve

Fox became acutely aware that Sapphire was sleeping again. He could sense her vibration shift into dream mode. He reached out to her, but she was blocking him somehow. He concentrated on her, pushing his energy further into her world. He sensed her need to rest: he picked up on a new barrier surrounding her. A wave of magic blew across his body as he saw her lying on her bed. He could see she was snuggled comfortably beneath her duvet; she was clutching her pillow, her arms above the cover. He observed her for a moment, watching her breathing deeply. She was sleeping peacefully but a slight frown was etched on her forehead.

He so desperately wanted to reach out and smooth the frown away from her beautiful face. As he pushed his mind further into her world he caught a glimpse of the crystal hanging around her neck. The black obsidian was nestled between her breasts. It was pulsing softly in the darkness; its magic was strong, very strong and it was protecting her from any intruders. He could only cross over when she allowed him to: tonight she was firmly planted in her own world.

The old woman had done well. She had put into place the necessary tools for Sapphire to make her own choices as to whether she travelled or not tonight … had given her a wall of protection that would keep her safe, not only from the gatekeepers but from Fox himself, if she so chose.

Fox withdrew his energy from her world. Tonight he would just observe. He was here if she needed him. If she called out to him he could push through the barrier and be there in a second. That was the nature of it. The tie between the traveller and the guardian … it was the way it had always been.

Fox was seated in his garden, the same garden he had held Sapphire in the night before when she had dropped into his world and they had talked and made love. He leant against the trunk of a huge tree that stood at the edge of his land; it was so old that even

Fox did not know its age. He opened his eyes and allowed the light of the day to filter through his mind. His planet was beautiful and magical. Everything here was shaped through magic, the creatures and beings who lived here all created through a web of ancient and mystical energy.

Fox was the son of a great magician. It had always been his path to become a guardian. Only a few of his people were ever initiated into such an honoured role. Since he had been born he had been moulded and guided into the world of travel through the dimensions, waiting for the time that he would step into his destiny of guardian. The people on Shaka lived timeless lives: they were not immortal but time had a different meaning on this planet. They did not keep track of how long they had existed: it was a journey and each individual played out their journey differently.

Fox had lived a thousand human lives. In his time on this world he had protected and watched only two other travellers and neither of those had been human: Sapphire was the first human to cross over to this world. From the moment she had been born Fox had been given the task of watching over her, waiting for her abilities to blossom. His father had warned him to be cautious with this traveller; he had told him of the myths of human dream travellers, for they were indeed very rare. It had been almost forgotten when the last human had travelled to their lands; it was virtually impossible – but Sapphire had, and she would continue to do so. Fox had become infatuated with her almost immediately. She was like nothing he had ever experienced – her vulnerability, her innocence, her complete oblivion to the way things were outside of her reality.

This knowledge was enough to make dream travelling very difficult for humans; their brains could not cope with the fact that there was a whole world outside their own that could be reached through vibrational changes. She was like a delicate flower which had blossomed but was so very fragile. His need to protect her surged powerfully through his body. He had never before experienced such intense feelings for a woman: even the women in his world, who were by far the most beautiful and intoxicating in many a galaxy, had not touched him the way she had.

He had already been severely punished for stepping over the mark with Sapphire. Saturating her with his magic when they had joined together was forbidden in the role of guardian, but he could not stop himself. If he did not behave himself his father had threatened to disconnect him from her, a process that would be painful – physically and emotionally – for both of them, as the link between them had been forged when she had entered her own world as a baby. It was unheard of for a guardian to be taken away from his charge.

Fox did not want to risk the wrath of his father again. The first punishment had been severe enough and he knew the gatekeeper Hecta was sniffing around her constantly, his curiosity also heightened by the uniqueness of Sapphire. He could not ever allow their link to be severed; he must be more disciplined, for her sake. She was like a newborn taking her first steps into a world she did not understand and it was his job to guide her, teach her, to protect her.

He was sitting cross-legged in a meditation pose, his back against the tree trunk, allowing him to link into the energy of the ground below him more easily. The rush of energy from below gave him a renewed sense of purpose. He would not fail her; he would abstain from touching her, from delving into her beautifully soft and wonderful body. He shuddered slightly at the thought of her wrapped around him, gloriously naked, riding him like a beast, the sensation of his cock pushed deep inside her pulsing in release.

Fox shook his head. This wasn't helping. He stood up abruptly and ran his hands through his wild hair. He needed distraction, anything to stop him falling into the world of Sapphire. He strode across his garden, birds startled from the tree above him flying off with a cry as he headed towards his armoury. Fox was an accomplished swordsman and he had a collection of arms that would impress even the greatest fighters. He pushed the door of his armoury open and stood in the large room, scanning the walls for something to take his mind off her.

His gaze fixed on to a broadsword, its hilt decorated with a large emerald set in gold. Grabbing the sword he flexed his arms, swinging the sword around him, warming up. The weight of the sword was substantial but Fox held it as if it were light as a feather. He moved around the large room, elegant jabs and thrusts warming his body up as he worked the sword, his muscles starting to respond to the movement. Like a dangerous dance he moved swiftly, practising his fighting skills with an imaginary opponent. "It looks like something has you riled, my friend."

Fox spun around, the sword held out in front of him at the ready to face the person who had entered without him knowing. A huge bulk of a man stood in front of him, his hands up in surrender. "Hey, my friend. It is only me. Calm down." Fox was panting slightly from the workout, a smile now curved on to his lips as he recognised his friend before him. "Bear, you know better than that to sneak up on a man with his sword in motion." He dropped his attack stance and stepped back, Bear watching him an amused smile on his face.

"Come my friend, let's eat. You look like you need sustenance." Fox nodded and placed the sword back in its place on the armoury wall. Bear ambled out of the door, ducking his head under the frame as he squeezed out. Fox followed him "What vexes you, my friend?" Bear gestured to a table that was now fully loaded with food under the tree Fox had just been meditating under. Magic was handy in this world. Fox joined him, sitting himself down and letting out a sigh. His arms were throbbing slightly now from the workout. Bear grabbed a piece of meat and jammed it into his mouth, chomping down on the bone with vigour. "You will laugh at me when I tell you, old friend." Bear licked his lips loudly. "Try me."

Fox joined him eating with a renewed hunger. "My charge, the dream traveller I have been watching – she has bewitched me, and I cannot stop thinking about her." Bear chuckled between bites. "Ah, the sweet scent of the female. Where is she from? You have not been tasked with the role of guardian for some time, Fox; perhaps you are a little rusty." Fox smiled, his amber eyes flashing in response to his friends gentle ribbing.

"She is human. She is like nothing I have ever experienced before. My judgement has been affected by her; I cannot seem to keep my hands off her." Bear let out a belly laugh, throwing his head back for full effect. "Oh, dear. By the gods, I'm sure that will have got you into all sorts of trouble, my friend." Fox nodded. "I am afraid for her, that my connection to her will put her in danger." Bear paused, watching his friend's face flicker with worry. "You are one of the oldest guardians, Fox, the best in our time. You will not fail her. If anyone has the strength to find a way around this problem, you will." He reached out for a goblet of wine and chugged it down in one gulp.

Fox pondered on his friend's words, "You may need to help me somewhat with that." Bear finished his drink, slapping his lips noisily with his tongue and wiping his mouth with the back of his hand. "I am here for you, my friend. You know that, whatever the task may be." Fox nodded. "The gatekeepers are watching her; she is vulnerable at the moment. The only guide she has in her own world is an old witch. She is helping her to slowly understand the ways of the dream traveller but I fear for her as she is alone in her world with this newly found gift. It is a huge burden to carry."

Bear was feasting with a vengeance upon the food laid out in front of them; he never seemed to satisfy his overly-large frame. "But the gatekeepers cannot harm her, you know that. It is forbidden. They can only stop her from changing the balance as she travels. Why are you so worried about them?" Fox took a goblet of wine and sipped it thoughtfully. "There has not been a human traveller for such a long time. She has caught the interest of Hecta himself ... He has been turning up in her world, threatening her."

Fox paused, the wine slipping smoothly down his throat, warming his belly. "He has also been playing games with me here, keeping me away from her. I've been watching him play with her. It's troubling me why he seems so interested in her." Bear paused in his eating spree. "Perhaps he knows something about her that you do not as yet." Fox regarded his friend, a frown on his forehead at the thought. "Maybe. They usually only observe, as do I. To appear in her world and threaten her is out of character for any gatekeeper."

Bear licked his fingers, seemingly full now he had demolished the table's contents. "I suggest you consult the Oracle. See what she has to say about your new charge." Fox's eyes lit up. Yes, that would be a very good idea, and the Oracle might be able to see if there was something more to Sapphire – with her newly-acquired gift of travel – than he was aware of. He pushed back his chair with a renewed sense of purpose. "You're not just a hunk of muscle, my friend.

That's a great idea; I shall go right now. I will see you again soon, I hope." Bear looked across at his friend with a grin. "You will, my friend. I have a date with the serving girl at the tavern today. Call me if you need me, but only if you really need me. I intend to get myself some alternative exercise this afternoon."

Fox laughed and stepped back from the table. He placed his hands together in front of his body in the prayer position and closed his eyes. Imagining the Oracle in his mind, he willed himself to travel to her house. In a flash of time Fox disappeared and reappeared outside a building made from glass and crystal; it glittered in the sunlight a shining beacon in the landscape.

Standing at the entrance of the crystal building were two men holding swords and shields. Their heads were covered with helmets, their bodies in leather armour: they were the guards to the Oracle, and no one entered without their permission. They stepped together, swords held up as a barrier, as Fox appeared in front of them. "Halt. Identify yourself." Fox eyed them cautiously. The Oracle was guarded by the best swordsmen on Shaka, and they were not to be approached lightly. "It is I, Fox, guardian to the dream travellers. I seek audience with the Oracle."

They stepped down slightly, pausing, as if waiting for the Oracle herself to give the OK for him to enter. They nodded silently and moved to one side, allowing Fox to walk through to the entrance of the building. As he did so a tremble within the energy made him shiver from head to toe. The magic was strong around this place; the Oracle had dropped her shield for a moment to allow him inside. She must be expecting him.

As Fox walked inside he felt his body tingle with anticipation. He had not seen the Oracle since he had been a child. She had given him her blessing, with his father's permission and guidance, to become a guardian: it was the greatest honour a man of Shaka could ever receive. He entered her receiving chamber. A small group of women were seated on the floor in front of her; they remained completely still as he walked between them. He kept his eyes lowered to the floor, aware of the Oracle herself seated on a plinth slightly higher than her priestesses. "Welcome, Fox. You honour me with your presence. It has been a very long time."

Fox knelt down and bowed his head respectfully. "Goddess, our most revered Oracle, I am grateful for your audience. I send you blessings and light from me and my family." The Oracle gestured for him to rise, a long white hand stretched out gracefully in front of her. "You have grown into an outstanding young man, Fox. It seems the role of guardian has been good for you."

Fox looked up into the eyes of the Oracle and was blinded for a moment by her light. She was beauty personified; a being so pure she shone like a star in her chamber. As his eyes adjusted he could see a slight smile on her lips, as if she already knew why he was there. "I need your guidance, Oracle. My new charge is causing me some concern. As you may already be aware, I have stepped off my path as guardian and been punished accordingly by my father. I do not wish to fail him or my charge again. I ask for your wisdom and insight to aid me in serving her better."

The Oracle laughed, a sound so light it twinkled in the air like a wind chime. "Ah, yes. The human dream traveller. She is a rare find, and to have travelled so far to our world is quite unique. This has not happened for a very long time." Fox waited with eager ears to hear of her thoughts on Sapphire. "This woman is very special. She has many gifts, all of which will cause her and you some difficult challenges ... but you must not lose yourself in her, Fox. She is precious and you must not lose sight of the fact that she is yours to guard, to protect from her own power – of which at the moment she does not have the slightest idea is so very strong."

Fox held his breath slightly at this news, "What other gifts apart from dream travel does she possess?" The Oracle continued to smile down at him. Her hair lifted softly around her face like a breeze had caught the air; sparks of light moved across her body like fireflies. "Some you must find out for yourself, but others I can tell." Fox waited with bated breath for her to continue. "She can sense the energy of nature and communicate with it when needed; summon the animals and insects at her will. She can harness the power of the elements and escape danger through illusion and magic, even in her own world." Fox took a deep breath in: this was indeed a lot of gifts.

"But the most interesting gifts are yet to be revealed to me, young guardian. That is why the gatekeeper is afraid of her; even he does not know exactly what she is capable of yet, which makes her very interesting and very dangerous. She is unaware of these gifts as yet, but they will come in time, and it is your job, Fox, to help her control them … because I have a very strong feeling that this woman is the key to changes as yet unknown within her world and ours." Fox stepped back slightly. He felt the need to run to Sapphire right now, to hold her and protect her. She was so very vulnerable; he could not believe he had jumped straight in with her when she was so very precious. The Oracle lifted her hands into prayer position, closed her eyes and shimmered for a moment. Fox watched her, mesmerised by the way she flickered in gold and silver light.

She opened her eyes once more; the smile was just a flicker on her lips. "Your link to her is very strong. The attraction between you will keep you together no matter where she travels, but you must not let it destroy you both. The balance between lust and love is fragile. She needs your judgement to be clear at all times. This journey has just begun for you both and there will be times when you will both be tested to your limits." Fox bowed his head. "Thank you, Oracle. Your guidance is gladly received."

The Oracle leant back in her chair; her eyes flickered purple and blue. "You are most welcome, Fox. Travel well, travel safe, and always keep a clear head … or you may just lose it." Fox smiled at her warmly. Stepping backwards with a bow to show respect he left the crystal building. He understood clearly now: Sapphire was not just a dream traveller. She was a new kind of dream traveller, one that did not as yet understand the extent of her power. The balance between love and lust? The Oracle's words played in his head. He thought he was already lost in both; clarity was a virtue that seemed to avoid him when he was near her. Fox realised he was going to need some help from his father, a fact that troubled him greatly, for he did not want to admit that he was in serious trouble … and the journey with Sapphire had indeed only just begun.

Fox travelled through thought and will to his father's house, a beautiful castle placed precariously upon one of the highest hilltops in Shaka; he had been raised here with the aid of servants and guards, as was his right as the son of the great magician. As he transported himself to the castle gates his awareness of his father's presence within trembled inside his belly, the link to him strong and clear. The guards at the gate bowed at him respectfully as he approached, moving aside so that he might enter. Fox acknowledged them with a tip of his head. He knew all the men who guarded the castle; he had grown up with their protection and guidance in the way of fighting and arms.

Inside the castle gates was a bustle of activity, women and men going about their business to keep the castle functioning. They had a courtyard, stables, kitchen, dining hall and many rooms to attend to. The town surrounding the castle spilled out before him in a maze of streets. Fox smiled at the women who scurried past him, arms full of baskets laden with linen to be washed, food to be prepared; it was a comforting scene. Life was full and vibrant within the castle walls. He headed up the spiral staircase to the side of the castle leading to his father's chamber; he sensed that he was working, as usual, high above the castle activity below.

His mother had died in childbirth and, as far as Fox knew, his father had no other women in his life other than the servants that took care of his everyday needs. Of course, being his father, he was sure that at least one or two of them took care of his other needs as well. He stood hesitantly outside the huge wooden door which kept the magical world his father ruled hidden to the rest of the castle. As he raised his hand to knock his father opened the door.

"Welcome, son. I have been expecting you." Fox regarded his father with wide eyes, dipped his head in respect. "Father, blessings to you on this day." His father stepped aside to allow him to enter. The room was warm, a fire burning brightly in the corner. It was a large room with a high turret ceiling; the walls were covered in strange and wonderful objects, the large wooden table in the centre scattered with scrolls and jars and bowls filled with magical herbs and powders. His father followed him inside, shutting the door behind him with a heavy thud. "Sit, my son. I feel your burdens weighing on your mind. Tell me what is bothering you." Fox made his way to one of the high-backed wooden chairs; they were intricately carved, with vines and patterns creating the image of a living thing.

As he sat his father crossed to the fireplace and stood opposite him, his hands within his cloak, waiting for Fox to talk. Fox watched his father's face for signs of his mood that day. He was a tall, imposing man, handsome and commanding in appearance. He fashioned a long goatee on his chin; his hair was also long, tied back into a braid which hung heavily down his back. He had the amber and black eyes that Fox had inherited. Magic wavered around him in a shimmer of gold light. Fox felt his body relax slightly as he acknowledged his father's calm mood.

"Father, as you know, I have already been punished for my weakness with the new dream traveller. I was foolish to jump straight in with her, but now I seek your guidance as I have gained new knowledge as to the extent of her gifts." His father raised an eyebrow in surprise and nodded gravely. "I do not like to punish you, my son. Luckily for you, the men of Shaka heal quickly. It was done more as a warning than out of following the rules.

"You must move forward cautiously with any dream traveller. The balance is delicate at the best of times, but with a human traveller who does not understand the way they can affect everything they touch as they travel. It is even more imperative that boundaries are set in place." Fox lowered his eyes for a moment, remembering the feel of the whip on his back when he had been punished for the first time he had joined with Sapphire in her dream state.

"I understand, Father. I have always followed the code of the guardian in the past. My previous charges have never affected me in the way that Sapphire has: they moved throughout space and time with no repercussion. After I was released from their service I never realised I would be tested so much as I am now with Sapphire." His father walked across to the table and picked up one of the scrolls laid out in front of him. He lifted the parchment and scanned the words slowly. "There has not been a human dream traveller for many, many lifetimes. The last one has been remembered almost as if it were a myth. They are unstable and unreliable: you are truly being tested now, my son. All your years of learning – all the magic and all the wisdom you have gained in your lifetime – will be pushed to their limits."

Fox nodded in agreement. "Yes, my father, and I come here today to share my new knowledge of this dream traveller with you." The magician scanned the scroll again. "The prophecy says that a human traveller – female – will arrive in our world and show us many things: she is very special and must be protected at all times. This Sapphire seems to be the same traveller they predicted would appear, hence the severity of my punishment to you when I found that you had become intimately connected. I fear your infatuation with her will be your downfall, my son."

Fox knew his father was right. Even now, while Sapphire slept in her own world, he could feel the link between them pulsing strongly. It throbbed deeply within his chest and awakened an aching in his groin. "She has many gifts, Father. I visited the Oracle today. She is aware of Sapphire and told me many things. I need help to protect her, to allow me to think and feel clearly. It is as if she has bewitched me; I find it difficult to abstain from touching her." His father smiled wryly, as if he understood the power of the female more than Fox would ever know.

"It was the same with your mother, Fox. Her magic was strong and she was the most beautiful thing I had ever seen. I, too, was punished for linking with her when it had been prohibited. We were very young and she was to be initiated as one of the Oracle's priestesses. We could not resist each other: by taking her body I destroyed her path to enlightenment." He paused for a moment, the smile still lightly etched on his lips, "But, luckily for us, this path was meant to be and she fulfilled another purpose by becoming my wife. Her magic, intertwined with mine, created an even greater power within me ... and, of course, she bore me my beloved son."

Fox felt a swell of love grow in his chest as his father spoke so fondly of his mother and the honour he gave Fox in acknowledging him as a favoured son. "Father, I thank you for being so understanding of my predicament and for sharing your thoughts with regards to my mother. I wish I had known her." His father placed the scroll back on to the table; it curled up and shuddered for a second as if a magic seal had been placed upon it. "I do not know how I can help you, my son. This path is yours alone and for you to take together; the destination is as yet unknown. The journey may be long and full of many challenges."

Fox ran a hand through his hair and leant back in the chair in frustration. "Can you give me a potion to at least dampen my ardour for her?" His father laughed, making Fox smile slightly. "My son, of course I can do that. This is a simple thing you ask of me, but I feel it is a challenge you must undertake without the aid of magic. Your connection to her is strong because you will it, and she responds to you because she wills it. This is something you must work out between you. I can, however, help you to protect yourself in her world, as I fear the normal rules of travel do not apply there."

Fox nodded, sighing loudly. "For a start, they have their own magical potions which allow the mind to travel without boundaries. This you have already experienced with her. It will make her unstable – and you need to teach her how to control the dream travelling, as well as the other gifts the Oracle foresees for her." His father started to move around his room, gathering various herbs and crystals.

"Luckily for me she has a witch in her world who is already helping her to understand and protect her energy. I have linked with her before as she dreams and I find her to be a very old witch. Generations of magic have passed through her; I believe it was also her destiny to meet Sapphire on this path." His father nodded, his eyes glowing slightly now as he began to mix the ingredients in a stone mortar. "Yes … Pearl … she was once of our world, many incarnations ago. She is intuitively aware of our world and our ways; she will be a valuable asset to you, Son."

He paused for a moment, the air in the room suddenly growing very thick and warm. Magic trembled around Fox and he grounded himself as he prepared for his father to finish the spell he was weaving. A sharp crack filled his ears and a flash of white light appeared over the mortar, his father clapping his hands over the concoction to close the spell. Fox had watched his father prepare a thousand spells and potions but he felt the power of this magic in his entire body. He knew this would be a very special talisman. His father lifted a small crystal, newly formed, from the mortar. It was a perfect egg shape, tiny like a wren's egg; it was mottled in green and blue, shimmering with flecks of silver. It seemed to flicker with a life force of its own.

His father passed it to him "This will keep you both safe when needed. Only call upon its magic when you really need to, but it will also alert you of any danger when you are with her." Fox held out his hand and felt a cool shiver trace up his arm as it slid on to his palm. "Thank you, Father. I shall hold it close to me at all times." He stood up, placing the egg in his pocket.

Heat travelled across his chest as he did so. He could sense a new invisible barrier forming around him. The magic was connecting to him instantly; it nuzzled his body like a familiar friend making its acquaintance with him. "Now go to her, Son. She needs you." Fox stood and bowed at his father, stepping back to leave. "Be careful, my son, and if you do find that you cannot resist her, try to be more discreet." Fox smiled at his father "I will, Father. Blessed be."

Chapter Thirteen

Fox returned to his own home, went to his bedchamber and stood at his balcony, looking out on to his garden; he was remembering the last time he had joined with Sapphire on his bed, tangled together with her while they had made love. He watched the wolves outside in his garden amble across his lawn. Sapphire had manifested them the last time she had arrived in his world and they still lingered. He laughed softly; thankfully the elephants had disappeared when she had left. The ripple effect his father had warned him of was clearly apparent.

He crossed the room and sat on the edge of his four-poster; the white linen canopy was pulled aside so that he could see all four sides of his room. He placed his bare feet on the marble floor and closed his eyes, concentrating on her energy, reaching out to her. He could see her still sleeping in her own bed. He had no idea how much time had passed in her world while he had been consulting the Oracle and visiting his father; time was different in each world and, clearly, she was still in a deep sleep, indicating little time had passed since he had last checked in on her.

As he pushed his mind across into her world he watched her stretch her body restlessly, as if she were aware of him. "Sapphire, I am here. Sapphire, can you hear me?" He concentrated on her form and willed himself to cross over the dimensions to push through the protective barrier the old witch had given Sapphire. She stirred again and her eyelids fluttered. His magic pulsed around him and he felt her give way slightly, allowing him to shift vibration and link into her. With a trembling in his belly he felt her catch his energy and pull him towards her.

A sharp intake of her breath swept him across time and he was suddenly in her room, standing next to her bed. He stood over her, watching her. She was breathing slightly more shallowly now, murmuring softly; he did not want to frighten her, so he crouched down so that he was not towering over her. "Sapphire … it is me, Fox." She jumped slightly and he could see her eyes open with confusion. She blinked in the darkness; she was awake now. "Fox? Is that you? Am I dreaming?" He reached out to her and touched her arm lightly. She jumped back, startled. "It is me, my beautiful lady. You are awake in your room. I am here; you are safe."

She fumbled in the darkness for her bedside light and switched it on, making him blink for a moment. Her hair was tousled messily around her face and she clutched the duvet to her chest, still unsure as to whether danger was near. As she focused on his face her expression softened and a small smile appeared on her full lips. She was beautiful, sleepy and temptingly soft around the edges in the glow of her bedside light. "You startled me. I was dreaming again, but I couldn't reach you. It was weird; I could see you in this big castle surrounded by people … a tall, older man with a long braid was standing beside you, then I lost you."

He smiled at her. She was truly growing in her abilities, casting her eye to his world but remaining here in her own. She reached a hand into her hair and ran her fingers through the silky threads, removing strands from her face. He wanted desperately to reach out and touch her; instead he slid up on to the bed so that he was sitting next to her. Sapphire reached out to touch him. Her fingers traced a line across his forearm and the familiar tingle of energy exchanged between them; he could see a trail of light linger from her touch across his skin.

"I'm glad you came. It's been a strange night. I saw Pearl earlier; she explained a lot to me. My brain was kind of frazzled for a while, but you are here now. Are you OK?" He was touched by her concern for him; he felt the pulse of magic surrounding him respond to her touch with excitement. "Yes, I am OK, Sapphire. I came to check on you, make sure you were sleeping safely. You pulled me through." She pushed herself upright against her headboard and let the duvet slip down, revealing her nightgown – which was a thin black silky number, her breasts pushed temptingly against the fabric.

Her nipples stood to attention. Fox was distracted momentarily by them; he shook his head, looking back into her deep blue eyes, which watched him expectantly. "We both have much to learn from each other now. It appears things have changed again since we last met; we will need to tread softly together now, my beautiful Sapphire." She blinked at him, biting her bottom lip as she digested his words. "Have I done something wrong?" He smiled at her, wanting to reach out and claim those soft lips with his own. "No, you have done nothing wrong, but we must be more careful not to upset the balance of guardian and traveller too much any more ... which, I have to say, will be much more difficult for me than you, my wonderful lady."

"I doubt that." Sapphire reached out again and grasped his arm, firmly pulling him towards her. He allowed her to move him closer, his face now inches from her own. He could feel the warmth of her breath on his lips; his eyes still locked with hers, he could feel the tingle of anticipation between them. Fox licked his lips, his heart beginning to bounce in his chest. She was just so goddam gorgeous. He trembled slightly, holding himself back just slightly so that they did not actually touch. Her smile widened and her eyes slipped to his mouth, a soft sigh leaving her lips in resignation. Letting go of his arm, she allowed him to move back again slightly, the connection between them lifting just a fraction. "This wild streak in you will be the death of me, Sapphire."

She giggled and lifted the duvet next to her. "Lie down with me, Fox, just for a while. I promise not to bite." Fox could not resist. He climbed over her, fully dressed. He slid down beside her and propped his head up on one hand; she did the same, mirroring him. They stared at each other for a moment, neither of them wanting to bridge the gap. The air around them seemed to spark and crackle, the intensity of being so close to each other becoming almost unbearable.

"Oh, for fuck's sake." She lunged forward and claimed his lips with her own. Fox, taken by surprise at her sudden break in willpower, ended up on his back with her body pinning him to the bed. She kissed him with a long slow rhythm; he responded willingly, his body giving in completely to the softness of her skin and body as it pressed against him. She moved across to his neck and fluttered across his skin with feathered kisses. Fox let out a low moan. "Woman, you are indeed going to be the undoing of me." She laughed softly as she continued to snake her tongue across his neck and catch his ear lobe between her lips. Sucking and licking gently, he gripped her waist and held her against him tightly.

She was doing her little lap dance again, moving her groin in tiny circles against him; he felt himself grow instantly hard, totally aroused within seconds. His breathing became rapid and he closed his eyes, coaxing her onwards, drawing her closer. She lifted her knees up and pushed herself completely into his groin, her need to be taken by him obviously causing her some distress, as she started to whimper between kisses.

Fox was lost in the moment. He could feel their energy begin to heighten and the magic between them began to swell. He allowed it to lift within him; his body pulsed with a new intensity, his muscles clenched with need and his body ached in frustration. She lifted her head and began kissing his mouth again; he took her greedily and she reached down to lift his shirt. As she touched his skin a new level of arousal over took him; they were totally lost in each other again, rushing to join, to become one, to reach the ultimate goal, the hunger inside them pushing them on, goading them to step over the forbidden line.

Fox reached down and lifted her nightgown up, revealing her bare, beautiful legs. He ran his fingers up her sides and felt her quiver in anticipation. As she fell back to allow him to lift it over her head the obsidian necklace fell forward from between her breasts and knocked against his chest. A sharp, almost red-hot pain hit him in the solar plexus and he yelped out in surprise. Sapphire shot backwards and let out her own cry of shock. "Ouch." Sapphire was panting now, clutching the obsidian, which glowed bright orange in the darkness. Fox felt his head clear instantly and he shook his head. Sapphire looked across at him, still stunned. He started to laugh; it rippled through his body, making him shake as the laugh grew louder.

Sapphire blinked and she too began to laugh. "Oh, my fuckin' God. This goddam necklace Pearl gave me ... I suppose it is meant to keep me safe from not only the bad guys, but from you, too." Fox put his hands behind his head, the laugh slowly turning into a chuckle. He was smiling broadly at her. "We have been warned, my hot-blooded lady." Sapphire sat back on his legs and let go of the obsidian. It returned to its dark black and she shook her head slowly. "I suppose I deserved that."

Fox nodded and pushed his groin up, knocking her off him. She tumbled back on to her side of the bed. "Yes, my lady, you most certainly did." Sapphire laughed again and punched him lightly on the arm. "OK, OK. No more getting carried away, I suppose." She lay on her back, her breathing still rapid from their brief encounter. Her skin was flushed and she looked utterly ravishing. Fox could not help but feel immediately tempted to claim her again. He smiled as he watched her continue to chuckle softly, knowing that this was just a little taster of how they would be punished if they pushed the boundaries too much. It was for their own good, after all.

"This is going to be extremely annoying, having you here but not being able to indulge." Fox reached across and ran a fingertip lightly across her lip. "We will learn restraint, Sapphire. We have a lot of time ahead of us. I am sure that eventually we will work out a way to be together without zapping each other." Sapphire turned her head to smile at him. It was just beginning to get light outside and he could see her features clearly now; she looked positively radiant. "I hope so; I've never been so frustrated in my life."

Fox sensed a new energy force begin to awaken near them; he stilled for a second, tuning in. "Your friend is awake. We may have made some noise and disturbed her. I should go." Sapphire cocked her head to one side, obviously not hearing anything. "It's too early for Charlie. She won't be awake for ages. Don't go, not just yet." Fox sensed differently but did not want to leave her. She blinked puppy dog eyes at him and he smiled at her. "I will stay, but just for a while." She grinned in triumph and tentatively reached out for him, pushing the obsidian to one side so that it did not touch him.

He moved down on to the bed and lay on his back; she snuggled into his chest immediately, causing his body to tremble. "I feel so safe when you are with me. Just stay until I fall asleep again." Fox placed his arm around her and squeezed her close, kissing the top of her head tenderly. "Your wish is my command, my beautiful Sapphire." She shuddered and sighed, deeply satisfied with his answer. He held her for some time, listening to her breathing become deeper again, and sensing her fall into a deep sleep. Fox switched off the bedside light and watched the dark turn to grey; a new day beginning to rise in this strange world. He could feel Charlie next door also return to her sleep, every vibration around him buzzing loudly in his ears … but, despite the white noise, the only thing he was acutely and exquisitely aware of was the humming energy coming from the woman lying on his chest and the strong, undeniable connection between them.

Chapter Fourteen

Monday

Sapphire stirred and shifted her weight as she slowly became conscious again; her head was pressed to her mattress, her belly flat against the sheet. She stretched like a cat and became aware that her pillow from earlier that morning had gone. Fox was no longer holding her: all that remained was his signature scent of sandalwood and patchouli. She smiled a lazy, satisfied smile and opened her eyes, slowly taking in the light of the new day. She felt a little sad that Fox was not there with her but knew it was probably best for both of them; she could not keep her goddam hands off him when he was around. They were both as bad as each other. The attraction between them was so very strong it clouded any sense of being responsible.

She rolled over on to her back and watched the sunlight that filtered through her curtains dance on the ceiling. It was another sunny day. A gentle breeze caressed her body and she ran her hands down her sides, revelling in the memory of Fox touching her. She felt constantly horny nowadays; Fox had relit her fire. It was frustrating as hell and totally wonderful. She could hear music coming from downstairs; the radio was on in the kitchen below her room and she could just make out Charlie singing quite badly and out of tune to the pop song she was listening to.

Sapphire smiled. Life was back to normal. Her magical man had returned to his own world and she was back in her reality. It was Monday and she was glad that she had absolutely nothing whatsoever planned. As she had worked the weekend she had a day off in lieu. After a long yawn she pushed herself up out of bed and grabbed her dressing gown. Pulling back the curtains to allow the day to enter her room she scanned the garden out of habit now, to make sure no one else was around. All was still outside; normal. She nodded and headed for the bathroom to brush her teeth and wash her face.

Looking at herself in the mirror as she brushed her teeth she could not help but giggle a little at her shenanigans in the early hours; it had felt like a dream, but she knew now that it had all been real. Rinsing her mouth out and then sitting on the loo for some relief, she went over the night spent with Pearl in her mind. So much was happening to her so fast; her life had changed overnight a week ago and everything felt like it was spinning out of control. Today she would be normal. Today she would be like every other human and do normal things: her washing, cook lunch, go for a walk, watch TV. That was her plan, anyway.

After finishing up in the bathroom she headed downstairs; she could smell bacon wafting upwards in belly-rumbling tempting waves. Charlie was still singing away, oblivious to Sapphire, as she stood at the kitchen door. "Don't give up your day job, hon." Charlie jumped as she turned around, holding a plastic spatula in her hand, the bacon spitting invitingly in the frying pan. "Oh, crap. You scared me, Saf." Sapphire headed across to the kettle to make tea. "Any spare for me? I'm starving." Charlie returned to her bacon, squashing it flat in the hot pan to crisp up the fat. "Of course. I'm making breakfast for Nathan; he's snoring like a pig up there."

She looked up and smiled at Sapphire, who was grabbing three cups to make tea – the kettle whistling softly as it began to heat up. "I thought I heard someone in your room this morning ... a man... Did you invite someone over late last night? Is there someone else who needs breakfast?" Her smile had a cheeky tilt. Sapphire shook her head, trying to keep her own knowing smile closed on her lips. "No, I don't have anyone in my room; you must have been dreaming. I slept like a baby all night ... just woken up. What time is it, by the way?"

Charlie frowned, a little confused. "Oh, that's weird. I was sure I could hear you with someone; it sounded like fun, too. It's 10.15." Sapphire tapped a spoon lightly against her cup, waiting for the water to boil. "Good. I didn't want to sleep too late today. It looks nice out. I might go for a walk today ... What are you two up to? Are you working today?"

Charlie had finished crisping the bacon. Lifting it on to a plate, she reached across for the eggs and began breaking them into the frying pan, bacon grease adding to the flavour. "No plans today, hon. We both decided to take a day off work. Nathan was due a day and I'm pretty up to date with my work, so we are around. I will see if lazybones fancies a walk – we could do with some fresh air." Sapphire began to pour the water in the cups, steam rising from them as she stirred in the milk. "Cool. There is a really beautiful tree in the woods I wanted to show you. It will be nice to have some company; I can put that chicken on for a roast later." Charlie flipped the eggs expertly; one thing she was really good at was bacon and eggs.

"Sounds like a plan. Grab me some plates, Saf. It's ready." Sapphire pulled three plates out from the cabinet and handed them across to Charlie, her mouth now beginning to water slightly from the smell of the bacon. "I think I'll have a bath before we go out. You guys are not in a rush, are you?" Charlie wrinkled her nose. "When are we ever in a rush, Saf?" I'll take this up for Nathan. Thanks for the tea." Sapphire nodded and sat at the kitchen table, ready to delve into her own plate of grease. Charlie headed up the stairs after grabbing a tray to place Nathan's and her own plate of food and drink on.

Sapphire tucked in. She was ravenous this morning, as if she really had spent the night with her lover; maybe it was just being around him that caused her appetite to spike. Whatever it was, today she felt happy and full of energy. After polishing off the food and washing it all down with her cup of tea Sapphire went up to run her bath. She wanted to float in hot water and give her body a chance to soak for a while; it might calm her spangled, horny nerves. She could hear Charlie laughing in her room. Nathan was obviously now awake. They were always laughing and joking; it was a good house to live in, with such a happy vibe.

Sapphire ran her water, running her fingers through the warm liquid. Everything felt heightened today. The fluid motion of the water as it touched her skin rippled across her body in little shivers. She smiled: it felt good. Adding scented bubble bath, Sapphire slipped out of her dressing gown and nightgown. As the material slid down her body the silk brushed like a feather touch, making her skin pop out in goosebumps. She dipped her toe into the water and felt a wave of arousal tingle up her calf towards her groin. "Oh, for goodness' sake." She laughed at herself and slid into the water, letting out a sigh as the water enveloped her. Had Fox scented her again? Was she covered in horny magic that was making her body respond like a quivering hormonal animal every time she touched anything?

She soaked in the bath for some time, waving her fingers through the water every now and then to enjoy the sensation of the water gliding across her skin. Charlie banged on the door, making her jump. "Saf, are you nearly done? I need to pee." Sapphire shook her head; she had no idea how long she had been wallowing in the tub. "Yep, all done. I'm getting out now; hang on." She hastily stepped out of the bath and wrapped herself in a towel, opening the door to Charlie standing outside with her legs crossed. "Sorry, Saf. You've been in there ages. I held on as long as I could – didn't want to disturb you." Sapphire bit her lip, feeling guilty. "I'm sorry, Charlie. I think I dozed off. I'll get dressed and get the dinner in the oven; we can head out for that walk." Charlie had already shut the door behind her, her need to pee obviously now at a desperate level. "OK."

After drying herself and smothering her body in moisturising lotion, which was gloriously perfumed with orange and geranium (everything smelt good today), she dressed in jeans and t-shirt, slipping on her flip-flops to head back down to the kitchen to prepare dinner for later. She bumped into Nathan on the stairs as she bounced down the two steps at a time. "Whoa, Saf. You in a hurry?" He beamed a big smile at her, hands in the air as he moved to one side to let her pass. "Sorry, Nathan. Gonna put the chicken in the oven before we go out for our walk. You nearly ready?" She eyed his bare chest; he was half-dressed in jeans, and that was it. "Yeah. Just grab a shirt; won't be long."

Sapphire skipped to the kitchen. Grabbing the chicken from the fridge she did a little dance around, finding all the dishes and herbs she needed. She started peeling potatoes and boiling a pan of water to put roasties on with the meat. She felt like she was literally flying around the kitchen today; a smile was planted firmly on her lips. I'm high. I think I'm actually buzzing from Fox magic. "Saf, what the hell are you doing?" Charlie stood in the doorway, an eyebrow raised, a thin smile on her lips. Sapphire continued to grab what she needed and smiled back at her friend. "I'm preparing lunch for later." Charlie laughed. "You look like a mad chef; be careful you don't hurt yourself hurtling around like that." Sapphire laughed. "You guys get ready. I'm gonna put everything in the oven really low. We can go for a long walk – work up an appetite."

Sapphire led the way into the woods; she had changed into trainers and stepped lightly over branches and brambles to find her way to the tree she had visited last weekend. Charlie and Nathan followed closely behind, laughing and pushing each other, sounding like two elephants trampling through the undergrowth. Charlie had prerolled a rather large joint for them to enjoy during their walk and Sapphire could hear that it was taking effect on the pair of them as they giggled loudly behind her.

The sunlight filtered through the trees in a shimmer of golden light. It was indeed a beautiful day. Sapphire could sense they were close to the old tree before she actually saw it; her fingers began to tingle and the cool breeze teased her bare arms with a heightened touch. "How much further is this tree, Sapphire? I'm getting scratched to bits here." Sapphire laughed. "You should have worn something on your legs, crazy woman." Charlie had opted for barely-bottom-covering shorts and a t-shirt for their walk. Sapphire didn't blame her for showing off her fabulous legs: Nathan was obviously enjoying the view.

She paused as the old tree came into view in front of her. A shimmer of heat seemed to rise from its branches and the trunk was positively glowing in the sunlight; she had never seen anything quite so beautiful. Charlie and Nathan came to an abrupt stop behind her, the noise of their feet trampling through the undergrowth now quiet. "Wow. That is a big tree."

Sapphire walked slowly to the tree trunk and reached out to touch it, like a familiar old friend. As her fingertips brushed the moss covering the bark she closed her eyes and felt a soft breeze rush across her face. She could smell the cool earth beneath her feet and the fresh scent of the grass and wood around her. She took a deep breath and felt the trunk beneath her fingers shift slightly, as if it too were taking an intake of the air around it.

"What an amazing tree, Saf. Did you find this last weekend?" Nathan was standing next to her, looking up into the huge canopy above him with wide, slightly hazy eyes. Charlie was equally dumbstruck, her mouth slightly open as she looked up. "Yeah, I did. Isn't it amazing?" Sapphire was smiling happily. The energy of the old tree hummed up her fingertips; she withdrew them reluctantly and looked across at her friends. "I never took you as a tree hugger, Saf." Nathan laughed and reached out to put his own hand on to the huge trunk. He, too, smiled as he placed his palm on the bark. "It feels warm."

Sapphire watched him with amusement as they stared up at the old tree. In their stoned state they too felt the amazing energy of the tree. "Cool, huh." Charlie joined him and they all stood around the tree. Looking up with one hand on the trunk now, Sapphire placed her forehead against it and closed her eyes again. As she did a silence enveloped them and the wood suddenly became very quiet, just as it had when Sapphire had stood at the gate at Pearl's house. She felt the warmth of the tree trunk begin to travel up her arm and she heard a slight crackle in her ears, as if electricity were building in her veins. The air became warmer and thicker and time seemed to stand still for a second.

Her head was buzzing now and in her mind's eye she could see right down into the tree's roots, down into the earth, through the mud and rock, deep down into a layer of crystal and heat. Her whole body felt like it was pulsing now and she could sense Charlie and Nathan next to her become very still and quiet. Sapphire felt a rush of energy come up from the ground through the tree roots. It was a bright white in colour and as it hit her in the chest she heard a loud crack. "Holy shit."

Sapphire opened her eyes. Charlie and Nathan were both on their backsides now, looking up at her as if she were an alien. The birds were singing again and the woodland had returned to life. "What the fuck was that?" Charlie blinked up at her; Nathan was shaking his head as if someone had just thumped him. Sapphire stepped back and shook her hands, which were still a little tingly. "Christ. Sorry, guys. Not sure what happened there." Charlie was frowning and looking slightly freaked out. "You zapped us. Have you been taking

Superman pills or something?" Nathan laughed loudly as he began to push himself up. Brushing his jeans down to remove any leaves or dirt, he reached a hand down to Charlie to help her up.

"That was super-freaky. That joint must have been really strong. One minute I was just standing next to you two, the next minute I'm on my arse." Sapphire wanted to giggle uncontrollably but thought that might be highly inappropriate. "I have absolutely no idea; you must have both slipped." Charlie allowed Nathan to pull her up, eyeing Sapphire a little cautiously. "I'm not touching that tree again, that's for sure." Sapphire laughed and stepped back, looking up at the tree.

"Shall we head back to the path and make our way back home? The food should be nearly done now: you two need to clear your heads." Charlie nodded, brushing her hands together. "Definitely. Let's step away from the crazy tree." Nathan hugged her and kissed the top of her head, still laughing softly. "Oh, poor baby, did you hurt your gorgeous butt? Here, let me kiss it better." He grabbed her and swung her up into her arms; she let out a loud cry of protest. Sapphire was glad they were laughing the whole episode off as a side effect from the joint. Now she was turning into a human lightning conductor.

They took a slightly quicker pace back towards the path, Sapphire wondering what the hell had just happened. She noticed, out of the corner of her eye, a deer standing in the ferns; it was looking straight at them as they made their way out of the undergrowth. Charlie and Nathan were making so much noise that Sapphire was surprised it had not been startled and scampered off. Instead, it took a step towards them. She turned her head to watch and slowed down slightly, letting Charlie and Nathan continue ahead of her.

The deer was moving towards her now, its ears pricked up, its eyes bright and alert. Sapphire stopped as it approached; it started to pick up a little speed and was heading straight for her. She was not sure what to do, then decided to stay put for a moment, enchanted by the deer and also a little nervous as to what it was going to do next.

The deer came right up to her. She had never been this close to a wild animal before. Slowly and timidly it stopped right in front of her and lifted its head up; Sapphire could see its nostrils flaring slightly, as if it were breathing in her scent. She very carefully reached out her hand to touch the deer: it did not move but bowed down slightly in front of her so that she could place her fingers on to the top of its head. She let her fingers move across its fur, felt the deer become still beneath her touch; her energy seemed to start to buzz again and the deer let out a soft grunt. She jumped back and the deer took off. It dashed through the undergrowth. Startled by the sudden change in tempo Sapphire staggered back slightly.

"Hey, Saf. You OK? What was that?" Charlie called to her from some way ahead. She blinked and shook her head. What the hell? First conducting energy via trees, now communicating with the wildlife ... What was happening to her? "I'm OK. It was a deer; just shot through the grass." Sapphire started to jog to catch up with them, suddenly wanting to get back to the safety of the cottage where no more weird shit could happen. So much for her normal day.

They made it back to the cottage with no further incident, the smell of roast chicken inviting them inside as they tumbled back in the door. Sapphire went straight to the kitchen to start the veggies, leaving Charlie and Nathan to their playfulness in the lounge. She could hear Charlie shrieking again as Nathan had obviously begun the tickling session he was so fond of. She smiled to herself as she began to lay the table. Her stomach was starting to rumble in anticipation of food and she felt that she had certainly worked up an appetite again.

"Shall I open some wine, tree girl?" Sapphire smiled at her friend, who had returned to the kitchen after escaping the clutches of her boyfriend. "Yes, that would be nice, Charlie. It's pretty much ready." They sat down shortly after to a table laden with food and drink, all three tucking in with gusto; Charlie and Nathan now clearly in the grips of the munchies and Sapphire just famished from the whole tree incident. She felt happy and a little stoned herself, even though she hadn't touched the joint.

It had been another strange day, but weirdly it did not worry her. She was taking this new set of events in her stride; after the last week's events the walk in the woods, connecting with the energy of the tree, and the deer did not seem that odd. She wondered if any more freaky abilities would show themselves to her. It was strangely exciting. Sapphire watched her two friends tuck into the meal, a sly smile on her lips. They had absolutely no idea what was going on in her life. The thought was thrilling and worrying at the same time.

The rest of the day passed without further incident. Sapphire did her washing, tidied her bedroom and cleaned out her underwear drawer. Charlie and Nathan were having a duvet day; after the big lunch they had settled into a drowsy state on the couch, watching an old black and white movie. They looked like two monkeys hugging each other under the duvet. Sapphire had left them to it, and buzzed around the house like she was on speed while they chilled out. They eyed her suspiciously as she popped in and out of the living room between her chores. She really didn't care; she felt overly energised and happy as a pig in shit.

The evening drew in quickly and Charlie and Nathan decided to pop down The Swan for a pint. Sapphire was actually looking forward to having some time on her own in the cottage; she had a good book she wanted to finish and a late shift at the cafe tomorrow, so she could relax for the rest of the evening. Charlie hesitated as they went to leave. "You sure you will be OK on your own, Sapphire? We won't be too long; we just fancy a quick pint. Call us if you need us." She was obviously still a little nervous leaving her after the last incident.

Sapphire actually felt confidently safe tonight; armed with her obsidian and her new knowledge she felt more empowered, and instinctively knew she would be OK. "I'm fine. You two go ahead. I've a good book to finish … I'll see you later." Charlie nodded, Nathan pulling her arm to hurry her along. "OK, hon. See you later."

Sapphire smiled as they shut the door loudly, the cottage becoming suddenly and peacefully quiet without their presence. She lit a few candles in the living room and an incense stick to create the perfect book-reading environment. After pouring herself a glass of red wine, she settled into the armchair next to the small table light and got stuck in. Sapphire read for some time, lost herself in the characters and plot of the book … the wine made her feel slightly fuzzy, but it was a nice feeling, and she felt her body at last start to relax; she had felt like a coiled spring all day. She leant back in the armchair and let her hands drop the book more comfortably into her lap. She read a little more, finding her eyes starting to become heavy, her lids dropping every now and then. A soft drowsiness started to surround her and she could feel the book start to slip from her fingertips. She let her head drop back and took a deep breath; her body was comfortably numb, her senses drifting away into sleep mode. Sapphire sensed the change in her energy but welcomed it. She suddenly felt utterly spent and wanted to sleep. She wanted to see Fox again. Eager to travel again, the thought left a trace of a smile on her lips as she drifted off.

Chapter Fifteen

Sapphire was standing on the edge of a lake. The water was blue-black like spilled oil, the huge full moon above her casting a silver glow across its surface. All was still. Nothing moved. The air was cool and clear; it smelt like snow was coming. Sapphire looked around her and could see a vast, open landscape. Apart from the lake in front of her there were few landmarks to distinguish where she was. It was night-time, but she knew she was not on Earth.

She let out the breath she had not realised she was holding and suddenly everything around her became alive again. The air moved once more. A light breeze ruffled her hair and she could hear a bird calling in the distance. The water lapped at the edge of the lake, the smell of pine trees lingered in her nostrils and she could now make out to her side the dark shadow of a dense forest. Sapphire looked down at her body and was amused to see herself clad in thick sheepskin clothing. Boots and mittens completed the outfit; without them she knew she would be freezing her arse off. This could not be Shaka; it was warm on that planet and the vegetation had been lush and fragrant.

She wondered where the hell she was, but of course, this was just a dream; it could be anywhere she wanted it to be. She smiled again, felt inside her sheepskin jacket to find the obsidian still hanging between her breasts; it was warm even to her covered hands. She decided to investigate, headed off towards the pine trees. Breathing in the fresh, crisp air Sapphire strode purposefully, wondering if she would bump into Fox. Hoping, of course. As before, Sapphire found that movement was wonderfully graceful in her dream state; she seemed to glide across the ground, her footsteps making no sound.

She cast no shadow in the bright moonlight. The sky was a black abyss that was never-ending, scattered with stars and what looked like several comets shooting across the inky darkness. Sapphire felt her energy quicken and her heart began to thud more loudly in her chest. She was aware of another presence and swung her head around to try and see who was near. At the edge of the trees she could see the outline of a rider on a dark horse. Warm breath came out in short bursts from the horse's nostrils; Sapphire felt her body being pulled towards the horse and rider with a sudden urgency. She gasped a little, surprised by the force of the speed she travelled at to reach them. Strangely, no fear gripped her body.

Within seconds she was standing looking up at the rider. Her eyes grew wide and her whole body began to buzz as she smiled with relief. "Fox." He reached an arm down, his wild amber eyes glistening in the moonlight, a grin spread widely across his beautifully handsome face. "Sapphire." She grabbed his arm and he flung her up on to the horse behind him. The beast stamped its feet with excitement and let out a snort, Fox holding the reigns expertly. Sapphire clung with her thighs to keep from falling back off.

Fox looked over his shoulder at her; he too was clad in thick sheepskin, his dreadlocks threaded with beads that shone dimly in the moonlight. "Hold tight, my lady." His grin was devilish now and Sapphire had no time to hesitate as he kicked the horse into a gallop. She clung to him tightly as they headed into the forest, a wide path leading them through the giant pine trees. The wind whipped against her face as they flew through the forest, her hair flying like a champion's flag behind her. She could see everything whizzing passed them in flashes, her adrenalin now pumping in her veins wildly.

Fox had his head down and was pushing the horse faster into the forest. She could hear him laughing. He was obviously enjoying himself immensely. Sapphire started to relax into the gallop; she had ridden as a child and had always enjoyed the sensation of being linked to an animal at such a fast speed. It was exhilarating. They spun around a sharp corner in the path, the horse scrambling for a moment to keep its balance. Fox pulled them to a stop and Sapphire laughed loudly, her breath coming out in fast, urgent bursts from the thrill of it all. Fox patted the neck of the horse, which was puffing and panting now from the exertion, "Good boy. Well done."

Sapphire pressed her face against Fox's back and hugged him tightly; he placed a hand on hers and squeezed. "Are you ready to see something amazing?" Sapphire lifted her head and felt Fox shift his weight as he moved to jump down from the horse. She watched him as he steadied the beast and reached up to help her down. She slipped into his arms and he held her at arm's length for a moment, staring intently into her eyes, a smile etched lightly on his lips. "Where are we?" Sapphire asked him, holding him lightly on the forearms. "Somewhere far away, Sapphire. A special place I have not visited for many lifetimes. You have brought us here."

Sapphire smiled up at him. "That really explains a lot." He laughed and pulled her into his chest, kissing the top of her head. "Come. I will show you." He led her through the trees, leaving the horse to graze behind them. Sapphire noticed that the area was becoming rockier; she could see a dark shape ahead – the face of a hill. As they approached she could make out a doorway cut into the rock; it was arched and surrounded by stones that glistened softly against the darkness. Fox stopped at the entrance and turned to face her. "This is a place of great healing. It has been here for longer than time itself, a place that few people have ever entered. You are greatly privileged to see it."

Sapphire nodded, not really understanding what he was talking about. He took her hand again and led her through the archway. As Sapphire stepped over the threshold she felt her body shudder and her energy shifted with a jolt. The room was a beautiful soft pink; everything around her was glistening like freshly laid snow. As her eyes adjusted she realised that she was surrounded by crystals; the walls, the floor, everything, was a sheen of light. Fox stood in front of her, his head tilted upwards as he looked up at the crystal ceiling. She could see a wide smile on his lips, his breath coming out in bursts of white mist.

Sapphire removed her mittens and placed them inside her coat. She turned around, taking in her surroundings. It was beautiful, unlike anything she had ever seen before. The entire cave was crystallized. The area seemed to be lit up on its own by some magical, unknown light source; it reflected off the walls and floor in an eerie glow. She could see several tunnels leading off from the cave they were standing inside. The energy around her hummed softly against her body; the whole place was alive with a soft soothing life force. Fox turned to face her. "The crystal chambers which lead off from this central cavern are all filled with a different type of crystal, each one giving a different energy source. It has been used for healing for thousands of years … I have not been here in a very long time."

Sapphire smiled back at him. The air was beginning to warm up around them. She could sense the shift in energy now they were inside the cave; her heartbeat quickened at its pulse. Fox opened his coat, the warmth obviously reaching his body too. She watched him with eager eyes, always happy to see him uncover his amazing body. He smiled at her with a wicked glint in his eye, aware of her hungry eyes. "Do you want to see the other chambers?" Sapphire nodded at him with excitement. "I've never seen anything like this before; it's amazing." He reached out for her hand; she shivered at his touch, his palms warm and tingling with promise.

He led her into the closest chamber. As they walked inside the walls lit up, allowing them to see all around them again. The floor and walls were all covered in crystals, this time a deep blue. Sapphire felt a pressing in her throat and raised her hand to her neck, taking a gulp of air. Fox stopped inside the chamber and looked back into her eyes. "The energy here heals the unspoken words, the trapped emotions that we are afraid to speak. This is why you are feeling it in your throat. If you have anything you need to say, here is the place to say it."

Sapphire let her hand drop from his grip and closed her eyes for a moment. A thousand thoughts suddenly spun through her mind … all the things she had ever wanted to say to the people she knew, the people she had lost… She saw her father in her mind, his face smiling at her kindly. A swell of emotion lifted up from her chest into her throat and seemed to choke her for a second. Tears began to fill her eyes and she gasped at the intensity. "I can see my dad. He is smiling at me." Fox was standing close; she could feel the heat from his body. "What do you need to tell him, Sapphire? Now is the time to speak." Sapphire took a deep breath, clearing the slight dizziness that had suddenly taken her. "That I love him and that I am sorry he is gone … sorry that I did not really know him." She felt a tear slip silently from her eye and slide down her cheek.

A shiver of warmth ran up her legs through her body and centred on her throat. It throbbed for a moment in that area then rose up through the top of her head. She let out a soft whimper and opened her eyes. Fox watched her, a kind smile on his lips. "Better now?" Sapphire blinked. Her head felt clearer and the gripping feeling in her throat was gone. She nodded at him. "Much better."

He nodded and took her hand once more. He pulled her forward and led her through to the next tunnel. The crystals in this chamber were a deep violet; she felt instantly dizzy. Fox tightened his grip on her hand. "This chamber is for healing the third eye, our imagination, our psychic abilities ... all the things that create vision in our worlds."

Sapphire tried to steady herself. Her brow throbbed painfully and she felt a little scared. Fox turned to face her. He looked down into her eyes and licked his lips slowly. "Open your mind, Sapphire. Free your spirit to the crystals. They will give you more power than you could ever imagine." Sapphire closed her eyes again and willed the throbbing in her forehead to stop; it was getting painful now. "Don't resist it, Sapphire. Imagine a door opening in the front of your mind; free your magic, go with the flow of energy."

He was holding her arms lightly, most likely to ground her as she seemed to reel under the immense pressure that was building in her head. The room around her was closing in; it was frightening the hell out of her. Sapphire took a deep breath and tried to calm herself. She pictured a door in front of her ... she pushed it open with her mind and allowed herself to give in to the pulsing energy in her skull. A loud cracking noise vibrated in her ears and with an almighty pop she felt her mind expand outwards. White light flashed in front of her eyelids and she felt all around her become still and calm.

She felt like she was floating on a cloud, in a nebula of clouds in a vast universe. The purple hues of the crystals around her held her in place; they caressed her softly. She felt amazing. She could see across time itself; it was magnificent, overwhelming and utterly spectacular. Fox gripped her forearms tightly, making her jump slightly from the pressure. "Back you come, my beautiful traveller. We don't want you flying off just yet." Sapphire opened her eyes.

Fox was grinning at her, his eyes flashing with amusement. "Wow. That was fucking awesome." Fox bent down and placed his lips on to hers. He kissed her firmly and she reeled again for a moment until he withdrew. "You are awesome. The energy shift was incredible when you did that." Sapphire laughed, suddenly feeling like she was stoned. "I think we need to move to another chamber. Is there one I can come back down again in?"

Fox nodded, still smiling at her. He pulled her forward, her legs feeling like they did not belong to her. They turned another corner deeper into the hill and entered another chamber; the crystals here were a deep, dark red. Sapphire instantly felt her body sink to the floor, a heaviness filling her limbs to the point that she stumbled slightly. Fox coaxed her forward gently. "Sit down, Sapphire. Regroup for a moment." Sapphire was glad to do just that. She felt so totally relaxed; she wanted to lie down, not sit.

Fox sat opposite her, his hands still holding her. She blinked at him and giggled, "I think I'm drunk." Fox laughed. "No, gorgeous. You are just feeling the effects strongly. You are very sensitive: we are in the base chakra crystal chamber. It will ground you but it will also heal your sexual energy ... your connection to the root source of your magic." Sapphire felt a warm tingle in her groin and her legs were super-sensitive. The heat began to travel up her body and she suddenly felt very horny. A sly smile grew on her lips.

Fox regarded her with a knowing smile. "Steady, my woman. Stay focused. We are grounding here." Sapphire shook her head. "God, I need to get a grip. I'm off again." She took another deep breath, bringing her senses back into alignment. Fox watched her intently. "I'm OK. I feel a little better now. Amazing, in fact. This is the most incredible place." Fox sighed with relief. "Yes. Yes, it is. The magic here is very strong. To bring us here was obviously meant to be, and I am glad you came here." Sapphire felt a shift once more in her body. The obsidian nestled between her breasts began to heat up; it was pulsing strongly, almost uncomfortably.

Fox frowned slightly. He reached into his coat and his hand stopped on something inside. Sapphire held her breath for a second, suddenly acutely aware that something had changed, and not for the better. "We have company." Fox stood up quickly. Sapphire wished she could move, let alone stand; her body was still remarkably relaxed and heavy. "Hecta is here; we need to leave." He paused, looking around himself in quick, alert movements. "Now." Sapphire looked up at him, her eyes wide. "Help me up; I'm kinda stuck here." Fox reached down and pulled her up, seemingly with little effort. Sapphire moaned a little at the effort she had to make. He grabbed her and picked her up like she were a small child. Sapphire felt her head roll to one side awkwardly as wind whipped against her face. Fox moved as quickly as a flash of light through the chamber into the entrance. Sapphire clung to him, her mind reeling with a stab of fear.

A second later they were standing at the cave entrance, the darkness outside suddenly foreboding. Fox dropped her feet to the ground. Still holding her against him, he whistled into the darkness. Sapphire strained to hear any other noise, afraid of what may happen next. The horse they had ridden earlier suddenly appeared from behind a tree and stamped its foot in response to Fox's call. As they hurried across to mount him, Sapphire gasped and pushed herself to an abrupt stop, causing Fox to bump into her.

A dark shadow had appeared behind the horse and it was moving very quickly towards them. The obsidian was pulsing with heat against her chest – as if she needed any more warning that this person was dangerous. Fox pushed her behind him protectively and stepped forward, "Hecta, show yourself." The shadow moved forward. The horse, startled by his appearance, reared up on its hind legs. The shadow revealed itself, lifted a hand to push the horse aside effortlessly.

Sapphire was suddenly very afraid. It was the same man who had been standing in her garden, the same hooded figure who had knocked on her door – and now he was here in her dream, dark and disturbing. Her body began to tremble slightly. "Fox, my old friend, it has been a long time since we crossed paths." Fox stood tall. Sapphire sensed his energy growing powerfully around him. "You are not my friend, Hecta, and you have no business with us here tonight."

Hecta stepped forward. Sapphire could now see him clearly in the moonlight. He was surprisingly easy on the eye, but a darkness to his eyes and the smirk on his lips caused her to tremble more. "She should not be here. This place is sacred; her travelling is not permitted to this place. You are breaking the law." Fox stepped forward, obviously pissed now. "We are breaking no law, Hecta. She has done no wrong. I am watching her, keeping her safe. You know that."

The sly smile vanished from Hecta's face now and the dark shadow surrounding him seemed to grow bigger. "She is not wanted here: not wanted anywhere." Fox pushed Sapphire back slightly and stepped forward again; he was inches from Hecta now. Sapphire could not see his face but sensed the anger rolling off him. "You are afraid of her, and you should be, Hecta. She is pure and powerful. You cannot control her and that is pissing you off." Hecta closed the small gap. "Be careful, Fox; for she may just break you, too."

Sapphire gasped as Fox raised his fist and punched Hecta full force in the face. Hecta stumbled back and laughed. "Already she has clouded your judgement, Guardian. You will fail in your task." Sapphire watched with horror as Hecta stepped forward and lunged at Fox. Without another moment's hesitation Fox engaged with him and Sapphire felt her mouth gawp wide as she watched them fight before her. They spun around, kicking and punching like two ninjas. They moved so fast that Sapphire could not keep up with them. But she could sense their anger and their pain as each blow made contact.

Sapphire was terrified. What was she supposed to do? This was her dream; she did not intend for this to happen. Her mind was spinning with confusion. "What should I do?" The air around her was cooling rapidly and a breeze was picking up. She felt her body start to thrum with energy, her panic making flashes of light appear in front of her eyes.

Sapphire looked up into the dark sky and closed her eyes. She concentrated on the cold air around her and drew it towards her, building it together, creating a crystal network of energy. Snow began to fall around her, flakes as big and thick as a penny landing on her hair. The snow began to fall heavily now. The wind picked up and she felt it spin around her in a whirlwind of cold, rushing snow and ice. She opened her eyes and aimed it at the men, focusing on Hecta.

The whirlwind of snow rushed at them and bounced off Hecta, knocking him back from Fox, who was pushed aside by the force of it. He stumbled for a moment, off balance by the sudden change of events. His head whipped back, his eyes wide with confusion for a second as he saw Sapphire standing behind them. She raised her arms and lifted Hecta off his feet. The snow enveloped him; she could just make out his dark shape. Inside the storm a low growl filled the air and made her shiver. She pushed her energy upwards and spun him off into the darkness, watching with mild amusement and a little horror at the strength of the snowstorm she had created.

Hecta thrashed within its centre, but to no avail; he was trapped within her magic. She smiled a little and flicked her hands, sending him off into the sky. A wail of frustration thundered across the landscape as he disappeared over the horizon. The ground trembled slightly and everything around them shook slightly, before turning suddenly silent once more. Fox strode back to her, his breath coming quickly now. He reached out and grabbed her, pulling her into his arms. He held her there for a moment, his breathing rapid against her.

"Are you OK?" She looked up into his eyes. He was shaking his head, somewhat bemused. "Am I OK? By the gods, Sapphire, you were magnificent." Sapphire laughed, a little shakily. "He was hurting you. I just wanted him gone." Fox lifted her chin and stared at her for a moment, his eyes wide, flashing amber and black. She watched him hesitate for a second before he bent down and kissed her hard. She responded feverishly, kissing him back with all her passion, their bodies pressed against each other with desperate need. He withdrew reluctantly, their breathing fast and heavy.

Lifting a strand of hair from her face he brushed his fingertips across her cheek. "You are the most amazing woman I have ever met, Sapphire." She blinked up at him, wanting to kiss him again; she pulled his head down to hers and wrapped her fingers into his hair, kissing him again and again. Melting into his body, holding him closer to her, Sapphire felt her body throb uncontrollably. The wind picked up again around them and she felt her body become lighter. Fox groaned inside her mouth. He was gripping her buttocks now, his groin pressed firmly against her. She allowed herself to become lost in him, felt the warmth of his beautiful body, smelt the strong scent of sandalwood fill her nostrils: they were falling into each other again, falling, falling, totally consumed. Sapphire wanted nothing more than to be in her own bed again, naked, with Fox on top of her, riding her with his big, beautiful cock inside her.

With a hard jolt against her back and a sharp crack in her ears she suddenly found herself doing just that. They were back in her room, on her bed, totally naked and totally intertwined. Fox was pounding her hard and she gripped him tightly with her thighs, feeling him inside her, filling her completely. She was thrashing like a wild thing, her head thrown back, a loud moan of pleasure escaping her lips. Fox gripped either side of her, pulling the bed sheets back, his mouth locked on to her neck, sucking her between growls of hunger.

She felt her body quiver in anticipation, heat building up in her groin, her legs becoming limp as the orgasm grew inside her. Fox continued to thrust deeply, relentlessly. Sapphire cried out as she was overcome by her release; her body shook with pleasure and she felt Fox withdraw from her neck. He let out a deep moan of ecstasy as he too came hard inside her. The room spun for a moment and Sapphire went limp. Fox fell on top of her, his chest heaving with exertion. They clung to each other for a moment.

Sapphire opened her eyes and blinked. Fox lay heavily on her, his hair covering her, his body hot and sweaty. Slowly and with some effort he raised himself up and stared down at her. His eyes were heavy and a satisfied smile sat firmly on his lips. "Sapphire, you have undone us both." She laughed now, a deep, almost hysterical laugh. Fox rolled himself off her, withdrawing slowly, her muscles clenching slightly as he did so, another moan escaping his lips as he lay on his back.

Sapphire reached between her breasts. The obsidian necklace was gone. She looked across to her bedside table and saw it sitting innocently on the side, glowing softly in the dim light. Had she done that? She reached across for Fox's hand and gripped him tightly. "I'm out of control, Fox. I don't even know how I did that." She felt him stretch slightly against her, a soft laugh coming from him. "I have no idea, either, but I'm not complaining." Sapphire rolled on to her side, watching him as he caught his breath "Are we in trouble again?"

Fox turned to look at her. He looked totally fuckable, his face covered in a fine film of sweat. "Most likely." Sapphire bit her lip. Feeling a little guilty, she reached across and touched his face softly. "You are here with me now. Am I still dreaming?" Fox sighed. "No. We are back in your reality; you have brought me back with you." Sapphire jumped up, looked across at her bedside clock. It was 3 a.m. "Oh, fuck. Oh, shit. I hope Charlie didn't hear us. Oh, my God."

Fox laughed again, sliding his hand up her waist. "Don't worry. I'm sure they are asleep. Come here." He pulled her into him, held her head to his chest and stroked her soft, silky skin. "I will stay with you for a while, just to be sure that Hecta does not follow us back." He felt her tremble against him. "Yes, that would be nice. That was pretty messed up."

He kissed her head softly and pressed his body against her, pulling the covers up over them. "I will never leave you, Sapphire. I will never let anyone harm you. That I promise as your guardian and as your lover." She took his hand and kissed his knuckles. "Thank you." Fox knew he was most likely in serious trouble again, but could not help smiling. She was beautiful, intoxicating … and his. He could not imagine any other place he would rather be right now.

Chapter Sixteen

Tuesday

Charlie sipped her tea, leaning back against the kitchen counter. She eyed the clock, noting it was way past the time Sapphire usually got up to get ready for her late shift. It was not like her to oversleep. It was also not like her to bring a stranger home and have very loud sex in her bedroom without giving her the heads-up first. She blew on the tea, took another sip, and pushed herself away from the counter edge. "Fuck it; I'll just give her a knock."

Nathan had left early that morning for work. Charlie had already done two hours of work on the wedding rings she was finishing off and had come back in from the workshop to have a break. She put the tea down and headed up the stairs to wake Sapphire. She felt a little nervous not knowing who was in her room with her. She stifled a giggle, hoping it wasn't some random guy Sapphire had picked up at the cafe; the local guys were slightly farmerish.

She stood outside Sapphire's door, hesitating, with her hand raised ready to knock. She placed her ear against the door, listening for any telltale signs coming from inside. Nothing; all was quiet. She knocked lightly. "Saf, it's me. Are you up?" No answer. It had been weird that Sapphire was not still up when they had come home last night. Her book was still on the chair she had been sitting on in the living room, the candles she had lit were still burning and Sapphire had obviously gone to bed early, but with no note. Not like her at all. It must have been a booty call.

Charlie knocked again. "Saf, you are going to be late if you don't get up soon." Still nothing. Charlie hesitated again, then placed her hand on the door handle, opening it slowly to peep inside. She really didn't want to walk in on Sapphire in a mid-morning tussle. Charlie looked around the door. Sapphire's curtains were open, as if she had not even bothered to draw them when she had gone to bed. As she glanced at the bed she let out a small gasp. Sapphire was lying on the chest of a man who was holding her tightly against him; both of them were naked, the duvet covering their legs and important bits.

Charlie could not help but stare. The man was absolutely jaw-droppingly gorgeous, with long, dark hair which was wild and decorated with braids, dreads and beads. He was sleeping deeply, as was Sapphire. His chest was broad and lightly tanned; he was as fit as fit could be. Sapphire had a very satisfied smile on her lips: she looked like she had been fucked every which way but Wednesday.

Charlie covered her mouth and stifled a laugh. She coughed before speaking, "Saf, hon. You need to get up. You are going to be late for work." The man jumped, his eyes suddenly wide open. Sapphire stirred slightly, stretching her body, giving Charlie an eyeful of her ample breasts. Charlie smiled at him; he looked utterly shocked and totally confused. He sat up abruptly and looked at Charlie. She saw his eyes clearly now, a deep amber surrounded by a dark black ring. They flashed at her mesmerisingly.

"Sorry to bother you, but Saf needs to be at work in an hour and she will be pissed if she is late again." He nodded at her, saying nothing. Charlie left them, giggling as she closed the door. Holy shit, that guy was hot stuff. Where the hell did she find him? She headed back downstairs, grabbed her tea and went back out to the workshop. Her face lit up with a massive grin. "Go, girl." she laughed as she sat back down to finish her work.

Fox shook his head. "That did not just happen, did it?" he thought. He looked down at Sapphire. She was starting to wake up but was obviously still jaded from the journey last night. He was still here. He had fallen asleep with her and now her human friend had actually seen him. This could be bad, very bad indeed. He ran a finger across Sapphire's cheek and kissed her lightly on her forehead. "Wake up, sleepy. You have to go to work, apparently." Sapphire squirmed and moaned softly. "I want to sleep. Leave me alone." He smiled, despite the predicament they were in. "Sapphire, you must get up now. I must leave you; I have lingered far too long already."

Sapphire opened her eyes and blinked up at him. A smile spread across her lips; she reached up and touched him. He could see a flash of new passion in her eyes. "You are still here?" He kissed her fingertips and pushed himself up so that he was sitting. "Yes, beautiful, I am, and I am so not meant to be. Your friend just came in. She saw us together. You will have a lot of explaining to do now."

That woke her up. "What? Charlie saw you? Oh, Christ. Shit. Oh, fuckitty fuck." He was laughing at her now as she jumped up, her naked body bouncing in all its glory. "You have to go. Quick, before she sees you again. Oh, my God." She was off the bed in a flash and dashing around for clothes. She threw on a ridiculous fluffy dressing gown and stared at him with horror on her face.

"How the hell am I going to explain this to her?" Fox grabbed his trousers and shirt, which had been discarded on the floor next to the bed, and began to dress quickly. He looked up at her with a smile. "Be creative, my love." Sapphire gawped at him then started to laugh, a real belly laugh; the whole situation was just too crazy. He stepped towards her and pulled her into his arms. "I will be watching you, beautiful Sapphire. Call me if you need me." She snuggled against him for a moment, burying her head into his chest. "I miss you already." He kissed her lightly on her head again and stepped back. She watched him with a sad expression, knowing that any second now he would be gone. And just like that, he was.

Sapphire stood and stared at the empty space where he had just stood; her heart was slightly racing now. She had totally fucked up. How was she going to explain Fox to Charlie, the girl who would absolutely not let her get away without a good and plausible explanation? She dashed to the shower and dived under the hot water. It was late. Her shift started in an hour, she needed to eat, her stomach was totally empty and she felt slightly bruised down below.

As she smothered her body in soap and washed her hair she could not help but smile. She felt fabulous; her body was singing like a canary and her mind was filled with the memories from her travelling last night. She rinsed her hair and the smile slipped slightly as she remembered the fight between Fox and Hecta; the sex they had enjoyed when they had returned had made her temporarily forget the dark edge to her dream.

She turned the shower off and stepped out, grabbing a clean towel. As she dried herself she caught a glimpse of her reflection in the bathroom mirror; she had another massive hickey on her neck. Fox really had a thing about sucking on her neck. Maybe he was part vampire. She touched it lightly. It actually felt quite tender. Her groin pulsed at the memory and she shook her head, "Oh, for Christ's sake." She ran back to her room and dressed quickly. Brushing her long hair out she watched herself in the mirror; she looked flushed, vibrant … and her eyes were the brightest blue she had ever seen.

She was changing; everything about her was different. She knew she would have to come up with a really good story for Charlie. As she headed down the stairs to find something to eat she tried desperately to think of something. Charlie was sitting at the kitchen table, a big Cheshire Cat smile on her face, her arms folded across her chest. She had been waiting for Sapphire to come down.

Sapphire stopped and stared at her. "So, Sapphire Whittaker, spill the beans. Is he still upstairs?" Sapphire walked past her and flicked the kettle on, her back to Charlie. "No, he's gone. He left when you went back out to the workshop." Sapphire hoped that this was at least a plausible reason for Charlie missing him leave. Charlie sighed loudly. "Shame. I would have loved another look at him before he left. So … come on, Miss. Tell me all the details. You can't get away with this one, you know. Where did you meet him? How long have you been keeping him a secret?"

Sapphire smiled shyly, turning around to face her friend. "I met him in the coffee shop a while ago; he's not from around here. He was visiting his grandmother … you know, Pearl … the crazy lady. He rang me last night when you guys left for the pub, and, well … He ended up staying over, that's all." The grin did not leave Charlie's face, and she nodded slowly. "Uh-huh. That's all, eh? Sounded like you two were at it big time in the early hours of this morning. Woke me and Nathan both up. Not that I blame you, hon. That man is fine."

Sapphire sighed, thankful her quickly made-up story had gone down as the truth. She smiled at Charlie. "Sorry we woke you. I kinda forgot where I was. It's been a while, you know." Charlie unfolded her arms, interrogation obviously over for now. "You go, girl. First a random stranger at Simon's party, now a one night stand with some hot guy you only met once. Is this a new Saf I am seeing?"

Sapphire laughed and busied herself with making tea. She looked into the fridge for something to eat. She was starving. "Well, I don't intend to turn into an old slapper ... but, yes; I'm having some fun for a change, if that's OK with you. I don't want to take liberties in your home." Charlie snorted a laugh. "Oh, Christ, Saf. You know that I, of all people, would never judge a woman for being a little promiscuous. Hopefully you will get to see him again. He looked totally wild; is he a model or something?"

Sapphire grabbed ham, cheese and pickle from the fridge. Taking the bread from the bread bin, she started slapping a sandwich together. "No. I'm actually not sure what he does ... but, yes, he is very hot – and very, very good in bed, before you ask – and no, I am not giving you all the juicy details." Charlie laughed loudly. "You don't have to, Saf. We could hear it. Does the mysterious man have a name?"

Sapphire felt herself blush furiously. She stuffed the sandwich in her mouth and ate quickly, avoiding eye contact. "His name is Fox." Charlie laughed loudly and pushed herself up from the table. "What kind of a name is that? Is he related to Bear Grylls? I'll get back to work. See you later, sexy lady." She was laughing all the way out the back door. Sapphire cringed slightly but could not keep the smile from her lips.

Chapter Seventeen

Sapphire almost skipped to work. She had managed to get ready super-quickly and was surprisingly full of energy, despite her night of adventure. The lie-in had obviously done her good. Of course getting laid had also done wonders for her as well. Thank God Charlie had woken them up or she may not have made it in at all today. She arrived on time and got stuck into her shift. The cafe was busy that afternoon and Sapphire was on form. Linda was suitably impressed at how quickly she managed to get the line down at the really busy moments throughout the afternoon. Sapphire felt like she had collected some kind of energy boost through her travelling. Maybe it had been the crystal caves. Who cared? She was feeling good, the best she had in ages.

But her mind was a little troubled by the fact that not only had she been careless bringing Fox back into her world with her but with the fact that Fox himself had slept by her side and been seen by Charlie. She wondered whether this would cause a ripple in the balance that Pearl had warned her of. She decided to pay the old woman a visit on her way back home that evening. She was the only human around that she could talk openly to without someone sending over the men in white coats. Sapphire finished her shift at 6.30 p.m. and left the cafe with a bag of chocolate cookies that Linda had given her.

"A suitable gift for Pearl," she thought, as she headed out towards the edge of the village to Pearl's cottage. The evening air was just beginning to cool and the breeze felt fresh and inviting as Sapphire walked with a spring in her step towards Foxglove. As she wandered down the pathway to the old cottage Sapphire sensed the old lady before she saw her. Pearl was standing at her gate, a big smile on her face. She held the gate open as if she already knew Sapphire was on her way. She probably did.

"Back so soon, Sapphire? It's lovely to see you again. I've just made a fresh pot of tea; you must be tired after being on your feet all day." Sapphire beamed at her; she was so very glad to see her friendly face and immediately felt a little relieved that Pearl had been waiting for her. They walked through the garden to the cottage that looked just as inviting in the daylight as it had last time she had visited. Pearl opened the front door and Sapphire followed her through to the kitchen. "Well, my dear. You have been busy, haven't you? You are positively glowing again. You must tell me what has added this new sparkle to your energy."

Sapphire sat at the little kitchen table, placing the cookies in front of her. "I've brought you some cookies, Pearl; thought you might like some." Pearl was pouring the tea. She looked over her shoulder at Sapphire and nodded, still smiling. "Thank you, my dear; that was very thoughtful. Now do tell me what you have been up to." Sapphire lowered her eyes, a little ashamed. After all, she had been treading on forbidden ground again; it was obvious Pearl could tell.

"Well, the travelling has intensified. Fox has been with me again, and I seem to be popping up all over the place. I'm a little overwhelmed by how often it is happening now." She paused for a moment. "And now my friend Charlie has accidently seen Fox. I'm a little scared. We have stepped out of line. What might the consequences be? I kind of need more help controlling all of this."

Pearl carried two cups over to the table and watched Sapphire with sparkling humorous eyes. "Yes, well ... I knew that he would not be able to keep his hands off you. The connection between you is very strong; it was inevitable that this would happen. Even the obsidian did not put him off for long." Sapphire allowed a small smile to grace her lips. "I think it is more my fault than his, actually; he seems to be trying hard to do the right thing. He did protect me from Hecta, after all, and he is always talking of taking care of me. I do feel much safer when he is with me."

Pearl lifted the paper bag with the cookies inside and opened it up, inspecting the contents. "Ah, chocolate chip; my favourite." She started to nibble one of the cookies, her eyes still watching Sapphire closely. "So ... really, you need to learn how to control the travelling more. Fox is merely following you around, which is of course his job, so we need to curb your enthusiasm a little. I know it must be like finding a new toy to play with, but as you must have realised, with Hecta also following your every move, it is probably best to limit the times you do actually leave this realm." Sapphire nodded. Lifting her tea to her lips, she blew on the edge before taking a sip. It was peppermint. Nice. "Yes, I need to do that. I can't keep pulling him over here, especially now that Charlie has seen him. I don't want to cause any more trouble; I would hate for anyone to get hurt."

She watched Pearl devour the cookie with amusement. "Hecta has already shown himself to Charlie and Nathan. I really do not want him and Fox to end up having a fight in our back garden – or worse, in the house." Pearl licked her lips, picking off a small crumb before taking a sip of her tea. "Of course not, my dear. That really would be very bad, so let's have a think, shall we? See what we can do to help you sleep without constantly popping up in some strange world."

Sapphire reached for a cookie, suddenly feeling peckish herself. "Any help you can give me will be gratefully received, Pearl. Seriously, I am starting to freak out a little now." Pearl leant back in her chair and closed her eyes for a moment, hands folded neatly in her lap. Sapphire assumed she was looking for inspiration somewhere in her head. "Now, we know that your abilities have grown from strength to strength very quickly and whatever you seem to be thinking of is manifesting just as quickly, whether it be a conscious thought or not." Sapphire ate her cookie slowly; it was a particularly good one.

"So the main element seems to be that thoughts becomes things… so we need to get your thoughts on track, to enable you to control the travelling more when you sleep. I'm getting a strong message through that the easiest way for you to do this is to try meditating a little every day. Focus your mind on what you want and put your intention to the forefront of your mind before you sleep."

She opened her eyes, a smug smile on her lips. "Easy." Sapphire nodded, her eyebrows high in response to Pearl's confidence in her. "I've never meditated in my life, Pearl, and as for my thoughts … well, they are random at the best of times." Pearl chuckled and reached inside the paper bag for another cookie; she obviously thought they were pretty damn good, too. "I can teach you. It's a matter of discipline … and, of course, my dear, you really should be drinking the herbal tea I gave you every day. I don't think by the looks of your aura that that has been happening. You are lit up like a firework again." Sapphire smiled a little sheepishly. "I'm not very disciplined, either, Pearl. Perhaps I'm a lost cause."

Pearl shook her head, a smile still in her eyes. "Of course you are not, my dear. You are a very special lady, and you will be surprised just how quickly you can get the hang of it. Just remember: thoughts can be controlled like everything else. The main reason you are travelling so much is because you have a strong and vivid imagination, and some of the places you are visiting you may have been to before in past lives, which makes it much easier for your mind to navigate."

Sapphire frowned a little. She was not really sure if she believed all this past life stuff; she could hardly remember last year, let alone another lifetime ago. Pearl watched her with bright smiling eyes as she tucked into the second cookie. "Don't doubt your abilities, Sapphire. Trust who you are, trust who you are becoming. You are in control of this and with time and practice you can be an amazing person … someone gifted enough to travel safely and see and experience things only some of us can only ever dream of." She laughed at her own joke. "Well, let's start now. No time like the present."

Sapphire felt a little uneasy. Suddenly the pressure was on and she wasn't sure if she could perform as well as Pearl seemed to think she could. Pearl stood up from the table after brushing off the last of the cookie crumbs. It was just starting to get a little darker outside and she looked out of the kitchen window for a moment before making her decision. "Let's go into the garden. It's still warm outside; a good place to sit and meditate is by my silver birch tree out front. We can ground you properly there and I can show you how to breathe and focus a little easier there." Sapphire nodded weakly. "OK."

Sapphire followed Pearl out into the garden. The light was fading fast but the sky had turned a light pink and orange, and cast a soft haze over the ground that made it look even more magical than usual. Pearl was humming happily to herself as she led the way; she had picked up two cushions from the house as they had walked through and was placing them on the grass under the silver birch tree, facing each other. She lifted her skirt so that she could sit down and proceeded to settle herself cross-legged, like a nimble young woman would – not like someone who was quite obviously very old indeed.

Sapphire followed suit, still feeling a little self-conscious. This all seemed a little silly, to be honest, something only hippies and New Age travellers did, but she was fairly desperate, and Pearl had seemed to know what she was talking about when she had helped her at the weekend. Pearl rested her hands on her knees and Sapphire copied her, sitting directly opposite. Her back was against the silver birch. She could feel the coolness of the trunk against her spine and the tingle of energy that she was beginning to become accustomed to whenever she touched anything lately.

Pearl smiled at her encouragingly. "The key to meditation is to empty your mind, or in this case to focus on something that you want to create in your mind. We could try a mantra or just work with breathing. What would you like to do first, Sapphire?" Sapphire fidgeted a little. She was not very comfortable. She needed to stretch more; her legs felt tight and she was already getting pins and needles in her right foot. "Well, perhaps the breathing first, I think."

Pearl took a deep breath in and then exhaled loudly, letting her shoulders lift and fall with the breath. "It's very simple; just take a deep breath in through your nose, right from the bottom of your stomach, and then exhale through your mouth. You might feel a little dizzy at first; probably the first time you will have taken in the proper amount of oxygen for a while."

Sapphire smiled and tried to follow Pearl's instructions. She did feel a little dizzy at first. Pearl encouraged her to continue breathing like this, but to allow it to flow more easily, with less effort. "That's right, follow the breath in your mind; allow your consciousness to go with the flow of the breath. Listen to it. Feel it in your belly. Follow your breathing so that this is the only thing you are aware of...focus..."

Sapphire did as she said and very quickly found that she could sense only her breathing, feel the air in her lungs, listen to the sound it made as it escaped her lips. It was soothing and slightly hypnotic. "Now you have the breathing right, just focus on your legs. Feel them on the ground; push your energy from the base of your groin down through your legs into the earth, breathing all the time as you have been."

Sapphire pictured her legs in her mind with her eyes shut. She could feel her energy shift and sensed a glow of light around her start to filter down into the ground. It pulsed softly. "That's good, Sapphire. Now you need to draw this energy up through your lower body to your stomach. Feel it inside you, hold it there for a moment and then continue to move it up your body all the way through your torso, your chest, throat, and forehead ... and then push it up through the top of your head."

Sapphire found with some surprise that she could do this very easily and quickly. The energy she felt beneath her moved with ease up the line of her spine and buzzed gently as it reached the top of her head. "Imagine a door opening on the top of your head. Allow the energy through it and let it go. It will find your true energy source to connect to ... and then you are fully centred, with the earth and with the universe. It will refresh you and heal you."

Sapphire visualised opening a wooden door from the top of her head. With a whoosh the energy spun off until it seemed to hit a bright, sparkling source of light that she had oddly felt somewhere before. The line of light ran straight down through her to the ground. She smiled, her eyes still closed. Her whole body was humming softly. It felt good. "Now you are connected to the true source of your energy you can focus your mind on what you intend. Either say the words or just visualise it."

Sapphire nodded. "So if I just want to sleep and stay home I can visualise myself in my bed for the night, safe and sound? Or if I want to see Fox I can just picture him?" Pearl laughed softly. "Yes. I am assuming that will work. Thoughts become things, remember." Sapphire continued to focus on the wonderful energy that was running up and down her body. Her breathing was still steady and she did actually feel very much in control. "To come out of your meditation ... just close your energy back down, bringing the energy back through your head, through your body and down to your feet again before you open your eyes."

Sapphire nodded and carried out Pearl's instructions; as she did so her body shivered a little at the shift. She opened her eyes slowly and stared at Pearl, who was watching her in the dim light with amusement. "Well done, Sapphire. That was wonderful; you are indeed a very quick learner." Sapphire breathed out a sigh of relief. She felt quite smug and happy with her first efforts of meditation; being able to sense the balance of energy from above and below was weirdly familiar to her. She had always been good at visualising things and it felt good to exercise this part of her brain again.

Pearl looked up at the sky and shook her head slowly. "It's getting darker now, Sapphire ... probably best for you to head back home before night falls completely. Remember, you have control now and you can practise meditating and focusing your thoughts any time you have free now. Practice makes perfect." Sapphire felt like she was back at school, being tutored by her old music teacher. He was always bleating on about, "Practice, practice," when she had been trying to learn the guitar – something she was, despite her efforts, totally rubbish at.

"Thank you, Pearl. Once again you have made me feel better. I really am very grateful for your time." Pearl pushed herself up gracefully, Sapphire watching her with envy as to how easily she could go from sitting to standing like that. Her own legs had now gone completely numb and she was having difficulty uncurling them. Pearl reached across to help her up, Sapphire taking her hand somewhat reluctantly, but grateful for some help. Pearl's skin was soft and smooth to touch and her palm was warm. She was still smiling at Sapphire with that knowing smile. Sapphire was absolutely convinced now that the old woman was indeed a mind reader.

"Now off you go, young Sapphire. It was a pleasure to spend time with you again. Take care; you know where I am if you need me." Sapphire nodded, brushing herself down and shaking her legs, trying to get some blood flow back into them. This meditating lark was going to take some getting used to if she had to sit still for so long. "Bye, Pearl. Thanks again."

They headed to the gate. Pearl hugged her tightly before opening the gate to let her out; Sapphire felt a rush of emotion run through her as Pearl let her go. She always felt the urge to cry when Pearl did that. She had no idea whether it was because the old woman was being kind to her, or that the situation she was in was just too overwhelming and that Pearl was the only person who truly knew what she was going through. Either way, it was a little weird. "Don't forget to drink the herbal tea, Sapphire. It keeps your aura clean and stops you getting so drunk on his essence," Pearl called out to her as she walked back down the path. Sapphire turned and waved back at her, smiling. "I will, Pearl. Goodnight."

Charlie was cooking something in the kitchen when Sapphire returned. She could not make out what it was from the smell wafting through the cottage, but it instantly made her stomach rumble. The radio was on loudly and Charlie was singing away again, as was her thing to do when she was cooking. Sapphire peeked around the kitchen door and knocked on the counter to try and alert her to her return. Charlie turned around and jumped in the air, the jar of sauce in her hand taking a leap up, spilling some of its contents on the floor.

"For fuck's sake, Saf. Will you stop doing that?" Sapphire laughed, grabbing some kitchen roll to help mop up the sauce. "Sorry, Charlie, but you will have the radio up so loud, and with all that noise you were making it's hard to get your attention." She looked up at Charlie with a cute smile. By way of apology she cleaned up the mess, Charlie returning to her saucepan. "I'm cooking spag bol. Do you want some?"

Sapphire threw the kitchen towel into the bin and went to find some wine glasses. She really needed a drink. "Yes, please, Charlie. That would be awesome. I'm starving as usual. Where's Nathan?" Charlie laughed. "He's at his house. I told him I needed a night off. Where have you been? Is more the question. You're late tonight. Anything to do with that super-hot Fox I saw in bed with you this morning?"

Sapphire knew it was too good to be true that Charlie had let her get off so lightly this morning. She was kind of hoping Charlie wouldn't bring him up again; fat chance of that. "No, not him. I went to see Pearl, though, just to see if she was OK. You know she's an old lady living on her own; thought it would be neighbourly to just check on her." She found the wine glasses and reached for a bottle of red that had been opened the day before, a nice Merlot. She indicated to Charlie to ask whether she wanted one. Charlie nodded a big, "Yes," a smile on her lips. "Uh-huh. You just thought you would check on the old lady who happens to be the grandmother of the said super-hot Fox, eh?"

Sapphire had the decency to blush and laugh at the same time. "It's not like that, honestly. I did go to check up on her, have some tea. Seeing him would have been a bonus, yes, but I believe he has left the area now." Charlie licked the wooden spoon she had been stirring the Bolognese with and nodded her approval. "Yeah, I believe you, but that's a nice thought. I've been waiting for you to come home. Got a surprise for you, babe."

Sapphire seated herself at the kitchen table. She wanted to go upstairs, get in the shower, and change before eating, but now she was curious as to what Charlie was about to drop on her. "What's that?" Charlie took a gulp of the wine and smiled a wide naughty smile at Sapphire. "I have tickets for all three of us for a festival being held this coming weekend, which is meant to be out of this world – and you, my lovely friend, are coming. No ifs or buts. It's time you had a little holiday from that cafe. I've already rung Linda and got the time off for you. Am I an amazing friend or what?"

Sapphire blinked at her, took a big gulp of wine and blinked again. "A festival. Where? What kind? I hope we are not sleeping in tents. Holy crap, Charlie, and how did you manage to sort that out behind my back?" Charlie was laughing now as she plopped spaghetti into the boiling water. "You will love it, honey. Simon got us the tickets; he knows one of the DJs playing and all the crowd are going. Linda had no problem giving you the time off; you haven't really had a break since you moved here. It will be fun. We can kick back for a few days, get wild, and yes – it is in tents – but I've got all the camping gear, so it will be fine. You can have your own little cute tent next to mine and Nathan's."

Sapphire was a little gobsmacked. She hadn't been to a festival since her twenties, and then it had been all rock and indie. Could she even do the whole no-washing-for-three-days thing again? Charlie was singing again loudly to the radio. Sapphire took another sip of wine and felt the idea slowly grow on her. Charlie turned and winked at her. Sapphire smiled back. How could she not get into the idea with her crazy friend instigating it? Fuck it. She did need a break from work and in the last week she had been struggling to live a normal life with all the changes taking place. It might be nice to just step away from everything for a while.

"So how much time have I got off, and how long is the festival, you crazy friend?" Charlie turned around and did a little jig; she was obviously pretty excited about the whole thing. "You have a whole week off work, and the festival is Thursday to Sunday. I've arranged with Linda that you take Thursday to Thursday off. Gives you time to get over it when we get back. You know, sometimes four nights of no sleep and lots of hard core dancing and all the trimmings can make you a little beat."

Sapphire was laughing at her now; it was hard not to get caught up in the excitement. "Oh, my God, you mean this week? So I only have to work tomorrow and then I'm off for a whole week?" Charlie danced across to her and landed a kiss on her cheek. "Yes, my lovely friend, a whole goddam weekend of dancing, drinking and downright debauchery." Sapphire giggled, clutching her wine. She was really getting into the idea now. It had been such a long time since she had taken more than a weekend off and life had been getting a little mundane, of course until she had started the dream travelling. This might be just what she needed to distract herself from the craziness she was up to her neck in.

"Go and have your shower Saf. Dinner's nearly ready." Sapphire nodded enthusiastically. She dashed up the stairs and threw her clothes off as quickly as she could before jumping under the hot water. Her mind was now reeling with the idea of camping under the stars, dancing with strangers again, having some fun, maybe seeing Fox in between as she slept. Oh my, oh my. That night she made sure she practised meditating before she retired for bed, concentrating on grounding her energy and visualising herself safe and protected in her bed so that she could sleep soundly before her last day at the cafe. She was jittery with excitement but determined not to ruin the next few days by exhausting herself by travelling in her sleep. She drifted off to a sound sleep with a smile on her lips.

Chapter Eighteen

Wednesday

Sapphire's official last day of work before her week off went by in a blur. Linda was indeed more than happy for her to take some time off; she had been working several more shifts than normal lately and Linda had managed to get cover for her quickly. She had worked her last morning shift and had the afternoon ahead of her to get packed and ready for the weekend away. When she returned home around 3 p.m. Charlie had already begun pulling the camping gear out of the garden shed and was busy sorting out sleeping bags, pots, pans and a few essentials she considered massively important for their adventure. Apparently a washing up bowl would double up as a pee bucket when needed in the middle of the night, an idea Sapphire found mildly horrifying, but she knew she would have to get over it.

"I have no idea what I'm supposed to pack, Charlie. You will have to help me; it's been years since I camped or did anything like this, to think of it." Charlie watched her with mild amusement, hands on hips, as Sapphire threw various items of clothing out of her drawer on to her bed. "Oh, Saf, it's not that hard. Just a couple of pairs of jeans, shorts, some t-shirts … just take stuff you know you love to wear. You will probably stay in the same clothes most of the time. Of course you will need your wellies just in case it does rain and some flip-flops and sunblock for the sunshine."

She headed over to Sapphire's wardrobe and started pulling out suitable clothing, helping Sapphire to roll up the t-shirts so that they would fit easily into her backpack. "Just take what you can carry; you won't want to be lugging too much shit with you, hon, believe me." Sapphire rubbed her forehead, a little anxious that she might not be able to cope without her hairdryer for a few days. She still had a little of the city girl in her and liked her creature comforts. "We will leave early tomorrow morning so we can get there when the gates open and get a good camping spot. There won't be much going on on Thursday night but we will all camp together and have a few drinks – get in the mood for the weekend."

Charlie was properly spiked up about the whole thing; her eyes were sparkling like a child before Christmas morning and she was having lots of fun helping Sapphire choose the prettiest tops and shortest shorts she could find. Holding up a camisole that held little to the imagination she swung her hips from side to side. "This will be good for the dance tent, Saf. Show off your amazing boobs." Sapphire laughed at her. "I wear that for bed, Charlie. I am not getting my tits out for everyone at the weekend."

Charlie gave her a mock frown, a smile on her lips. "Oh, for goodness' sake, Saf. Let your hair down. You are a beautiful lady; show off your assets – you might just pick up another gorgeous man to play with. Or of course you could phone the sexy Fox and get him to meet us there. I am sure there will be tickets available on the gate." Sapphire narrowed her eyes at her friend; she just wasn't going to let the Fox situation drop. "I'm not sure he would be free, but I'll see."

Charlie rolled the camisole top up and put it in the backpack. Grabbing a hairbrush, some face wipes and a few of Sapphire's necklaces and bracelets, she nodded at her. "Uh-huh. We'll take some nice make-up just in case he does turn up. We can make you look stunning and have him melting in your arms, hon. With all the music and booze you two could have an awesome time."

Sapphire could not help but smile back at her. She picked out a few make-up items, some dark kohl eyeliner and red lipstick (she hadn't worn lipstick for absolutely ages, but now seemed an appropriate time to start the habit again). "I'll finish packing my stuff. We can load the car in the morning. Make sure you get a good night's sleep tonight, my lovely … and I would suggest a bath, as we might not get another chance to wash for a while, unless of course they have some showers tucked away." Sapphire wrinkled her nose up at the thought. "I will definitely have a bath in that case, but I'm taking shower gel and shampoo anyway, just in case."

Charlie nodded and headed out of her room to finish her own packing. Sapphire sat on the edge of her bed for a moment, looking at her backpack. She was excited but nervous at the same time. She didn't really know anyone except Charlie, Nathan and, of course, Dave and Grace, but it was time for her to make some new friends. She hoped that her dream travelling wouldn't be a problem while they were away. Remembering the bag of herbs Pearl had given her she ran down the stairs to the kitchen to find them. Best pack them and take them with her; she did not want to have any problems with Hecta, and Pearl seemed to think they dampened her aura so they might help.

She could hear Charlie in her room talking away to herself as she packed; she was so into having a good time. "I'm going to have that bath, Charlie. Do you need to use the loo before I go in?" Charlie peeked out from her room, holding a bikini in her hand. "No, you go ahead, hon. What do you think? Too much?" The bikini was bright red and looked like a piece of string with two tiny triangles sewn on to it. "Not for you, Charlie. Take it; I'm sure you can use it in the dance tent." Charlie laughed loudly and spun back around into her room. "Now you're getting it, Saf."

Sapphire laid in the bath, revelling in the sensation of warm water and bubbles. She rinsed her hair under the water and tried to remember exactly how it felt to be really, really clean. It was most likely going to be some time before it happened again. She visualised how the next few days might turn out: sleeping in a tent, listening to the thump, thump of bass music and the laughter and shouts of partygoers. A smile played on her lips; she was actually really starting to look forward to the weekend.

After giving her legs a proper shave and using the pumice stone on her feet she slowly stepped out of the bath. Pulling out the plug she watched the water start to lower. Drying herself slowly, she felt ready for a good sleep, and finished her bedtime routine: brushing her teeth, combing out her long hair and braiding it into plaits ready for the weekend. She smothered herself in body lotion (the good one) and dressed in her rabbit t-shirt ready for bed.

Charlie was talking on her mobile in her room; Sapphire hesitated at her door before knocking to say goodnight. "Yep, Saf's ready and packed. A little nervous, I think, but I know she will love it. We will be ready for you to pick us up at 10 a.m. Can't wait to see you, babe; sooo excited. Hope you have all the gear. I'm up for a mental one.

OK; see you tomorrow. Luv ya." Sapphire waited for her to switch off from Nathan before popping her head around the door frame. "I'm going to bed now, Charlie. See you in the morning." Charlie was sitting on her bed, still dressed. Her packing had obviously taken a serious amount of time and concentration. She beamed at Sapphire, pupils wide with excitement. "OK, sweetie. God, I'm so excited. Not sure how I'm gonna sleep; might go out for a quick joint to calm me down. I'll set the alarm for about 8am; I'll make you a cuppa." Sapphire smiled at her. "OK, Charlie. See you in the morning."

Sapphire headed back to her bedroom, lit some candles and an incense stick. She had checked her salt boundary was double thick, as she really needed to sleep, and made sure her obsidian necklace was properly secured around her neck. Sliding into bed she closed her eyes and savoured the softness of her sheets and duvet, the clean smell of fresh bedding and the comfort of a proper bed – another thing to remember before she slept on a blow-up mattress for a few nights.

Taking a few deep breaths, she allowed her body to relax and her mind to let go. She desperately wanted to reach out for Fox but knew it would be dangerous. Instead she allowed her mind to whisper to him softly. "Fox, I am going away for a few days. I know you will be watching me, but I will try hard not to wander too far. I miss you and look forward to seeing you again when the time is right." She hoped her thoughts would reach him and turned on to her side, pulling her pillow closely to her chest for comfort as she willed for a peaceful night's sleep.

Chapter Nineteen

Thursday

Nathan stood by the car, his arms folded in front of his chest, tapping his foot, a frown on his forehead. "What the hell, babe? You cannot seriously be taking all this shit." Charlie was loading the car up to the roof. She had every single thing you could possibly think of stuffed in the boot from food to rope to raincoats and lots and lots of boxes of wine. "It's not that much, Nathan. Come on; you will thank me when you need a cup of tea in the morning and I'm the only person with a kettle and camping stove."

Sapphire watched the pair of them, laughing softly. She felt refreshed and alive after a particularly good night's sleep. She had dreamt of Fox, seen his face smiling at her in her thoughts, his beautiful amber eyes flashing sexy unspoken words at her. She knew instinctively he had been watching over her but because she had practised Pearl's visualisation as she had drifted into sleep last night and asked for a peaceful night in her own bed she had not travelled any further than her own room.

"OK, that's enough. We really need to get going now, babe. Si and the others are already well on their way. It's going to take about an hour to get there; we want to get in before all the good camping spots go." Charlie shoved one last blanket into the boot with her hip and stepped back with a satisfied smile on her lips. "All done. Let's go. You ready, Saf?" Sapphire nodded. She had packed a small shoulder bag that she could take with her in the back of the car with some cash, tissues, lip gloss, and the mobile phone she rarely used nowadays, but that Charlie had insisted she bring so they could get hold of each other if they were separated over the weekend.

They climbed into the crowded car and headed off, Charlie leaning back to smile at Sapphire. "The weather report says 'Sunshine all weekend,' so it should be a good one, but I've got all the rain gear just in case." Nathan snorted. "You've got the bloody kitchen sink in there as well, Charlie. I think every possible scenario is covered." Sapphire smiled back at her friend and settled into the seat ready for the journey. A little buzz was tingling in her belly. She assumed it was excitement, but she noted that the obsidian was also buzzing a warm glow against her chest as well and it made her shiver slightly in anticipation.

Just over an hour later they arrived at the festival site. Cars snaked their way along the side of fences which had been erected around the site to stop people jumping over and gaining free entry. Charlie was literally bouncing up and down in her seat. Nathan was on the phone talking to Simon, who was apparently already inside with the rest of the group. He switched off from the call and swivelled around to face the girls. "Si's made a space for our tents. I know roughly where they are; we have our names on the gate so we should be able to get in ahead of the queue. Just need to get through this traffic and park."

Charlie clapped her hands with glee. "Oh, goody. I'm so up for a drink; can't wait to see what's inside. Tell me again, Nathan. Who is playing?" Nathan smiled at her, put the car into first gear as they crawled forward an inch. The traffic was crazy. "No big bands or DJs: it's all new up-and-coming artists … but they make a big effort with the stages and have some crazy chill-out areas and arty stuff. I think they also have a funfair and a place you can go and get a massage … you know, like at Glasto where you can have some healing and stuff."

Sapphire was getting twitchy legs. She wasn't very tall but she did not like sitting still for long, and sitting in the queue waiting to get parked was taking its toll. "Sounds brilliant," Sapphire nodded, rubbing her hands up and down her thighs to get the circulation going. "Do you guys mind if I get out and just walk by the car for a minute? My legs are going dead." Charlie smiled at her. "Yeah, sure. Actually … open the boot, Nathan. There are a couple of cans of beer on the top of the blankets in the boot. Grab them, Saf, so we can have a drink while we are waiting to get in." Nathan laughed. "I suppose we could get the party started. It is after lunch, after all."

Sapphire jumped out and lifted the boot. She looked around at the other cars and people milling around. Groups of people were walking alongside the cars, loaded up with bags and camping gear. They ranged from hippy-looking types to hard core clubbers in fluffy boots and fluorescent clothes; it was a weird and wonderful mixture of people. As she rummaged for the beers she could not help but smile at the happy feeling building up around her. Everyone was smiling, laughing, having fun already – just queuing up to get in. She could feel the energy buzzing around her. She was super-excited.

Handing the beers back through the car window she opened herself a can and started to walk slowly alongside the car, people-watching as they made their slow pace towards the entrance. They were pretty close now; it had taken them over half an hour already but the time had passed relatively quickly. Her legs were starting to feel normal again as she walked and she sipped her beer looking up at a clear blue sky, thankful that the weather report was at least right for today. Putting a tent up in the pissing rain would have been a real downer.

"Hey, beautiful. Hope to see you inside." A young guy had stopped walking as he passed her and was smiling at her appreciatively. He was blonde, his hair touched his shoulders in soft curls and he had laughing blue eyes ... not bad-looking, and a fit body. Sapphire smiled at him shyly as he continued to walk by her; his friends were laughing and nudging him in jest. She had pulled already. The weekend was looking better by the minute. Charlie stuck her head out the window. "Her name's Sapphire; she is single, you know."

Sapphire choked on her beer. "Charlie, shut up." The blonde guy winked back at Sapphire and they continued their walk to the entrance. Sapphire felt her cheeks turn a deep shade of red. She rolled her eyes at Charlie, who was laughing loudly. "I cannot believe you just did that." Charlie saluted her with the beer. "Well, you are single. Can't pass up on a good opportunity like that." Nathan was also laughing. Sapphire reached for the car door and jumped back inside; she was mortified, but a smile slipped on to her lips. She ducked down a little, not wanting to make more of a scene, "Just get us inside, Nathan, before she embarrasses me any more."

Within an hour they had at last managed to park and were loaded up with bags and gear ready to go in. As promised, Simon had put their names on the gate for a speedy entrance and they jumped the queue – much to Sapphire's embarrassment – but she was glad they did not have to stand in the really long queue of rowdy people, which trailed a very long way back into the distance. She eyed the bouncers at the gate a little nervously as they did a very quick check in her shoulder bag; a sniffer dog was walking excitedly through the people grouped at the entrance. Sapphire looked across at Charlie, suddenly dreading the thought that her friend might get pulled to one side for carrying a bag of weed. Charlie grinned at her mischievously, obviously picking up on her thoughts, as they were ushered through to the main entrance to the festival site.

As they stepped through Sapphire felt her eyes grow wide. It was like stepping into another world, a world of fantasy and fun. She could see tents already pitched either side of her and in the near distance larger tents, more suitable for a circus, were dotted around, with flags flying in the gentle breeze. Charlie nudged her. "What do you think, hon? Good, eh?" Sapphire gawped for a moment. It was like nothing she had ever seen before; a new world of fantastical fun and frolics waiting for her to enjoy.

Nathan was marching ahead, on a mission. "Come on, you two. Si and the others are over the back near the side gate." Charlie giggled and lugged her overly-stuffed bag and tent higher on to her back. Sapphire was totally loaded down with several other bags Charlie had handed her, and her backpack. She really wanted to put it all down and stretch her body out. After treading carefully around guy ropes and bodies they found Simon and the rest of the group in a cool area off to the side of the festival site – obviously a prime camping site close to everything, but far enough away that they would not be too bothered by other campers.

Sapphire counted five other tents in a circle, some large, some small, surrounded by windbreakers and a large canopy that covered the centre for a convenient seating area everyone could meet up in. Simon greeted them with a big smile and a brotherly hug for Nathan. "Great to see you guys. Did you get in OK? No problems at the gate?" Nathan nodded, smiling broadly. "Yeah man, no problems. Thanks for that. Charlie carried the stash." Sapphire cringed, knowing that she had been absolutely right about Charlie and her big bag of weed, or worse. "Cool. Let's help you get those tents up, then we can chill for the night before the party gets started tomorrow. I've got us some backstage passes for the weekend and know a couple of the guys playing on the main stage Saturday night. It's going to be a good party."

Charlie was positively busting with excitement. She was already pulling the tents out and stacking the poles to one side. Sapphire put the bags down with a sigh of relief and regarded the pile of tent poles dubiously, not having one hell of a clue where to even start. "Sapphire, you help me put the poles together. Nathan, you put Sapphire's little tent up over there. We can start on the big one." Nathan saluted a "Yes," and started working on the little dome tent Charlie had brought for her. They spent the next half an hour laughing and falling about while deciding which pole went where. Eventually the tents were up and they could start to chill.

Dave and Grace had pitched next to them and were starting up a small barbecue, the rich smell of sausages wafting over their little group invitingly. Sapphire felt a happy buzz in her belly as she pulled out a hoody from her backpack. The air was just starting to feel a little chilly and she noted that the day had passed quickly while they had unpacked and pitched up. She left her shorts on and grabbed a beanie hat to cover her head just to keep off the chill. She knew she must have looked a scream with her plaits and flip-flops but it really didn't matter here; there were people all around her in fancy dress and crazy outfits – no one gave a shit what you looked like.

Everyone was smiling and laughing. Blankets and cushions had been thrown on the groundsheet under the canopy and a low wooden table had appeared from somewhere in the middle for a few candles to be placed on. The scene was chilled and funky. Sapphire recognised the girl Simon had been with at his party and several other faces she could remember vaguely seeing at his place. Some of them she remembered bumping thighs with in his lounge; the thought was somewhat embarrassing, but everyone seemed really friendly and included her in their group with no hesitation.

As the daylight began to disappear Sapphire could hear music start up around her. Some people were playing music on their portable speakers, others were drumming … so much laugher and talking and noise but, strangely, it was totally comforting, as if a tribe of people had all descended on this one place and were meeting again after a very long winter apart. This is what it must have felt like when people did actually congregate together thousands of years ago. She remembered her very first dream with Fox, when they had danced around the fire, bodies moving together as one ... perhaps this would be the same.

Charlie and Nathan were curled up together to one side on one of the big cushions, the light of the candles giving their faces a warm glow in the growing darkness. They were smiling and whispering sweet nothings to each other. Sapphire had seated herself a little way back from the others; she was propped back against her backpack, her knees up, her back against the ground. She could watch the group but look up at the sky at the same time. "Here, Saf, do you want some wine?" Grace was standing over her with a plastic cup filled with dark liquid in her hand. "Yes, thanks. That would be nice" Grace smiled at her sweetly, handing her the wine. Sapphire took it and sipped slowly; it was good, despite the plastic cup. She had turned down the food offered earlier and as she sipped the wine she noted how quickly it was going to her head; probably not a bad thing if she was going to get any sleep at all that evening. The excitement of arriving had totally stolen any appetite she may have had. She sat back and listened to the easy conversation that travelled around the circle ... watched as her friends enjoyed a smoke and a drink. The night was still young and Sapphire knew it was just the beginning of a possibly very eventful weekend.

Chapter Twenty

Several glasses of wine later and the party was officially starting. Simon had propped his iPod speaker against the wooden table and they now had their own little dance tent going. Charlie and a few of the other girls were dancing around, laughing and bumping hips. Sapphire had declined – despite Charlie's insistence that she, too, should get up off her backside and have a dance; she was nicely fuzzy but wanted to just watch tonight and save her energy for the rest of the weekend. A smile rested happily on her lips and she tapped her feet to the music. The boys were chatting and laughing; all around her she could hear groups of people partying in their own way. Lights scattered between the tents gave the area a surreal feeling, everyone separate but joined in happiness.

Sapphire could feel the obsidian warm between her breasts and her body was slightly tingling now; she assumed it was the wine. She decided to stand up for a while and have a little wander; she had her pocket torch and figured that their little camp would be easy enough to find again in the dark. She pushed herself up slowly, trying not to get a head rush. Charlie saw her and motioned for her to come and join the dancing. Sapphire smiled back and shook her head. "I'm going to have a look around; I won't be long." Charlie nodded and carried on with her pelvic circles ... the girl could dance.

Sapphire realised that she only needed the torch to navigate the guy ropes. There were strings of lights along the camping area pathways and people were wandering around, like her, to scope the site. Everyone smiled at her and she felt completely safe ... a strange feeling surrounded by people she did not know, but her instinct was telling her all was OK. The larger circus-looking tents were dark – no music or movement tonight – but she could make out each area and the seats and gazebos scattered around looked inviting for the start of the festival tomorrow.

She did not wander too far and was happily people-watching when she felt the obsidian start to burn hotly against her skin. She reached inside her hoody and held it in her hand; it was glowing abnormally hot. Her heart started beating a little faster and she stopped for a moment, her head swinging around, looking for danger. Why would it start alerting her here? She did not have to wonder for too long. Standing to one side was Hecta. He was slightly obscured by a group of people dancing around their own little disco; he jumped in and out of her sight as they moved.

A sharp breath caught her throat. He was smiling at her, that dark nasty smile he seemed to find so attractive. No one seemed to pay him much attention: perhaps they could not even see him. He lifted his hand and waggled one finger in front of his face, shaking his head as if to tell her off. Sapphire stood her ground. She suddenly felt pretty pissed off. How dare he follow her here? This was her time out.

The anger grew in her belly and she could feel her energy start to crackle. Her hair became slightly static and she knew it wasn't good to lose control. He was grinning now, mocking her, goading her to make her move. Sapphire took a deep breath and tried to regain control. With all the weird shit that had been happening in her dreams she could not take the risk that suddenly a snowstorm would arrive and start whipping innocent people up into the air around her. Instead she smiled back at him and flipped him the bird. Before she could see his reaction Sapphire turned on her heel and marched back towards her tent and the safety of her friends. The obsidian grew cooler the further she stepped away from him. Thankfully, he did not seem to be following her.

She arrived back at the tent a little breathless. Her retreat back had been a little hurried, and dodging people, tents, and guy ropes was hard work. Charlie flung herself at Sapphire as she entered their camp. "Hey, sweet thing. Was starting to worry where you were. All OK?" Sapphire hugged her back, really glad to see her friend. "I'm fine. It's brilliant: the site looks amazing. Can't wait to see it properly in the daylight tomorrow." Charlie nodded enthusiastically, totally unaware of Sapphire's flushed cheeks and heightened heart rate. "Me, too. Do you fancy a smoke before bed? Might need it to help you sleep with all this noise going on."

Sapphire hesitated for a moment, not sure if that would be a good idea, but she was on holiday and her friends were right there with her, watching over her. "Yeah. Why not?" They sat down with the rest of the group. Charlie had prerolled and lit up expertly, passing it immediately to Sapphire after one tug. Sapphire was not a smoker and coughed painfully for the first two pulls; they all laughed at her but she wasn't offended. She knew after the third go that it had been a mistake to mix wine and weed – the cardinal sin. Sapphire felt a little sick and dizzy. The others seemed to be fine and had started to laugh at pretty much nothing, such was the effect of Charlie's magic bag of weed.

"Charlie, I think I'm going to lie down; feeling a bit weird, hon. I'll see you guys in the morning." Charlie stroked her arm. "Oh, hon. Sorry. I know it's strong gear. You OK? Take some water. Call me if you need me; I'm just next door." Sapphire smiled at her feebly. She really needed to lie down now and take a load off.

After taking a rather wobbly pee in a dark corner behind the tents, something she had not done in years, Sapphire climbed inside her tent and rummaged around, using the torch to find some toothpaste. She gave up in the end and decided to suck a mint; it might help with the sick feeling. She wrestled out of her clothes and changed into some loose joggers and a camisole top; she untied her hair and slipped into the sleeping bag Charlie had provided her. Nathan had been a darling and pumped up the air bed when they had arrived. She lay down and was grateful that she did not have the dreaded head spin she was expecting. Instead everything felt incredibly heavy and the sounds of laughter, music and talking were a comforting blur in the background. White noise. Sapphire curled up and snuggled into her pillow, willing sleep to come. She had no other thoughts before falling into a deep and heavy sleep.

Sapphire assumed she was dreaming again. Everything was quiet around her; she was lying flat on her back with her arms above her head. She could sense dawn approaching; she was comfortable and half-covered with the sleeping bag, but the dream was making her feel weightless like she were floating above the ground. A warmth was skimming across her chest and neck, like fingertips trailing her skin. She could feel her body start to respond to the warmth in slow sensual pulses. A small moan escaped her lips; her eyes felt heavy and she could not open them. Soft lips were placing light feather kisses on her neck and ear; a wet tongue licking slowly across her ear lobe was making her body start to tingle in all the right places. A hand was moving slowly, leisurely, in tiny circles across her stomach that was exposed now, making her squirm. She tried to roll over on to her side and open her eyes, but a large warm body prevented her from moving.

As she tried to open her eyes again the lips moved to her mouth and crushed against her, taking her in a sweet deep kiss. She opened her mouth and allowed the kiss to grow, tongues linking and dancing together. She knew this kiss; she knew this touch. He was here with her, wherever this was. At last her eyes opened and she sighed in relief at the sight of Fox hovering above her, a firm smile on his lips. He raised a finger to them and whispered, "Sshh." She stretched and smiled back at him, nodding. As she blinked she realised that they were in her tent and she was actually awake and not dreaming at all. Fox was here with her at the festival. She giggled at the thought and raised her hand, placing her fingers behind his neck into the depths of his wonderful hair. His eyes flashed at her and she knew he was anticipating her next move. As she pulled him towards her for another kiss he sighed and she felt him push the sleeping bag down, away from her legs. She surrendered completely and allowed him to remove her clothes and make sweet, slow love to her in her tiny tent surrounded by people only one foot away. It was the most intimate, exciting and wonderful thing she had done in quite some time.

Chapter Twenty-One

Friday

Fox held Sapphire in his arms. They were both naked, lying on the ground, covered by her sleeping bag in the dome tent. She had fallen asleep again after their lovemaking; it had been tender and excruciatingly wonderful as always but the location was somewhat different from what he was used to. Being surrounded by humans but separated from them by a thin piece of sheet was a whole new experience for him; this world was indeed very strange. When he had reached out to her in her sleep state she had welcomed him willingly and he had slipped through to her realm with ease. He had been somewhat bemused by the tent he had found her in and the fact that there were so many other people around her but it had not stopped him from wanting to touch her and feel her body wrapped around him, as was becoming their pattern.

She was so utterly intoxicating to him. The obsidian had not bothered him this time: he had slipped it off over her head while he kissed her and she had not protested during their coupling. They had been silent and intense in their joining and she had quivered like a bow during her climax. He had held her close to him as the dawn had arrived and he could hear people beginning to stir around him. He knew he would have to leave again very soon as it would be unwise for other humans to know of his existence; they had already been treading on very dangerous ground lately. He sensed Hecta lingering close by and he did not want to leave her side but knew he must be very careful. In this strange world that she lived in anything could happen with their magic: she was growing stronger by the day. He could sense that more than ever now and she was quickly becoming more aware of her gifts.

He scanned the area in his mind and could feel the presence of Sapphire's friend and housemate in the tent next to them; she was stirring in her sleep but had not yet fully awoken. This place was most strange. He could see the intense joining of energies around him and the fact that many people here were quite intoxicated on various levels. He would have to watch over Sapphire carefully while she was here. Fox felt her move against him; she snuggled her head further into his chest and he sighed deeply, taking in her wonderful scent. He would do anything for her, to keep her safe and to keep her happy. She was his life now. He kissed the top of her head and she moaned softly. He wanted to say goodbye to her before disappearing, knew she would be agitated if he did not give her the courtesy.

As if she sensed his thoughts he felt her begin to wake and press her body more tightly into his. "Good morning, Fox," she whispered, with a smile in her voice. "Fancy meeting you here." He chuckled softly. "My lady, it is a pleasure as always." She glided her arms up and circled them around his neck, lifting her head to look up at him. "Thank you for staying with me until I woke up." He kissed her lightly on the lips. "I knew you would be annoyed if I was not here after our lovemaking this morning." He watched a sweet blush grow on her cheeks. She was always so bashful, a quality he found endearing in her. "I know you can't stay long, but I'm glad you came. I saw Hecta in the crowd last night. He's watching me again." Fox frowned slightly and traced her lips with his fingertip softly.

"Yes, he is here. But so am I. Nothing will happen to you. I will be watching you, too, and I will be with you whenever I can, my beautiful Sapphire." She withdrew her hands and pushed herself up slightly, looking down at his magnificent naked body, licking her lips with approval. "Good. That means I can have some fun without him pestering me." Fox laughed softly. "Yes, have fun ... but be careful. This place is most strange and there are a lot of humans all in one place who are very intoxicated. Could be troublesome, I think." She stretched against him, the smile still firmly on her lips. "I can take care of myself, you know that now; but please come see me again when you can." He nodded and pressed his lips to hers once more. She felt a brief shift in her energy, and as his kiss probed deeper the familiar pop sounded in her ear ... and then he was gone.

Sapphire laid still for a moment, relishing in the afterglow of being with Fox. His scent was all over her and she thought it would be a good idea to make some of the herbal tea she had brought with her, just in case. The campsite was slowly waking up around her; she could hear people starting to rise and chatter. She pushed herself up and looked down at her naked body; she felt a little hot and sticky and would have loved to jump straight in the shower. Realising this was a fantasy right now she reached into her backpack for the trusty wet wipes Charlie had given her; she gave herself a sleeping bag bath and used deodorant and talc to freshen up. That would have to do for now.

She was hungry. Her head felt a little thick from the wine and smoke last night but she was amazingly alert, her energy heightened from being around Fox again. She pulled out some jeans and a t-shirt after finding fresh underwear for the day. Tying her hair up into a loose knot on top of her head, she dressed awkwardly in the confines of the dome tent. Using the compact mirror in her make-up bag she checked the damage out before applying a little make-up. Mornings were not her greatest look but she had a certain glow about her today and she smiled at her reflection smugly: the cat that had certainly had the cream. The hickey on her neck was almost gone now, fading fast. She hoped it didn't look too obvious; she had been cleverly covering it with scarves and her hair for the past few days. What the hell? No one cared, anyway.

Tentatively, she peeked out of the tent and surveyed the little camp area they had created yesterday. The only other person awake at this time was Simon's girlfriend, who was squatting down under the canopy next to a camping stove – boiling water for some tea by the looks of things. Sapphire reached back inside her bag for the herbs; perhaps if she smiled nicely she could pinch some water and, even better, some food. Her stomach rumbled at the very thought of sustenance. Clambering with little style out of the tent she noted that the day was warm and bright and dry. Perfect camping weather. She was glad she had brought the sunscreen Charlie had nagged her about.

Pulling on her flip-flops, she stood up and stretched fully. It felt amazingly good, her muscles sending warm, approving signals down her legs and ribs as she put her arms over her head and leant from side to side. The blonde girlfriend looked up and smiled at her. She was a typically pretty blonde, with big blue eyes and big tits to match: Sapphire could see why she belonged to Simon. "Hi. Do you want some tea? I'm Caitlin, by the way. Simon's girlfriend. We didn't get properly introduced last night. I remember you from the party. Sapphire, isn't it?" Sapphire dropped down beside her and sat cross-legged on a cushion, smiling back at her. "Yes, that's right. I have my own tea, but would love some hot water, and I don't have a cup. Charlie has all the stuff in her tent and they are not up yet." Caitlin nodded. "No problem. I have plenty. I'm always an early riser: doesn't matter what time I put my head down I'm always awake with the dawn chorus. Pretty annoying sometimes, but it can be handy on occasion. What woke you up so early?"

Sapphire could feel her cheeks flush a little. "Oh, just an early riser, too, I guess. It's a bit strange, camping. I haven't done it in ages. I think the light woke me." Caitlin looked up at the sky. "Yeah. It's a beautiful day. Gets light pretty early now the summer's here. Should be a really fun weekend. This crowd are good fun to party with and the music here is good. We came last year. Had a ball." The kettle started to sing, steam rising from the spout. Caitlin grabbed some cups, filled hers with a tea bag and, Sapphire noted with amusement, a massive spoonful of sugar. This girl obviously liked her sugar.

She handed Sapphire a mug. "Here you go. Put your tea in. I will fill it up for you. What you got, peppermint?" Sapphire dug out her bag of herbs, a little self-conscious now. "Erm, no. It's herbal tea that a friend of mine gave me. It's actually really good – a little spicy – wakes you up in the morning." Caitlin watched her spoon some of the herbs into the bottom of the mug. She raised an eyebrow. "Looks like skunk." Sapphire laughed. "It's not. Don't worry, it's completely legal." "Well, I think it is," she thought in her head. Caitlin laughed, pouring the hot water into the mug. "How boring."

They sat back on the cushions. Caitlin had produced some biscuits from her food supplies and offered one to Sapphire, who nodded, quite famished. "When the others get up we can head to the main site and get some breakfast from one of the stalls. The food here is pretty good." Sapphire munched on the custard cream. "Cool. I'm starving." She waited for the herbs to settle at the bottom of the mug before taking a sip and was surprised by the smooth warmness of the concoction on her lips. Her body shivered a little as if the potion was already altering her vibration. Damn, this tea was good. They sat and chatted amiably for a while before the rest of the group began to slowly emerge in various states of hangover from the tents.

Charlie and Nathan appeared last. Sapphire was positively champing at the bit, her stomach was so empty. Charlie was dressed in a suitably eye-catching over-the-top outfit of extra-tiny shorts, red bikini top with a thin camisole in bright pink over the top; her curls were pinned in little swirls on her head complete with flower clips. She looked like a flower fairy. "Morning, Saf. You were up early, hon. Couldn't sleep?" Sapphire had finished her tea and was feeling bouncy and full of energy. "Yeah. Caitlin has been keeping me company. Are you guys ready to go and find some breakfast?" Nathan was scratching his head sleepily, nodding with enthusiasm. "Defo. We are both starving"

They headed off as a group through the tents and crowds of people, all milling around now towards the food vendors, settling on a good old-fashioned breakfast bar with bacon butties and sausage sandwiches. Sapphire had ordered a huge all-in-one breakfast bun filled with sausage, egg and mushrooms. She ate it like a woman on a mission. Nathan laughed at her. "I've never seen someone so slim with such a big appetite, Saf. How do you burn those calories off?" Charlie snorted a laugh. "Don't ask her that question, babe. You would be shocked." Sapphire continued to eat, trying not to blush again.

Once they had all had their fill of food and drink they headed off to scout the festival site, splitting off into little groups. Charlie linked her arms in between Sapphire and Nathan, dragging them in the direction of the stalls, where she wanted to have a browse at the clothes and nick-nacks. "We need to get you some suitable festival attire, Saf. Those jeans and t-shirt will just not do." Nathan rolled his eyes. "If you two are going shopping I'm heading over to the main stage to see who's playing later." Charlie let him go. "Off you go then, babe. I'll call you when we are done." Sapphire allowed her friend to drag her off to the stalls. She was nicely full now and her energy was still buzzing. Charlie's enthusiasm was catching and she liked the idea of having a browse.

The stalls were a mixture of clothing and jewellery, bits and pieces you would expect to find in a flea market; all very New Age and hippy-like. Charlie spotted a tent that had a few boutique items hanging outside. "Oooh ... this one looks promising." They entered the makeshift boutique and Sapphire was hit with the smell of incense and music playing chilled-out tunes from some invisible speakers. The clothes were all really funky and outrageous, almost like a fancy dress shop – flowing skirts and long dresses with lots of lace, sequins and pearls. Charlie was clapping her hands in glee as she began to push through the rows of clothes on the rails. Sapphire wandered around a little, picking up a few items but putting them straight back, thinking she wouldn't be seen dead in any of them.

"Saf, look at these. They are perfect for you." She was holding up a bustier top in baby pink, complete with lace-up back and tiny sequins on the front panelling; a long skirt in the other hand, in the same baby pink, with lace and flower detailing trailing down its sides. Sapphire eyed them doubtfully. "Just try it on. I think you will be surprised." Sapphire took them from her friend, more out of humouring her than anything else. She couldn't think of anything less flattering. Charlie brushed her away towards the little fitting room with a gentle push and turned back to the rails.

Sapphire reluctantly went inside and began to undress. She pulled the bustier over her head with a slight tussle to get it down over her chest, which seemed to want to pop out over the top, and wiggled around a little to get it in place. It did seem to fit her perfectly. Next came the skirt; it sat on her hips just below her belly button, exposing her flat stomach, something she had always been quite proud of, and fell heavily to the floor just above her ankles. It actually felt really comfortable, and surprisingly very familiar, as if she had worn this type of outfit before. She had no idea what it looked like as the mirrors were outside the fitting room.

She pulled the curtain aside warily, looking for Charlie, who happened to be standing directly outside holding an armful of clothes. She jumped up and down with joy at the sight of Sapphire. "Oh, Saf, come out. Take a look. You look amazing." Sapphire pulled the curtain back fully and stepped out, a little unsure of herself. She walked over to the mirror and stood in front, staring at her reflection in wonder. She did in fact look awesome. The bustier top was very pretty and flattering, her breasts spilling just slightly over the top, giving her the look of an eighteenth-century barmaid, and the skirt sat on her hips, showing off her hourglass figure. Despite the fact that she was not very tall the length of the skirt was just right and the whole effect was definitely aesthetically pleasing to the eye.

Charlie stood behind her and placed her hands on her shoulders. Looking into the mirror, Sapphire saw her clock the hickey and raise a questioning eyebrow before a giggle escaped her lips. "Naughty Fox." Sapphire laughed with her. "Right. We need to find some clips for your hair and then the outfit is complete. God, I'm good." Sapphire, caught up in the experience, now nodded with a smile. They found some tiny diamond clips and feathers which Charlie said would look funky and cool.

Within twenty minutes they had purchased an entire outfit for Sapphire, and Charlie had collected herself another three tops and two more miniskirts. Sapphire was pleasantly surprised that it cost her no more than £20 for the whole thing. She had been slightly dreading the cost before the dreadlocked young girl behind the makeshift counter had added it all up. Charlie was over the moon at her purchases, which came in at the grand total of £40. Bargain. Sapphire kept the clothes on, feeling like she now fitted in more with the rest of the crowd, who were all collectively dressed in various weird and wonderful clothes.

They practically skipped back to the tent to meet up with the rest of the camp. On arrival Nathan gave Sapphire an appreciative wolf whistle, causing her to blush even more as everyone turned to look at her.

"Wow, Saf. You look good enough to eat. Like the new look; it suits you." Charlie bustled past into her tent to gather further implements of beauty.

Sapphire did as she was told and sat down while Charlie produced brushes, combs, hairspray and the hairpins to begin her hairdressing magic. The day was moving on. Before long lunchtime drinks were being produced and the others were keen to get back out to start the real partying. Music had begun to start in the main arena and Sapphire could feel the energy of the site lift as everyone headed in to begin dancing and partying.

Chapter Twenty-Two

The sun was shining down on the site with a bright intensity that seemed to highlight the overall positive mood everyone was feeling. Music was playing all around them now, from live folk music to a drum and bass tent, and the main stage was kicking off with some funky indie band. Sapphire walked around with the others, her eyes wide and her mouth slightly open in awe. Her body moved without hesitation to the music. They seemed to continually sway and spin around each area instead of walking, stopping every now and then to grab a drink from one of the beer tents. The afternoon was warm and hazy; a few clouds dotted the sky and a gentle breeze kept them cool as they danced away. Charlie beamed like the Cheshire Cat all afternoon and Sapphire could not help but smile back at her. It was infectious, a collective grouping of happiness which seemed to be spreading throughout the festival site.

Sapphire could feel it in her bones, the pulsing throbbing magic of music and dance, making complete strangers smile and laugh with each other. She was starting to feel relaxed in a way that had seemed long forgotten to her. She could not even remember the last time it had felt so normal to let go of her body, her mind and her inhibitions. They danced for some time before Charlie grabbed her hand and led her out of the dance tent they had ended up in. "I need a pee, Saf, and a sit-down for a while. Will you come with me? Nathan is busy dancing."

Sapphire nodded. Her skin was covered in a fine film of sweat from the sunshine and dancing and she was thirsty. "What time is it?" Charlie shook her head. "Who cares? It's still light, but looks like it could be around 6 or 7 p.m." Sapphire was shocked at how quickly the day had gone by. She followed Charlie to the line of portable loos. The smell was not too bad, considering how warm the day had been, but then again it was only day one of the festival. She dreaded to think what it would be like by Sunday. She waited for

Charlie to take her pee. She had obviously sweated all her fluids out; hence the dire need of a drink of water right now.

As she looked around absently at the people around her she noticed a group of guys off to her right. They were looking directly at her and nodding at each other. She turned her head to see if there was someone behind her they were looking at. Then she saw the blonde-haired guy with them, the one that had spoken to her as they had queued up to get in yesterday. His friends were obviously winding him up to come over and talk to her. Sapphire lowered her eyes and looked at the grass below her feet, not really wanting to make eye contact any more. She was not really in the mood to talk to a strange man, not with Fox on her mind and possibly watching her from wherever it was he disappeared to.

Charlie reappeared and grabbed her arm. She was laughing. "Those guys were all talking about you over there, about your killer boobs and fabulous outfit. God, men are so hormone-driven. You could just flutter your eyelashes right now and I think the blonde one would fall at your feet." Sapphire kept her head down and turned quickly to move out of the line of sight. "Oh, crikey, Charlie. You know how to make me feel self-conscious." Charlie looked back over her shoulder, one arm interlocked with Sapphire's, the other raised as she waved at the group of guys. "See you later, fellas."

Sapphire wanted the ground to open up. She hurried Charlie along as quickly as she could towards a stall to buy some water from and to hide again. "You are such a shit, Charlie. How am I going to stay out of trouble with you around?" Charlie was really laughing now. "Why stay out of trouble here, hon? This is a playground, to play and have fun in." Sapphire shook her head at her friend, smiling now. They queued for water and found a place to sit for a while, Charlie unloading her smoking paraphernalia out on to her lap so that she could roll a joint.

They sat with the sun on their faces, watching people go by, listening to the music and sharing the smoke. They sat for some time watching the sun slowly start to go down and the daylight fade. The air started to feel a little cooler but Sapphire was not cold; she felt like an internal fire was burning inside her now. It was comforting and soothing, her body was relaxed and humming softly from the effects of the smoke, which she was now getting the hang of smoking without coughing up a lung. Charlie leant her head on her shoulder and let out a deep, contented sigh "This is the life, Sapphire. This is the life."

As the daylight began to fade they decided to head back to camp to freshen up before heading out again for the real partying to begin. Charlie had texted Nathan and told him to meet them back at the tent. They found their way back as the sky began to turn a spectacular shade of pink and orange, the daylight finally disappearing over the horizon, leaving them to fumble for candles and the torches again so that they could freshen up. Sapphire decided to keep her outfit on; she was enjoying the feeling of exposing her arms and chest to the world and she was still warm, knowing that she would be getting hot and sweaty again in a while when the dancing started.

Charlie had changed into hipster jeans and a tiny electric blue top that left little to the imagination. She insisted on making a few finishing touches to Sapphire's hair by adding a few white feathers to the clips that stuck up in strategic places in between the swirls of hair she had placed around her head. Pieces of hair fell softly around her shoulders and Sapphire felt utterly feminine and fabulous by the time Charlie was finally happy with her creation. She had reapplied her eye make-up in a smoky grey that highlighted the purple tones of her big blue eyes and added the red lipstick.

Stepping back to admire her handiwork, Charlie smiled at her widely. "You look like a gypsy princess, Saf: sexy as hell. Can't wait for tonight to kick off ... it's gonna be a good one." Sapphire nodded enthusiastically at her, just as Nathan stumbled back into the campsite. "Wow. You girls look hot. I'll be the most envied guy in the dance tent with you two by my side." Charlie laughed, bending down to rummage in her bag. "Right, let's have a pick-me-up ... get us in the mood. Where are the others, Nathan? I've got some wraps for us and Simon and Caitlin if they want one."

Sapphire watched her produce a little bag of goodies that she had obviously been holding back for them to enjoy for the evening. Her heart started to flutter again, excited at the thought of taking the drug she had taken at Simon's party, although her excitement was mixed with some trepidation as to how dangerous it would actually be for her to do this again in a strange place. Fox had warned her that taking drugs would change her vibration and cause problems. She pushed the thought to one side. She was on holiday, after all. Nathan nodded eagerly; he clearly had no doubt in his mind about jumping into Wonderland again. Charlie grabbed them a bottle of water and handed out a small wrap to Nathan and passed one to Sapphire, who paused for a moment.

"Come on, Saf. It's perfectly safe. You were fine last time. We will take care of you. It's only a little drop of sparkle; it will be fun." Nathan was already consuming his little drop of joy, gulping the water down greedily. "Don't worry, Saf. I will be with you both to take care of you. No one's going to hurt you while you fly; I'll make sure of that." Charlie kissed him on the mouth. "Our guardian for the night. You can't say "No," now, Saf. Come on: bottoms up."

Sapphire took the wrap and held it in her palm for a moment. Her body tingled in anticipation. For a brief moment she saw Fox in her mind and wondered whether he would be angry with her. "Oh, fuck it. OK, but promise me you won't leave me alone, I'll never find my way back to the tent without you guys later." Charlie winked at her and passed her the water bottle, after knocking back her wrap and chugging some water down. Sapphire followed suit, allowing the drug to wash down into her belly. She took a deep breath and let her shoulders go. "I'm ready"

The festival was now in full swing, music pumping from all areas, the stages lit up with flashing lights and lasers swinging across the sky. Somehow they had managed to find their way back to the dance tent and meet up with their group again. Charlie had passed out her goodies to Simon and Caitlin, who had also seemed more than happy to join them on the other side. Sapphire had started to feel a little floaty and the music was lifting her up nicely. She danced with a soft sway of her hips and her body started to buzz nicely. The obsidian was hanging low between her breasts beneath the bustier and it sensed her change in energy and pulsed warmly against her skin.

Charlie and Nathan were grinding provocatively next to her, eyes locked in a sexual stare that Sapphire recognised as the start of something much more primeval. She envied them for a moment. Her body was trembling slightly with arousal and she felt herself start to

171

come up, slowly, seductively, with a shiver of silver and gold flashes around her skin. Sapphire was flying again, flying with the crowd, with the music. It was wonderful, intoxicating, and dangerous. She knew she was smiling like a wicked woman with a need to claim and conquer. She closed her eyes and let the music take her away, her body swaying with the beat, her arms above her head tracing patterns with her fingertips, touching the soft, soothing air around her.

Bodies moved beside her, their energy brushing against her own. She was linked with them intimately and connected to everyone around her. She could almost feel their individual heartbeats, hear the sound of their breath leaving their lips as they danced together, as one, linked by this amazing, crazy drug. The bass grew stronger, the music louder. Sapphire spun in little circles, watching her energy flicker around her body in purples, blues and pinks. It was fascinating to watch; she was smiling and laughing, aware of her friends so close but enclosed in her own little bubble.

A warm hand caught her around her waist as she swished her hips to one side … pulled her into an even warmer body, placed firmly against her back. His groin pressed into her back. Her breath caught in her throat and her eyes opened in surprise. Dark hair fell across her shoulder as the man placed his head down against her cheek. She leant back into him and breathed in his scent; patchouli and sandalwood filled her nostrils. She smiled. Fox kissed her neck and pulled her tightly against him; he growled a low, sexy moan into her ear and licked her slowly, like an animal scenting his mate. Sapphire felt her body ignite from the groin outwards. She was on fire again; her energy pulsed and her vision flickered for a moment, making her lose her balance for a second.

"Naughty Sapphire. You are flying again, aren't you? My beautiful, gorgeous, sexually edible woman, what am I going to do with you now?" Sapphire grasped his arms and spun herself around so that she could face him, her eyes wide now, her pupils black and huge. He stood in front of her, magnificent in black leather trousers, waistcoat and beads around his neck. The tattoos on his arms seemed to glow under the fluorescent lights and his eyes were lit up, amber and black, with gold sparkles that caught the lasers like cat's eyes. She was temporarily blinded and stunned by his beauty; this magnificent man was here with her, in her world, showing himself to everyone around her to see him in all his glory. He was smiling broadly at her, his face slightly in shadow, casting a dangerous edge to his handsome features. "You can do whatever you want to me Fox. I am yours for the taking ... do your worst."

He threw his head back and laughed loudly. The music was so loud she knew no one would hear him, but she grinned at him, a little crazy, totally overwhelmed by the situation. There was no way she could hide him now: Charlie and Nathan were dancing right next to them; the rest of the group was close by; they would see him dancing with her, holding her intimately. There would be no holding back now. He pulled her roughly into his body, crushing her against him, his arms holding her face either side as he claimed her for a deep, slow kiss.

She fell into him, into the kiss that deepened and grew stronger and harder as she let him devour her. Her head fell back as he released her momentarily. The intensity was so strong that her head spun for a moment; he spun her around again so that she had her back to him once more. He slid down her body and placed his hands either side of her thighs, grabbing handfuls of her skirt and lifting it up her legs slowly, seductively uncovering her calves and thighs so that his fingertips brushed her skin, igniting her in a trail of fire. His hands moved around to the front of her thighs and brushed up towards her groin.

She groaned out loud. She was instantly turned on to the point of exploding. She could not believe he was doing this in front of everyone, exposing her body, touching her in the most open display of sexual foreplay. Sapphire opened her eyes again as he rubbed his groin hard into her buttocks. He was obviously as turned on as she was; he was hard against her and pushing himself into her body like a man about to bend her over and fuck her from behind. Sapphire realised she did not care ... he could take her here right now. She was putty in his hands, panting like a dog.

She could see Charlie and Nathan beside her. Charlie was looking right at her; she was smiling and dancing and seemed to be completely oblivious to Fox ravaging her in front of their very eyes. Sapphire giggled uncontrollably. It made no sense, none whatsoever.

Fox laughed softly against her ear. "They cannot see me, my beautiful Sapphire. We are cloaked in magic, our magic, which is blinding them to the truth. All they see is a gorgeous woman dancing wildly in the dark, losing herself to the music. I can do whatever I want to you right now and they will be oblivious to the fact."

Sapphire pushed back against him. She believed him. She knew he was working some kind of spell over her friends and the people around her; he was invisible to the crowd right now. Fox slid his hand up further into her underwear and pushed his finger underneath to find her warm, very wet pussy which was positively crying out to be touched. She shivered and groaned again as he pushed his finger very slowly and gently inside her. His body pressed against her, his mouth on her neck again, sucking, kissing, licking.

They were still dancing together, Sapphire with her skirt hitched up around her legs, Fox wrapped around her, fucking her with his fingers as he held her in place with his other hand around her waist, his mouth claiming her neck. Her legs were weak from pleasure but he held her up, moving in small circles against her body, the dance becoming a sexual release. She could feel her body starting to push against him, her hips grinding into his wonderfully clever fingers so that he could push deeper inside her, slipping in and out with the beat of the music. Sapphire moved her head to one side so that she could kiss him. As he lifted his head to accept the kiss she knew it would not take long for her climax to come.

Fox held her like that, hard against him, kissing her, fucking her with his fingers, the music lifting them both, people almost bumping against them. Sapphire felt her core begin to tremble uncontrollably as a wave of absolute pleasure began to rise with pure white hot pulses from her groin up into her belly and cascade out through her mouth into Fox. He swallowed her climax greedily as it tumbled out like a spray of red-hot wax from her body into his.

For a moment time stood still. She felt Fox lift his head from her and release her mouth. She fell limply into his arms as he pulled his fingers out from inside her to catch her fully before she fell to the floor. He lifted her up into his arms and with a swift stride took her out of the tent to the cool night of the air and laid her on the grass as she gasped and trembled in the afterglow. Sapphire could hear him chuckling softly as he lay down alongside her, resting her head in his lap, stroking her hair. Her eyes were heavy and she could feel her limbs lying like jelly against the coolness of the ground. Slowly she regained some form of consciousness and blinked up at him. His face was in shadow but she could see the smile on his lips, a lazy satisfied smile. She knew he was totally amused by her state of sedation, that he had taken pleasure in making her bend to his will, give herself to him freely and completely in front of a whole tent of people who were dancing and having fun. They had perhaps seen a woman high on drugs coming up so fast that she looked like she might combust at any moment, but they would have had no idea that she had indeed just exploded on the dance floor.

Sapphire started to laugh, her body shaking now with the full reality of what had just occurred. He had finger-fucked her on the dance floor. Fox leant down to kiss her again, softly now, with a gentleness that made her toes curl. She held his head in closer for the kiss to continue. She was aware of the people around her, the music still playing, the breeze caressing her hair. But all that was important was him, the man she was with: this wonderful, sexual, glorious man who was hers to have whenever she wished. Slowly and with some reluctance he released her from the kiss and stared at her with an intensity that made her body tingle with goosebumps.

"How do you feel now, my beautiful Sapphire?" She smiled and pushed herself up so that she was sitting now and facing him on the grass. She placed her hand on his cheek and brushed away a hair that had slipped across his mouth. "I feel wonderful. Alive and amazing. You are amazing. How did we get away with that? Did we get away with that? Oh, my God. I hope you did cloak us in magic. That would be hideously embarrassing if it were witnessed by all my friends." Fox laughed and stroked her arm with his fingertips softly.

"No one saw us, only you dancing like a gypsy woman, wild and free. Do you want to go back in?" Sapphire raised her eyebrows in mild horror. "God, no. I need a drink, maybe a stiff one, after that." Fox laughed and pushed himself up to standing, his hand reaching down to help her up. She took it and let him lift her up with ease. They stood for a moment holding hands and looking into each other's eyes. Sapphire could not help but feel like the luckiest woman alive to have him here with her now. They turned slowly, Fox placing his arm across her shoulder and pulling her gently into his side as they took a slow walk off to find Sapphire a drink. No one paid them any attention, the gypsy princess and the gorgeous, wild, leather-clad man. Sapphire felt like she was floating an inch above the ground and the only thing stopping her from actually flying off into the dark night sky was the strong arm draped around her shoulders.

They found a small tent which was selling beers and a few strong liquors. Sapphire went for a shot of whiskey to help bring her back to earth. The drug was still coursing through her veins and although Fox had well and truly grounded her with his fantastic finger dance she was still buzzing nicely. He sat next to her on a high bar stool, leaning against the bar edge with one elbow propping up his chin. He was smiling at her, a soft, amused smile, as he watched her sip the straight whiskey with a slight grimace on her face at its sourness. "This has to be the strangest place I have visited with you yet, Sapphire. Yet it feels quite normal to be sitting here with you in your world, watching you drink your drink."

She laughed, slamming the shot glass down and shaking her head at the taste that burned a trail down her throat. "I'm glad you are enjoying yourself. I'm still a little freaked out, but happy you are here with me. Are you planning to stay a while?" His gaze stayed fixed to her, the smile flickering on his lips. "You are in control of that, Sapphire. I can stay as long as you wish, but the cloaking magic can only hold for so long before people will actually start to see me again, and of course we have to be careful we don't upset the balance too much or Hecta may pop up again."

Sapphire frowned. "Mmmh … and I was just starting to really have some fun. Did you really have to mention him again?" She waved at the bartender. He stepped over to her and leant forward to hear her order. "I'll have two more straight Jacks, please." The bartender looked at her oddly but poured two straight Jack Daniels shots, sliding them across the bar at her as she handed him a £10 note. Sapphire pushed one across to Fox. He looked at her a little confused. "I'm not drinking alone. Try it; sample some of Earth's naughty pleasures." He laughed, took the drink and licked his lips, watching her intently "You mean other than your wonderful body." Sapphire blushed again, lowering her eyes as she picked up her drink. "Just drink and enjoy." Fox knocked the shot back down his throat as if he was born to do so. Sapphire realised he had most definitely drunk shots before. They both slammed the shot glasses down on the bar at the same time and laughed out loud. Sapphire knew the night was still young and the possibilities endless.

They drank several more shots together, Sapphire feeling the effects more than Fox seemed to. He cut her off after the fourth shot; her eyes were starting to become a little blurry and she was grinning like a crazy person. "Let's go back to your tent; I think it's time to come back down for a while, gorgeous."

Sapphire nodded happily at him. She was fuzzy and feeling a little wobbly. She could think of nothing better than to be wrapped up against him in the privacy of her little tent. She had no idea what the time was – it seemed irrelevant – but she suddenly realised she had been gone some time and her friends might be wondering where the hell she was. She reached inside her small shoulder bag and pulled out the mobile phone to check for messages. There were three from Charlie, ranging from, "Are you OK?" to "Where the fuck are you? Call me." She began to text Charlie back, not wanting to cause her friend any more distress.

Fox stood next to her, watching in wonder, as her fingers tapped into the phone. "What are you doing?"

Sapphire finished her message, clicking the Send button. "I'm letting Charlie know that I'm OK and that I'll meet them back at the tent."

He shrugged his shoulders "This is a strange world, indeed."

People were still partying hard all around them. The music seemed relentless and Sapphire had absolutely no idea when the whole thing would start to wind down again. Her stomach was completely empty but she had absolutely no appetite; she felt warm inside and her happiness was keeping her sated. Fox took her hand again and began to lead her through the crowds back to the camping area. It was as if he could see in the dark; he did not hesitate through the tangle of tents and led her back to their camp with a swiftness she found somewhat funny. As they stepped into their clearing Sapphire was glad that all was quiet and still. She did not want to face her friends right now.

Fox opened her tent and lifted the flap, pulling it to one side for her to step into. As he followed closely behind, a glow of light seemed to appear from nowhere, illuminating the inside of the tent so that she could see a little more clearly in the dark. Fox sat next to her. In his hand was a small round crystal the size of an egg; it gave off an orange light that lit up the dome tent softly. He was smiling at her. "Magic."

Sapphire smiled at him and began to pull some fresh clothes out of her backpack. "I need to change, pee and brush my teeth." She paused looking, back at him. "Human stuff."

He laughed and nodded. "Don't be long, my beautiful lady." He helped her undress, slowly lifting the bustier over her head, his eyes drifting over her body with an expression of wanting ... but he did not touch her or kiss her, allowing her to disrobe and re-dress in joggers, t-shirt and jumper. Suddenly she felt quite cold.

Grabbing some tissues, her toothbrush and toothpaste, a bottle of water, and a torch, she shuffled out of the tent to find a spot to pee. The drink and drugs were making this quite difficult; everything was slightly lopsided, and she giggled at herself as she stumbled a little awkwardly away from the tent so that she could crouch down and do her business. After swaying a little and doing the deed she cleaned herself up with some tissues and wipes and crouched over to brush her teeth – her mouth was as dry as a birdcage – before she headed back into the tent.

Fox was lying down with his head propped up in one hand. The tent was warm now and he patted next to him for her to lie down; the sleeping bag was laid out invitingly and another bottle of water had appeared from somewhere to one side. She kicked off her flip-flops and settled down on the air bed next to him, taking the bottled water for a good long drink.

He watched her the whole time, a soft smile on his lips. "OK now?" He brushed the back of his hand across her cheek and moved a little closer. As he took her into his arms and kissed her again she was glad she had managed to brush her teeth hastily after the pee. They lay down together under the sleeping bag and kissed each other softly and intensely for what seemed like hours, his hands caressing her gently between mumbled words in the strange language she did not understand. Words of endearment? Words of love? She was starting to come back down now and her body was fluid and limp within his arms. A comfortable heaviness surrounded her and she noted that he did not push her for further sexual release. Right now she was just content to just lie and kiss him.

Fox lay with her, watching her sleep. After they had kissed and held each other for quite some time she had started to show signs of sleepiness and he knew she was about to pass out at any minute. He had lifted the jumper off over her head and settled her into her sleeping bag; she was out cold within minutes. He felt a strong need to stay and watch her for longer but knew he must return to his own world for a short time to regroup and recharge his energy. This place was strangely draining; all the human activity around him seemed to be a massive pull on his magic.

As he pushed himself up to focus on returning to his own world the tent flap suddenly zipped open with a forceful jerk and Charlie threw it to one side, her head popping in, with a worried expression drawn strongly across her face. She stopped abruptly as she noticed Fox sitting upright next to a sleeping Sapphire. Her eyes grew wide and a small O shape formed on her lips. Then she smiled widely and nodded at him, winking, with a chuckle. "That makes sense," she said, before letting the flap fall back down again. Fox smiled. Caught out twice by the human friend; this really was getting very complicated. He closed his eyes and tuned into his home planet Shaka. His energy rippled around him and with a push inside his solar plexus he left Sapphire and returned to his home.

Chapter Twenty-Three

Saturday

Sapphire woke up feeling hot and heady. She was lying on her side with her pillow tucked under her arm; her head was on the jumper that she vaguely remembered Fox removing over her head last night. Or was it this morning? The whole night had been a little hazy after the dance tent and the Jack Daniels showdown. She opened her eyes slowly and smiled. God, he was so mind-fuckingly gorgeous, that man. Memories of the night came flooding into her mind as she stretched out her body and scratched her head sleepily. Despite the heavy amount of drinking and drug taking she actually felt quite good. Her senses homed in on any activity around her. She could hear people talking outside the tent and realised that she had absolutely no idea what time it was.

With some reluctance she pushed herself out of the sleeping bag and sat herself up to open the tent up. As she stepped out of the tent she was met by the smiling, knowing faces of her friends. Everyone, including Charlie, was up and sitting around enjoying morning coffee, or was it afternoon tea? "Morning, sleepy head." Charlie grinned at her and winked. "Have a good sleep, did you? Is that gorgeous man of yours still sleeping, Saf? Did you wear him out?" Sapphire blushed again, for the millionth time. "No he's gone. It's just me. What time is it?"

Charlie pouted at having missed him again. "It's 11.30, so you just made the morning. How are you feeling? Do you want some tea?" Sapphire wandered over and plonked herself down on a big cushion next to Nathan, who was building a rather large joint. God, they started early here. "Yes, please. Hang on. I have some tea; I'll just grab it." Charlie jumped up to get a mug and hot water. "Oh, and I'm a little pissed at you, Saf. You scared the shit out of me, disappearing like that last night. One minute you were there with us dancing, the next gone, just like that. Mind you, I don't blame you if the sexy Fox turned up; I would have done the same." Nathan slapped her bottom playfully. "Hey." She stuck her tongue out at him and wiggled her bottom.

Sapphire grabbed her bag of herbal tea and handed it to Charlie, who stared at it for a moment blankly. "This is skunk, Saf. What the fuck?" Caitlin laughed. "No, it's not, apparently, Charlie." Sapphire shook her head. "Look, I'm really sorry I tripped out on you guys last night. I was having such a good time, then Fox did just turn up and, well … we kinda left the dance tent for a while, had a few drinks … you know." Nathan raised an eyebrow. "Yeah, we know, Saf."

She was so damn fed up with being embarrassed she raised her chin and smiled back, determined not to blush even more. "Well, this is party land and I am officially partying." Everyone laughed and Sapphire took her tea, taking a big sip, the warmth of the herbs making her slightly thick head start to disappear quickly. Perhaps this brew was a strong one; Pearl may have known she would need some help. They spent the next hour or so drinking tea and smoking again, chilling for a while. Dave and Grace had left earlier to get some food and wander around the stalls; some of the others had gone to investigate the funfair. It was just Charlie, Nathan, Simon, Caitlin, and Sapphire, sitting in a circle, passing the joint around while they drank tea and laughed at nothing.

Sapphire took very little of the smoke; she wanted to clear her head from the night before and didn't want to risk stepping out of her body again while Fox was obviously out of the picture. Although she was relaxed and contented she could sense an uneasy feeling in the pit of her stomach that Hecta was still out there somewhere. She pushed the thought to one side and thought of other things instead, like what was she going to wear today and how badly was she starting to smell now, without a shower.

They picnicked at the campsite on some snacks Charlie had brought in her abundant supply bag, munching on crisps, biscuits, and some cheese and ham that had survived in the chiller box. Nathan's smoke had given them the serious munchies. After everyone was suitably full Charlie pulled Sapphire to one side. "Do you fancy a walk over to the massage tents? I could do with one after last night, plus I want some time on my own with you so that you can tell me all about last night. I want all the details this time; no leaving anything out." Sapphire sighed; this was going to be difficult, but inevitable. They changed clothes after freshening up. Sapphire really wanted a shower and hoped to find some when they ventured out again into the festival site. Nathan was happy to spend some time with Simon and Caitlin while the girls went off to do girl things.

The day was slightly more overcast today but the air was still warm and dry. They wandered at a slow, comfortable pace through the crowds towards the massage tents. Charlie hugged Sapphire around the waist and squeezed her, giggling a little. "So ... come on. What happened last night? How did the mysterious Fox just appear and then disappear again this morning, without any of us seeing him leave? Is he coming back later?"

Sapphire took a deep breath. She continued looking forward, not wanting to make eye contact with her friend in case any lie she told was more than obvious. "I had no idea he would be here, Charlie, honestly. He turned up at the dance tent and we danced for a while. It was nice, then I got hot and needed a drink and he took me outside so we could get some fresh air." Charlie let go of her waist and swung around so that she was walking backwards facing Sapphire, a grin planted firmly on her pretty face. "Uh-huh, and so he just turned up without any of us seeing him? You were dancing alone and then you were gone. Is he magic or something?" Sapphire laughed softly "You guys were as high as me. You probably just didn't notice him slip in; we left quite soon after he found me."

Charlie shook her head, not buying it. She stepped back in line with Sapphire as they continued to the massage tents that were coming into view ahead of them. "So what happened back at the tent? When I peeked in, expecting to find you alone, you were crashed out, fully clothed. He was wide awake sitting up next to you, looking very fuckable, of course. I can't believe you didn't take advantage of having him in your tent in that state, Saf. How terribly boring of you." Sapphire brushed the hair away from her face that the breeze had swept into her eyes. "We made out for a while, but nothing else happened." Charlie did a little excited skip and giggled. "Oh, God. I bet he's a good kisser. He is, isn't he?" Sapphire laughed. "Yes, he is a very good kisser. I was just too bombed to do anything else. He was quite the gentleman, seeing me back to the tent and making sure I was OK."

Charlie looked up at the sky and sighed deeply. "Oh, my. He sounds too good to be true. You must get him to come back later, Saf. I want to meet him properly. Call him, text him; just get him to meet up with us later." Sapphire squirmed a little. She really did not want that to happen. It would just be too hard to explain, plus Fox was just a little too out of this world to pass as a real human. His eyes would give him away immediately. "Maybe. We'll see later."

They had reached the massage tents and Charlie stepped up to the table, where a row of ladies were taking bookings. "We will talk about this later, Saf. Have you got anyone available for a couple of massages today, ladies?" A young brunette with piercings and tattoos looked down on her booking sheet. "Actually, yes. I have two therapists free in about half an hour. Would you like me to book you both a slot? They can do Thai or aromatherapy massage." Charlie clapped her hands with excitement. "Oh, goody. Yes, please. I will have an aromatherapy. What do you want, Saf?" Sapphire shrugged; she had not had a massage in years. "I'll try the Thai massage; I think I need a good stretch." Charlie laughed. "I bet you do."

As they had half an hour to kill they went off to sit in the Zen garden that had been erected within the massage site; a lovely little garden of potted bamboo plants and low seats around a proper sand garden, complete with raked patterns in the middle. It was all very serene and calm in the midst of all the chaos. Sapphire lay back, resting her head on the triangular Thai cushion, and stretched her legs out, wiggling her toes in her flip-flops. She had worn shorts and a camisole top today, no bra: she was feeling wanton today. Charlie did the same and they gazed up at the hazy sky for a while in silence.

"I wish we could live like this all the time. No work, no worries, just partying and chilling. Wouldn't that be lovely?" Charlie said, lifting her arms above her head and stretching out her long limbs. "I don't think you could do it for too long, Charlie. It might become a bit boring after a while, plus the hangovers would get to you after a while." Charlie turned to face her. "Actually, I feel pretty damn good today ... plus tonight is the big night, and I've got some more niceness for us to take later if you want." Sapphire raised her eyebrows. "Two nights in a row? Christ, Charlie. Is that why you booked so much time off after the festival?" Charlie laughed. "Look, you have to go for it while you are here, hon. It's par for the course."

Sapphire shifted her body to a slightly more comfortable position on the grass and contemplated the thought. Could she do it all again so soon? Should she? The waiting time for their massages went by quickly and before Sapphire knew where she was she was inside a yurt with a twenty-something hippy wearing fisherman's trousers and a camisole top, lying on a mattress and being kneaded heavily, to the point of melting into a puddle. The therapist was good; she had asked Sapphire a few questions before getting her to lie down on the padded mattress and beginning her magical routine.

Sapphire had never felt so utterly relaxed. The rhythm of the therapist's hands padding up and down like a cat was hypnotic and she knew just where to apply a little more pressure. All the knots she did not even know she had were being worked out with a slow, steady dance up and down her legs and arms. Sapphire felt her eyes start to close and her body became heavy and weightless. The soft music playing inside the yurt along with the smell of strong incense was making her slip into a light sleep; she let her head fall to one side and allowed her mind to wander.

She was not sure if she was actually dreaming but Sapphire could sense another person in the room with them. It was not Fox and it was not Hecta, thankfully. She could not open her eyes now but could still feel the steady rhythm of the massage therapist. A voice in her head – female – whispered to her softly. "Sapphire, dream traveller, you must be careful in this place. Your energy is growing and your vision is strong. Do not wander too far from the path, for it is a dangerous place to go. Be safe, my child."

For a brief moment Sapphire saw a beautiful blonde woman in her mind. Her eyes flashed blue and silver, not unlike the way Fox's eyes did when he made love to her. The woman was smiling at her, hair splayed out around her head as if she were floating in water. She raised her hand and blew Sapphire a kiss, a shower of light escaping her lips and rushing towards Sapphire like glitter in the wind. Sapphire jumped, her eyes opening suddenly wide. The therapist stopped her cat-walking and stared at Sapphire, a little frown etched between her brows. "Are you OK?" Sapphire blinked and took in the room, knew she was still here on earth at the festival, having a massage; she breathed a sigh of relief. Who was that? "Yes, I'm fine. Sorry. I must have dozed off." The therapist smiled at her serenely and asked her to turn over so that she could work on her back. Sapphire complied; she was definitely not taking any more drugs this weekend.

After the wonderful massage Sapphire dressed again and left the yurt to find Charlie, who was sitting in the Zen garden with a contented smile on her face. She looked up when Sapphire approached and waved at her lazily. "That was awesome. How was yours?" Sapphire sat down next to her. The sky was no longer overcast and the sun was shining again. She could feel the warmth of the rays on her skin, knowing that she was catching a lot of sun this weekend despite the sunscreen she had applied this morning. "It was great; I feel good." She did feel good. Despite the vision she had experienced during the treatment she felt refreshed and her body felt alive and supple again after sleeping awkwardly for two nights.

"Shall we head back to the main site, have a look around, find the others again?" Sapphire nodded. She really wanted to find a shower, if there was one. "Sounds good. I'm going to see if there are any showers around, Charlie. I really need to freshen up." Charlie nodded. "I'll ask at the booking desk … see if they know where there are any, if at all." They walked back to the desk and asked one of the ladies if there was such a thing. With much relief she said that there was a block of showers that you could pay for over on the far side of the site. Charlie was just as excited at the thought as Sapphire was. They headed back to the tents to grab toiletries and towels before texting Nathan to let him know their plan. Half an hour later they were stood in a queue waiting for a hot shower. Bliss.

They chatted while they waited, the sun warm on their faces. Sapphire couldn't wait to get clean; she had fresh clothes to wear. Charlie had lent her one of her new tops; it was a beautiful lilac with pretty flowers and lace on the tiny straps. She had decided to go for the gypsy skirt again, as it was getting hot today. When it was Sapphire's turn to step into the shower she took off her dirty clothes with glee. The water was hot and the pressure was good. She stood under the water, lathering up her hair and closing her eyes, revelling in the clean smell of shampoo and body wash. God, it felt good. Such a simple thing, which could bring so much pleasure. They both felt wonderful after cleaning up. Heading back to drop off their toiletries and old clothes Charlie insisted on helping Sapphire with her hair again and they spent half an hour applying fresh make-up and sprucing themselves up for the rest of the day. In high spirits they laughed and joked all the way back to the festival site.

"I'm hungry, Saf. Fancy a bite to eat before partying again?" Sapphire agreed; she hadn't really eaten very much at all in the last two days. They found a van that sold jacket potatoes and got stuck into some serious carbs, Sapphire washing it all down with a bottle of water. Happily full, clean and totally refreshed, they headed out to find Nathan and the others, who were at the main stage watching one of the bands. Sapphire smiled, genuinely contented, and they spent the rest of the afternoon dancing and having fun in the sunshine.

By the time the evening started to fall she could tell the night was going to be a big one. Her skin was starting to turn a nice shade of brown and she was keen to take in all the sights without getting off her head. Simon had given them all backstage passes for later that night so they could have cocktails and champagne with the musicians, something Sapphire found very amusing. She wondered if she would bump into anyone famous.

The festival was in full swing again; people everywhere were dancing and laughing, drinking and having fun. Sapphire watched everyone start to unwind; the alcohol was flowing and she knew at some point her little group would be participating in some extra fun. She knew Charlie would be pushing her to take the leap again but instinctively knew it would be a bad idea. As time passed they danced and drank heavily. Sapphire found her energy was already lifting high and she felt the buzzing happiness start to tingle throughout her arms and legs.

Charlie caught her by the arm and pulled her aside. "Here, Saf, have another wrap. You enjoyed it last night, and if Fox is around I have a spare." Sapphire smiled at her but shook her head slowly. "I'm OK, Charlie, really. One night was enough for me, but you guys enjoy. I'm happy to just dance and have a few drinks; in fact I'm looking forward to the champagne in the VIP tent." Charlie pouted a little. "Oh, really? Are you sure?" Sapphire continued to dance while they shouted over the music at each other. "Really. Charlie, I'm fine. You go ahead." Charlie shrugged her shoulders and swallowed the little wrap of happiness with a slug of water.

Sapphire knew where it would take her but wanted to stay grounded tonight. She was curious to see if Fox would arrive any minute, cloaked in magic and ready to do his worst to her on the dance floor. She started to blush at the thought.

Simon was waving them over and pointing to the backstage area. Nathan and Charlie nodded and pulled Sapphire with them. A square-shaped bouncer was standing at the entrance of the VIP tent. He looked at their passes – no expression on his face as he let them through. Charlie giggled at Sapphire as they walked passed him, "Mr Personality. Not."

Sapphire agreed, but was instantly sidetracked by the interior of the VIP tent. There were lots of people backstage, but the area was spacious and had hard flooring and sofas and comfy chairs dotted around low tables. The music was not as loud inside and the lighting was dim with a funky bar at one end, lit up with pink and blue tube lighting that gave it a high-class nightclub look. Everyone was attractive and glamorous. Sapphire wished she had dressed up a little, although Charlie had done a great job on her hair again; it was braided and laced with ribbons and clips, making her look like a Grecian goddess. Charlie always looked glamorous whatever she wore. Charlie was on fine form, hugging everyone and smiling and wiggling her hips. A few heads turned in their direction.

Sapphire was suddenly wondering what the hell she was doing backstage with all these people. They landed at the bar and Simon ordered them all champagne. Sapphire took her glass and savoured the cool, dry bubbles; it was deliciously crisp. No doubt it would get her totally pissed very, very quickly. The group was in high spirits, and not just with the champagne.

Sapphire noted that they were all coming up at the same time. It was more than just a little interesting to her that she could see their energies shift in front of her eyes. Little swirls of light were exploding from them in different colours. She blinked a few times, wondering if Charlie had slipped some into her drink but realised that bodily she felt fine – a little drunk, but by no means flying. She realised that she could just see everything without the aid of the little bag of sparkles. Sapphire remembered her vision, the beautiful, mysterious lady telling her that her powers were growing. Perhaps this is what she had meant; a new second sight.

She leant back against the bar, nodding her head in time to the music, which had started to crank up a notch. The bass was heavy and the VIP crowd were starting to get down and dirty. She smiled as she watched; it seemed that the glamorous and gorgeous also liked to let their hair down. Charlie and Grace were doing their little bump and grind routine, Nathan and the other guys watching and laughing as they started to draw a small crowd. Caitlin was keen to join in and, before she knew what was happening, Charlie had grabbed her arm and pulled her over. Sapphire laughed and thought, "What the hell?"

They began to dance provocatively together in the VIP tent, rubbing shoulders with God knows who. As Sapphire let herself go she closed her eyes and drifted with the music; the girls were all moving together, hugging and kissing, as was the nature of the beast.

Sapphire suddenly felt hands place themselves on either side of her waist and pull her into an unfamiliar embrace. She opened her eyes and came face to face with the blonde guy she had avoided for the last two days. He was smiling broadly at her, his blue eyes wide and inviting. Holding her lightly on the hips he moved with her as she danced a little stiffly now. She did not want to encourage this guy. Charlie was watching, laughing; she thought it was highly amusing. Blonde guy leant in to speak, his hair brushing her cheek softly. He smelt a little too strongly of aftershave, possibly Calvin Klein.

"Hi, I'm Michael. Nice to bump into you again." Sapphire looked around a little nervously now. She had no reason to be resisting but her heart was elsewhere. His hands remained on her hips as she danced. "Sapphire … nice to meet you." He licked his lips, his eyes darting to her chest for a moment. "I've been wanting to talk to you since I saw you in the queue to get in on Thursday. It must be fate that you are in here tonight. My brother is in one of the bands playing here; he got me the VIP pass." Sapphire nodded and smiled a little weakly. "Oh, that's nice." He started to step forward a little more into her personal space, obviously taking her interaction as a green light. "Very nice for me, Sapphire. You are totally gorgeous."

Out of nowhere a hand appeared firmly on Michael's shoulder and pulled him with some force away from Sapphire. Fox stood, eyes dark, face stern, behind him. Michael stumbled, a little taken by surprise for a moment. "This lady is taken. You will move away and not remember speaking to her or seeing her. Do you understand?" Michael stood very still. Sapphire held her breath, afraid of his reaction. He nodded silently and moved away back into the crowd, not even looking back over his shoulder at Sapphire, who stood her mouth slightly open in shock.

Fox stepped forward and stood inches from her, his eyes now flashing gold and black, his lips curling up slowly into a sexy, dark smile. "Hello, beautiful." Sapphire laughed and flung her arms around his neck, pulling him into her body, her face lifted to his, expecting one of his wonderful kisses. Instead he responded by grabbing her backside with both hands. Cupping her cheeks tightly and swinging her legs around his waist he carried her off to one side of the tent and pushed her up against the wall, his breathing heavy and frustrated. She looked straight into his eyes, her heart starting to race again, wondering if he was cloaked in magic or if the whole of the VIP tent had just witnessed the little display of testosterone. He paused for a moment, the wicked smile still lingering on his lips. "No one touches my lady but me. Understand?"

She was starting to feel a little dizzy; her pulse was jumping up and down like a kangaroo. She nodded obediently, a little turned on by this primitive show of possessiveness. He leant down and kissed her hard; she responded with a raw need to have some possession of her own. His hands went up into her hair and he held her head tightly as he kissed her, his tongue pushing into her mouth with a hunger she matched just as strongly.

They fell into each other, his body pushing against her with a renewed thirst, as if they had not seen each other for a very long time. His hands moved down her neck and caressed her, before sliding down her body to grip on to her buttocks again. She squirmed against him, not caring if the whole tent was watching. The need to have him, to feel him inside her was so great she could feel her body start to tremble and her energy ignited into a wild heated frenzy.

After what felt like aeons of time he pulled away from her, his breathing heavy and laboured. She was just as frantic, but caught her breath before smiling up at him. He laughed then, his body still pressed firmly against her. She started to giggle, looking over his shoulder with some trepidation that the whole tent would be standing their gawping at them. Of course they were not. In fact everyone was still dancing and doing their thing, seemingly oblivious to the show. She sighed heavily, still smiling. "You really know how to say 'hello' to a girl, don't you?"

He kissed her lightly on the lips and ran his finger down her arm, sending shivers into her groin. "This place makes me do strange things. I need to fuck you, Sapphire. It's been too long." She blinked at him, her bottom lip starting to tremble slightly. Oh, God. This guy was too much. "And where do you suggest we do such a thing, with all these people around us?" He smiled at her, a lazy tilt to his lips. "I can do whatever I like whenever I like with you, my beautiful woman. You know that."

She glanced over his shoulder again. Charlie and the others were partying hard now. The VIP tent was rocking. A DJ in the far corner had started to crank the tunes up and the lights were now turned down low. In the corner up against the wall she and Fox were almost invisible to the crowd. She felt a dangerous thought flicker through her mind. What if they just did it now, right here up against the wall, cloaked in magic and darkness. How would that feel? He smiled at her, reading her thoughts. He nodded with a slight flick of his head and pushed her further back to one side of the tent.

They were hidden slightly by a large pillar, which held a vase full of fairy lights. It cast a soft glow across his face and she suddenly melted against him. He started to kiss her again gently now as he traced patterns across her breast with his fingertips, slipping his hand inside her camisole top so that he could pinch and tease her nipple. She moaned at the pressure he applied; it sent flickers of arousal down into her groin, her legs suddenly feeling quite unsteady. With his other hand he lifted her skirt and expertly pulled down her pants,

190

slowly, steadily, with a promise of what was to come. She felt him tug at his own trousers and release his beautiful, more-than-ready cock.

Her hands were wrapped around his neck and she let him do all the work. He was still kissing her and stroking her; his fingers had found her point of pleasure and he was stroking her clit with just enough pressure to make her head spin. One minute he was using his fingers to get her off, the next she felt him lift her up and pull her down on top of him. She felt him slide with exquisite sensual control up inside her. Inch by inch he claimed her until she was full of him. Her head was thrown back now; he held her against him and started to push with a slow, almost painfully silky rhythm into her pussy. She was lost, totally and utterly gone. He fucked her in time to the music, his body hot and pulsing against her. His head was low against her neck; he bit her gently and sucked on the tender skin.

She expected him any minute to draw blood. Perhaps he was a vampire, after all. She felt her body start to shake with anticipation as her climax started to creep up slowly, building with intensity as he pumped in and out. He whispered in her ear, "You are mine, only mine." It turned her on even more, tipped her over the edge and she climaxed hard, her legs gripping him tightly as she convulsed around him. He growled deeply and thrust one more time hard inside her and found his own release, with his hands gripping her so tightly she thought he would break her in half. He kissed her tenderly, lifting her back up and off so that she could put her feet back on to the ground.

As he slowly released her she looked up into his eyes and saw such intense emotion flashing across them that it made her stomach flip in wonder. He smiled at her and bent down to help pull up her pants and straighten her skirt. He was already safely tucked back into his leather trousers. Magic. Sapphire wanted to fall down on the floor and rest her legs, which were like two spaghetti strings. He took her hand and led her over to one of the couches, motioning for her to sit. She did.

All around her the party continued. She spotted Charlie across the room. She was dancing and laughing. The rest of the group were either at the bar or dancing; no one had even seen her slip away. Fox stood and held her hands for a moment before he turned and walked casually across the room, through the crowd and to the bar. She watched him, a little stunned, still full of oxytocin, as he spoke to the bartender. No one else seemed to notice him – which she noted, with some amusement, would be impossible, as he was so damn sexy – if he were not cloaking himself. He walked back to her with two glasses of champagne in his hands. She laughed as he handed one to her and sat down beside her, draping one hand across the back of the couch behind her. "Are you having a good time now, my lady?"

Sapphire took a sip of the champagne and raised her eyebrow. "Are you kidding me?" He laughed and ran his fingertips across her shoulders in a slow light tease, sipping the champagne as if he had not just fucked her up against the wall with a room full of people. She snuggled down into his side and swung herself around so that she could drape her legs over his long, lean limbs. He watched her intensely, the smile never leaving his lips. "I am glad you are happy, Sapphire, and I am glad you did not choose to fly away too far tonight. I have enjoyed being with you here in this strange place."

She sipped the champagne and thought how wonderful it was to just sit with him in the VIP tent after committing such debauchery. "There you are, Saf. You disappeared again. Where did the blonde guy go?" Sapphire turned her head a little too quickly and sloshed some of the champagne down her skirt. Charlie was standing in front of them, her hands on her hips, her face flushed, her eyes wide, her pupils big and black. "He went away," she stuttered.

Fox shifted his weight slightly against her; she could hear him chuckle softly. "Oh, really? Well that's a shame. Anyway, where is the handsome Fox tonight? Did you text him earlier? He can't have just disappeared again. Get him to meet us at the entrance; I'm sure Simon can get him in." Sapphire watched her friend, totally bemused. She obviously had no idea Fox was sitting right in front of her. Cloaking magic. Fab. "I, erm … I will try to find him." Charlie nodded and started a little dance again; she was finding it hard to stand still. "OK. Let me know if you get hold of him. Come and dance when you are done drinking that."

She headed back off to the bar. Sapphire turned to face Fox; he was smiling that sly smile at her. "She can't see you, can she?" He shook his head. "Not unless you want her to, no." Sapphire took another sip of her drink, finishing it off. Placing the glass on the floor she pushed herself back off him and stood up. He watched her with dark, predatory eyes. "No, I don't want to share you with anyone. I want to dance; come on." He laughed and put his drink down. Holding her hands they walked back out into the crowd, just slightly away from her group so that they could dance. He held her close and moved with her to the beat; they were intertwined in time with the music, swaying and touching. Sapphire felt wide awake, flying high in a completely different way from the night before; she was high on him, high on the magic surrounding him.

As the night disappeared around them Sapphire felt herself melt further and further into the man before her. He never left her side and they danced for hours, the sexual tension between them crackling like electricity as they kissed and moved on the dance floor, people all around them moving with the music soaking up the vibe. Eventually she saw Charlie searching for her again in the crowd. "I will have to go back to them soon, Fox. They will be getting worried." He nodded and kissed her lightly on the forehead. "I will meet you back at your tent. Don't be long." She squeezed his hands and smiled at him. He stepped back and closed his eyes. For a moment she saw his image flicker in a glow of silver light, then he was gone. Again.

Chapter Twenty-Four

Sapphire was shocked to find that the time was now 4 a.m. They had been dancing and partying for a long time. Charlie, Nathan and the rest of the group were as high as kites, and although ready to head back to the campsite were by no means ready for bed. Sapphire wandered back with them, wondering how she could get away with a quiet exit to her bed, with Fox waiting for her. Charlie was hugging her and kissing Nathan alternately, between playfully giving Sapphire a hard time about her disappearing act again in the VIP tent.

When they reached the campsite everyone settled on the cushions under the canopy, with candles lit and music low so they could have a smoke and chat before the dawn would come again. "I'm going to bed, Charlie. I'm totally done for the night, hon." Charlie was rolling again, her favourite pastime for the weekend. She looked up and smiled at her with a slightly wobbly expression. "OK, Saf. Sure you don't want to have a nightcap with us?" Sapphire shook her head. "No, honestly. I'm fine. I'll see you in the morning." Charlie laughed. "It is the morning."

Sapphire said goodnight to everyone and unzipped her tent. Climbing inside, she reached out to find Fox. She was disappointed to find it empty. She grabbed her backpack and fumbled for a torch so that she could go and take a leak, brush her teeth. She changed her clothes again into something a little more appropriate for sleep, joggers and a loose t-shirt. Her hair was still up in braids and she did not have the energy or inclination to start undoing pins. She left the tent and headed over to the fence to find a spot to clean up. The campsite was still fairly active and she could hear people talking and laughing; Saturday night seemed to be an all-nighter for a lot of people.

As she stepped carefully back over the guy ropes she realised that her little dome tent was now softly lit inside by a warm glow. She did not remember leaving a torch on. As she climbed back inside she was greeted by the smell of patchouli and sandalwood and a long, lean pair of leather-clad legs stretched out in front of her. Fox was lying on his back, his hands behind his head. His chest was bare; the smile on his lips was playful and promising. She could not help but smile back, thankful for his return. After zipping the tent back up she climbed on all fours – her legs either side of him – up his body. He watched her, his eyes glowing in the soft orange light he had magically conjured for them. She wondered if their shadow would be cast on the tent walls.

She hovered above him for a moment, watching his expression, "I'm glad you came back." He shifted his weight and released his hands from behind his head, placing them on her hips and pulling her against him. "I never left." She bent down and kissed him softly on the lips. She was starting to feel tired but her body responded to his with an urgent need to get closer again. Without breaking the kiss he started to slide her joggers back down her legs. She scrambled a little to help him, giggling slightly at the difficult position they were in. She lifted up a notch so that he could lift her t-shirt over her head.

Her obsidian necklace swung forward as he pulled it up. He raised an eyebrow and she took it off over her head and placed it on her clothes to one side. She was naked now except for her pants. She felt wonderfully feminine and powerful, with her breasts free and voluptuous so close to his face. He licked his lips slowly and raised his hands to cup them softly. Sapphire closed her eyes as he squeezed them gently and rolled her nipples between his fingertips. He knew which buttons to press.

Without warning he pulled her over and laid her flat on her stomach. She let out a little yelp in surprise; he chuckled softly. "Sshh, my woman. You don't want to draw any attention to us." Her head to one side, her skin was now tingling in anticipation as he rose above her. She could hear him start to remove his trousers. She felt his skin brush against her, the hairs on his legs tickling her slightly, making goosebumps travel up her body. He bent over her and kissed her neck. Travelling down her back, his hair trailing across her skin, a soft moan escaped her lips; he stroked her expertly and started to gently pull her pants down so that her buttocks were now completely exposed.

She gasped as he kissed the top of her hip and ran his hand over her pert bottom cheeks. Her pussy was responding with a warm, pulsing sensation, making her raise her hips up slightly to meet him. He was whispering to her again in his language, his voice deep and sultry. She was so turned on she could not wait much longer for him to take her. "Patience, Sapphire. Patience." She moaned again in frustration as he continued to kiss her across her back, her buttocks, stroking and caressing her, brushing her pussy just slightly, making her quiver. She tried to move so that she could hold him but he held her down with a gentle push and she gave in to him.

Without another word he placed his hands either side of her hips and lifted her up slightly, so that she was almost on all fours again – her head still down on the mattress but her buttocks up in the air so that he could position her where he wanted. And where he wanted was inside her. As he pushed his wonderful cock inside, slowly, inch by inch, she found it hard not to cry out. The pleasure was almost painful. He held her waist and worked her, sliding in and out with a slow steady rhythm. She could hear his breathing become faster and her heartbeat thumped in her head as he continued to make sweet love to her.

She had no idea if anyone outside the tent could see or hear them but at that moment in time, as Fox pleasured her for the second time that night, she did not give a flying fuck. This man was beyond pleasure; she was lost in the moment, her body floating on the edge of orgasm as he fucked her softly, then harder, slightly faster. She knew that at any moment she would have to let go. She gripped the mattress and tried not to cry out too loudly. As a wave of extreme, wonderful climax swept up from her groin to the tip of her head she felt Fox push himself completely and deeply inside her and her whole body shook with release. She tried so hard not to cry out that she felt tears of joy spill from her eyes, and Fox came with a hard grunt into her as she wept softly with happiness.

He held her for a moment before pulling out very slowly and dropping her hips back to the ground again. He lay down beside her and flung his arm over her waist; his breathing was still heavy and he was hot and sweaty. His eyes were dark and the flashes of gold and amber gave him a primitive animal look. He lifted his head suddenly, realising she was crying, and leant forward to kiss away her tears. She rolled on to her side and he took her into his arms, cradling her head now into his chest. He held her there for some time, holding her so tightly, kissing her hair, his legs wrapped around her. "You are the most amazing woman I have ever met, Sapphire," he whispered quietly.

She noticed that the light he had conjured earlier was no longer glowing in the tent and the grey beginning of dawn was softly illuminating them now. The voices outside had grown quiet and Sapphire realised everyone had gone to bed. She lifted her head to gaze up into his beautiful eyes. The tears had stopped now but her heart felt like it would burst any moment. "Stay with me a while?" He nodded. "Always."

They fell asleep, wrapped around each other under the sleeping bag, as the new day dawned. Sapphire drifted into the most comfortable and soothing sleep she could remember, with the man that she knew she was falling head over heels for holding her closely.

Chapter Twenty-Five

Sunday

Sapphire woke suddenly, her body pinned to the mattress by Fox's arm, which was lying heavily across her hip. She had her back to him and his body spooned her perfectly, naked and warm. He was still sleeping and she realised with some confusion that he had stayed with her the whole time she had slept. He had not left her, returning to his world as he had done previously, and she wondered if this was a good thing. She shifted slowly to lift herself up. He stirred and moaned a little as she moved. Facing him now, she looked down at him in wonder. His face was relaxed, his eyes still closed. He was the most gorgeous thing she had ever seen; his hair fell across his face, giving him a ruffled, slightly wild look.

She traced a finger across his cheek. He opened his eyes slowly and blinked, a smile creeping slowly across his lips. He stretched and lifted his hand to brush her cheek. "Good morning, beautiful." Sapphire returned the smile and leant in for a kiss. He responded with a deep probing of his tongue. Her body instantly turned on, she pulled away softly. "Should you be here?" He frowned a little, suddenly aware of their location. "Probably not. I am breaking all the rules with you, Sapphire."

She sat up and looked around for her clothes. The inside of the tent looked a mess; clothes and bedding tumbled all over the place. "I had better get dressed and see if anyone is around." He nodded and, it seemed, with some reluctance, grabbed his trousers and pulled them back on. He did not seem to have a shirt but at that moment she was still enjoying the view. "I have lingered longer than I should, but it is getting harder to leave you, my lady, such is your magic to me."

Sapphire smiled as she dressed, pulling on shorts and another camisole top. "Do you want to borrow a t-shirt?" He laughed. "No, I don't think you would have anything that would fit me. I must go now, Sapphire. I believe our time together for the moment is up." He pulled her towards him and kissed her hard again. "Enjoy your day. I will be back when you need me." With a deep sense of loss, Sapphire sat back and nodded. He winked at her once and then vanished before her eyes, leaving a very empty space behind him.

Staring at the empty spot that Fox had just been in, Sapphire shook herself back into reality. She felt an urgent need to pee again and her stomach rumbled loudly. She unzipped the tent to find outside completely quiet and empty of friends. All the other tents were still closed and she assumed her friends were still sleeping. She rummaged in her bag for the mobile phone and checked the time. It was 10 a.m.

She decided to head off to the food vendors and grab herself some breakfast and maybe a shower; after the night's hot and sweaty activity she could really do with one. She took some toiletries and fresh clothes along with her money, and headed out to find the showers and food. Texting Charlie as she walked to let her know where she was she noted that the day was slightly more overcast and, although still warm, the air held a promise of a possible storm. People were up and about wandering the campsite and starting the final day of the festival. Her body felt a little heavy today and she noticed with a shy smile that she felt somewhat bruised underneath. Twice in one night with such a hot guy was obviously taking its toll.

She found the showers and was grateful that the queue was not too long. She stood waiting patiently, going over the last few days in her head. It had been an amazing experience: the festival, dancing, Fox … everything was just like a dream. She realised with a little alarm that her guardian had been spending more and more time with her in this world. The crossing over had become more frequent. Would there be consequence for this? Would Fox be in more trouble because of her? She felt her chest tighten at the thought of him; he was constantly on her mind now. She wanted to be with him now. Her need for him was out of control.

She was suddenly at the front of the queue and glad to step into the little shower cubicle. She undressed quickly and turned on the shower; the water was just as hot and wonderful as before. She washed away the scents and secrets from the night before. It felt so good to clean her body and hair again, but she was sad to remove Fox's magic from her.

She dried herself and dressed again just as quickly, knowing there would be other people wanting to jump into the cubicle. As she left the showers and headed to the food vans she realised that it would not be too long before the festival would be over and she would have to return to normal life. The thought was a little depressing. She had enjoyed the freedom of this wonderland, but decided there and then to make the most of the last day and night. Finding the breakfast bar she ordered a sausage baguette and a coffee, to satisfy her rumbling stomach. She sat on the grass watching the crowds and munched happily, totally unaware that her last day would be the most eventful of them all.

Chapter Twenty-Six

Fox was kneeling down on one knee, his head bowed in submission in front of his father, Conloach, the great magician. "I am beyond punishing you now, my son. You have been pushing the boundaries of guardian with this traveller far too much for me to even comprehend what is going on in your head." On his return to Shaka that morning after leaving Sapphire in her tent he had been summoned somewhat abruptly to his father's castle. He knew he was in deep trouble again. His father paced in front of him, the agitation in his body coming off in waves of dark red sparks.

"I am in love with her, Father. I cannot help myself. She has bewitched me." Conloach stopped his pacing and looked down on his son. Placing his hand on his head for a moment he took a deep breath. "Rise, Fox. You need not cower before me. What is done is done." Fox lifted his head and saw that his father was no longer scowling at him; a slight smile was now on his lips. He stood up slowly, uncurling his long, lean body to its full height. "Your love for her will be a challenge when it comes to making the right decisions, but I understand this passion and longing. It was the same between your mother and me."

Fox let out a sigh of relief. He had had no idea what his father had planned for him when he had been ordered to attend his chamber. "But you must be careful when travelling to her world so often. It is affecting your magic and very soon people will begin to notice and question the changes you are making to her." Fox nodded. "I am aware of the risks, Father. I have been as careful as I can. No one but her friend has seen me." Conloach laughed. "You have been running around fornicating with her at every opportunity, my son. You must have more self-control. You are her guardian, and she needs to be as focused as she can with the new magic that is growing inside her." Fox shook his head slowly. "How, Father, do I refrain from consuming such a wonderful thing when she draws me so?"

The magician placed his hands inside the sleeves of his robe and closed his eyes, breathing heavily for a moment. "That, my son, will be your challenge. But for now you must gather your senses, recharge your energy. You are saturated in that place. The energy there is strange and draining. You need all your strength to protect her. It is much easier here on your home planet, but on Earth you become weaker and Hecta is still lingering there, waiting for her to make a mistake." He paused, opening his eyes. "Go to the mountains and meditate for a while. Allow the energy that flows from deep within them to fill you once more with the power that by your birthright you can absorb. I sense a shift in the balance coming and you will need to be ready."

Fox ran a hand through his hair, a slight frown on his brow. "I sense it too, Father, which is why I have been staying with her longer each time. But you are right. I need to cleanse myself and regroup. I do indeed feel a little weak from visiting her last night." Conloach raised a brow, a slightly amused smile on his lips. "It is no wonder you are weak. Your activities with her have all but worn you as defenceless as a kitten."

Fox had the decency to lower his eyes for a moment. He was glad his father seemed to understand his obsession with Sapphire. His need and growing love for this woman were clouding his judgement constantly, but, as his father had said, what was done was done. There was no going back now.

"Do you still have the crystal I gave you?" Fox nodded and reached inside his pocket to touch the small egg-shaped crystal his father had given him previously. It was warm to touch and sent flickers of energy up his hand. "Yes, Father." Conloach nodded. "Go now, son, and take some time to reflect on the past few days of travels. I am here if you need me."

Fox stepped back and took a deep bow before leaving. He left the castle and went back quickly to his home to gather some provisions. He knew he had plenty of time to recharge in his own world before he would need to return and check on Sapphire again. As he grabbed some food and bathed and re-dressed his mind was fully occupied with her, memories of holding her, possessing her, watching her face light up with wonder as they danced and made love.

He knew that he had fallen completely and utterly for this woman. He had never known such intense feelings, and the sensations of jealousy and protectiveness he had experienced last night when the human had approached her had been unknown to him before then. He must stay focused. Without focus he could put her in harm's way. He headed out to take the journey to the mountains to the west of his home; he had travelled to them many times and it took just moments for him to visualise and transport himself to one of the highest peaks.

He stood above the cloud line and looked out on the magnificent vista before him. The air was clean and fresh here and the energy was high and powerful. He took a deep cleansing breath of air into his lungs and then settled himself in the lotus position to meditate and clear his mind. The sun was shining down on him and as he started to ground and pull the energy from the great mountain up through his body a shiver of anticipation ran up his spine. As Fox channelled the energy from his homeland his body grew stronger. He could sense the awesome flow of energy from the root of the mountain travel up through his body as he focused his mind and cleared his body from the negative draining aura of Earth.

Shaka was a light and powerful place. Magic was strong here and all around him. He was unaccustomed to the draining saturation of human energy and had not realised how much it had affected him while he had been on Earth. As he breathed in the powerful refreshing energy of the mountain he began to feel more like himself. His muscles began to grow stronger and his head began to clear. Each chakra in his body began to hum and vibrate at the perfect pitch and he linked into his higher self to listen to any words of wisdom it may have for him. In his mind he could see a clear vision of himself and Sapphire standing together, strong and connected. The link between them was forged so greatly now that their destinies were intertwined and ran the same path. She was his now and there was no going back.

As he focused on the higher vibration that buzzed in his third eye and crown he saw a vision of Sapphire standing alone in the dark. She was frightened and fighting someone or something with a flash of power that ripped from her fingertips in silver sparks. He frowned and concentrated harder on the vision to make the picture clearer. As he pushed to see further into the scene it wavered in his mind and was then gone.

He opened his eyes and gasped. If this was a true vision, something terrible was about to happen. He stood and looked out over the mountain to the range below him. All was calm in his world. Fox felt recharged and strong; he knew he would need to return to Earth quickly, but not without a weapon. He closed his eyes and willed himself to his home. Standing suddenly inside his armoury he scoured the walls to find the most suitable piece to take with him to her world. He did not even know if it would be possible to transport such a thing with him.

His eyes wandered across the walls at the swords and bows, axes and chains. His gaze fixed on the perfect item. He lifted it off the wall and prepared to transport himself again. He focused on Sapphire, seeing her in his mind asking for her permission to join her. His magic pulsed around him as he pushed the boundaries of time and space to reach her.

A dark invisible field pushed against him and prevented him from shifting. He tried again and felt sweat begin to form on his brow at the exertion. Nothing happened. The dark veil wavered in his mind for a moment as he probed heavily to push through. Nothing. Frustrated, he opened his eyes and paced the armoury for a moment, trying to think clearly. What was happening? Why could he not reach her? He was feeling a slight panic in the centre of his chest. It started to swell and overwhelm him. Focusing once more, he pushed harder against the wall. In his mind a face appeared in clear focus, a dark smile on its lips. Hecta. Fox dropped to his knees, the force of the barrier pushing him down and preventing him from shifting to her world. He could not get through. She was alone in her world, and the thought of her, defenceless and scared without him, made his heart break in two.

Chapter Twenty-Seven

Sapphire walked back to the campsite, a smile on her lips. She was watching the crowds and enjoying some time alone. The music had started up again in some of the smaller tents and she could sense the energy lifting again around her. She hoped that Charlie and the rest of the crew were up and about now; she wanted to make the most of the time they had left. As she wandered back into the campsite she was pleased to see everyone was up and moving around, making tea, laughing and joking. Charlie was bouncing around as usual, dressed in tight hipster jeans with a bright red top. She stood out in the crowd.

As Sapphire entered the campsite Charlie flung herself at her and hugged her tightly. "There you are, Saf. I was wondering when you would get back. How are you feeling today?" Sapphire laughed at her enthusiasm. She had no idea where the girl managed to get all her energy from. "I'm really good. I've had a shower and eaten so I am up for the last day with a capital H for Hello." Charlie whooped with glee. "Me, too, hon. Let's make it a day to remember. We are heading back to the dance tent for the afternoon before watching the grand finale fireworks tonight at the main stage." Sapphire nodded. "Sounds good to me."

After some last minute faffing everyone headed back out to the main festival site. Sapphire was dressed in a borrowed miniskirt from Charlie and her baby pink bustier ... hair loose today around her shoulders, with flowers pinned around at various points to make her look a little more funky (Charlie's words). She had decided to ditch the flip-flops today and had worn some sheepskin boots instead, much to Charlie's disgust, but her feet were starting to get a little sore from all the dancing and she wanted to walk and dance in some comfort on her last day. Besides, the outfit did look kinda cool in a retro-chick way.

Nathan was giving Charlie a piggyback and the rest of the crowd were in high spirits. Despite the fact that they had all been drinking, smoking, and flying for the last few days no one seemed to be experiencing any sort of comedown as yet. Sapphire knew that would most likely come very soon, when they returned home. The main site was fully charged now, everyone dancing and having a crazy time. The urgency to make the most of it seemed to be spreading across the whole of the site. They went straight to the beer tent, did a few shots and headed over to the dance tent. The music was pumping and it was only 12 noon. Sapphire was up for it, big time. This was their last day, after all.

The dance tent was packed and people were really getting into the hard beats the DJ was spinning. Sapphire was feeling alive and full of energy; she flowed with the music and picked up on the heightened happy energy bouncing around the tent. As she moved in time with the crowd she noticed that her new second sight seemed to be in full force today. She could see waves of energy coming off the people around her. Some were cloudy and dark; others were bright and sparkling. She noted that Charlie's energy seemed to be a bright green today, speckled with spots of silver.

Sapphire wondered what she looked like herself. Lifting her hands in front of her face she concentrated on the edges of her fingers and was pleased to see a light violet colour coming off her fingertips. Sparks of white light shone through the hazy violet, making her look like a glowing disco ball. Closing her eyes again she pushed her energy outwards. Working through the crowd, she could feel the buzzing happy vibe surrounding her. The thump of the bass vibrated through her chest and lifted off out of the top of her head. The smile on her lips grew wider. This was totally cool.

Charlie and Nathan were bouncing around like two bunnies, their eyes wide and full of laughter. The rest of the group seemed to be on an equally high vibe, dancing and flowing with the tunes. They danced for some time. The tent was literally jumping with energy. After what seemed like hours Charlie approached her and placed her hands on Sapphire's hips, leaning in to speak to her against the noise. "Fancy a drink and a rest for a mo?"

Sapphire nodded and followed her friend outside. The day had moved on quickly and the overcast sky was now becoming even darker, due to the heavy cloud. The air was thick with the scent of rain, an oppressive weight coming down on them. They wandered over to one of the food vendors to grab some water and find a spot to sit on the grass. Charlie looked up at the sky as she caught her breath and took gulps of the water. "Looks like rain's on its way. Hope it stays off for a while for the fireworks later."

Sapphire nodded. They had managed to get away with perfect weather all weekend, and she had turned a lovely shade of brown in the last couple of days from all the sun exposure. Charlie was also a wonderful healthy colour, her nose a little pink. "It's been a great weekend, Charlie. Thanks for pulling me along. I haven't had so much fun for ages." Charlie grinned at her. "Yeah, it's been awesome. Shame Fox didn't come back. Did you manage to get hold of him again?" Sapphire shook her head, her eyes downturned for a second. "No, he must have gone home." Charlie shrugged. "His loss."

They sat for a while, Charlie smoking a roll-up while they people-watched. Sapphire watched two guys walk past them with appreciative eyes. They winked at them and Charlie giggled. "God, there are horny men everywhere here. Just as well I am loved up with Nathan or I would be in serious trouble." Sapphire laughed. "You are always in serious trouble, Charlie, but that's what I love about you." Charlie eyed her with amusement. "You haven't done too badly this weekend. The blonde guy, Fox ... you never know ... tonight you might get lucky again."

Sapphire leant back on her forearms, smiling. "No way. I'm happy in my own space, Charlie. Kinda like partying with you guys but I'm not up for any more romance." Charlie nudged her. "I'm not talking about romance, Saf." They both laughed. Drinks finished and legs ready for another bout of dancing, they headed back to find the others. Sapphire gazed up at the gathering clouds and the darkening sky and wondered how long the rain would actually hold off.

They found the rest of the group, who were ready to head over to the main stage and grab something to eat before the evening started. After munching rice and noodles from a Chinese food stall, they were all ready for the finale. Simon was keen to get to the main stage. His friend was mixing a set before the main band and he wanted to catch him. The evening drew in quickly and it was dark by the time they reached the main stage for the final show. Around the edge of the crowd small fires were lit tonight, giving the whole thing a tribal feel; the last gathering of the masses.

Sapphire was starting to feel a little cold and wished she had changed before they had headed back out. "Charlie, I might go back to the tent to change, hon. I'm feeling a little cold." Charlie frowned at her for a moment. "Really? OK, but don't be too long. We will stay right here in this spot. Will you find us?" Sapphire nodded. With this new sight she had no doubt she could trace her friend in the pitch black if needed.

She wandered back out of the crowd and headed to the tent. Her thoughts returned to Fox. She knew he would be back; she shivered in anticipation of seeing him again. In her mind she could see him facing her, reaching out to embrace her. For a moment she felt a strange, cold sensation in the centre of her chest. It pushed into her solar plexus and made her stop still for a second. Her body trembled slightly and she suddenly felt very uneasy. Looking around, she reached for her necklace to see if any warning signals were being given off. Nothing. Shaking her head and pushing the feeling aside she headed back to the tent.

The campsite was relatively quiet. She could hear the main stage music start to kick off and a loud cheer rose into the air as the crowd greeted the beginning of the night. A few stragglers were wandering around but most people were in the main site now. Sapphire found their little camp and unzipped her tent. Fumbling for her torch, she rummaged through her backpack for warmer clothes. Undressing quickly she lay on her back and pulled up her jeans, shuffling into them with a little difficulty. She grabbed a shoestring top (unsure exactly of the colour in the torchlight) and a hoody. She felt instantly warmer.

Checking her mobile again for any messages (there were none) she made sure she had some money and lip balm before heading back outside the tent. As she bent down to rezip, the obsidian necklace began to throb steadily against her chest, a warm quickening that she instantly recognised. She stood up double quick and swung the torch around behind her.

A dark shadow crossed quickly in front of the beam and disappeared again. "Who's there?" She spoke firmly, a slight tremble to her voice. As she stood quite still, her heart beginning to thump a little loudly in her chest, the shadow stepped into the light.

Hecta stood before her, a slight smile on his lips. He wore a long dark coat that swept to the floor. His hood was pushed back and she could see darkness swirling around him in thin tendrils. Within the darkness she could see red and orange flashes, as if he was very angry. "Sapphire. How nice to meet you again." She stepped back slightly, her legs pressing against the tent. "I think you owe me an apology, traveller. Last time we met you were rather rude."

Sapphire could feel her breath coming fast. Her adrenalin was starting to pump strongly through her veins and she could sense ... smell ... the fear starting to rise within her. "What do you want, Hecta?" He chuckled, a deep almost sarcastic tone to his voice. "I want you to stop playing games and go away." Sapphire felt her hands curl into fists at her side; he was really starting to piss her off now.

"I'm not playing any games or bothering anyone. You provoked me last time. Leave me alone." Before she could even think he lunged forward and grabbed her around her throat, squeezing just tightly enough to make her gasp and stumble backwards into the tent. He held her steady, his face inches from hers. "Don't make me angry, Sapphire. You really wouldn't like to see me angry." Sapphire felt her energy shift. Her muscles were trembling slightly as it gathered around her. How dare he touch her?

She flexed her body slightly and pushed her energy outwards, making Hecta loosen his grip on her throat. He gasped and stepped backwards, his eyes wide now. "Don't touch me." She took the opportunity to make a run for it and took off, away from the tent. She had dropped the torch when Hecta had grabbed her but she could see quite clearly in the dark. She leaped through the maze of tents, over guy ropes, and dodged a few startled people. She could hear Hecta behind her, shouting into the dark. "You can run Sapphire, but you cannot hide."

She kept running, her heart thudding loudly in her chest, her bag bouncing against her side, as she headed towards the main stage. She only stopped for a breath to look over her shoulder once before pushing her way back into the thick crowd of people to find Charlie and the others. She was gasping for air by the time she spotted them. They were facing the main stage, dancing and totally oblivious to her presence, until she almost crashed into Charlie. "Fuck, Saf. Are you OK?" Charlie held her at arm's length, looking into her eyes with a look of shock. Sapphire slowed her breathing and nodded slowly. "I'm OK. I just got lost for a moment and panicked."

Charlie pulled her into her for a hug. "It's OK, hon. You found us. Slow down. Your heart is bouncing all over the place." Sapphire smiled at her weakly, taking one last look over her shoulder. Hecta was nowhere to be seen. The people standing next to her eyed her suspiciously. She must have looked like a nut job.

Sapphire reached out in her mind for Fox. Where the fuck was he when she needed him? She felt no response to her probing. He must be coming soon. It was unlike him to not respond to her call, especially now. Gradually her fear started to subside and she stayed close to Charlie, who put her arm around her. She took a deep breath and concentrated on the music and allowed her body to relax. What could Hecta do now? She was surrounded by people. He could hardly start making a scene with all these people around her.

After some time she started to push the thoughts of Hecta from her mind. The obsidian had returned to its normal warmth and she wanted to focus on enjoying herself. The main stage was set up for the final band of the night and the crowd was growing rowdy. People were cheering and catcalling for the band to start; the build-up was electric in the air around her. Lights began to pulse and a steady beat of drum started. Sapphire saw a beam of light on the drummer start to flicker on and off and the other band members moving on to the stage.

As she watched, mesmerised by the show, she felt a shift of energy above her. The sky started to rumble with the low groan of thunder, flickers of lightning began to flash across the dark sky and she looked up in wonder as the storm above her began to grow and expand. In time with the music a blast of fireworks shot sparks of red and gold upwards into the night sky. The crowd were ecstatic now. Everyone was jumping. Waves of people bouncing to the beat moved and rippled before her. The loud bangs of the fireworks and intermittent thunder heightened the atmosphere; Sapphire could feel the energy around her lifting higher and higher. Charlie and the others were lost in the building tension.

Sapphire looked around her, ever hopeful that Fox would suddenly appear. Without warning she felt hands grab her from behind her and spin her around. "Found you," Hecta growled at her, his eyes now flashing a nasty shade of red. She pushed back against him, but he was gripping her arms now with a painful intensity. Charlie, suddenly aware of Sapphire struggling next to her with a stranger, stepped to her side and grabbed his arm. "Hey. Fuck off. She's not interested, buster."

Hecta stared at Charlie, his grip still tight on Sapphire's arms. A smile curled sadistically on to his lips. He released Sapphire and out of nowhere produced a knife which he swiftly pushed up under Charlie's chin, against her neck. Her eyes grew wide with terror and she let out a squeal so loud that the people around them suddenly stopped dancing and stared at the commotion. Sapphire could not believe this was happening. The band continued to play loudly, accompanied by the bursts of fireworks which lit up the sky. Thunder started to rumble above their heads and Sapphire felt as if she were dreaming, a horrible dream that was quickly turning into a nightmare.

Hecta was holding Charlie against his body now, the knife glinting silver in the flashes of lights against her neck. He was smiling directly at Sapphire as she stood transfixed, unable to move.

Now he had really pissed her off. Nathan, suddenly aware that his girl was being held against her will by some madman with a knife to her throat, lunged at him. Sapphire gasped as she watched him bounce off an invisible shield that seemed to have gathered around Hecta and the now-crying Charlie.

The people around them were backing off. Panic was gathering in the air and Sapphire could hear a few of the women starting to scream. Sapphire felt her anger rise within her stomach. This was not going to happen. He was not going to hurt her friend. She felt a darkness begin to swell in the pit of her stomach. Anger, thick and heavy, pushed up into her chest. She closed her eyes for a moment and gathered her energy inside her. The thunder grew louder and the sky began to light up brightly with shards of lightning. The electricity building around her began to flash and crackle.

Her body was vibrating now, humming with power. She opened her eyes and lifted her hands above her head, calling the lightning to her, willing it to bend to her will. She watched everything turn into slow motion around her. A crack of lightning came down from the sky and shot through her body, making her light up like a Catherine wheel.

Hecta stood perfectly still. The smug expression on his face was fading slightly now. Sapphire absorbed the lightning bolt and then flung her arms forwards, aiming it directly at him, focused purely on one intent only: to remove him from this world, to blast him into tiny pieces and away from her friend.

Charlie was watching the whole thing with an expression of utter disbelief. The lightning shook through the shield Hecta had placed around them. She watched it ripple slightly and give way. It hit him directly in the face and he dropped the knife, Charlie crumpling to the floor as he stumbled back at the force of the blow.

Sapphire moved forward now, her anger crashing in waves around her as she pulled energy from around her, ready for another attack. Arms suddenly gripped her tightly, holding her back, keeping her own arms pinned to her side. She felt a warm breath sweep over her cheek, soft hair brush her face.

"Stop, Sapphire. Stop now." Fox. He held her closely to his chest. Her breathing was rapid and she was suddenly aware again of the utter chaos around her. He released his grip for a second and stepped gracefully around her so that he now shielded her from Hecta, who was starting to take a run at them.

All around them people were shouting and pushing away from the fight. Terror ran thickly through the air. The storm above them now grew into a crescendo and rain started to fall heavily from the dark clouds. The band played on, strobe lights and fireworks still flashing across the crowd. Sapphire was trembling. With a sudden wave of exhaustion she suddenly felt light-headed and ready to buckle. She watched with horror as Hecta leapt at Fox. They connected with a loud crash and began to fight with an intensity that made her flinch. This was really happening in her world in front of a whole crowd of people and all her friends.

She blinked and looked down on to the floor. Nathan was holding a heavily-weeping Charlie. She knew the whole situation had now become completely out of control. She looked around and saw the crowd starting to part as Security pushed its way towards them. Sapphire wanted to cry. Her stomach was churning and her legs felt weak.

In her mind she saw a flash of the beautiful woman who had appeared to her during her massage. She was smiling at her. "You can make this stop, Sapphire. Will it so."

Sapphire took a deep breath. Fox was holding Hecta to the floor. He had his own knife in his hand and was wrestling with him to keep him pinned down. She stepped towards them and took a deep cleansing breath to steady her nerves. Moving closer, she placed her hand on Fox's back and pushed her energy outwards, visualising them away from this place, away from the chaos. Anywhere but here.

She visualised Hecta being thrown away from this world, to be imprisoned somewhere, far, far away. She felt the air around her ripple and bend. The rain fell heavily on her back and dripped down her face. There was a loud crack of lightning above them and with a twist of pain in her head she felt them flicker and shift.

Everything went still and quiet. The festival disappeared from around them and she was suddenly lying flat on her back in sweet-smelling grass. The sky was still dark above her but the rain had stopped. Everything was quiet and she could smell the remnants of a fire in her nostrils. Her body was smouldering as if she had indeed been on fire and the fire was now extinguished. Her head was spinning and she felt like she were about to throw up at any second. She tried to move but her body was limp and sore.

As she struggled to make sense of where she was a hand gripped her own and she heard someone calling her name. She took one last gasp of air before her mind went black and she lost consciousness.

Chapter Twenty-Eight

Fox paced his bedroom floor up and down, wringing his hands, combing his hair back away from his face. His father was seated on his bed next to the motionless body of Sapphire. "Be still, my son. She is fine. Her body is recovering from using so much magic. No harm has come to her." Fox continued to pace, a deep frown etched on his forehead. "She should be awake by now, Father. It has been hours."

Conloach looked across the room at Fox. Watching him fret so over this woman made him worry. He had never seen his son this way before. He was truly lost to her. "She transported you back to Shaka from her own world without even being in a dream state and blasted Hecta with a bolt of lightning. I think she is doing rather well, considering." Fox stopped his pacing and walked across to the bed; he sat down on the other side of Sapphire and brushed a hand across her cheek, willing her to wake up. "You are right, as always, Father, but I will be happier when she comes back to me." Conloach took Sapphire's hand and closed his eyes.

A ripple of magic washed from him down into her body and she trembled and groaned slightly. Fox watched with wide eyes. "This woman has immense power, power that even I have never seen before in a dream traveller. She is going to be fine." He looked across at his son. "The balance has been shifted between our worlds. The fact that humans have witnessed such a scene will cause massive consequences. I cannot begin to imagine the confusion this will have caused. You have created quite a mess, my son."

Fox sighed deeply. "For that I am deeply sorry, Father. I could not stay away and let Hecta harm her." Conloach regarded him solemnly. "I believe she is quite capable of taking care of herself, Fox." Fox nodded and bent forward to kiss her softly on the lips. His father stood and watched the tenderness before him with a knowing in his heart. Fox was incapable of making rash decisions when it came to this woman. He stepped back from the bed and noted that she was beginning to awaken. Her energy was shifting before his eyes. He had healed her to the best of his ability. She had all but drained her life force using the magic within her to bring them back to Shaka. He had no idea where she had sent Hecta but he knew it would not be long before the gatekeeper would come for her again.

The fight was now on. "I will leave you now, my son. You will need to help her recover her state of mind. She will be confused and troubled. Call me if you need me." Fox looked up into his father's eyes, which were full of a deep sympathy he had never seen before. He watched his form shimmer for a moment before he disappeared. Sapphire murmured his name and twisted on to her side. He slipped on to the bed next to her and drew her into his arms as he felt her wake up. She took a deep, gasping breath and suddenly let out a loud sob. "Fox." He held her close and ran his hand across her cheek. "I am here, Sapphire. You are safe; be still."

Sapphire clung to him as the realisation swept over her that she was in his arms again. "Oh, Fox. I was so afraid, so angry. Has it all gone away? Is Charlie OK? Where are we?" Her words tumbled from her mouth between gasps and soft whimpers. "We are home, my home, in the land of Shaka. Your friend was fine when we left, after you removed Hecta from the picture and brought us here, my powerful, wonderful woman." The slight trembling in her body was subsiding now and she was growing calmer within his arms. She lifted her head and looked into his eyes.

Her expression was fraught with worry; he could feel his heart swell with thanks that she was with him again, safe and well. "How? How did I do that, in front of all those people? Oh, my God. What a mess." He smiled now she was almost back to her old self. He leant down and kissed her softly, a deep sweet kiss, to let her know that all would be well, he hoped. As he withdrew from her she looked at him with soft watery eyes and sighed deeply. "I've really fucked things up now, haven't I?"

He chuckled and kissed the top of her head "We will work it out somehow. I might have to bend time a little to stop your friends losing their sanity, but I'm sure we can fix this." Sapphire pushed herself up and took in her surroundings. She was on the four-poster bed she remembered in her dream … the night she had travelled to Fox and they had sat in his garden and then made love right here. She sensed a new energy inside her now. It trembled in her core and made her shiver with awareness that everything had changed. Nothing would ever be the same again. She had been living in a bubble thinking she could control this – the travelling, the growing power within her. But that had just been wishful thinking.

How could she hide this new world she had discovered any longer? Charlie had seen her take the lightning and blast Hecta with it. She had been witness to the whole crazy scene. Maybe she could put some of it down to three days of heavy drug-taking, but in her heart Sapphire knew her friend was not stupid and would question every moment. Would she be wondering where she was right now, or would time have stayed still and would Charlie still be weeping on the floor at the festival, unaware that Sapphire had shifted herself, Fox and the mad, crazy Hecta to another realm?

Her head was throbbing again with all these thoughts. "Sapphire, calm yourself. You are draining your energy again, thinking too hard. Rest for now. I sense your friend is well. We can deal with that when the time is right." Sapphire hoped he was right and willed it so. If everything that had happened to her lately was destined to be and was true, she knew that she had the power within her to do great things and to put this right.

She had not asked for this gift, not consciously anyway, and she had never done any harm to anyone before. Hecta had pushed her to the point of no return, goaded her into pulling her powers into force in front of all those people. She had to be more careful, not let him push her into making more mistakes. "Have I been sleeping again? I think I lost consciousness. Everything went black and I could feel you beside me and then another man; I've seen him before in my mind." Fox nodded, his amber eyes lighter now … less worry in the dark swirls. "My father. He helped you to heal."

Sapphire watched his face, his beautiful handsome features starting to warm her heart again. "Thank you. Thank you for coming for me. I know it was dangerous. How did you know? I had been calling to you but you did not come until the last moment." Fox looked down for a moment; she watched a flicker of pain cross his face. "Hecta had created a barrier preventing me from crossing over to you; it was not until you broke it with the lightning strike that I could break through and reach you. I failed you as your guardian and for that I am truly sorry." Sapphire frowned and lifted his chin with her hand, forcing him to look back at her. "You did not fail me. Don't ever think that. You saved me. You have saved me more than you will ever know."

He blinked, his expression filled with wonder and awe. "Sapphire, you have stolen my heart. You are my life now. I will never leave you alone again to fight without me by your side." Sapphire smiled, a swell of pure and unconditional love sweeping up through her body. She cocked her head to one side and bit her bottom lip before speaking. "Well, I'm kind of hoping we will be doing less fighting and more fucking in the future."

The seriousness of the conversation was suddenly broken, and he laughed loudly. Grabbing her either side of her face, he brought her lips to his own and kissed her with a ferociousness that took her breath away. They fell back on to the bed and began to kiss each other, their energy swirling around them in a mist of white and gold sparks. For that moment nothing else mattered and Sapphire wanted him to consume her again, to wash away the memory of the night. She wanted to return to her dreaming, feel lost within his lust, lose herself to him completely. As he removed her clothing and kissed her body she closed her eyes and let herself go. In fact as he took her into his arms and made love to her again she wanted nothing more than to stay right here with him, forever.

Chapter Twenty-Nine

Charlie was wrapped in a blanket, Nathan holding her closely, back at their camp. After the chaos of the fight, and Sapphire and the two men who were grappling on the floor disappearing before her very eyes, she had blanked out for a while. She had come to with several security guys and a medic standing over her. The confusion of what had actually happened seemed to be clouding everyone's judgement of what she had seen. Nathan and the others had no recollection of Sapphire throwing a bolt of lightning at the man who had held her by knifepoint.

She shivered at the memory and Nathan hugged her a little more tightly. "It's OK, babe. You are safe now. That crazy fucker is gone. Security can find neither head nor tail of him. He must have made a run for it. Believe me, no one is going to hurt you again." She nodded slowly. "Has anyone found Saf yet? I'm so worried about her. She just disappeared, Nat, honest to God. I saw the guy she's been playing around with come rushing to her side. He took that twisted fucker out and then they just vanished." Nathan held her quietly, obviously thinking she had lost her mind. Had she?

"Babe, Saf must have got pushed away in the crowd. She will make her way back soon. It got pretty crazy out there. I didn't see much after that guy somehow managed to push me to the ground, just heard a lot of commotion and fighting. He must have got scared by the security which turned up and grown a conscience. I reckon he must have been trying to mug you."

Charlie sighed deeply. She knew no one was going to believe what she saw, damn it. She didn't even believe what she had seen herself. The security people had asked her a few questions but the turmoil had quietened down pretty quickly once the mad fucker had disappeared. It was as if it had never happened. "Pass me my phone. I'll call her again." Nathan released his hold on her. The rest of the group were quietly talking among themselves; the mood for the evening had been dampened somewhat by the strange turn of events. It was still raining, but the thunder and lightning had ceased after Sapphire had disappeared. The band had finished their set and the rest of the festival-goers had no idea what had occurred.

Charlie was so confused. Was it possible that Sapphire had been struck by lightning and that it had bounced off her, hitting the mugger? Where was Sapphire? Was she OK? Why was she not answering her mobile? Charlie let out a little moan. She was worried sick. Nathan rocked her gently in his arms trying to soothe her; she would not be able to relax until her friend was with her again. "Nathan, get one of the guys to go to Security and ask them to try and find her. She might be hurt out there and no one knows. Please." He kissed her softly and nodded. "OK, babe. I'll ask Simon to go. Let me make you some tea and a joint to calm your nerves. Trust me. It will all be fine." Charlie looked like a sad puppy. Her makeup was smudged and her eyes were slightly bloodshot. She just wanted to find Sapphire and go to bed. She knew it was going to be a long night.

Sapphire had drifted off into a peaceful sleep after their urgent lovemaking. Fox had held her in his arms, whispering her name and talking in his language softly to soothe her. The passion between them had washed some of the night's memories away. In the pit of her stomach she knew that she would have to return soon. She could not stay here; there had been enough confusion tonight. Charlie would be wondering where the hell she was. But for a short time she had allowed herself to sleep in his arms and feel safe again.

She woke up feeling sore all over. Her body was curled up on the bed in the foetal position. She reached out for Fox, finding an empty space. Her eyes flew open. "I am here, my beautiful lady. I have brought you some food." She rubbed her eyes sleepily. Daylight was filtering through the windows. She had no idea what time it was. "Oh crap. How long have I slept again?" He sat on the edge of the bed, a plate of bread, cheese and fruit laid out before her. Her stomach growled. Fox laughed softly. "You need to eat. You are famished. Here, take some; it will make you feel better."

Sapphire pushed herself up. She was naked except for the white sheets lying across her body. She began to devour the food, ripping the bread into pieces and stuffing it into her mouth with a renewed hunger. Fox watched her with shining eyes. He certainly looked better; a hazy white shimmer surrounded him and Sapphire noted that the edges of his body were cloaked in a dark blue aura. Between mouthfuls he handed her some water, which she gulped down greedily. She was famished.

"We will return to your world together, Sapphire. I am not leaving you to deal with this on your own." She stopped chewing and looked at him, her eyes wide. "No. You can't. It will be more confusing. How can I explain all of this?" He smiled at her. "They only need to see me if you want them to, remember." Sapphire let out a sigh and continued to eat. The food was good; every mouthful was as delicious as the next. "I remember now. I will feel better if you are there but I have to think about what the fuck I am going to say to Charlie. How the hell am I going to explain all of this?"

Fox leant forward and kissed her forehead. "You are a clever woman, Sapphire. You will think of something. Trust yourself." She wanted to believe him but her stomach, although now nicely satisfied from the food, was starting to churn suddenly with anxiety. After Sapphire had finished eating Fox took her hand and led her to another room, where a large, sunken bath was waiting for her. She was anxious to get back to her own reality but the bath was far too tempting to miss out on.

As she slipped into the hot water filled with rose petals she let out a sigh of bliss. Fox stood in front of her and undressed. She watched him with hungry eyes. He was magnificent naked, his body firm and muscular, but in a lean and wonderful way. Perfect. He was smiling that wicked smile she was beginning to love as he stepped into the water beside her. She felt her heart begin to flutter again in anticipation. He moved her so that she was lying back against his chest, his legs both sides of her, and began to wash her hair. She closed her eyes and revelled in the sensations of water flowing across her head and body. He was pressed against her and she felt him become aroused. "We really don't have time for any more fun, Fox, as much as it would please me to take advantage of you right now."

He chuckled softly and continued to lather her hair, massaging her scalp with strong fingers. "I cannot help the way my body responds when it is close to you, Sapphire." She smiled and allowed him to rinse her hair. He was using a soft sponge now to clean her chest and arms. Slow, long strokes across her skin with a beautifully scented body wash; she could smell tones of orange and rose drifting up from the water and soap. She was in bath heaven. He kissed her neck tenderly and she found her body responding to his touch eagerly. A sly smile crept on to her lips. "If you carry on doing that I might just have to give in." He laughed again and ran a finger across her cheek, lifting his head from her for a moment.

"We have all the time in the world to enjoy pleasuring each other, Sapphire. For now, I believe you are right: we must return to your Earth. We can come back here soon." Sapphire opened her eyes and shook herself to stop the surges of lust that had started to travel through her body. She moved away from him so that she could turn around and face him. He was leaning back against the side of the bath tub, his arms stretched out in a relaxed and lazy fashion across the sides. His smile was sexy and full of promise. "You are one naughty man, Fox. I'm getting out."

He laughed and watched her step out, taking in the view of her wonderful bottom and breasts as the water trickled down her back from her long hair. She walked over to one of the chairs and grabbed a towel to dry herself. With a deep sigh he finished washing and did the same. They dried themselves in silence, Sapphire wrapping her hair up on top of her head. "Where are my clothes?" Fox was dressing in leather trousers and a loose white shirt; he looked as sexy as hell as usual. "They were somewhat ruined; I have laid some other clothes out for you in the bedroom." She nodded, wondering where her bag had gone, and her mobile phone. It seemed that material things from her world could not transport themselves over with her.

She found a long dress in a deep blue made from velvet on the bed, along with some pretty blue underwear; no bra, but that was not really a major problem. The dress was amazingly soft and as she pulled it over her head she shivered as it slipped down her body. It fitted her perfectly. The top was laced together so that her breasts pushed up and spilled over the top slightly. "Medieval barmaid outfit number two," she thought. Shaking her hair out she found a brush on his dresser and began to pull through the knots.

Fox stepped up behind her and took the brush from her hand. He began to brush out her hair gently, with slow, sensual strokes. "I love your hair … so wonderfully long and beautiful; it makes me want to bury my face into it and breath in your scent." Sapphire closed her eyes again and took a deep breath. Everything he did to her made her quiver in anticipation; his touch was like a long slow tease of what was to come. After he was satisfied that her hair was knot-free he stood back and turned her around to face him. She looked up into his amber eyes. His hair was also still a little wet, the beads twinkling slightly. "Are you ready to go back?" Sapphire bit her lip and held on to his forearms. He was warm to touch and she felt instantly calmed by him. "I'm ready."

Fox had somehow managed to bend time and provide Sapphire a cloak, which she thought was rather amazing, as when they suddenly arrived back at the festival site it was still dark and raining. She had opened her eyes to the sight of him standing with her in the Zen garden of the massage and healing area. There was no other soul around but she could hear music coming from (she assumed) the dance tent and people buzzing around them. She wished she knew exactly what time it was here.

Fox drew her into his arms and held her close to him for a moment. He too was now wearing a cloak and his hood was up, sheltering him from the fine film of rain that was persistently falling around them. "Are you OK, Sapphire?" She was trembling a little and was not sure if it was from the drop in temperature or the fact that she was now back, having to face the music. Literally. She nodded silently and stepped back a little so that she could look up at him. His eyes were smiling at her and she felt a touch better. "Let's go find the others."

He draped an arm around her shoulders and they headed back towards the camping site. Stepping out of the healing area they were surrounded once more by people and Sapphire's eyes darted around warily, looking for danger. "You are safe, my lady. Do not fret." She trusted him and took a deep breath as they walked through the crowds towards the campsite. It must have been getting very late but quite a few stalls were still open and people were making the most of the last of the festival activity. It did not take them long to find the small campsite that had been her home for the last three days.

As she moved towards the canopy area Fox moved his arm away from her shoulder and stepped back a little into the shadows. She could see Simon and Caitlin standing to one side, and huddled on the cushions she saw Charlie wrapped in a blanket, with Nathan smoking. As she stepped into the candlelight Charlie looked up, her eyes growing wide with a mixture of relief and confusion. She jumped up, almost knocking Nathan over. "Saf. Oh, my God. Thank goodness you are OK. Where the fuck have you been? I've been worried sick."

She ran towards Sapphire and flung herself at her, embracing her tightly. Sapphire held her, feeling tears begin to prickle her eyes. Charlie pushed back slightly and looked her up and down. "What are you wearing? Where are your clothes?" Sapphire shifted her weight, her eyes downcast. "It's a long story, but I will explain it to you later. Are you OK?" Charlie was frowning slightly now. "Yeah. I'm OK. Why didn't you answer my calls? Where is your phone? What happened to you?" Sapphire looked over her shoulder nervously. Fox was nowhere to be seen. "I lost my phone. Everything was crazy after that guy ran off. I got separated from you and then covered in mud and really wet from the rain. I headed off to find some clean clothes and, well, here I am."

Charlie was looking more like her old self. She wasn't buying it. "Uh-huh, and where is Fox? I saw him; he came crashing in to the rescue. Has he just disappeared again? I would love to speak to him about what happened." Sapphire could feel a warm blush start to spread across her cheeks; she really had no idea how to get out of this one. She felt a surge of warm air beside her and knew that he had stepped forward. "I'm right here." Charlie's face was a picture as he stepped up beside Sapphire and put his arm around her shoulder. The hood to his cloak was now down and his face was softly cast with shadows by the candlelight. He looked totally gorgeous.

Charlie gulped a little overwhelmed by this change of events. She had only managed to catch him at brief moments and the full-on effect of the man himself was causing her to become speechless. Sapphire found this highly amusing. "I brought her back after finding her something to wear; she really was rather wet, you know." Charlie nodded, her mouth slightly open. "But I can see that you girls will need to do some catching up so I will leave you for a while." Charlie continued to gawp at him. The rest of the group were watching the scene silently; they too had all been rendered speechless, suddenly. He kissed Sapphire on the lips tenderly and brushed his hand across her cheek. "I will come back and find you later, Sapphire." Sapphire nodded and smiled at him, knowing full well that he would not be going anywhere but would just step back into the shadows to cloak himself in darkness while she talked to her friends, ever there protecting her.

Charlie took Sapphire's hand and led her back to the cushions, plonking herself down, her face still a picture of slight disbelief. "Fuck me, Saf. That guy is one hot piece of ass. I didn't even get a chance to thank him for helping me out." Sapphire laughed now. The awkward moment had passed and Charlie was now totally sidetracked, just focusing on the fact that Sapphire had a gorgeous man at her side. Wonderful.

"I still don't know how you just managed to disappear, Saf. One minute you were there and Fox was wrestling the guy to the ground, the next thing you had gone." Sapphire sat next to her and prepared herself to tell a few lies. "Charlie, you were terrified and probably in shock after that creep attacked you. We didn't disappear. You passed out, Fox and security took him away, I just got pushed into the crowd and lost you for a while. Honestly, nothing sinister: just some weird, dangerous, probably-taken-too-many-drugs idiot."

Charlie took the joint she had been smoking back from Nathan, who was smiling widely at Sapphire now, nodding his head. "I think I'm the one who has taken too many drugs this weekend, Saf. Honest to God, I seriously thought you shot a bolt of lightning at him and then disappeared." The rest of the group started to laugh. Nathan shook his head. "Babe, you are funny. No more sparkle dust for you for a while." Her face began to soften and a smile appeared slowly on her lips. She looked across at Sapphire and let out a big sigh. "I'm just glad you are here now. You really freaked me out. I was so worried about you."

Sapphire reached across and took her hand, feeling a little guilty that she had just convinced her friend she was seeing things and that what she had actually seen quite clearly was not real. "I'm so sorry, Charlie. I would have been here sooner but Fox said I looked a state and we went for a drink to calm my nerves before I changed my clothes. I didn't mean to worry you, honestly. I lost my bag in all the chaos." Charlie took a drag on the joint, allowing the smoke to filter slowly from her nose. "Yeah, what's with the medieval wench look anyway? That outfit is out of this world. Did Fox buy you two matching cloaks or something?" Sapphire laughed. If only she knew.

Nathan passed Sapphire a paper cup with what looked like some form of alcohol in it. "Here, Saf. You look like you need warming up. Have a shot of whiskey." Sapphire took the cup and sniffed it a little hesitantly before throwing it back down her throat in one swift motion. It burnt her throat all the way down before settling in her stomach, giving her a warm, glowing feeling. The rest of the group had started to gather around now and were chatting again about the night and all the craziness that had happened at the main stage.

Sapphire listened to them discuss different ideas as to why a total stranger had approached her and then tried to mug Charlie for no apparent reason. After a while the topic moved on and Sapphire was relieved to think that she had got away with the whole magical side of things and that they had missed some of the crucial pieces of the puzzle. She could sense Fox on the sidelines; in fact she could see him in the dark, standing perfectly still, just waiting for her to return to her tent. She wanted to go to him but knew it would seem out of line after she had frightened Charlie so much with her disappearing act.

"What time is it, Charlie?" Charlie was looking a lot more relaxed now the joint had most certainly done its thing in calming her down. "I have absolutely no idea." "It's 3 a.m.," Caitlin called out from across the campsite. She was sitting inside her tent with her head poking out. "We are going to bed now, guys. It's been emotional. See you tomorrow."

Sapphire felt like it should be 3 p.m. the next day; her mind was all over the place from the travelling she had done tonight; bending time certainly did weird things to you, like jet lag but worse. "It's later than I thought." Charlie smiled hazily. "Is that man of yours coming back to spend the night, Saf? What's going on with you two, anyway? You're not giving me any info on him. It's not fair."

Nathan laughed. "I'm going to bed, Charlie ... leave you two to that conversation." Sapphire smiled up at him. She desperately wanted to go to bed and lie down with Fox, hold him again, but she knew it would be unwise to step out right now, with Charlie probing so. Sapphire took another sip of whiskey that Nathan had refilled for her; she needed it for this conversation. "He'll be back; we have become kinda close in a short space of time."

Charlie leant forward, excited now. "Do you think this could be the start of something wonderful, hon? He's uber-gorgeous. Oh, my God ... the way he just took that guy off his feet. I don't care what the others think or what you said, Saf. I saw him like a ninja; it was pretty amazing. I wouldn't mind a piece of that." Sapphire choked on the whiskey and laughed; she could hear Fox in the darkness, laughing softly. "Yes, he is rather wonderful. I'm starting to let him in, I think he may be around a lot more in the future."

Charlie grinned at her. "Fabtastic. You need a good man in your life, Saf, even if he dresses a little funky and puts you in a wench's outfit." They laughed together and Sapphire could feel the last remaining tension of the evening beginning to lift. "I really need to get some sleep, Charlie, before we have to get up and take the tents down tomorrow." Charlie pulled a face. "I know. It's all over tomorrow. I don't really want to go back to reality. It's been such fun. Even the weirdness of tonight has been kind of exciting in a fucked-up kind of way. I certainly won't forget this festival in a hurry."

Sapphire leant forward to hug her friend, who returned the gesture with a kiss on her cheek. She held her for a moment and let her energy wash over Charlie, sending her big love. Charlie leant back, looking a little tearful. "You are a good friend, Saf. I can't imagine you not in my life now. I'm glad you came to live with me." Sapphire smiled at her, the warmth of their friendship shining through. "Me, too, Charlie. Sleep well tonight. I'll see you in the morning." They parted company, Sapphire standing up and stretching a little before she looked across into the dark to see if Fox was still standing waiting for her. She noticed that her tent was now glowing a soft orange and knew he was already waiting for her.

Unzipping the tent, she found him waiting for her in his usual relaxed manner, hands behind his head, his legs crossed at the ankles, a soft smile on his lips. She closed the tent entrance and started to take off her cloak. She wanted to feel his arms around her as quickly as possible. "You did well, Sapphire. Your friends seemed satisfied with your side of the story; it was not too difficult to mislead them after all." She crawled over to him and kicked off her shoes (Fox had magically conjured her some new shoes at the point of re-entry to Earth – very handy).

He sat up and reached for her, taking her into his arms and lying her down with him. She nestled into his chest and soaked up the smell of patchouli and sandalwood. He was so warm; her body instantly started to throb with the thrill of being close to him again. "I'm so glad you are here, Fox. I cannot begin to even understand what is happening between us any more: what is real; what is not. I feel like I am constantly dreaming now: it's been the strangest few days for me."

He kissed her gently and stroked her cheek. "It is all real, beautiful lady. You have made it real. We have crossed over now. There is no going back; we will just work through each moment as it comes." She lifted her head and looked up into his eyes, mesmerised by the tenderness held within them. "Will Hecta come for me again?" He nodded solemnly and held her closer. "I believe he will. He has become obsessed with stopping you using your new magic and travelling, but this is something he cannot do; it is your destiny and your right. I will make sure no harm comes to you, Sapphire. He will never stop me from reaching you again."

Sapphire wanted to make that part of her crazy life just go away, disappear. She wondered where he was right now, but wanted any thoughts of him removed from her head. There was only one way she knew that this was possible. She kissed Fox, started to remove his shirt and trace her fingers across the firm warm skin on his chest and arms. He moaned softly as she undid the lacing on her dress to allow her breasts to spill out before him. His eyes turned a darker shade and the smile on his lips turned into a slow promise. She watched him in the soft light as he helped her slip the dress off over her head. He shuffled out of his trousers, an action that seemed oddly strange for him. Usually they just magically disappeared.

When they were both naked Fox lifted the sleeping bag and blanket and motioned for her to climb inside. She did so willingly. Her body was tingling in anticipation now. She could not get enough of him. Every moment alone together seemed to be an opportunity to step across the line between reality and fantasy. He kissed her softly, with a tenderness that made her body quiver. Stroking her and murmuring to her she lay back and closed her eyes. He lifted her hands above her head and whispered silkily into her ear for her to keep still. She felt him move down her body, stopping at each breast to suck and tease her nipples, making her groin clench in arousal.

When she tried to bring her hands down to touch him and push her fingers into his hair he placed them back above her head. "No touching," he whispered again, making her body light up with its own internal furnace. He was really turning her on. He was kissing her softly on her right hip bone; his fingers were tracing light patterns across her thigh, close enough to the entrance of her pussy to make her groan with delight. She kept her hands above her head, making her breasts rise up higher. Keen to play the game now, she allowed him to tease her gently.

His mouth moved down towards her most intimate of places. His head was under the covers and she felt like the virgin on prom night waiting to be deflowered. She let out a sharp gasp as his mouth slipped down and his tongue gently probed the opening to her pussy. She was wet and more than willing for what was to come. Her hips started to rise up and he chuckled softly between kisses, his fingers finding the soft folds of her opening ... and he pushed one inside slowly and licked her clit, making her shake with pleasure. Her hands drifted down and pushed the blankets back away from his head so that she could watch him as he pleasured her with his tongue and fingers; the sight of him working his magic tipped her further over the edge.

He looked up at her and smiled, continuing his finger work before dipping down again and licking her expertly, a little harder this time. She clung to his head; he growled softly and let her guide him to the perfect angle. She knew that at any moment he was going to make her come and she let the energy flow without holding back now. She was so ready for him to push her over the edge, his head moving with a rhythm that matched her arching hips, the tension building wonderfully inside her groin was starting to make her head spin. As her climax peaked and burst outwards and upwards to the rest of her body in one big head rush, she threw her head back and cried out, not caring if the whole damn campsite heard her.

Her body trembled with the sweet sensations that swept over her, her body becoming limp with pleasure, her legs shaking slightly from the intensity. As she gasped for air he moved up her body and pushed his cock inside her. She was so wet he slid inside in one quick action. He claimed her mouth and kissed her hard, their tongues meeting in a wild dance. He pumped inside her, his heart beating hard against her breasts, sliding up and down her body. She gripped him with her thighs and pushed him in deeper; he released her mouth and groaned loudly.

There was no doubt everyone around them would be hearing them now. The thought turned her on even more. She urged him on faster, wanting him to consume her fully. She could not get enough of him, this man of hers – this wild magical man who was making her do crazy things, things she had never dreamt she would do before. Fox thrust hard into her and she felt him shudder before coming deeply inside her. She clung to him and felt her own second climax rush upwards to the top of her head and spill out, making sparks appear before her eyes. He slumped down heavily on top of her, his breathing fast and hot against her ear. She released her grip on him and let her body go limp, her head to one side as she tried to regain her senses. He was laughing softly as he rolled over on to his back beside her. "I think we may have woken up a few people."

Sapphire giggled and slid over into his arms, burying her head into his chest. He wrapped his arms around her and kissed the top of her head, their hearts still beating quickly like a jackrabbit. "We most definitely woke up more than a few," Sapphire whispered. He squeezed her tightly and pulled the sleeping bag up over their legs again. She had never felt so utterly ravished and satisfied. Her heart was fluttering like a butterfly; she felt his love for her and it consumed her completely. Lifting her head so that she could look into his eyes she kissed him softly one more time before whispering softly into the night, "I love you, Fox." At that moment Fox knew that his world had been completed in every way possible; he had been holding back on saying the words to her in fear that she did not feel the same way. He knew they shared an undeniable lust and passion for each other and he had seen a flicker of her emotion for him when they had made love before. But now he knew, and it filled his heart with joy. He kissed her back and held her close. "I have always loved you, my beautiful Sapphire, and always will, my love; my only love." They fell asleep wrapped in each other's arms, safe in the knowledge that the feelings they had for each other were mutual and that whatever challenges they may face from now on, they would face together.

Chapter Thirty

Monday

"Wake up, you two sleepy heads. Breakfast is ready." Sapphire woke with a start. Charlie had her head poked through the tent flap. She was grinning at her with a happy, wide-eyed expression on her face. Her eyes wandered over the body lying next to Sapphire with appreciation. Fox was draped over her, his leg flung across her body. The blankets were pushed down low so that most of their naked bodies were exposed. Charlie winked at Sapphire and then disappeared again, zipping the tent back up behind her.

Sapphire blinked sleepy eyes. She looked down at Fox. He began to stretch his body as he awoke. She felt her own happy smile spread across her lips. "Good morning, beautiful," he murmured, as his eyes opened and he traced a finger across her breasts. Sapphire pushed herself up and rubbed her eyes. "You are still here?" Fox was sitting now and facing her, wide awake. He leant forward and kissed her lightly on her nose. "Yes, I'm still here." Sapphire knew in her heart that he was taking a massive risk by fully exposing himself to her friends but he had stayed and chosen to remain in her world again. "We need to get dressed."

He was smiling at her, his eyes bright and alert. She wished she could feel quite so optimistic. Reaching for her backpack she began to pull out fresh clothes for the day. As she dressed silently, her mind still trying to make sense of it all, Fox ran his hand down her back. "Stop worrying. Everything is going to be fine." When she turned around to face him, after pulling a t-shirt over her head and clambering into her knickers and shorts, he was now fully clothed in jeans and a black fitted t-shirt with the Jack Daniels emblem slashed across the front. She gawped for a moment. He looked very human, apart from his eyes ... like any other guy in normal clothes at a festival. He raised an eyebrow and smiled. "I'm blending in." She laughed and kissed him. He pulled her into his arms for a moment and they held each other, kissing softly. Reluctantly, Sapphire withdrew before they got too carried away. She knew they had to get moving as the others would be packing up soon. Brushing hair away from her face, Fox nodded. "Let's get some breakfast, then."

A little nervously, she opened the tent and crawled out. The day was bright and sunny. The rain had cleared and soft white clouds drifted across the blue horizon. Charlie and Nathan were sitting making tea and frying up some bacon. The smell wafted over to Sapphire and her stomach rumbled. As she stepped out Charlie looked over and smiled at her. "Morning, Saf. How was your sleep, or should I say, 'Did you get any sleep?'" Sapphire blushed furiously. Fox had appeared beside her and he had pulled her into his chest, hugging her in clear view of Charlie. "We slept well. Thank you, Charlie." He spoke on her behalf. Charlie beamed at him. "Yeah, I bet you did. There's coffee and bacon sarnies. Help yourselves; the others are just getting ready."

Fox released her from his arms and they wandered over to join Charlie and Nathan, Fox holding her hand tightly. As they sat down under the canopy Nathan stood up and leant across with his hand out to Fox. "Good to finally meet you, Fox. I'm Nathan. Thanks for helping out with that creep last night." Fox shook his hand and nodded. "No problem." Sapphire could not believe they were actually having this interaction, that Fox was sitting relaxed and at ease about to have breakfast with her in her world.

As Charlie poured hot water into cups filled with coffee Sapphire watched Fox grab a sandwich and tuck in. Normal. Weird. Amazing. "So where do you come from then, Fox?" Nathan started to chat to him, guy to guy. Fox watched him, amusement in his eyes. Sapphire was starting to feel slightly on edge. "I get around, but I visit Pearl from time to time. That's how I met Sapphire." Nathan was sipping his coffee, sussing this new man in Sapphire's life out. "Oh, yeah? What do you do?" Charlie laughed. "Stop interrogating him, Nathan. Let him eat."

Sapphire was surprised her friend was being so relaxed. She would normally be the one doing the grilling. Fox seemed to be perfectly happy to chat. "I travel a lot; I work as a bodyguard." Sapphire spat coffee across the grass. Charlie eyed her suspiciously;

Nathan's eyes lit up. "Cool, man. That makes sense." Charlie was giggling as she flipped the bacon in the pan. "Oh, your own personal bodyguard, Saf. You could be like Whitney Houston and Kevin Costner." Fox's eyes went blank but he remained silent, having no idea whatsoever who she was referring to. Sapphire felt her body start to relax and laughed a little. "Yeah, that's funny, Charlie." As they sat and ate the rest of the group started to emerge from the tents and gather under the canopy. The girls all stared at Fox with wide eyes and slightly parted lips, such was his effect on the female species. Simon and the rest of the guys seemed amiable enough but were a little more cautious.

After everyone had eaten and were ready to get moving Fox helped Sapphire to pack her bag and roll up the mattress and sleeping bag. He smiled at her with a knowing tilt to his lips as he folded the blankets that not so long ago they had spent time rolling around in. With a swiftness that was almost inhuman he dismantled the tent. She was almost waiting for him to just magic it back into the bag but that would have been too damn obvious.

Once the campsite had been disassembled and the area was scattered with bags he lifted as much as was humanly possible ready to carry back to the car. Sapphire was more than happy to let him help her; she remembered the long slog on the first day they had arrived. Nathan wandered along beside him, chatting away, as they headed back to the car. Charlie walked behind with Sapphire and nudged her jovially. "He seems like a great guy, Saf. I hope we get to see more of him."

Sapphire watched the two men in front, Fox tall and elegant, moving with a grace that was unlike any other man – the weight of the bags he was carrying causing no apparent effort on his part. She smiled; there was a warm sensation in her stomach at the sight of him pretending to be one of the guys. When they reached the car Charlie walked across to Fox. Standing before him, squinting in the sunlight, she asked him, "Do you need a lift?" He had helped Nathan load the car in double quick time and was now standing with his hands tucked in his jean pockets, looking like a supermodel. "I have my own transport, thank you, Charlie."

Charlie shrugged and then leant in for a hug. Fox was a little taken aback but returned the gesture warmly. Charlie withdrew from him reluctantly; her hug had been a big one. "I hope to see you again very soon, Fox. You know where we live. Don't be a stranger." Sapphire could not help but smile at the scene. Fox nodded at Charlie with his best serious face then waved goodbye to the rest of the gang. Charlie and Nathan jumped in the car, Charlie winding down the window. "Say goodbye, Saf. I'm making a smoke so you have a minute to make it a good one."

Sapphire laughed and stepped away from the car into the waiting arms of her man. Fox held her to his chest, his head resting on top of hers. She breathed in his scent, felt the warmth of his body against her. "I will see you again soon, Sapphire. You know I will not be far away." Raising her head to look up at him she smiled, and stood up on tiptoes to kiss him. They kissed for some time, Fox cradling her head in both hands. The kiss was filled with passion and love.

"Come on, you two lovebirds. We are ready to get going," Charlie shouted out of the window at them, laughing. Fox released her slowly. She watched his amber eyes flash with amusement. "I'll see you soon, then?" He nodded at her and kissed her hand before stepping back. She climbed into the back seat of the car and wound down the window. He stood watching them, a faint smile on his lips. Raising her hand to wave, they pulled away. She watched his tall figure stand perfectly still, growing smaller as they drove further away from him. Sapphire could see the air around him waver like heat on a car roof for a moment, then he was gone. Just like that.

The journey home seemed like a long ride. Sapphire nodded in and out of sleep in the back of the car, her thoughts drifting through the many events that had occurred and what seemed real and what did not. She could not wait to get home and run a bath and then slip into her clean bed for a proper nap. Charlie chatted to Nathan in the front; the sound of her voice faded in and out as Sapphire catnapped.

When they arrived back at the cottage they all agreed that they would unpack the car later, or even tomorrow. Grabbing her backpack Sapphire headed up the stairs, her body suddenly very weary.

"Charlie, I'm going to run a bath, if that's OK?"

Charlie had put the kettle on. Nathan was sprawled out on the sofa flicking through the TV channels. He had obviously missed some of the comforts of home.

"Sure, hon. There should be plenty of hot water. The immersion heater has been on timer while we were away."

Sapphire dropped her bag into her room, pausing for a moment as she looked around at the bed and the familiar things she had forgotten about in the last few days. It had felt longer than a long weekend away. Undressing and pulling on her dressing gown she went to the bathroom and began to run the hot water. She could no longer sense Fox's presence around her and guessed he had returned to Shaka to recharge. The night and morning on Earth must have taken a toll on him.

When her bath was run she slid out of her dressing gown and stepped inside the tub. Her mind took her back to the memory of bathing with Fox in his huge sunken bath; she smiled at the thought. She had told him that she loved him and she did. The fact that he had returned her feelings and said so in such a passionate way made her body tingle. The water enveloped her and she slid right down so that only her head was lifted out, resting back against a towel. She closed her eyes and allowed its warmth to soothe her body, the body that had been taken to places she never knew existed until recently.

As she wallowed in the tub, moving her hands through the water, her mind drifted and she could see a dark place filtering into her vision. The obsidian necklace was still around her neck and it started to pulse softly against her chest. The vision became clearer and she saw Hecta clearly in her mind. He was standing inside a darkened cavern, his face shrouded in shadows. As she started to back away from the vision, a little scared by the clarity of the picture in her head, he looked up and his eyes flashed red, a snarl on his lips.

Sapphire jumped, opening her eyes and gasping a little. The water in the bath sloshed around her as she felt her heart jump in fright. He was out there somewhere, waiting for her. Waiting to return. The sun was still shining outside and the bathroom was warm and comforting but she suddenly felt very cold. She finished washing quickly, not bothering with her hair now.

235

Getting out of the bath she wrapped herself in a towel and hugged herself tightly. It wasn't over. This turning of events was moving forward before her and she knew that at some point soon it would begin again. She knew that she would need to protect herself and that the best person to help her besides Fox would be Pearl. She would visit her again tomorrow and try to find some peace once more.

Heading back to her bedroom Sapphire dried herself properly before sliding naked in between her sheets. The feel of cotton against her skin and the softness of the mattress and pillows soothed her wonderfully. She could hear Charlie and Nathan downstairs talking, a murmur of voices in the background that made her feel safe.

The salt around her bed was still in place and she visualised in her head that she was protected and able to stay grounded in this world. She needed to sleep for a while without any disruptions. Placing her head on the pillow and snuggling against her duvet she closed her eyes and relaxed. Thoughts of Fox drifted through her mind, filled with colourful moments from the festival, dancing and laughing drinking and flying high. It had been an amazing time and she had learned a great deal more about her growing power. With a deep sigh she felt her body start to drop into sleep state. She was absolutely exhausted and desperately needed to recharge her batteries.

Chapter Thirty-One

Fox sat in the tavern with his friend Bear and shared a tankard of ale. His face was lit up as he talked to his closest friend about his latest trip with Sapphire. Bear was nodding as he talked with excitement about her confessions of love for him. Bear was grinning now in between taking great gulps of the ale, his nose slightly ruddy. "She is the most amazing woman I have ever met, Bear ... the power she can wield ... I have never seen anything like it." Bear leant back in his chair. People were drinking and eating all around them, talking loudly; he had one eye on the barmaid, who was giving him the come-on.

"Yes, my friend. You have already told me several times. I am pleased for you; she sounds wonderful." Fox grinned and ran his hand through his hair. "I am sorry, Bear. I have been talking about her too much, but she has bewitched me." Bear laughed loudly and thumped his tankard down on the table. "Your enthusiasm for her is amusing, Fox, but it sounds like she is also causing some trouble between this world and her own. The fact that Hecta showed himself to the other humans and you had to stop him is a problem. I feel you should stop fucking her for a while and get your focus back." Fox took a sip of his ale and contemplated for a moment. "We both know the risks and consequences of our actions, Bear ... but it is as if we are unable to control our desire for each other when we are in the same room. You are right, of course, but each time I have tried to refrain from joining with her I have been unable to stop myself."

Bear chuckled. "Ask your father for a potion that will dampen your ardour for her. That would be a good start." Fox shook his head slowly. "I will not, I cannot. Our energy together makes us stronger. I sense it, and we will need to be strong for the next time Hecta returns." Bear frowned. "There has never been such a time when a dream traveller has provoked the gatekeepers so much. I can understand their interest in her to a certain extent, but I am feeling there is more to it than just her coupling with you and throwing a few lightning bolts. Truly, my friend, I believe he knows more about her than he is letting on."

Fox scratched his head. His friend was right the last time when he had guided him to see the Oracle. Perhaps he was right again. "You really do have brains as well as brawn, don't you, Bear?" They both laughed together and continued with their drinking. Fox found solace in spending time with this man and being in his own world, enjoying simple pleasures. It was wonderful being with Sapphire but her planet was strange to him, the people there even stranger. He knew he was being tested each time he travelled to see her and it was getting harder.

Fox reached out in his mind for her and sensed her sleeping soundly. She was not reaching out for him and her mind was calm and peaceful. She had wrapped a protective shield around herself, but he could still push through if needed. He could always connect with her now; the love between them had stopped any doubt of that. After several tankards of ale Fox was feeling a little woozy; alcohol in his world was a whole different ball game from that on Earth. Bear, on the other hand, looked like he was ready to take on the world or, at least, the barmaid who was giving him the eye from across the bar.

"I will see you soon, old friend. I am going home to refresh myself." Bear stood as he started to leave and embraced him heartily, "Be safe, my friend. Think about moving forward with this woman with caution. I fear a little for your sanity now that love is in the equation." Fox smiled at him, knowing that his friend was only looking out for him but feeling a little frustrated by his words of restraint. They parted company, Bear heading over to the bar to talk to the more-than-willing barmaid. He stepped out of the tavern and walked for a while, spending time to think rather than just transporting himself back home with magic.

He could feel the drain on his body and mind every time he visited Sapphire on Earth, the last trip being especially hard with the interaction with her friends. It was a necessity for her but it pulled on his magic and made him weary. He wandered the pathway back to his home, soaking up the sunshine which seemed to be especially fulfilling here on Shaka. The fields surrounding him were lush and green, ripe with corn ready for harvest. This world was flowing with abundance and it gave him a warm pulse of energy as he walked. He wished that Sapphire was from this world and could live here with him permanently, they would be safe here and he would give her everything she could possibly want. They could be together without having to constantly watch over their shoulder for Hecta or any other predator. He knew this would most likely be impossible, but it was a thought that he could not remove from his mind as he made his way home.

After a short time he stood before his beautiful house, the gardens laid out before him fragrant and welcoming. He entered the hallway and realised how quiet it was; he had been alone for a very long time. He imagined walking through the door and Sapphire greeting him, barefoot and smiling. It was a fantasy that made him smile as he walked up his stairs to his bedchamber. He stood at the balcony and looked out over the vista before him. Sensing his own need to rest he stepped back inside eventually and undressed to bathe, before taking some time for himself to sleep and recharge his energy. He wished she were with him now, but smiled at the vision of her climbing into his bed with him and knew if that were the case he would not be getting very much sleep at all.

Sapphire was dreaming again, but this time it was different. She sensed the shift in her energy as she began to move out of her body. A thin thread of light was connected to her body which still remained within the bed, safe at home. She was watching the dream as if from afar, an observer rather than a participant. She could see a darkened cavern before her ... two people sitting around a fire which burned brightly in the centre, reflecting orange and red flames off their faces.

As she moved closer she could see that one of the figures was Hecta. He was crouched over the fire, his head down slightly, his face troubled. She watched, a little afraid that he might see her, but he did not even look up. "You have failed me again, Hecta. I am most disappointed in you." A woman's voice carried across the fire and into Sapphire's mind. She could clearly hear the words spoken by her, although she had her back to Sapphire and she could not see her face. Hecta looked up at the figure before him, a scowl etched across his forehead. "She is more powerful than I anticipated. Her strength has grown quickly and with her guardian constantly at her side my attempts to take her have been futile. I will not let you down again." Sapphire watched, horrified and mesmerised at the same time as they talked about her, oblivious to her watching in her dream state.

"I do not think you realise how important it is for me to have her, Hecta. The power she holds is the key to everything." Hecta was still scowling, and poked the fire with a large stick angrily. "You have made it quite clear how important she is. I do not underestimate that, and I will bring her to you when the time is right." The woman huffed. Sapphire wished she could see her face. "It took me a great deal of time and energy to retrieve you from the barren planet she sent you to, Hecta. Next time she does that I will not bother to find you."

Hecta sighed deeply, obviously trying to rein in his anger, as a large vein in his forehead bulged with frustration. "I am in your debt, Priestess. I will not fail you again." The woman stood up, her back still to Sapphire as she watched from afar. "You do understand that the only place she is vulnerable is on her own planet. When she travels or visits her guardian's world it is much more difficult for her to be extracted as the magic there is strong and gives her protection. You must plan your next move carefully." Hecta shifted his weight and nodded. "I understand."

Sapphire felt her energy begin to shift again and a sharp tug on her solar plexus pulled her back into her body. The silver line of light that was holding her was swallowed up as she landed abruptly back on her bed. Her eyes flew open and she gasped out loudly for breath. Sitting up in her bed she found the room was a soft shade of grey; the daylight was disappearing fast and dusk was upon them. She had obviously slept the afternoon away and was now more than a little troubled by what she had witnessed while sleeping.

Pushing herself up and out of bed she pulled on some clothes and headed back down the stairs to find Charlie. She wanted company and something to calm her now-frayed nerves. Charlie and Nathan were curled up together on the sofa; the TV was on playing to itself in the background as they were both asleep. Sapphire wanted to wake them but knew that would probably be a bad idea. Instead she headed into the kitchen to make herself a drink and something to eat.

Her dream was still bouncing around in her head. What did this mean? Who was the woman and what did she want with her? As she made herself a coffee with a shot of whiskey to steady her fluttering heart she knew that her next visit to Pearl could not come soon enough. Grabbing some bread, she made a sandwich and went back into the lounge to sit with her friends. As she slumped back into the armchair Charlie stirred and lifted her head, her eyes opening slowly. "Hey, Saf, did you have a good nap?" Sapphire munched the sandwich a little sadly. "Yeah, I'm OK. A bad dream woke me up."

Charlie sat up and rubbed her eyes. "Oh, hon, really? You and your dreams, eh? Never mind, we will all be feeling a little jaded after the weekend. I'm sure it will fade, that's why it's good to have some time off this week." Sapphire nodded, starting to feel a little better now she was back in her own reality again with her friend. "Are you and Nathan going to be around tomorrow?" Charlie nodded. "Yep, we have both taken a couple of days off to recover … most likely sleep a lot. I suggest you do the same."

Sapphire finished her sandwich and sipped the liquor-laced coffee slowly. "Mmmh … I will try to get some sleep. I have already slept the afternoon away, but I think I'll go and visit Pearl tomorrow for a while." Charlie was watching her with concern in her eyes now. "OK, sweetie. Are you OK?" Sapphire smiled, not wanting to alarm her friend. "I'm fine, Charlie, honestly." Charlie nodded and settled back down, snuggling into Nathan, who was snoring softly now. They watched TV in silence for a while – Sapphire going over the dream in her head, wishing it would go away and give her some peace. She knew Fox would never let anyone harm her, but she suddenly felt very vulnerable with this new piece of information. She almost did not want to sleep again that night in case she had another horrible revealing dream.

What was left of the day had turned to night quickly and eventually Charlie and Nathan headed up to bed. Sapphire followed them and took time in the bathroom, brushing her teeth and combing out her hair before going to bed. She made sure all the doors were locked and the windows closed before retiring. Lighting a candle beside her bed and rechecking the salt boundary, she slipped back under her duvet. She stared up at the ceiling for a long time before eventually she could no longer fight the need to sleep again. She asked Fox in her mind to watch over her and drifted into a restless and somewhat troubled sleep.

Chapter Thirty-Two

Tuesday

Sapphire woke the next morning to grey skies. Heavy cloud hung as if suspended by invisible thick ropes with the promise of more rain. It suited her mood. That was definitely bleak. The cottage was quiet and she knew Charlie and Nathan were still sleeping off their comedown. After washing and dressing she slipped quietly downstairs to have some breakfast before heading out to find Pearl. Sitting at the kitchen table she ate some cereal in silence. Despite the fact that no more dreams had filled her mind she had not slept well, and she felt drained and tired today.

It was 10 a.m. when she left the cottage. Walking through the village with her hoody up over her head she felt nervous and a little shaky. This was becoming a joke, feeling like she was being watched; totally paranoid all the time. Perhaps it was the effects of her own comedown. She reached the gate to Pearl's cottage quickly and paused for a moment before pushing it open to enter the beautiful garden. The sky overhead had released the rain it had been promising earlier and it started to fall heavily as she reached the front door.

Before she could knock the door opened and Pearl stood before her, a big smile on her face. "Good morning, Sapphire. Come in, my dear." Sapphire all but flung herself at the old woman, who laughed softly as Sapphire hugged her, a little damp from the rain. "There, there, my dear. It's OK: everything will be all right. Come in ... I will make us some tea ... the kitchen is nice and warm ... come in out of the rain." Sapphire released her reluctantly and followed her into the kitchen, which was indeed warm and inviting. Everything about Pearl's house was welcoming: the smell of fresh bread wafted in the air and, despite the dark sky outside, the cottage was lit with candles and incense, giving everything a warm glow.

Sapphire sat at the kitchen table and watched Pearl move around with grace and ease, making tea, gathering plates for some delicacy she had no doubt made that morning. Sapphire propped her head in her hands and felt a slow swell of emotion lift from her chest up to her eyes. Tears began to spill over and she found that she could not stop them. Pearl turned around with two mugs and sat opposite her; she frowned as she noticed the tears sliding silently down Sapphire's cheeks. "Oh, my dear Sapphire. What is wrong? Don't cry, my love. Things can't be that bad, can they?"

Sapphire sniffed and rubbed away the tears with the sleeve of her hoody. "I don't even know where to begin, Pearl. The last few days have been so crazy: things have escalated to the point that I don't know what I am doing any more. I'm not sure I can do this, whatever it is I am supposed to be doing." Pearl pushed the mug towards Sapphire and grabbed a handful of paper towels, passing them across to her. She was smiling softly at her, making Sapphire want to start crying again. "Start from the beginning, Sapphire. I'm sure that a problem shared is always halved, as they say." Sapphire took the paper towel and blew her nose loudly.

"I've been to a festival over the weekend. We got back yesterday. It was fun, but lots of crazy stuff happened and Hecta actually appeared and tried to hurt my friend Charlie. He made me so angry that I threw lightning at him and everything got totally out of control, and then yesterday when I was sleeping I had another dream. It was different this time: I was just watching instead of being in the dream. I saw him with a woman ... they were talking about me ... it was horrible ... she was telling him to 'extract me,' whatever the hell that means, and that my power is the key to everything. It freaked me out completely, and today I just feel like utter shit."

Pearl's eyes were wide now and she had stopped sipping her tea. Sapphire knew she was babbling but she didn't care: she needed to get it all of her chest. She looked at Pearl sadly. "I'm scared, Pearl. Even with Fox watching my back I'm so worried something is going to happen to me or, worse, to one of my friends, because of who I am. I'm in over my head and have no idea how to sort this out." Pearl sighed deeply and took another sip of her tea. "Well, that does change things, doesn't it? We really don't want you feeling so scared and upset, do we?"

Sapphire shook her head, taking a sip of the tea. It was delicious as always: lemon with a tang of orange and ginger and something else she couldn't identify. "I can see that there has been a massive shift in your energy. You are changing very quickly now, faster than I could have anticipated, and this new twist with Hecta is certainly interesting. We may have to consult the cards to see what the future has in store for you. Of course I can help with some protection spells, but I am really not sure what is going on here. Nothing like this has ever been recorded by any other dream traveller." Sapphire continued to sniff a little miserably. The tea was comforting but she still felt totally lost.

"And what is happening between you and your guardian is also unheard of. No guardian has ever crossed over to our world the way Fox has with you. It seems your paths are intertwined somehow – again a first." Sapphire frowned. "Why me, Pearl?" Pearl chuckled softly. "That I cannot answer, Sapphire, but the path of the dream traveller is a magical one. It is like walking along a road made of diamonds – so beautiful to look at and experience but painful at times to walk on. Such is the way of being gifted." Sapphire let out a deep sigh. "I'd rather just walk a normal path like everyone else, Pearl." Pearl laughed and stood up, moving over to the kitchen dresser, rummaging through the drawers, looking for something.

"But if you did that, Sapphire, you would not have met Fox or fulfilled your destiny and you would most likely spend the rest of your life feeling unfulfilled and miserable." Sapphire laughed at the irony. "But I'm miserable now." Pearl found what she was looking for and turned around. She was holding a bundle of silk cloth in a deep purple colour, wrapped around something in the shape of a small box. "Ah, here they are. Misery is something we all have to experience to understand the depths of joy, Sapphire. You will understand in time. Now, let's have a look, shall we?"

Sapphire watched her with interest now, wondering what was in the silk bundle. Pearl sat back down at the table and unwrapped the package to reveal a set of cards – the Tarot, she presumed. Although she had never had her cards read she had seen them before and was anxious to find out how they worked. "Take the cards and shuffle them. Clear your mind and relax your energy so that we can get a clear reading." Sapphire took the cards and held them for a moment, sensing a slight buzzing in her fingertips as she touched them. She closed her eyes for a second and took a deep breath. She had never been very good at shuffling, and one of the cards flew out of her hands as she tried to shuffle them. Pearl picked up the card and placed it down to one side. "That one wanted to be seen. Carry on, my dear. Lay them out in front of you and then pick five more cards. Lay them face down."

Sapphire did as she was told, fanning the cards out in front of her. She scanned them slowly. "Don't think about it too hard; just feel which cards are right for you." Sapphire closed her eyes and ran her hands over the line of cards. As she hovered over them her fingers began to tingle again as she stopped at one of the middle cards. She pulled it out and did the same along the spread until she had six in total. Pearl watched her with a serious expression. "Now turn them over in the order you picked them and we will see what they have to say."

Sapphire found herself shaking a little in anticipation. What if the message was bad? As she started to turn them over she felt herself gasp a little at the pictures: some of them were clear to her, although she did not know the meaning fully, and others made no sense at all. Pearl, although looking across the table at the cards that would appear upside down to her seemed to have no trouble in interpreting them. "OK, so we have the first card that jumped out: The Lovers." She looked at Sapphire and raised her eyebrow, smiling. "This is the coming of sexual awareness and the importance of love in your life, most likely between you and Fox." Sapphire looked at the card – the picture of the naked male and female standing below the angel above them. She felt slightly exposed and blushed a little.

"Second card is The Devil. This represents bondage … feeling restrictions in your life. You may feel that you are not in control of your life, but don't worry, Sapphire. Although he looks scary the card's meaning is slightly different. When you are feeling restrained you nearly always hold the keys to your own freedom; you can choose to free yourself from whichever restrictions are holding you back." Sapphire picked up her tea and took a big gulp. It did not take a pack of cards to tell her that that was exactly how she was feeling right now. "The third card is The Nine of Swords – again, a card that can be a little intimidating, but it is voicing your anxiety and worry. You have the ability to change this."

Pearl paused, looking at the next card before speaking again. "Fourth card – The Tower. There are big changes coming your way: a shattering of what is real to you now and new beginnings. It reminds you that dreaming is important, but it is also important to be living in reality, too. You will get through this time just fine, particularly if you remember that you have all the resources you need already inside you to deal with life and to do what you need to do."

Sapphire found her head nodding in response: this was like someone was reading her mind, but reassuring her at the same time, The Tower card looked as equally scary as The Devil, but Pearl was making them sound more positive than they actually looked. "And then we have the fifth card, The Two of Cups, which shows me that you are feeling more than usually loved-for and contented. There is a true love scenario here; a balanced partnership or commitment." She smiled at Sapphire and winked.

"And last, but not least, we have The Four of Wands, which symbolises a celebration or special event, and a potential marriage. There. That wasn't too bad, was it? Nothing nasty jumping out there at all, just a few indications of change and that you must stop worrying so much." Sapphire relaxed a little as Pearl smiled at her. "Oh, and I forgot that sometimes The Four of Wands can also mean that you will be moving your place of residence." Sapphire raised her eyebrow and shook her head. "I'm not intending to move anywhere or get married just yet, Pearl."

Pearl started to pick the cards up and pat them back into an orderly fashion. "Well, they are just a guide, my dear, but if there was anything to worry about I am sure it would have come up for you." She placed the bundle on the table and reached across to hold Sapphire's hands gently. "Do you feel a little better now?" Sapphire griped her hands and nodded. "Yes, I do. Thank you, Pearl." She continued to hold Sapphire's hands and closed her eyes. "Now let me just get a feel for your energy, see what is actually happening to you in the magical realm." Sapphire felt the warmth of Pearl's hands start to travel up her arms. It was comforting and soothing.

"Ah, yes. You have downloaded a new strain of magic. It helps you harness the elements at your will – hence the ability to control the lightning – and I can feel something else, as yet unclear, growing inside you. It has great strength and power; maybe that is what the woman in your dream is coveting." Pearl opened her eyes. "But I don't think we will have to worry about that for a while; I do not sense any danger at the moment. I will mix you some more herbs for protection, to drink and to scatter around your bed for when you sleep … but you must remember, Sapphire, that you have the ability to control your travelling. This is your choice, your free will."

Sapphire nodded as she released her hands. "What about Fox? I know that every time he comes here to help me it affects him. Will he be safe around me now?" Pearl contemplated the question. "You must understand, Sapphire, that Fox is not of this world. He was born from magic and cannot stay in our realm for great periods of time without it draining him. It is impossible for you to be with him in a normal relationship here on Earth." Sapphire looked at Pearl with anguish. "So you are saying that we cannot be together?" Pearl shook her head slowly. "No, it is not impossible, but there may come a time when one of you must make a choice – whether to stay or leave. If he crosses over to you to live on Earth he will eventually lose his magic and become like any other human male. If you jump across to his world the possibilities are endless, but your life here as a human woman would be over."

Sapphire gulped. "Heavy, Pearl. Heavy." Pearl laughed. "Yes, it is, but I doubt that it will come to that. We shall see what happens in time." They sat for a while, finishing the tea and nibbling on some cookies that Pearl had baked. Pearl left the room for a while and told Sapphire to relax while she gathered fresh herbs to make new potions for her. Sitting in the kitchen alone Sapphire looked around, and wondered how she had ever ended up in such a place. The information she had just gained was buzzing around her head. She was trying desperately to live a normal life, but nothing was normal any more. Pearl was right: she could sense the changes taking place within her. Everything felt different. A new awareness was growing and she could feel her body shifting with it.

Pearl returned with a bag full of herbs; she gave them to Sapphire and reached for her to give her a motherly hug. "Go home now, Sapphire. Enjoy the rest of your day and take time to rest and nurture yourself." Sapphire stood to leave, and tucked the bag inside her hoody so that it would not get wet in the rain which was still falling quite steadily from the sky. She headed out the door of Foxglove and down the garden path; she knew Pearl was watching her in the doorway. At the gate she turned to wave and noticed that Pearl was glowing slightly against the door frame. Magic. It was all around her and she could see it clearly now. The second sight she now had was as clear as day. It was like seeing someone for the first time, and the picture of Pearl glowing in a soft gold was breathtaking. She smiled and raised her hand to wave goodbye. "I'll see you again soon, Pearl. Thank you." Sapphire walked home with her bag of herbs and a slightly lighter heart. At least the future looked brighter than she had thought this morning.

By the time she had reached her cottage the rain had stopped and the sky was looking less ominous. Entering the cottage, she could hear movement upstairs. "Hey, Charlie, it's me. I'm back." Charlie came down the stairs looking slightly the worse for wear; her usual sparkle was definitely on the back burner today. She scratched her head sleepily. "Hey, Saf. I wondered where you were. Have you been to see Pearl?" Sapphire went into the kitchen to put the kettle on. Tea made everything better. "Yeah, she's a nice old lady, I just needed to ground with something normal for a minute."

Charlie shuffled in to the kitchen, dressed in a pink fluffy onesie that made her look much younger than her actual years. "Mmmh, normality – something I'm finding difficult today. Are you making tea?" Sapphire nodded. She was actually feeling a lot better, and her energy had lifted greatly since her visit to Pearl. "What are you guys doing today?" Charlie yawned and sat at the kitchen table. "Not much, hon … probably just chill today, unpack the car later…Nathan crashed hard last night … might go into town tomorrow, do a bit of shopping. We need food and I could do with some new undies."

Sapphire laughed. Shopping was Charlie's favourite pastime. "Can I come with you tomorrow?" The kettle clicked off, and Sapphire busied herself making fresh tea for them both. "Yeah, sure. I was also thinking that at some point we could go down to the farm in the next village and pick ourselves some new chooks. I'm already missing the fresh eggs." Sapphire smiled, handing, her a mug of steaming tea. "Sounds good."

Charlie blew on the tea before taking a sip. "Are you going to see Fox this week before you go back to work?" Sapphire sat opposite her, watching her friend's expression change into a subtle question. "I'm not sure. Possibly." Charlie eyed her suspiciously. "Getting cold feet already, Saf?" Sapphire laughed. "No, not at all, it's just that he is a little unpredictable. I'm never really sure when he will be around ... don't want to push him too much." Charlie smiled softly. "Ah ... the mysterious sexy man, eh? Yeah, you don't want to scare him off by being too keen, eh?" Sapphire sipped her tea, smiling... if only Charlie knew the complications of her new relationship. It was hard for her not being able to share the secrets with her friend, but she knew it would just blow Charlie's mind if she revealed all. Plus it would put Charlie in an even more dangerous position than she was already in by being around Sapphire.

They sat at the kitchen table and chatted about normal stuff for a while, going over the weekend and the fun they had at the festival; it now seemed like a long time ago. After their tea and Charlie finishing two rounds of toast they decided to put some washing on and make a start on the car. Charlie went back upstairs to wake Nathan, whom she needed to help shift some of the heavier stuff. The rest of the afternoon passed by quickly as they unloaded the tents and supplies they had taken to the festival, sorting out where everything should be stored and washing their dirty clothes.

As Sapphire loaded the machine for the second time she paused as she held the pink bustier and gypsy skirt in her hand. It brought back memories of dancing with Fox and all the wonderful things that had happened between them. She felt a hot flush of arousal run through her body. God, she missed him already.

It was a normal day and they did normal things. The sun came out again later in the afternoon and they sat in the garden for a while, chatting and laughing, Nathan was feeling just as jaded today and they did very little else after that. Sapphire had started to feel a little more relaxed, in the knowledge that Pearl had given her more herbs and that the Tarot had given her some positive news for the future. She pondered over parts of the reading: the love commitment, possible marriage and moving of residence. Could that really happen to her? The way her life had been lately anything seemed possible.

The daylight hours were moving on and before Sapphire knew it the day was over. She had managed to get all the washing done and was cooking dinner for them all. Tuna pasta was all she could find in the cupboard: they really did need to get some food shopping. Charlie and Nathan were still on a comedown and had hunkered down again in the living room in front of the TV. Sapphire was glad she did not feel quite so jaded. She was also glad the weather had changed again. For early July it was certainly a little changeable at the moment – good old English weather.

She wondered absently as she stirred the boiling pasta if she could focus on it being a long, hot summer for them all. Now that was a thought. After the pasta had boiled and she had spread it into a dish with the tuna and sauce she grated some cheese. Turning the grill on to hot she lifted the dish and turned around to place it under the grill.

Fox was standing in the kitchen leaning back on the counter, his arms crossed in front of him, his long, lean legs crossed at the ankles. Sapphire jumped an inch off the ground and nearly dropped the dish on the floor. "Fuck." Fox jumped forward to steady her. He was laughing. "Oh, my God, Fox. Please stop doing that." He helped her guide the dish under the grill and hugged her tightly to his chest from behind. She closed her eyes for a moment and just let him hold her; his warmth and smell enveloped her and she sighed with happiness. "I could not wait for you to sleep, my love. I wanted to be with you."

Sapphire turned herself around and wrapped her arms around his neck, looking up into his eyes, which flashed deep amber and gold. "I've missed you." He kissed her softly in response. The kiss was a good one and only interrupted by a soft cough at the kitchen door. "Hi, Fox. When did you get here?" Sapphire broke away from him and peeked over his shoulder. Charlie was still in her onesie standing in the door frame, a big smile plastered on her face. Fox released his hold on her slowly and turned around, draping his arm over her shoulder. "Good evening, Charlie. How are you feeling tonight?" Charlie sauntered over – putting on the charm – to grab a bottle of wine, her eyes watching him with each step.

Fox was watching her with amusement. Her strange outfit was making him want to laugh out loud but he felt that would definitely be offensive as she was flirting somewhat with him. "I've felt better: nothing I didn't expect. Are you staying for dinner?" He raised an eyebrow and looked down at Sapphire. "Why not?" Sapphire felt her heart start to flutter in her chest. He was doing it again; interacting with her normal human life like it was the most natural thing in the world. "Cool. Do you two want some wine?" Sapphire nodded. She could do with a drink now: her body was doing an internal shimmy dance and a smile had crept on to her lips. "That would be nice," Fox responded, in a soft, warm, teasing voice.

Charlie uncorked the bottle and grabbed some glasses from the cabinet. "I wondered when you might come and visit Sapphire again. She was missing you today." Sapphire felt the familiar blush travel up from her neck on to her cheeks. Fox squeezed her and kissed the top of her head. "The feeling was mutual. I had some time free so thought I would drop by and make sure you were all OK." Charlie poured the wine expertly, looking quite funny in her pink outfit, trying to be provocative. "Our own personal bodyguard for the night. How exciting." He laughed, and Sapphire wanted to punch Charlie for her teasing.

Realising the pasta was still under the grill she grabbed some oven gloves and pulled it out before it burnt. Fox sat down at the kitchen table watching her with sexy eyes, a sly smile on his lips. Charlie passed him a glass of wine. "Cheers." They chinked glasses and Fox smiled his easy smile at her. Charlie giggled a little; she was turning into a giddy teenager around him. "Give Nathan a nudge, Charlie. Dinner's ready." Snapping out of her hormonal spell Charlie sipped the wine and left the kitchen, smiling her own sexy smile at Fox as she left. When she had left the room Sapphire laughed loudly. "Do you have that effect on all the women you meet?" He regarded her with an innocent expression over the rim of his glass as he sipped the red wine. "I don't know. Do I?" Sapphire shook her head, the smile still on her lips. Her hands were shaking slightly with the excitement of having him in her space again.

Dishing up the food, she took her own drink and sat next to him at the table. Charlie and Nathan came back into the kitchen. Nathan still looked slightly dishevelled but smiled warmly as he clocked Fox sitting at the table. "Hey, man. Good to see you again. I didn't hear the doorbell ring." Fox smiled at him, the lie he was about to tell coming easily from his lips. "I came in the back. Sapphire let me in."

They sat at the table and began to tuck in. Their appetites were most obviously back, despite the comedown. Fox ate with them, Sapphire watching him from under her eyelashes, her face tipped down to avoid staring. He seemed quite at home. She noticed the blue hazy aura around him was filtered with sparks of silver that moved around him like fireflies; he certainly looked recharged.

He smiled at her softly between mouthfuls. Charlie munched happily between sips of wine. She regarded Fox across the table. "So – apart from your work – what interests do you have, Fox?" Sapphire held her breath for his answer. "I like beautiful women and magic." She laughed a little too loudly and everyone stared at her. "Magic?" Charlie said, a little amused. "What kind of magic?" Nathan was chomping loudly on his second helping of pasta. "Kids' party magic or Dynamo magic, Fox?" Charlie giggled.

Fox looked at them both with a blank expression for a beat, then smiled. "The kind that makes you think and explore the endless possibilities of life itself." Charlie stopped eating, her mouth slightly open. "Wow. That does sound impressive. Perhaps you can show us some later." Sapphire was trying not to burst out in hysterical laughter; she stifled it between mouthfuls of food. Fox turned his head to her and licked his lips slowly. "If you like." They finished the meal in silence, a weird kind of atmosphere hanging in the air between them. Sapphire was not sure if it was her or the joining of their energies, or the fact that he seemed such a mystery to Charlie and Nathan, who were smiling at each other with that "What the fuck?" look. After dinner Charlie told Sapphire and Fox to go and relax in the lounge while she cleared up with Nathan. She winked at Sapphire as they left the kitchen and licked her lips suggestively.

Sapphire raised her eyebrows at her. Fox took her hand and led the way. She watched him move like a big cat into the lounge. He was dressed in jeans again, with a long-sleeved, fitted black top that showed all his muscles in the right places. Fit. He made himself comfortable on the chair by the window and patted his thighs, indicating she should sit on his lap. She stood and looked at him for a moment before smiling and jumping on. He pulled her into him, arranging her legs across the arm of the chair. She nuzzled into his neck, holding him tightly. They sat in silence for a moment.

"Are you OK, Sapphire? I sense some anxiety in that pretty head of yours." She smiled, winding her fingers around a lock of his hair and breathing in his scent. "I'm OK. I visited Pearl today. She helped me feel a little better." He took her other hand and kissed her fingertips, sending shivers down her arm. "What is troubling you?"

She could hear Charlie and Nathan laughing in the kitchen. "I had another dream yesterday. When we got home from the festival I took a nap and I dreamt about Hecta again." She had his full attention now and felt his body tense slightly. "Tell me." Sapphire could feel her breathing quicken as she recalled the dream. "I was observing rather than participating, as I normally do in a dream. I saw Hecta with a woman. I could not see her face; she had her back to me. They were talking about me. She was angry with him because he had failed in bringing me to her."

Fox swung his head around so that he could face her properly. "What do you mean?" Sapphire could not look him in the eye. She felt her bottom lip tremble a little. "I don't know. I'm not sure what she meant, but she said that I would be most vulnerable here on Earth and that he should plan his next move carefully." Fox was looking straight at her; he raised her head with his hand gently and made her look at him. "No one will harm you, Sapphire. I will never let that happen." She nodded and smiled weakly. "I know. It was just a very strange and scary dream. I woke up after that." He closed his eyes for a moment and let out a deep sigh. Opening them again, he leant in to kiss her; it was a hard kiss, filled with passion. She gripped him tightly, understanding his unspoken words.

"Can't leave you two for a minute without you sucking face." Charlie was back in the lounge, smiling at them. Sapphire blushed again. Fox brushed her cheek gently with the back of his hand. "Fancy showing us some of that magic now, Fox?" Nathan was standing with Charlie, holding her hips from behind, his chin resting on her shoulder. They were both staring at him, waiting for a response. Fox laughed softly. "Of course." Charlie clapped her hands and skipped to the sofa, Nathan following. Fox kissed Sapphire softly before lifting her legs from him; she stood up so that he could get up from the chair. He uncurled himself, the big cat again – or should that be the big fox?

Sapphire settled into the chair, wondering what the hell would happen next. Fox stood and faced them, ready for the show. He smiled at Charlie. "OK. Give me something, a piece of jewellery or an item you hold dear to you." Charlie laughed. "Are you going to make it disappear?" Fox smiled at her, his legs positioned slightly wider than his hips giving him a look of strength and power. "Maybe." Nathan laughed and took off his watch. Leaning forward, he handed it to Fox. "Here, use this. Charlie is too scared to give you anything of hers." Charlie nudged him in complaint.

Fox turned the watch over in his hand, inspecting it. Sapphire watched with anticipation. He held the watch in the palm of his hand and brought his hand out in front of his body so that they could all see it. "OK. Keep your eyes on the watch. Don't stop focusing on it. Imagine it changing shape, moving before you. Keep the image in your head." Sapphire felt like her eyes would pop out of their sockets any minute; she was gripping the arms of the chair tightly. Charlie was giggling softly. As Sapphire looked more closely at the watch she saw a shimmer in the air around it; as she focused more intently she saw it begin to twitch on the palm of his hand. Charlie stopped giggling. The watch started to lift up from the palm of his hand so that it was suspended in the air about two inches from his skin. It started to rotate in a circle, slowly at first, then faster and faster.

Sapphire heard both Charlie and Nathan gasp in surprise. She could make no sound. She was utterly speechless. As the watch turned so fast it began to blur out of shape. The air shimmered and pulsed around it. Without warning she heard a pop in her ears and the watch fell back down on to his palm, but it was not a watch now. It was a gold ring, chunky and decorated with diamonds. Nathan shook his head. Charlie was just gawping. "No way, man. That's totally fucking crazy. I was thinking about my old man's ring; it's gold with diamonds. No way." Fox just smiled and handed it back to Nathan.

Charlie was still stunned to silence. Sapphire did not know whether to laugh or cry. Charlie whispered softly, "Am I still on drugs? That wasn't magic. It's fuckin' unreal." Nathan was turning the ring over in his hand, inspecting it, with a big grin on his face. He looked up at Fox, who was also smiling a rather large smug smile. "Can you magic it back to my watch?" Fox laughed and stepped forward. Taking the ring back, he held his hands together, the ring now hidden inside. He winked at them and then blew into his hands. Opening them again he revealed the watch, back to normal.

Charlie shot up and grabbed it out of his hands. "No way. No way. That's mental." Nathan was laughing loudly. Sapphire started to laugh, too – this was just too damn freaky – but they seemed to be enjoying the show. Charlie was standing right in front of him, a frown on her face as she looked at the watch that had returned to being a watch again in her hand. She was shaking her head. Nathan was laughing softly. "That was one hell of a show, man. How do you learn something like that?" Fox returned to Sapphire and she stood up so that they could return to their former position, curled around each other. "Practice, and a little faith." He kissed Sapphire softly on the lips. She could not help but smile at him as he pulled away from her, his eyes dark and sparkling.

The rest of the evening passed with music and wine. Charlie and Nathan chatted about the festival and, luckily, neither of them brought up the incident with Hecta again. Sapphire remained unusually silent, giving only the briefest of input when needed. Fox also talked only when directly spoken to. His eyes were permanently fixed on her; he kissed her every now and then softly between conversations – just a gentle reminder that he was always there, holding her, protecting her.

Eventually Sapphire decided enough was enough. She needed some time alone with her magical man. "I think I'm ready for bed, Charlie. We are going to head up now; see you tomorrow." Charlie smiled across at her with that knowing smile, a somewhat envious tilt to her brow. "Of course, honey. See you two tomorrow. It's been fun, Fox. Glad you came over."

Fox lifted Sapphire up and placed her on to her feet in one graceful sweep. She caught her breath and he took her hand, interlocking his fingers with hers. Leading the way again out of the room he paused, and looked back at Charlie and Nathan curled up together on the sofa.

"It's been a pleasure to spend time with you both. Sleep well."

They smiled back a little crazily, not sure how to respond to his weird way of talking.

Sapphire trailed behind him, waving, with a wobbly smile on her lips. Her legs were feeling a little shaky. As they reached the bottom of the stairs Fox faced her and swept her off her feet into his arms. She gasped as he cradled her in his arms and carried her up the stairs, his eyes fixed on her own. Silently he reached her bedroom and kicked the door open with his foot, making Sapphire feel like she were some damsel in distress about to be devoured. She certainly hoped she would be devoured. He dropped her on to the bed and turned to close the curtains. She watched him, a little breathless.

"I need a minute, Fox. I won't be long."

He turned around and nodded without speaking his face lit up with amusement. She jumped up off the bed and headed to the bathroom, her body on automatic pilot. She stood in front of the bathroom mirror and looked at her reflection. She looked back at herself and was amazed at the bright-eyed, slightly flushed woman staring at her – eyes big, wide and blue, shining like two large gems. Sapphires. Shaking herself back to reality she brushed her teeth and took a pee. She undressed quickly and took the fastest shower humanly possible; she wanted to feel squeaky clean before returning to her man.

Opening her bedroom door dressed only in a towel she found Fox sprawled out on the bed before her; he had removed his shirt and was wearing only his jeans and a smile sexy enough to make her toes curl. She closed the door softly behind her and walked over to her bed. He had lit some candles and her incense was burning on her dresser. He patted the bed beside him and shifted over so that she had room to lie beside him. Dropping the towel to the floor with no shame she climbed naked on to the bed. His eyes followed her with appreciation – predatory eyes, dark with lust.

As she slipped down beside him he turned on to his side and traced a line with his fingers across her lip, down her neck, across her breast to her stomach. Sapphire closed her eyes and trembled.

"Open your eyes, Sapphire. Look at me." She did. He flipped himself on to all fours above her in the fastest move she had ever seen. He blurred for a second – most definitely part vampire. He grinned at her, his hair falling forward across his face in a wild tumble of braids and beads. God, this man was sexy with a capital S. She felt her chest rise and fall in quick succession. He was watching her, tracing patterns across her skin with just his gaze. The silence and stillness was unbearable.

"Undo my trousers, Sapphire." She gulped and reached out to unbutton him. He watched her the whole time, never moving his gaze, burning a hole of desire into her. She lowered the zip slowly. He pushed himself up and knelt before her, his jeans undone to his waist. She could see the soft, dark hair from his navel trail down to the place of forbidden treasures. He smiled at her lazily before shimmying them down to his knees, uncovering his wonderful, amazing cock that unleashed itself like a spring-loaded cannon waiting to be fired. She felt like giggling. She was nervous, for some reason, as if this was the first time they had been together. She realised that every time felt like the first. Falling back down on to all fours he kicked the jeans off his lower legs until he was naked in all his beautiful glory before her. She could see his cock bob gently as he moved up her body … so close, but not quite touching. She was on fire again, lit up like a shining star. Every particle of her body was quivering with anticipation.

He leant down and began to kiss her, softly at first, his body still an inch from hers. She could feel his heat against her; the energy around him caressed her own, teasing and sensual. The kiss became fevered and she fell into the deep, wonderful pool of Fox. Her own body began to move now, her internal fire rising up, causing her to grip tightly to his buttocks. He remained steadfast, inches above her, waiting, teasing, making her whimper softly between his kisses.

As she began to feel slightly light-headed and, just as she couldn't take the pressure building up in her groin any more, he slid down very softly on top of her. With the gentlest of movements he pushed himself into the very outer edges of her pussy. She was more than happy to invite him in; her body was soft and palpable, like butter warmed to the point of melting.

He raised his head slowly and looked at her with a smile on his lips. "Are you ready, Sapphire?"

She nodded, still gripping him tightly. Without hesitation he pushed himself fully inside her, making her gasp out loud and fling her head back against the pillow. He pushed his hands into her hair and held her in place as he began to fuck her with the perfect rhythm and depth to send her off into pleasure heaven. Moving down to her breast he sucked and teased her, while his cock continued to slide in and out of her body. Sapphire was trembling now, out of control.

She could feel her climax start to rise inside her. He continued to pound her relentlessly, his tongue tracing white-hot fire over her nipples. Her muscles began to contract and she came quickly with a ferociousness that surprised even her. She continued to tremble beneath him, her climax still quivering within. He held her against him and lifted his head so that he could watch her face. His breathing was hard and heavy and she could see him shift before her eyes as his energy changed. Sparks of white shot from his body and she watched him wrestle with the flames that began to erupt across his skin. He came hard, so hard she felt them lift off the bed – so that for a moment they were suspended in the air in white light. He growled loudly and cried out her name, followed by words in his language that she did not understand.

Landing back on the bed with a bounce Sapphire gasped for breath. Fox was flat against her. The air smelt suffused with smoke, as if they truly had just been on fire. She started to laugh softly; he was heavy on her chest, pinning her down.

Slowly he lifted himself up and smiled down at her. "You are magnificent, Sapphire, magnificent." He rolled over so that he could lie on his back; she was unable to move at that precise moment but continued to laugh gently. He joined her and before long they were laughing loudly, Sapphire running her hands through her tangled hair in an attempt to bring some reality back into her mind.

Fox pulled her into his side and wrapped his arms around her, kissing her cheek ... her neck ... her hair ... over and over, between her peals of laughter. "You have officially fucked me silly, Fox." They held each other close and recovered their breath before Fox pulled the duvet up over their naked bodies and stroked her gently, lulling her into a slow, drifting, peaceful sleep. Sated and satisfied, they were both totally unaware of the danger heading their way in the darkness, slipping silently into the shadows, waiting to make its move.

Chapter Thirty-Three

Fox jumped up suddenly, on full alert, his energy expanding outwards into warrior mode. The room was dark. The candles he had lit earlier were long extinguished but he could see clearly in the dark. Sapphire was sleeping beside him. He could smell smoke; it was snaking under the door from the hallway. Reaching out in his mind he could sense a fire downstairs, which was clearly in full force. He dressed quickly and put his hand up against the door to feel for any heat. The door was cool to touch but he could feel the fire's intensity on the ground floor. Someone – or something – was smoking them out.

His mind began to spin with thinking about what action to take. He had to get everyone out of the cottage. Opening the door just slightly the smoke rushed in, engulfing him for a moment. He slammed it shut quickly and gathered his magic around him, creating a bubble of oxygen. He moved back to the bed and grabbed Sapphire, shaking her roughly.

"Sapphire, wake up quickly. We have to leave." She mumbled in her drowsy state, her eyes fluttering open. "What? What's wrong?" He literally pulled her up out of the bed. She woke up quickly at his insistence, her eyes wide and frightened. "Put your clothes on: there is a fire downstairs. I will get Charlie and Nathan. Hurry."

Sapphire scrambled out of the bed, grabbing clothes that were on the floor. He had switched on the light and she was squinting at the sudden brightness in the room. Fox moved quickly to the room across the hall. Sensing that Charlie and Nathan were in a deep sleep, he threw the light on.

"Charlie, Nathan … Get up now. There is a fire downstairs; we have to get out." Charlie opened her eyes, her body jerking in response to the intrusion. She stared at Fox wide-eyed for a moment, not registering what was happening.

"Quickly, Charlie: you must get dressed now." Charlie grabbed Nathan, who was still snoring softly, and shook his shoulder. "Nathan, wake up. Wake up, babe."

Fox dashed back towards Sapphire's room and found her standing in the doorway looking like a ghost. "What's going on, Fox?"

He grabbed her arms and looked at her with a seriousness she had not seen in him before.

"Hecta has been here. The downstairs lounge is on fire; it is burning quickly. We have to get out before the whole cottage sets alight." She gasped, trembling now. Charlie and Nathan appeared at their doorway, Nathan pulling his jeans up hastily. They both stared at Fox, who looked down the stairs. The smoke was gathering in momentum now, curling up the stairway in slow grey wisps that had started to rise above waist height.

Fox closed his eyes and reached out with his mind to sense the damage. He could see the whole downstairs lounge burning brightly. The flames were licking up the walls. Thankfully, they had shut the stairs door before going to bed. Sapphire grabbed his arm. "Fox, what should we do? Can we get out?"

Charlie was starting to whimper now, Nathan holding her into his chest trying to soothe her. "Not that way. We will have to climb out the window. You need to get help to put out the fire." Sapphire nodded. "Charlie, where is your mobile?" Charlie was beginning to cry softly. Nathan looked up. "It's next to her bed, Saf." Before Fox could stop her she pushed passed them into Charlie's room. The smoke was getting thicker now: it made her eyes smart but she visualised a protective barrier around her and pushed the smoke away as she dashed to the bedside cabinet to find the mobile phone. Grabbing it quickly, she ran back into the hallway and nodded to Fox. "Got it."

Fox grabbed Charlie and Nathan by the arms. "This way. Follow me." They did without hesitation and shut the door firmly behind them to stop any more smoke entering the room. Standing in Sapphire's bedroom, Fox began to strip the bed. Pulling the sheet off the mattress, he then removed the duvet cover and tied it to the end of the sheet.

"Nathan, open the window. Help me get this out. You go first: I will anchor this end. You help the girls get down." Sapphire was on the phone; she had dialled 999 and was now speaking in a rushed, scared voice to the operator. "Yes, that's right, a fire. We need help. The address is Rookery Cottage, 6, Mulberry Lane. OK. Thank you. Please hurry."

Fox and Nathan were hanging the sheets out of the window. Nathan was looking down at the ground with a frown on his face: the smoke was growing in thick clouds now and, despite the door being closed, it pushed under the gap with a frightening intensity. Charlie was standing still, looking totally shell-shocked. "I don't understand. Everything was switched off when we came to bed. I don't smoke in the house; how can there be a fire?" Sapphire grabbed her and hugged her tightly. "It's OK, Charlie. It will be OK." Nathan was looking back at the girls and then at Fox somewhat fearfully. "It's a long way down, Fox."

Fox held the end of the sheet and placed his hand on Nathan's shoulder. "I've got you. You won't fall ... now go." Nathan nodded, looking over at Charlie, who stared at him with scared doe-eyes. He stepped up on to the window ledge and grabbed the sheet. Fox held on and closed his eyes. Sapphire could see the air around him start to ripple and she knew he was using his magic to steady Nathan and prevent him from falling. Nathan backed out of the window slowly, using the sheet to climb down, his head disappearing as he moved down the outside wall of the cottage. The girls stood holding each other tightly, Sapphire keeping an eye on the amount of smoke coming under her door. It was starting to fill the room and Charlie was coughing now. Nathan shouted up loudly, "I'm down."

Fox nodded at Charlie, "You next. Quickly, Charlie." Charlie was not moving. She had gone into shock very quickly. Sapphire grabbed her arms and turned her so that she could look at her properly. "Charlie, come on. I'll be right behind you. We have to get out." Charlie nodded, speechless. Sapphire all but lifted her over to the window, Fox helping her to stand on the ledge. She was shaking now. "I can't do it. I'm afraid of heights." Fresh tears were forming in her eyes.

Fox took her hand and placed it on the sheet. "Grab this. Just slide down. I will not let you fall ... remember the magic? I can help you; trust me." Charlie nodded, her bottom lip trembling, as the tears began to slip down her cheeks. Sapphire felt her own tears begin to rise up. She hated seeing her friend so afraid: she knew this was all her fault and that Hecta was trying to trap her. Lifting Charlie up on to the window ledge Fox held her with one hand, the other gripping the sheet. The air around him shimmered again for a moment and then Charlie was gone. Sapphire heard her shriek in fright as he sent her down the side of the house, most likely using magic rather than her ability to walk down the wall. He looked back at Sapphire. "Now you, Sapphire. Quickly, my love."

Sapphire nodded and stepped up on to the window ledge. She was glad she had put her trainers on rather than go barefoot. He kissed her on the lips before she stepped out. Sapphire felt a warm rush of air around her and, rather than having to grip on to the sheets as Nathan had, she was suddenly standing on the grass in the garden next to Charlie and Nathan. Another second passed before Fox stood next to her; she did not even see him exit through the window. He pulled her into his arms and held her firmly against his chest.

The lower part of the cottage was now lit up in an eerie orange glow. The entire ground floor was on fire. Charlie and Nathan had moved back further down the garden as the heat began to build up. Fox pulled Sapphire back with him, knowing that at any minute the windows would most likely shatter. As they stood huddled in the garden watching the horrible event unfolding before them Sapphire could hear sirens in the distance, moving closer and closer. Everything seemed to be in slow motion. Charlie was weeping loudly now, crying out, "My house. Oh, my God. My house." Nathan was trying to soothe her but was obviously as shocked as she was.

Sapphire felt like her whole world had been turned upside down. In front of her the cottage burned brightly, the windows starting to shatter with the added oxygen. The flames licked up with a roaring sound to the upstairs of the cottage. Sapphire watched in horror. How could this be happening so quickly? The cottage was being consumed in a matter of minutes. She could hear the fire engine pull up in the street and people starting to shout out from outside the other cottages either side of them. Nathan was trying to pull Charlie further away; she looked like she would crumple any second. Fox held Sapphire tightly, but she sensed something else in the air around them, a new shifting of energy separate from the fire. Fox sensed it too and he suddenly went very stiff. Hecta.

"We need to leave now." Fox pulled her back into the shadows of the garden. Sapphire was so afraid she nearly stumbled and fell over as he pulled her backwards. "Nathan. Get Charlie out of the garden. Take her over the fence if you have to. Use the chairs to climb over. We will meet you out front." Fox barked the order at Nathan who nodded in response, grabbing Charlie by the arm and taking her across to the far side fence. Sapphire watched him take one of the garden chairs and push Charlie up and then over the fence. She was protesting loudly but he was persistent, and then he jumped over with her.

Once they were out of sight Fox took Sapphire by the hand and led her to the very end of the garden. She could feel the ripples of power around him pulsing angrily. Suddenly, out of the darkness, Hecta stepped into their escape path. She stopped abruptly, bumping into Fox. She gasped loudly in fright. Fox let go of her hand and pushed her back slightly, ready for a fight.

Hecta was armed this time, with a long chain which he was swinging around his head. The smile on his face dark and ominous. "You cannot save her, Guardian. You are weak on this planet."

Fox did not seem to be bothered by the taunt. He launched himself at Hecta and dodged the chain as Hecta swung it around his head. Sapphire watched with horror as they made full contact, the air around them bending and swirling with flashes of white light. They became a blur, Sapphire cringing as she heard the clash of bodies and the crunch of flesh and bone as it made contact. Behind her Sapphire could hear glass shattering and the shouts of the firemen who were out front trying to control the fire. She looked up at the sky that was as black as ink; there was no lightning to harness tonight. Her body was shaking uncontrollably now; she was frightened and angry. Fox and Hecta were fighting on the ground, beating the hell out of each other. She wanted to scream at them both. Distracted by the fire and by the two men in front of her Sapphire did not sense the new presence behind her.

A warm pulse started to pound steadily against her chest. The obsidian necklace was on full alert. Sapphire spun around and was faced with a new opponent. A figure shrouded in darkness – clothed in a long dark hooded cloak – stood in front of her. Before she could react the figure reached out and touched her. She felt her energy shift and tremble and – without warning – felt herself being pulled almost out of her body, upwards, rushing so quickly it made her feel sick. It was like being propelled through a dark tunnel, a wormhole, into another realm.

Sapphire reached out for Fox, screamed out his name. The darkness enveloped her and she felt her head begin to crush inwards at the pressure that was building. She could not see a thing; her eyes were pinned shut by some invisible force and she felt herself spinning in the darkness. The hand that had reached out for her was gripping her arm tightly and pain travelled up from the fingers that were pushing into her flesh. Her mind flashed with the image of Fox trying to reach out for her; she felt his anguish and pain. Without warning the spinning stopped and she landed hard on a very cold solid surface. It knocked the wind from her and her head smacked back with a loud thump. Everything stopped still. There was no sound … nothing, and then Sapphire lost consciousness. Again.

Chapter Thirty-Four

Sapphire regained her senses slowly, coming to. She was lying flat on her back. Her body felt like it was pinned down by a very heavy weight. She tried to lift her head but it was too painful, making her cry out. As she opened her eyes she became aware of her new surroundings: she was in a cage, a dim light to her left casting shadows up the wall that flickered like flames. The fire. Her brain switched on and she let out a loud gasp, sitting up suddenly and panting for breath. Where was she?

Gradually her vision began to clear. There was a fire in the room, but she was not watching her home burning down. It was in the cave she remembered seeing in her dream, when she had watched Hecta and the woman discuss her. Her head was pounding now, the pain intense. She brought her hand to the back of her neck and felt a warm sticky wetness. It made her feel a little sick. She could see shapes across from the fire … movement.

Her eyes grew wide as she realised that Fox was on the other side of the fire. He was held up against the wall by chains, his arms above his head, which fell limply down towards his chest. He was out cold. She started to shiver uncontrollably. Was this real? Out of the shadows a woman stepped towards her; she was beautiful and intimidating at the same time. The hood of her cloak was down and Sapphire could see her clearly now as she walked towards the cage. Long black hair cascaded around her shoulders. Her face was young and serene; cherry-red lips curled into a wicked smile that made Sapphire back up on her backside further away.

The woman bent down to look through the cage bars. Her smile grew wider. Sapphire could see her energy flickering around her, dark swirls of red and black interlaced with flashes of gold. She was powerful, very powerful. "Hello, Sapphire. What a pleasure to finally meet you in the flesh." Sapphire frowned. "Who the fuck are you? Why have you brought me here?" The woman laughed, showing perfect white teeth. "Humans … how funny you are." Sapphire tried to calm her energy; she did not want to appear weak in front of this creature, whatever she was. Maybe she was actually dreaming the whole thing. Fox had not really woken her up earlier to a house that was burning down; she was not really here in a cage in a dark cave. She was at home, safely snuggled up in bed with Fox, sleeping soundly. This was just a dream. Of course it was.

The woman stopped smiling and brought her face closer to the bars. A slight snarl began to form on her beautiful Cupid's bow lips. "You are here for one purpose only, Sapphire, and that is to fulfil your destiny … to give me what I have been looking for … something that is very precious, something that you cannot even begin to understand." Sapphire could feel her anger begin to rise inside, pulsing softly, growing stronger and stronger. "What have you done to Fox? Release me from this cage now."

Sapphire was willing herself to wake up. This was not a dream: it was a fucking nightmare. Pearl had told her that she could control her travelling; it was her will that made it so. She began to draw her power from within her and harness it to make everything go away. The woman raised an eyebrow and tilted her head to one side, as if she sensed this change in energy. She stood up and stepped back slightly. "My, my. You are an interesting thing, aren't you?"

Sapphire was getting more and more pissed off now. Pushing herself up, she crawled towards the front of the cage on all fours and grabbed the bars in both hands. She narrowed her eyes at the woman, who was standing very still in front of her. "Let me out now, or I will make you let me out." The woman laughed. "Oh, please, my dear Sapphire. You have no idea who you are talking to, or what I am capable of. Stop fighting and relax. It will all be over for you very soon."

She turned her back on Sapphire and walked around the fire towards Fox. Sapphire watched her walk up to him and trail her finger down his cheek. She looked over her shoulder, a new smile on her lips. Lust. "I shall enjoy claiming your guardian as my own when you are gone. He will make a good plaything for me." Now she had done it. Sapphire's button was pushed full on and she flexed her energy outwards, visualising the bars snapping and this very irritating and clearly up-her-own-arse woman on her backside after Sapphire had punched her in the face.

Sapphire heard a loud popping noise in her ears and the bars began to shake. She gripped them tighter and with a shudder and groan they snapped; the front of the cage tilted forward and then slammed down on to the ground with a loud crash. She had let go just as it had started to tip forwards. Sapphire crawled out and stood up to her full height. The woman was still standing with Fox; her face was lit up by the fire and Sapphire noticed that her expression was now one of excitement. Sapphire just felt crazy-angry. She stepped forward towards the fire, scanning the cave quickly to look for Hecta. She realised he was nowhere to be seen.

Sapphire felt her energy swell inside her. She gathered it within, willing it to come at her command. Lifting her hands up, she focused on the flames from the fire and drew them towards her. Pulling the heat into her fingertips she watched as the flames rose and flickered, moving upwards and curling to join her. The woman moved cautiously, watching Sapphire with interested eyes. "Ah … the ability to harness the elements, Sapphire. How wonderful." Sapphire drew the fire up into her hand and held it there, watching with interest as it formed a ball within her palm. She looked across at the woman, at Fox still chained behind her, his face bruised and cut from a beating he had taken. Her anger swelled and gave her more confidence. "Move away from him now."

The woman stepped forward and smiled. Sapphire raised her hands and pushed the fireball out, aiming it at her with all the force she could muster. The fire rushed towards the woman in a loud whoosh. The woman raised her hand and batted it away; it fizzled out as it hit the cave wall. "Nice try, Sapphire, but you will have to do better than that." Sapphire felt deflated for a moment, but she was not defeated. Without hesitation she stepped forward again and gathered her power. "You want me to do better? I'll show you better."

Sapphire rushed towards her. She wanted nothing more than to take the smug smile off her face. The woman looked confused for a second as Sapphire rugby-tackled her to the ground. She had not been ready for Sapphire to actually try to bodily challenge her in a catfight. Sapphire grabbed her by the hair and pictured in her mind that she was strong and more than capable of fighting off this enemy. The woman gasped a little, taken by surprise, but threw Sapphire off easily with a surge of power that knocked her on to her backside. The woman stood up and shook herself as if irritated by a fly. Sapphire took a deep breath and pushed herself back up; her head was spinning now with what to do next.

There was only one thing she could do. Before the woman could react Sapphire ran to Fox and threw her arms around his waist. She held his body to her own and felt the warmth from him wash over her in a soothing caress. In her mind she pictured them back in his world, in his home, in the safety of his bedroom, lying on his bed wrapped around each other in a state of happiness. She willed it so. She felt a trembling in her chest; it grew as she focused on the image. Her love for him was so intense, so pure and clear that she drew on its magic and created a new surge of power.

She heard the woman cry out from behind her; she was rushing toward them now. Sapphire knew she could do this. She made it happen. Just as the woman reached out to grab her she felt the air around them shift and the energy changed. Sapphire and Fox were travelling together, across time and space, away from the cave and the woman who had held them there. Sapphire could sense Fox with her, their energies now intertwined, connected by the love they shared. She felt a huge pressure in her head build up to create a pure white light that filtered through her closed eyelids and blinded her. The white light consumed them both, brilliant and perfect. It pushed them through to his world, to the world of Shaka.

Sapphire opened her eyes. Fox was still in her arms, hanging limply against her. He was starting to regain consciousness. They were standing in his bedroom. She all but dragged him to his bed and dumped him on the mattress, his weight making the action a little difficult for her. Her breathing was coming out in fast gasps as she tried to calm herself again. Looking around the room she was grateful that they had made it back to his world, away from the cave and that horrible woman. Fox started to moan. His eyes were fluttering open and he rolled on to his side. "Fox … oh God … are you OK, Fox? Wake up."

He opened his eyes fully and stared at her, a frown on his forehead. He lifted his hand and touched her face as she stood over him. "My love, you are safe?" She breathed out a sigh of relief. "Yes, we are both safe, here in your bedroom. I brought us back here." He pushed himself up slowly, shaking his head. "After you disappeared Hecta trapped me in the chains and transported me. I could not defeat him; my strength was weakened from being with you on Earth. I am so sorry."

She sat down on the bed before her legs gave way beneath her. "You do not have to apologise. I think we were a little outnumbered and overpowered by the woman who was with him, and neither of us saw that coming." He pulled her into his arms and held her close. "I could not defend you, Sapphire, which is unforgivable." She looked up into his sad eyes. "Stop. Stop punishing yourself; we are safe now."

He pulled her into him, holding her tightly, pushing his head into her neck, breathing heavily now. It sounded like he was trying not to cry. She pushed him away gently and looked into his eyes. "Please don't, Fox. You did everything you could to save me. You saved my friends from being burnt to death; there was nothing more you could do." He shrugged, looking totally downtrodden, unlike anything she had ever seen in him before. "It does not matter what you say, Sapphire. I failed you as your guardian. It will never happen again. You must stay here where it is safe until we can work out what happened, who this woman was who took you from your world and who imprisoned me."

Sapphire stroked his hair, trying to soothe him. "I have to go back, Fox: I cannot stay here. Charlie needs me. Her house is gone … I need to find out if she is OK." Fox sat up abruptly and held her arms, gripping a little too tightly. "No, you cannot, it is not safe." Sapphire frowned. "Fox, I have to go back; there is no question about it. I can defend myself, you saw that – I brought us here. She underestimated me. I won't be caught out like that again." He released his grip and shook his head, battling with the idea. "I need to consult my father; he may know who she is. He may be able to help us."

Sapphire nodded. She desperately wanted to jump straight back to Earth, if she could even do that now; she had no idea how much time had passed since she had been in the cave and whether Charlie and Nathan were safe back on Earth or were still standing in the garden watching the cottage burn to the ground. The thought made her feel sick to her stomach. Fox stood up, his strength returning now. He was still battered and bruised but his expression was turning from despair to anger now. "I will call my father. Please stay here with me until I have spoken to him." Sapphire nodded. Her hands were still shaking and she felt like she had been hit by a truck.

Fox went to the balcony and stood motionless for a moment. She felt his energy change and a soft shimmer of white light rippled around him. He was obviously making a call, she thought with irony. Seconds later, as Sapphire remained sitting on the bed, a man appeared in the room with them. He stood towering over her, his eyes a deep amber with black rings that flashed with gold specks. There was no doubt he was Fox's father. Dressed in a deep purple robe he was a formidable figure and she gasped a little, surprised by his sudden appearance.

Fox strode back into the room. "Father, thank you for coming so quickly." The man nodded his head, his eyes remaining fixed on Sapphire – who was starting to feel a little uncomfortable under his stern scrutiny. "So this is the human dream traveller. You are indeed a beautiful woman, Sapphire. I can see why my son has fallen so hard for you." Sapphire felt her mouth open in an attempt to answer him, but nothing came out. "Father, a new predator has surfaced in Sapphire's life – a woman, working with Hecta – whom I have never seen before. She extracted both Sapphire and me from Earth and took us to some another realm that I am not familiar with, trying to trap us both. I do not know the reason why, but they burnt the house Sapphire has been living in to the ground, a move quite obviously meant to harm anyone who stood in their way."

The man remained still. Sapphire found that sweat was beginning to bead on her forehead. She felt like she was awaiting the headmaster's punishment after getting caught doing something very naughty at school. "I will need to reach into your mind, Sapphire, to recall the events, before I will be able to make any judgement or be of any help to you both." He took a step towards Sapphire, his arms now reaching out for her. She withdrew, afraid of him suddenly. "Do not be afraid, dream traveller. I mean you no harm." Fox was suddenly by her side, sitting next to her on the bed. He did not touch her but nodded, smiling, trying to make her feel more comfortable. "It is OK, Sapphire. He needs to touch you to see what has happened." Sapphire took a deep breath and looked up at the great man before her; she nodded her head slightly and closed her eyes.

She felt his hands rest softly either side of her head. Warm and soft to touch, they were not unlike Fox's gentle caress. Without warning her mind began to flash with images like a movie through her head; she watched from afar the last hour's events, which tumbled across her vision like a disturbing film ... waking up in her bed, with Fox urging her to get up and dressed ... standing at the window about to jump out ... watching the house burning brightly in the darkness from the garden. She then saw Hecta and Fox fighting and sensed the intrusion of the female behind her as she reached out to grab her ... the darkness that surrounded her as she was pulled through the wormhole ... then the woman standing before her as she sat in the cage, the struggle with the fireball and knocking the woman to the ground ... then her mad dash at Fox and her shifting of time and space as she willed them back to Shaka.

She gasped out loud as Fox's father released his hold from her head, and her eyes flew open in surprise. He regarded her solemnly, a deep frown on his face. "Her name is Ebony. She was a priestess serving our Oracle on this world a very long time ago. She was sent to exile after committing crimes on this planet that even I am unable to speak of; she is darkness personified and very powerful." Fox took Sapphire into his arms and held her close, kissing her head gently. His father stepped back and closed his eyes, taking a deep breath of his own.

"I do not know why she covets you so, Sapphire, but it must be something of great importance that you hold for her to move to your planet to trap you. The fact that she has enlisted Hecta's help is not a surprise; he would be easily brought for the right price." Fox growled softly, his energy rippling with anger. "I will not let them harm her, Father, but how can I keep her safe on her own planet? The energy there weakens me so." His father began to pace slowly, gracefully, like a panther, across the marble floor. "She will never be completely safe on Earth; the magic there has gone to ground and is buried deep within its mother. You are unable to feed from its source and this is why you, too, are vulnerable on Sapphire's home planet."

Sapphire watched him with anxiety swelling in her chest. "I have to go back; my friends need me." He turned to face her and smiled softly. "I understand your concern for them, Sapphire, but you must understand that the magic inside you is growing at an alarming rate. You are no longer technically human; you will find it more and more difficult to function in your own world. This is your destiny. It was always meant to be so; I see this now. Your connection to my son has intensified the magic and it cannot be undone. Events are unfolding now that even I cannot stop."

Sapphire stood up; she was getting agitated now. "Fuck this; fuck her. I need to go back and make sure my friends are OK. I am human. I have a life there; I have family and friends; I have a bloody job." Conloach regarded her with amusement now. Such passion, such anger; it really was quite amazing to watch. Fox stood up and tried to grab her arm. She shook him off. "Fox, don't try to stop me. I love you, I really do, but I have to go back. I need to clear my head, sort things out. I can't just stay here hiding from this Ebony woman, just because she is some crazy fucked-up priestess, damn it. I'm not going to let her scare me."

Sapphire realised she was shouting now and both men were staring at her like she was some animal that had gone a little bat shit crazy. Fox sighed and nodded. "And I would never stop you from doing whatever you pleased, my love, but I will not leave you to travel alone. I will come with you." Sapphire laughed shakily. "And get the shit kicked out of you again? No way; I'm not letting anyone else get hurt because of me."

Fox's father laughed now, a deep belly laugh. It made them both stop still for a moment and stare at him. "This woman has fire in her blood, Fox. I don't doubt her ability to take care of both of you. If she insists on returning to Earth then so be it. I will do my best to watch over you from here and protect you as much as I can, but first I must heal you both." Sapphire could feel her heart thumping loudly in her chest. Despite her bravado she was feeling decidedly light-headed. Fox reached for her cautiously and took her hand; she let him interlock his fingers with her own. "Please, Sapphire, let my father recharge and heal us. Then we can return together."

She felt the warmth of his love travel up her arm into her body and her legs started to give from under her. This was all too much. He swept her up then into his arms and she started to cry. He held her, whispering to her in his beautiful mysterious language, carrying her back over to the bed. She closed her eyes, just wanting everything to be normal again. None of this should be happening – the dreaming, the travelling, the crap that was going on around her – all the horrible things that were happening to the people she cared about. Fox stroked her cheek gently and kissed her lips tenderly. She felt a rush of warm air surround her and suddenly she really didn't care any more; it was if someone had turned off the light switch and nothing really mattered any more. She could just sleep for a little while and then deal with all the shit. The last thought that crossed her mind as she slipped into unconsciousness once more was that Fox's father also smelt like patchouli and sandalwood and how absolutely wonderful that was.

Chapter Thirty-Five

Wednesday

Charlie was wrapped up in a blanket one of the firemen had found for her. Nathan held her to him, rocking her gently. The fire had finally been put out and smoke now smouldered from the blackened frame of the cottage. They had managed to save the actual structure of the cottage and it had not spread to the cottages either side of them but the inside of her little cottage had been completely ravished by the fire. The fireman who stood talking to her was telling her that the upstairs had been saved but that pretty much all their belongings were now burnt to a crisp or ruined by smoke. She heard him say that her workshop out back was OK and that everything inside, including all her tools and computer, were undamaged. His voice continued to drone hazily into her head but she could no longer hear exactly what he was saying.

She was in total shock. Where the fuck had Sapphire and Fox disappeared again? Nathan had tried to find them but without much luck. An hour had passed since then and her neighbours had brought them sweet tea and sympathetic smiles.

Daylight was starting to filter gently over the horizon; it had been a long night. She wanted to just lie down and keel over. Nathan thanked the fireman for all the hard work they had done. She watched him head back to the rest of the crew, who were starting to coil up the long fire hoses. "I'm sure Saf will be back soon, Charlie. I saw her and Fox at the bottom of the garden before we went over the fence; he may have taken her with him somewhere." Charlie sniffed. Her face was smudged with black splodges from the smoke. "I wish she would just stop disappearing on me, Nathan. It's getting beyond a joke." He nodded and pulled her in closer, kissing her cheek.

"I need a smoke; can you get me one, Nat?" He laughed softly and nodded. "Yeah, I'm sure I can find someone who smokes. Stay here." She watched him leave into the crowd of people which had gathered outside the cottage, everyone standing around discussing how terrible it all was. She needed a stiff drink, too. Thank God she had insurance, but what the fuck? How had a fire started in her home? It didn't make any sense at all. She was scared, knackered and pissed off all at the same time. She was also thankful that they had got out alive, but confused as to how this had actually happened. Fox had saved them all but then whisked Sapphire off somewhere out of sight. There was definitely something odd about him; she just couldn't put her finger on it.

Nathan returned with a lit cigarette and as if he had read her mind a glass with amber-coloured liquid in it. "Here. Fred from next door thought you might need a whiskey. I got the fag from his wife; she is chain-smoking herself right now."

Charlie could not help but smile. Nathan could always make light of any situation. She took the cigarette from him and tugged on it greedily. The smoke filled her lungs and she felt instantly calmer. God bless nicotine. Taking a generous slug of the whiskey, she let out a big sigh. "Well at least all my insurance paperwork and cash is in the safe in my workshop. I'll have to get on the phone tomorrow and sort out all of this fucking mess."

Nathan sat back down next to her, watching her with sympathetic eyes. "You can stay at mine as long as you need to, babe, you know that. Thankfully my car keys were in my jeans pocket so I can drive us back when you are ready."

Charlie nodded, taking another swig of whiskey. It burnt the inside of her throat but she didn't give a shit. "I'm not leaving until Saf comes back. I need to make sure she is OK." He nodded. "Sure, babe, whenever you are ready. I'll call work later and let them know I need some time off." She felt another swell of emotion rise in her chest and fought back a fresh bucket of tears. "Thank you, hon. You are too good to me." He smiled and reached for the cigarette. She passed it to him so that he could have a puff. "Anything for my beautiful lady."

Charlie suddenly felt her stomach lurch as she realised Sapphire was pushing her way through the crowd towards her. Fox was right beside her; both of them looked like they were about to kick someone's arse big time.

"Charlie ... Oh my God, Charlie. Are you OK?" Sapphire ran towards her and flung herself at Charlie, who had stood up just in time. She nearly dropped the whiskey glass as Sapphire clung to her, sobbing.

"Saf, for fuck's sake. Where have you been? I'm OK. Honestly, I'm fine." Sapphire released her and looked up at her friend, tears in her eyes. Fox held back slightly. Charlie could feel the heat and tension radiating off him. "I'm so sorry, Charlie, I really am. Fox took me out back away from the fire. We didn't realise how much time had passed before we came back out front here to find you. I'm so, so sorry."

Charlie frowned and held Sapphire away at arm's length. Looking into her wide, scared eyes she felt a wash of love rush over her. "Saf, come on. It's OK; we are all alive and safe. I was just worried where you guys were ... no harm done." Sapphire had stopped sobbing and was trembling slightly. She looked weirdly guilty. "I am sorry I worried you again. It's unforgiveable; what's happened to your home is unforgiveable. I will do anything I can to make this right for you."

Charlie smiled now at Sapphire forever trying to do the right thing for everyone. "Saf, this is not your fault. Seriously, hon, stop it. We are all OK; it's just the shock of it. Fuck, I'm in shock. I'm pretty pissed ... I've lost my entire wardrobe. Some of that shit was vintage, you know." Sapphire smiled and then laughed. They both laughed, a little hysterical now, both laughing and crying some more.

Nathan stood next to Fox and nudged him. "Women, eh?" Fox nodded, allowing a thin smile on to his lips. He was on full alert. After his father had healed them both and given him his word that he would protect them as much as possible he had transported them back to Earth, much to his disapproval. He knew how vulnerable they both were now, but he also knew that Sapphire would hear nothing of staying on Shaka until she was reunited with her friends and knew they were OK. He watched his beautiful woman cling to her friend and felt a sadness within his heart; it was unfair to ask her to leave this place. Unfair that she had to face such danger; unfair that he wanted nothing more than to take her away forever and claim her as his own in his world, to live together within the safety of his magical home.

As if she felt his sadness she turned to face him and smiled; it pulled at his heart even more. She released Charlie and walked the two steps to his side and looked up at him. "I'm going to stay at Pearl's until everything is sorted, I'm sure she won't mind. Charlie will go to Nathan's. Everything is going to be OK."

He blinked and nodded; his heart was telling him that this was far from the truth. They eventually parted company, Charlie and Nathan heading off in his car back to Nathan's house so that they could get some sleep before Charlie called the insurance company and sorted everything out. The police had taken a statement and the fire crew were satisfied that everything was safe to leave. They had told Charlie that an arson investigation team would come in the day to go over the cottage with a fine-tooth comb to try and find any evidence of either foul play or some electrical fault. Sapphire could not help but feel like she had a big arrow pointing at the top of her head saying "Guilty as charged".

The new day had begun and dawn had risen by the time they left Mulberry Lane to walk to Pearl's cottage. They walked silently, holding hands. Fox could sense her turmoil and squeezed her fingers gently. "You are an amazing woman, Sapphire. To return here after everything that has happened is admirable indeed."

She laughed softly. "Stupid and crazy, you mean."

He looked at her, a tenderness in his heart. "You are neither of those things, Sapphire." Sapphire stopped walking and turned to face him. He stood motionless, looking into her eyes. They shone a deep blue filled with so many questions, so many thoughts, that he could almost feel her slipping emotionally away from him. "A few weeks ago, Fox, I would have agreed with you, but now ... now, everything is different. I'm not sure who I am any more."

He lifted his hand and brushed his fingertips across her cheek, a gesture so familiar to both of them now. "You are a powerful, wonderful woman, one who has proven time and time again that she is not afraid to fight for her friends or for what she feels is right in this world." Sapphire raised herself up on tiptoes and kissed him, a soft, teasing kiss that spoke of so much more. As she withdrew slowly he noticed that a slight smile played on her lips. "You are just a little biased about my abilities, Fox." He chuckled and kissed her again, harder now, pulling her into his chest. They kissed standing on the pathway as the sun began to rise above them, the birds chirping happily in the trees. Everything was calm and fresh, a new day, a new beginning.

Reluctantly Sapphire let go and pulled his arm. "Come on. We need to get to Pearl's house before some other tragedy befalls us." Before long they stood at the gate of Foxglove cottage, Sapphire finding a deep calmness filling her belly as she placed her hand on the gate to push it open. Fox hesitated behind her as she stepped through the gate; she turned to look at him, questioning his resistance to enter. "There are powerful wards around this house, Sapphire. You will have to ask Pearl to invite me in." She smiled at him. "Are you sure you are not part vampire?" He laughed, "No, I am not, but the wards are meant to keep all magical creatures out, and I am born from magic, my love. It is impossible for me to step through this gate without an invitation."

Sapphire nodded and walked to the cottage door; as usual it opened before she could knock. Pearl stood in the doorway; she was wearing a dressing gown and looked oddly dishevelled. A smile was, however, firmly placed on her lips. "My dear Sapphire, welcome. I am so glad to see you. I had the most awful dream last night; it really did give me quite a fright." Sapphire wanted to rush in and hug the old woman but looked over her shoulder, indicating to Pearl that she had company. "Pearl, it would be really nice if you would invite Fox in; it seems he cannot enter your garden without your permission." She looked back at the old woman who was now staring, eyes wide, at the man standing at her gate. She laughed and nodded. "Why, yes, of course. Enter, Fox. You are most welcome."

Sapphire felt a shift in the energy around her and Fox stepped through the gate, shutting it behind him – a gesture Sapphire found quite funny, considering all things done. He walked up the path with his eyes shining brightly, definitely happy to make Pearl's acquaintance. She stepped aside and let Sapphire walk through, kissing her on the cheek warmly as she passed – something she had never done before, and Sapphire found herself wanting to cry again. Damn it, Pearl just had that effect on her. Fox followed and bowed at the waist as Pearl closed the door behind him. "It is an honour to meet you, wise woman." Pearl chuckled and gestured for him to follow Sapphire through to the kitchen which was, as usual, filled with the smell of herbs and baking.

"Sit, both of you. I am sensing a rather big shift in events. I have just made a fresh pot of tea; you must be thirsty and hungry, I am sure." Sapphire flopped down into one of the kitchen chairs. Fox remained standing for a moment, looking around the room with a faint smile on his lips. Pearl busied herself with the tea, a ritual Sapphire was so comfortable watching now that it made her feel safe again. Fox pulled out a chair and sat next to Sapphire, who watched him curiously. He seemed a little nervous here, as if he was visiting the Queen.

Pearl was humming to herself in her usual sweet way; as she turned around with a tray filled with cups, plates and flapjacks Sapphire heard her own stomach growl loudly. Fox smiled at her and sat up a little straighter. This was funny, like bringing her man to meet her grandmother for approval. Pearl sat and started to pour the tea which smelt like cinnamon and honey. "Now, young Fox, what brings you here to our world? Something of great importance must have happened to push you outside the safety of your own realm." Fox shifted in his chair. Sapphire was actually enjoying this now.

"Sapphire is without a home. Last night we were attacked and her house was burnt to the ground by Hecta and a priestess called Ebony. They tried to take Sapphire away; it grieves me to say that in my weakened state here on Earth I was unable to prevent this from happening." Pearl was nodding her head slowly as she poured the tea. She said nothing. Sapphire reached for a flapjack; she was suddenly starving. "I see ... and you, Sapphire, what are your thoughts on the matter?" Sapphire was munching on the delicious flapjack now. Her mouth full of oats, she swallowed slowly.

"My thoughts, Pearl? God, I can barely think clearly at the moment. To be honest, I think I've finally lost the plot." Pearl laughed, and Fox tried not to choke on the tea he had just lifted to his lips. "Well, it seems that you are both in a bit of a pickle, aren't you?" Sapphire took a mouthful of the tea; it was wonderful, of course. "You could say that, Pearl. I was kind of hoping that I could stay with you for a while, seeing as I no longer have anywhere to live, which actually – now I think about it – you did warn me about when we did the card reading only yesterday." Pearl paused and looked up at the ceiling. "Why, yes; you did have several indicators for change, and the chance of moving residence. I did not think it would happen quite so quickly, though, my dear ... and of course you can stay with me for as long as you like. It will be nice to have some company, although you may find it a little quiet. I do not have a TV or anything remotely twentieth-century here."

Sapphire laughed. Fox was keeping quiet, sipping his tea politely. The whole situation was like something out of the Mad Hatter's tea party. "To be honest, Pearl, a bit of peace and quiet would suit me fine for a while. I think my head is about to explode with everything that has been happening." Pearl turned to Fox and gave him one of those stares that your mother gives you when you have been very naughty. "Fox, I thank you for returning Sapphire home safely and it has been a pleasure to meet you at last ... but I feel that it would be to both your benefit if you were to return home for a while so that Sapphire can rest and clear her mind."

Fox twitched. Sapphire could sense his energy shift and anger rise up within him slowly. "But she is not safe here any more, wise woman. I need to protect her." Pearl picked up a flapjack and nibbled the corner, regarding him coolly. "And you will, young man, from your own realm. I am quite capable of protecting her here in my home. As you can see, my own magic is strong enough to repel any persons wishing to do us harm." He looked down for a moment, his energy shifting again as he tried to remain calm. "Forgive me, Pearl. I did not mean to offend you. I am aware of how powerful you are, and I trust you implicitly. It just makes me nervous now to not be at Sapphire's side." Pearl smiled a warm understanding smile. "Ah, yes. The love you have for her is overwhelming. I understand, but you must give her some time ... time to think, time to consider what needs to be done next. You understand this, don't you?"

Fox looked at Sapphire then back at Pearl, his handsome face a little sad. Sapphire felt her chest pull tightly; she hated seeing him like this. "Yes, I understand completely. You are right; I will return to Shaka and wait for you to call me when you need me, Sapphire." Sapphire had stopped eating. They were making decisions for her;

talking about her like she was twelve. But it actually felt right; she wanted someone else to decide what she should do next and, quite frankly, she wanted to chill the fuck out for a while. Her house had burnt to the ground; last night she had been whisked off to some other realm and had a major catfight with some crazy power-possessed priestess. She needed a reality check.

She tilted her head to one side and regarded Pearl and Fox, who sat quietly, watching her eating flapjacks and drinking tea. As if living in a magical cottage with an old witch for a while could be reality, but what the hell? It was the only choice she had without getting grabbed again. Sapphire nodded. "I think that sounds like a great idea." Pearl nodded. It was decided, then. They finished their breakfast and Pearl headed back upstairs to fix the spare room for Sapphire, whom she said looked like she needed a lie down. Sapphire couldn't agree more; she was totally fucked. And not in a good way.

Sitting in the kitchen, Sapphire turned to Fox. He looked like a man who had lost the winning lottery ticket. She reached out and touched his hand gently; he raised his eyes to hers and smiled weakly. "I know you want to stay with me, Fox – and believe me, I cannot think of anything better than going upstairs and snuggling up with you under whatever duvet Pearl has up there – but at the moment I really do think that what she is suggesting is just what I need. Some time out. But just for a little while." He nodded solemnly. "As you wish, my love."

Sapphire stood now and pulled him up to stand with her. "Come here. Don't be sad. I will see you again soon … in my dreams, most likely." She laughed softly, trying to make light of the situation. He held her close and kissed her hair. She lifted her head and looked into those beautiful, magical eyes which swirled and danced with gold light. He kissed her softly and stroked her arms, making her body tremble slightly. She felt his love for her, his undeniable passion and longing for her. It was the most wonderful feeling in the world, but for now she needed to just be Sapphire again. He withdrew this time, sensing her need to step back away from him. He kissed her hand softly and stepped back from her, his eyes swimming with unspoken words. He nodded slightly and licked his lips slowly. "I will see you again soon, my love." Sapphire smiled at him, and watched him disappear before her eyes.

The kitchen was strangely silent, as if the tiny fairies that were hiding in the corners had held their breath while they had said goodbye to each other. Sapphire suddenly felt very, very tired. She wandered out of the kitchen and stood waiting for Pearl at the bottom of the higgledy-piggledy stairs that led up to the bedrooms. She could still sense Fox's energy and the twining of silver light that held them together now, strong and pulsing with his love for her. She stepped up slowly, wearily. Pearl was at the top holding blankets, a warm smile on her face. "Here you go, Sapphire. The bed is freshly made. You lie down and rest; you are safe now, my dear."

Sapphire nodded and entered the little bedroom, which was clean and fresh with white bed linen and a vase of wild flowers on the dresser. Pearl lingered at the door for a moment. "I will check on you, my dear. You can rest at ease here; nothing can harm you while you are in my home." Sapphire believed her and sat down on the bed; as Pearl closed the door she took off her shoes, which were dirty and a little black from the fire. As she undressed and slipped into the wonderfully soft and sweet-smelling bed she realised that she was crying again, silent tears to release her from the trauma that she had been holding inside. They washed away the fear and the guilt and she slowly felt her body give in and slip into a deep, much-needed state of sleep.

Chapter Thirty-Six

Sapphire woke to darkness; she had slept the entire day away. The room was lit by a candle that Pearl had placed on the dresser next to the wild flowers. She rolled on to her back, stared up at the ceiling for a moment and stretched her body out, letting her muscles release any last remaining tension. She did feel better; a lot better, in fact. Stepping out of bed she noticed that a pile of fresh clothes had been laid on the trunk at the end of the bed frame. She smiled as she lifted them and found jeans, a t-shirt, a sweatshirt, and clean underwear, still in the packet. Dressing slowly, she headed back down the stairs to find Pearl. She was in the kitchen, preparing a meal. It was warm and inviting and the smell of food wafted deliciously from the oven.

"Ah, Sapphire, you are awake. Did you rest well?" Sapphire pulled out a chair at the kitchen table and sat down, rubbing her eyes, still a little sleepy. "Yes, I did … thank you, Pearl. No dreams, just a lovely, restful sleep." Pearl bent down to retrieve whatever she had been cooking from the oven. She was dressed now in one of her long, flowing hippy-style outfits; her hair was tidy and she looked much more like her old self. Sapphire watched her place a ceramic dish on the table; she had already laid out plates and cutlery and glasses with fresh water. "I've made us a nice vegetable stew; I know it's summer but I thought you might like something a little more warming, considering the circumstances." Sapphire nodded and smiled; it smelt wonderful.

They sat in silence for a while. Pearl had dished them up both a sizeable plate and produced a loaf of her freshly-made bread to dip into the gravy. Sapphire tucked in, not realising how hungry she was. She noticed with a smile the warm hint of chilli in the mix; it made her body tingle nicely. "Thank you for the clothes, Pearl. How did you get those?" Pearl watched her from across the table. "Oh, I popped out when you were asleep to the village charity shop. I hope you don't mind second-hand clothes. I have washed and dried them, of course, and the underwear is new; thankfully, the little boutique in the high street had some, and the lady was very helpful in guessing your size."

She paused and took another mouthful of the stew. "Oh, and I brought you one of those mobile phone thingies from the supermarket; I thought you might want to call your friends and make sure they are OK. I'm sure there is nothing left at your cottage now and I am afraid I don't have a phone here." Sapphire nodded. She mopped up some of the gravy with her bread and licked her lips. She felt much better; the food had done wonders to her energy. "I will pay you back, Pearl. I will go to the bank tomorrow and get some money out; I'm not sure how without my card and ID, but I'm sure I will find a way."

Pearl smiled at her kindly; she was delicately dotting her lips with a napkin. "Not to worry for now, my dear; money is not really of importance to me." Sapphire smiled at her; this woman had turned out to be a complete godsend in her life. "Pearl, I can't thank you enough for everything you have done for me. I know we haven't known each other very long, but you really have been the most helpful and kind person to me. I don't really have any other friends or family here except Charlie and I don't know what I would have done without you."

Pearl reached out to pat her hand. "It has been a pleasure, my dear; you do not need to thank me. I think we have both been waiting to meet each other for quite some time, in fact it was rather boring until you arrived." They both laughed. Settling back in her chair, Sapphire looked at Pearl. Her heart was fluttering a little. "Pearl, I need to spend some time just thinking this through, clear my head a little. Everything that has happened recently has become so overwhelming. Would it be OK for me to use your garden to meditate and recharge?"

Pearl smiled at her kindly. "You take as much time as you need, my dear. My house and garden are yours for as long as you like. I know you have a lot to think about and some decisions to make, but I will guide you as much as I can. Nothing can harm you while you stay within my grounds. When you need to leave I will come with you; I know Fox wishes to be by your side but for now I do feel it is best for him to remain on his world. His influence on you does tend to cloud your judgement a little."

Sapphire blushed. She knew what the old woman was talking about and she was absolutely right; with Fox around everything became fuzzy with sex and passion – not that that was a bad thing, it just caused her a big distraction. Pearl put the napkin down and pushed her chair back. "Well, my dear, if you wanted to take a walk in the garden tonight and find some solace it is still fairly early and the night is clear and warm. I will be here making some new remedies, so just call me if you need me." Sapphire nodded. "Do you want some help with the washing up?" Pearl chuckled. "Oh, no, my dear; I have my little helpers for that. You run along to the garden and enjoy some peace and quiet."

Sapphire raised her eyebrows at that statement. Perhaps there really were fairies in the kitchen, after all. She left the cottage barefoot. Pearl had obviously not thought about shoes and her trainers were still dirty from the night before, but as she stepped on to the grass she was glad she had no shoes on as the texture of the lawn was soft and warm. She walked silently through the garden, looking around at the flowers and herbs laid out beautifully in well-kept beds. The garden was truly magical and the light from the moon cast the trees and shrubs with a silver glow. The night sky was completely clear and she looked up at the stars scattered throughout the darkness, wondering which one might be Shaka. Her heart swelled at the thought of Fox waiting patiently for her.

She found the silver birch tree and sat down with her back to the trunk, her legs wrapped in the lotus position. Taking a deep, calming breath she closed her eyes and settled into meditation. The ground beneath her grew instantly warm and she felt the energy start to travel up her body, pulsing gently. It felt wonderful; her mind was calm but images of the past two weeks' events began to play in her head. She knew that it was time to make a decision, to plan her next move; she would need to decide what to do about all of this – her new awakening, her new abilities, the new man in her life. The thought pressed heavily on her shoulders. As the refreshing energy of Mother Earth washed through her she felt a guiding light shine down from above. It cleansed her and cleared her thoughts. The light filled her with new hope and a new future. She knew exactly what she must do and a smile lifted her face at the thought. It was time. Time for a change.

She had no idea how long she had sat in the garden under the silver birch tree but eventually she started to feel a little cold and knew it must be late. Standing up and stretching, she noticed that the garden was now lit up a little brighter and the plants were shining like little lanterns. Everything seemed to be covered in fairy dust. As she walked back towards the cottage she brushed her fingers across the petals of a rose bush and the dust flew upwards in a shower of tiny sparkles. Sapphire laughed and knew that her second sight was allowing her to see the energy of the plants as they recharged in the moonlight. It was breathtaking.

She was suddenly aware that Pearl was standing next to her. She jumped a little, then smiled. "It's beautiful out here in the moonlight, isn't it Sapphire? Can you see the plants bathing in the energy?" Sapphire nodded. "Yes, I can. Everything is illuminated like they are fluorescent." Pearl chuckled softly. "Yes, nature is wonderful. Every plant has its own life force, its own story to tell. It is a shame that most humans do not take the time to see it."

Sapphire rubbed her arms to try and take off the chill. "I think most people would be a little freaked if they could actually see what was going on around them." Pearl nodded, smiling. "Yes, you are probably right. Shall we go in now? It is rather late. You have been out here quite a while; I thought I would just check on you." Sapphire stepped towards her, heading back to the cottage. "I'm sorry, Pearl. Have I kept you up?"

They walked back to the cottage. The door was open, soft candlelight lit the hallway. "Oh, no, my dear. To be perfectly honest I often spend the night doing just this, walking among the flowers and talking to the animals." Sapphire laughed. "You really are rather odd, Pearl." She did not seem offended and closed the door behind them softly. "Well, my dear, I think I will retire for the remaining part of the night. I know we have some things to do tomorrow and we should head out early to get things sorted." Sapphire wondered if she knew what she had been meditating on, or if she was just very intuitive. Possibly both. "Yes, that sounds like a good idea. I am actually feeling a little tired now. Goodnight, Pearl, and thank you again."

Pearl hugged her warmly, leaving her to retire to her new room while she blew out the candles and tidied the kitchen before bed. Sapphire noticed that she did not lock the door, but then why would an old witch with magical wards surrounding her property need to? She headed up the stairs and paused before she reached the top, looking down for Pearl. "Pearl, can I please use your bathroom? I could do with brushing my teeth and having a wash." Pearl appeared at the foot of the stairs. "Of course, Sapphire. There is a fresh toothbrush for you, and a clean flannel. Help yourself to towels."

Sapphire smiled, suddenly feeling very weary. It wasn't hard to find the bathroom; the cottage was even smaller than Charlie's. Everything was clean and white; an old cast-iron bath sat against the wall, standing on lion claws. The sink was a lovely old square butler sink, and Sapphire noticed a new toothbrush still in its packet sitting on the cabinet next to the bathtub. She ran some hot water and found soap and a flannel. She undressed slowly and stood in the bathtub; it was close enough to the sink for her to wash herself down, reaching over to dip the flannel in the water between washing her body parts.

She felt like she was in the Middle Ages but it was strangely soothing, standing in the moonlight that filtered through the window, naked, and bathing using just a flannel and soap. After she had cleaned herself she dried and wrapped the towel around her middle. She had a pee and then washed her hands and brushed her teeth. Normal things; things that she had not remembered doing for a while. Heading back to her room she met Pearl in the hallway. "Sleep well, Sapphire. I am right here across the hallway if you need me, but remember that no harm can come your way while you are in my home." Sapphire nodded and reached over to kiss her lightly on her cheek. Pearl smiled and headed into the bathroom; she obviously needed to do normal human stuff sometimes as well.

Sapphire opened the bedroom door and found that Pearl had straightened her bed and lit a fresh candle and some incense while she had been out in the garden. It was like staying at the best hotel in the world – well, the best magical hotel in the world. Folding the towel and placing it on the trunk next to her clothes she climbed into bed and snuggled down beneath the duvet, hugging a pillow to her chest. She felt the obsidian necklace warm and soothing between her breasts. For the second time in one day she allowed herself to fall asleep, safe in the knowledge that the bogeyman could not come and get her.

Chapter Thirty-Seven

Sapphire had slept without dreaming again. It was bliss. She had not realised how draining it had been lately, with all the travelling and extracurricular activities she had been carrying out with Fox. She had smiled at the thought. This really was a much-needed break from all the weirdness that had been happening. She had woken feeling fully refreshed and ready to take on the world.

Pearl had cooked them scrambled eggs and warm muffins for breakfast with hot ginger tea. Delicious. She had no idea what the time was: there were no clocks in Pearl's cottage. After breakfast Pearl had gathered a small cloth bag with God knows what in it. Sapphire wondered if it was filled with magical herbs that could fight off gatekeepers and bad priestesses. She giggled at the thought. Pearl was waiting for her at the door while she put on her trainers; she noticed they were now sparkly-clean again. Fairies, perhaps? As they headed out the door Sapphire was pleased to see that the sun was shining brightly; it was a pleasantly warm day with a light breeze.

Pearl tucked her arm into the crook of Sapphire's elbow and they opened the gate to enter the real world. As they walked towards the village Sapphire felt strangely calm and centred. The fear she had been carrying was gone. It was a very liberating feeling. They walked in silence, Sapphire knowing exactly where she wanted to go first. Pearl did not even need her to explain what she wanted to do. They headed to the coffee shop. Opening the door the bell tinkled indicating a new customer.

Linda was behind the counter and her face lit up, firstly with surprise, then happiness, then concern. "Oh, Sapphire. Oh, it's so good to see you. I heard about the fire; I did not expect to see you here so soon." Sapphire smiled at her warmly and headed around the counter to give her employer a big hug. Linda was gushing now, chattering non-stop about how awful it must be to have no home and what was she going to do about her belongings? Pearl had settled into one of the chairs by the window and was watching with a smile on her lips. Sapphire knew this was going to be hard, but necessary.

She stepped back from Linda and held her arms lightly. "Linda, you have been an amazing person to work for and I am so grateful for everything you have done for me since I came to live here, but I am not going to be able to come back to work for you tomorrow." Linda was nodding, concern on her face. "Of course, Sapphire. I totally understand. My niece has been covering for you, anyway, while you were on holiday, and she is here for the summer while college is on its break, so that's not a problem. Take as much time as you need to get things sorted."

Sapphire watched, her sadness filling her chest. She took a deep breath. "And I am very grateful for that, Linda … but, you see, I won't actually be able to come back to work for you any more. I am moving away again. I am sorry to give you such short notice, but with everything that has happened I have no choice." Linda looked gobsmacked. Her mouth opened into a little O shape. "Oh … Oh, goodness. Really? Oh, that's such a shame, Sapphire. You have been such a pleasure to have here … We will all miss you so much … Are you sure?"

Sapphire smiled at her and nodded. "Yes, Linda. I am quite sure you will find someone to fill my space no problem; it's a great place to work." Linda nodded slowly. "Well, OK, then. I will get your money paid into your account straight away. Oh, it really is such a shame. Stay and have a coffee before you go. I have just baked some fresh cupcakes." Sapphire hugged her one last time. "Actually, Linda, I have a few errands to run and really need to get going, but thank you so much for the offer and don't worry about that final pay cheque. Put it towards something nice for yourself."

Sapphire left the coffee shop with Pearl at her side; she did not look back as they closed the door behind them. They walked up the high street to the bank; it was the only bank in the village and Sapphire knew the girl behind the counter, as did everyone who lived here and who conducted their everyday business there. She walked to the counter and smiled at Stephanie, who looked as shocked as Linda had at seeing Sapphire standing before her. She wondered if the rumour mill had sent word around that she had actually been burnt to death. "Good morning, Stephanie. As you most probably know, Charlie's cottage was burnt down last night and I have absolutely no ID, clothes or anything for that matter now – but I need to draw a cheque and I am hoping that you will be kind enough to authorise it."

Stephanie was smiling a little inanely now; she nodded and pushed her chair back to stand up. "I'm sure we can sort something out, Miss Whittaker, considering what you have been through. I will just have to check with my manager." Pearl was standing next to Sapphire and she smiled at her reassuringly. The manager appeared quickly; Sapphire did not know him but recognised his face from working in the coffee shop. He smiled at her warmly. "Good morning, Miss Whittaker. I am so sorry to hear of your tragedy last night. Stephanie has told me you would like to draw some money out. Is that right?" Sapphire nodded. "Actually I would like some cash, if that's possible, and what's left in the account I would like made out as a cheque to my friend Charlie."

He blinked at her and then smiled again. "Well, normally we would need your bank card and some ID, depending on how much money you need the cheque to be made out for, but considering the circumstances I am sure I will be able to bend some rules for you today. How much would you like?" Sapphire smiled at him. Her heart was beating faster now. Pearl had placed her hand lightly on her arm, sending her warm soothing vibes. "I would like £100 cash and then whatever is left in the account to be made out to Miss Charlotte Daines." He nodded.

"I don't suppose you remember your account number, do you?" Sapphire laughed softly. "Yes, I do, actually." She gave him the numbers and the sort code and waited. He keyed everything into the computer and then looked back at her with a blank expression on his face. "You want everything that's left in the account made into the cheque?" Sapphire nodded slowly. "Yes, that's right. Everything." He licked his lips slowly. A small bead of sweat began to form on his brow. "Well, that is rather a lot of money, Miss Whittaker, but of course it is your money to do with as you wish. I will have that drawn up for you now and Stephanie will give you the cash. We can sort out the ID and paperwork once you have new copies to put on file." Sapphire let out a sigh. Well, that was easier than she thought.

Pearl winked at her. They waited five minutes in the lobby before Stephanie came out to hand her the cash and the cheque. She was holding it tightly, staring down at it with what looked like envy in her eyes. Sapphire took it from her gently; she did not seem to want to let it go. "Thank you, Stephanie. You have a good day." They left the bank, Pearl saying nothing as Sapphire tucked the cheque and cash into her pocket.

They walked down the high street and headed towards her old cottage. Standing outside, looking up at the shell of the cottage, Sapphire felt a lump rise in her throat. It was cordoned off with black and yellow police tape; small wisps of smoke were still curling up lazily from some of the debris. A group of men were walking around in fluorescent jackets; firemen, possibly.

She walked up to one of them and tapped him on the shoulder. "Hi, I'm Sapphire. I used to live here; can you tell me if there is anything left in the upstairs bedrooms?" The man looked at her a little confused for a moment then shook his head. "No, Madam. Nothing worth keeping, anyway. We have done a thorough check and it looks like a possible electrical fault in the kitchen started the fire, but of course the investigation could take some time before we have a final report. I'm sorry."

Sapphire nodded. The lump was stuck and had started to make her feel like she wanted to gag. Pearl touched her lightly and the lump disappeared. "OK. Thank you; has another young woman been here yet today? She owns the cottage. Her name is Charlie Daines." The man shook his head "No, not yet, but we do have her details and will be contacting her shortly."

Sapphire nodded and stepped back. She looked at the cottage one last time, remembering all the good times – her room, the garden, the chickens out back, Charlie's workshop. Wonderful memories. Without saying another word she turned her back on the cottage and they headed back towards the edge of the village towards Pearl's place. Pearl walked silently beside her, Sapphire pulling her new mobile out from her pocket. She tapped in Charlie's number and listened to it ring for a while. She answered after the fourth ring.

"Hey, Charlie." "Saf, is that you? I didn't recognise the number. Hey, hon, are you OK? I was going to contact you later. We have only just got up and I need to make a shit-load of calls. Everything OK with you staying at Pearl's? We can go shopping for clothes as soon as I get the cheque from the insurance company. I'm standing here in Nathan's jeans and a big fat-arsed t-shirt." Sapphire laughed. "Charlie, I need you to pop over to Pearl's cottage this evening, if that's OK. I've been to the cottage already. It's still cordoned off, but they are doing a good job investigating. I'm sure everything will be sorted soon for you."

Charlie was silent for a second; she had her hand over the mouthpiece and was talking to Nathan. "Yep, that will be OK. Nathan can run me over later ... say around seven? I need to sort stuff out this afternoon. It will be good to catch up with you. I miss you, hon." Sapphire smiled. The lump was back. She said, "Goodbye," and hung up. Pearl looked at her and nodded. They walked back to Foxglove cottage in silence.

When they reached the cottage Pearl made tea, quietly humming to herself. Sapphire took the cash and the cheque out of her pocket and sat at the kitchen table. She stared at it for a moment then pushed both under the little pot of wild flowers in the centre of the table. Pearl placed a cup of hot steaming tea in front of her and sat down. "Are you OK, Sapphire?" Sapphire looked at her and smiled warmly. "Yes, I'm fine. I just need to see Charlie, then I'm done." Pearl nodded and sipped her tea. "Yes, of course, my dear. Would you like something to eat?" Sapphire sighed. "Actually Pearl, I seemed to have lost my appetite right now."

Pearl placed her teacup down and placed her fingers together in her lap, sitting back in her chair "Is there anything you would like to ask me, Sapphire?" Sapphire sipped her tea and then sighed heavily. "Fox's father is a great magician. He told me that our planet has lost its magic – that it is buried deep inside the Earth and we no longer have access to it. Is that right?" Pearl contemplated the question for a moment. "Not exactly. He is right that the magic is buried deeply, but I believe our mother is sleeping right now and that she will eventually awaken and we will be able to access that magic again. In fact I sense that she is stirring right now. Slowly, our consciousness is changing; we are on the verge of a new beginning for all our kind."

Sapphire nodded, a slight frown on her forehead. "I think I know what it is that I hold inside me, Pearl. I am beginning to understand what it is that Ebony wants from me, but I am not ready yet; I need to keep it safe." Pearl nodded and smiled. "Yes, my dear, I think you are right. None of us are ready yet, but you are strong and clever and, I sense, wiser than anyone can imagine. I am glad that you are realising this."

Sapphire reached for the cash under the flowerpot. She took it out and handed it to Pearl. "This is for you, just to cover the clothes and my keep for the time I have been here." Pearl chuckled. "Not necessary, but I thank you for the gesture, Sapphire. It is most kind of you." They sat in silence for a while before Sapphire decided it was time to take a bath and properly wash away what was left of yesterday. She ran the bath and undressed slowly. Her mind was clear but her thoughts played heavily on her conscience. Slipping into the hot water she leant back and allowed her hair to float around her like a sea anemone, waving gently as she drifted her fingers through the water. She felt a little numb, like she was on autopilot.

The water was soothing and Pearl had given her some shampoo and conditioner that smelt of lavender and roses. She washed her hair and rinsed it using a porcelain jug that sat beside the sink. She lay in the bath tub for quite some time and closed her eyes, thinking of Fox; his beautiful handsome face, those magical eyes flashing at her wild with passion, his braided hair, his long, lean, muscular body. The way he kissed her, made love to her, she could feel her body respond to just the thought of him; she missed him terribly, even though they had only been apart a very short time.

Opening her eyes she smiled softly and lifted herself out of the water. She dried herself, taking her time, before wrapping her hair in a towel. Pearl had laid out fresh clothes again; somehow she had now managed to produce a summer dress which had tiny shoestring straps and pretty yellow flowers on it. She slipped it on, wondering who it had belonged to. She found some flip-flops at the end of the bed and pushed her feet into them, wiggling her toes. Heading back down the stairs with her hair still wet and slightly tangled around her shoulders she found Pearl sitting at the kitchen table reading a book. She smiled as Sapphire entered the room.

"Ah, that looks pretty on you, Sapphire; the perfect dress for the occasion." Sapphire raised an eyebrow and smiled. This woman could definitely read minds. "Pearl, do you have some writing paper and a pen?" Pearl put the book down; Sapphire noticed it was a book on herbs and wild flowers. She smiled. "Why, yes, I do my dear. Let me find some for you." Sapphire sat down at the table and looked out the kitchen window at the sunshine filtering through; it was such a lovely afternoon. Pearl had left the room but returned quickly with a pad of paper and a pen; it was a soft vanilla colour and good quality, Pearl obviously did a lot of correspondence but to whom? Pearl sat back down and regarded her quietly, a serious expression on her face.

"Would you like some privacy while you write your letters?" Sapphire nodded. "Yes, that would be nice, Pearl." The old woman nodded and left the room; she took her book with her. Sapphire set about writing her letters, one for Charlie and one for her mother. It took her some time, as she was finding it a little hard to write exactly what was on her mind in exactly the right way. Eventually she finished and folded them neatly; Pearl had provided two envelopes with the paper, apparently aware of exactly how many letters she needed to write.

She wrote her mother's address on her envelope and Charlie's name on the other. She put the cheque inside the latter, folding it in half before putting it behind the letter. Pearl appeared again just as she finished sealing the last envelope. "Are you feeling better now, Sapphire? Would you like to eat now? I thought we could sit in the garden and have some something light, enjoy the sunshine."

Sapphire nodded; she was feeling a little hungry. "Yes, actually. I am ready to eat now." Pearl whipped up a lovely fresh salad in no time; everything was from the garden and she had put some pretty nasturtiums on top to decorate the salad leaves. Sapphire took the tray laden with food and some lemonade that Pearl had made and followed her out into the garden. They sat on a blanket Pearl had laid out for them under the silver birch. Sapphire felt like it was the Last

Supper; she was glad she was spending this time with Pearl in her beautiful garden on this glorious summer's day.

After they had eaten Sapphire stretched out her legs and admired the colour they had turned from her time at the festival. She felt at peace. Pearl sat quietly cross-legged, watching her. "You will be fine, Sapphire; you know that, don't you?" Sapphire smiled and nodded. "Yes, I know." The afternoon passed with them chatting about this and that, nothing of importance. Sapphire lay in the sunshine and enjoyed the warming and revitalising sensation of the rays on her skin. As the day disappeared Pearl stood up and gathered the plates and glasses to go back inside. "Your friend should be here soon, Sapphire. I will put the kettle on." Sapphire smiled up at her.

"OK, Pearl. Have you any of those fab flapjacks left?" Pearl chuckled and nodded. Heading back to the cottage with the tray she left Sapphire on her own for a moment. She sat up and looked around her at the flowers and shrubs bobbing gently in the warm breeze. She heard a car pull up outside the gate and her heart started to beat a little faster. Charlie had arrived. Just as she stood Charlie came bounding through the gate; she was dressed in shorts and a tiny vest top, looking very much like her old self – a bright red handbag slung over her shoulder. She was beaming at Sapphire.

Charlie rushed to her and took her into a big bear hug, squeezing her hard. "Oh, Saf, it's so good to see you. I'm glad you are staying here. You look good today; this place must be doing wonders for you" Sapphire laughed and hugged her back. "Yeah, it's so peaceful here, and Pearl is the best hostess ever." They headed back inside the cottage, arm in arm. Pearl was setting out the tea things; she smiled warmly at Charlie as they entered the kitchen.

"Pearl, this is my friend Charlie: Charlie, this is Pearl." Charlie was looking around the cottage with wide eyes. "It is a pleasure to meet you Charlie. Would you like some herbal tea?" Charlie raised an eyebrow. The only thing herbal she ever had was slightly different from Pearl's tea. "Yes, thank you, Pearl. That would be lovely." Pearl straightened the napkins she had placed next to the plate of flapjacks. "I will leave you two ladies to chat in privacy; I will be in the lounge if you need me." Sapphire smiled at her with gratitude in her eyes. When Pearl had left the room Charlie flopped down on one of the chairs. She was grinning. "This place is a blast, Saf. It's like something out of Grimm's Fairy Tales." Sapphire laughed and started to pour the tea. "I know. It's kinda cool, don't you think?"

Charlie snorted. "Yeah, in a fairy godmother kind of way. Talk about Hansel and Gretel. Are you sure she is not going to stuff you in the oven and cook you for dinner?" They both laughed. "Did you manage to speak to the insurance company? Here, have a flapjack: they are delicious." Charlie eyed the oatcakes suspiciously but picked one up anyway. "Yep, all done. Thank God I had full cover and contents insurance; they are sending over an assessor tomorrow, but apparently I am covered for all works that need to be done to fix the cottage and once I can work out how much all my stuff is worth they will get some money wired to my account. Nathan took me shopping this afternoon with his credit card to get a few clothes; I couldn't walk around in his stuff any more."

Sapphire watched her friend chatter excitedly; she was obviously over the trauma of it all now. "That's good. Is Nathan still OK with you bunking at his until it's all sorted out? I presume it could take some time." Charlie looked up a cheeky glint to her eye. "He's more than happy. Actually, it is quite nice; we have become really close lately and I suppose it's a kinda trial run in case we decide to move in together – that's if you don't mind having him around in the future."

Sapphire looked down at her teacup for a moment and blinked. "Of course I don't mind at all, Charlie. It's your home; you can have whoever you like staying with you. I'm really happy for you guys; you are good together." Charlie was nibbling the flapjack now and pulling a face as she discovered the chilli kick. "Where's Fox?" Sapphire bit her bottom lip. "He's gone home for a while, but actually I wanted to talk to you about that." Charlie stopped nibbling for a second. Her face lit up in anticipation. "Mmmh … give it up, girl. What's going on now?" Sapphire laughed softly. "Well, although it's lovely here he has offered to take me away for a while, kind of like a road trip … you know, some time out from everything for a little while." She felt her cheeks blush at the lie she was telling. Charlie just thought she was blushing from her confessions of love for him. "That sounds cool. Have you asked Linda for some more time off?"

Sapphire nodded, not looking directly at Charlie. She was finding it hard to meet her gaze now. "Yes, it's all sorted." Charlie put the flapjack down and pushed the plate away from her, wrinkling her nose up. "They are hot, man." Sapphire sipped her tea. She was really finding this hard. "So everything is cool, then – you off to have a bonking time with your sexy man and me waiting on my insurance cheque. God, who would have thought ... The whole thing has actually made me realise how bloody lucky I am, Saf. I mean, we were kissing death's backside the other night. It could have turned out a whole lot worse if your man hadn't been staying over. Fuck. It doesn't bear thinking about, does it?"

Sapphire wanted to cry. She held it in well. "Mmmh, I know. It puts things into perspective, doesn't it." Charlie nodded, taking a sip of tea. She cocked her head to one side. "Now, this shit is actually good." Sapphire laughed again, the tears going back down again to the centre of her chest. God, she loved her friend.

Charlie leant back in the chair and sighed. "I don't know, Saf. Sometimes I wonder if there isn't someone up there throwing stuff at us every now and then, just to make us think about life a little differently. You know, like a challenge. After the fire and spending some time with Nathan I realised how much I've become wrapped up in my little world and all the material stuff we have. It actually doesn't mean shit, does it? Just like that it can all be taken away. But the stuff that does matter is around us all the time, and we forget that, don't we?" Sapphire smiled at her, nodding.

"I mean, I realised – after several whiskeys, of course – that my home is wonderful and all that – and, of course, my vintage stuff was dear to my heart. But it can be replaced – God bless insurance – but the things you can't replace are the people you love and your friends." She smiled sweetly at Sapphire. "And you and Nathan are everything to me. I'm just grateful we can still be together."

The room suddenly fell silent, Sapphire gulped before speaking. "Yes, I agree, Charlie. That's what's important in the world." Charlie regarded her, a little frown suddenly appearing on her pretty face. "You OK, Saf?" Sapphire smiled her best smile. "Of course, honey.

It's great to see you again; I missed you, too." Sapphire pushed her chair back. "I'll show you around the garden while it's still light; it's amazing." They headed out front again, Sapphire linking arms with her friend leading her around the flower and herb beds. Charlie made all the right noises of appreciation in the right places, but Sapphire knew it wasn't really her thing; she just wanted to spend a little more time with her.

Dusk fell and Sapphire knew it would be time for Charlie to leave soon. They went back into the cottage, which was lit with candles and soft table lights; it seemed just a little more magical tonight. Pearl was back in the kitchen making more food; she was cooking something in a frying pan that consisted of what looked like rice and vegetables, a risotto of some kind. It filled the kitchen with delicious smells that made Sapphire feel hungry again. "Would you like to stay for supper, Charlie?" Pearl asked as they came back into the kitchen. Charlie stood in the doorway, hovering, taking in the smells and sights of the darkened room.

"Actually, yes; I would love to, Pearl. Nathan is meeting some friends tonight. He can pick me up later." Sapphire was more than happy that her friend was staying a little longer than she expected; it was an added bonus of time together. They settled down at the table, Sapphire helping to lay plates and cutlery; they chatted amiably for a while as Pearl finished preparing the meal. Charlie was telling Pearl about the heroic Fox and how he had rescued them all and what a godsend he was and how wonderful it was that Sapphire had at last found herself a man. Pearl smiled as she stirred the rice, looking up occasionally at Sapphire with a knowing glint in her eyes.

As dinner was served Sapphire had the overwhelming feeling of contentment to be sitting with two such wonderful women, completely opposite in personality but both close to her heart. They tucked into the food, which was wonderful, of course. Pearl had even produced a bottle of cold, crisp white wine. It was totally delicious and Sapphire wondered where the hell she had found it. "I can see why Sapphire likes it here so much, Pearl. That was the best meal I have had in ages. No offense to your culinary skills, Saf, but this lady can cook." Pearl poured them both more wine; she seemed in the party mood.

"Why, thank you, Charlie. It is such a pleasure to entertain two such wonderful young ladies. As you can imagine I don't get to spend much time with other people – to be honest I have always kept myself to myself – but it has been such fun to get to know Sapphire, and now meeting you, Charlie." Charlie took a sip of the wine and nodded her head, giving a thumbs-up; she was in supper heaven. "Well, I shall come and see both of you more often while the cottage is being renovated. Nathan is great, but you can't beat a good girlie night, can you?" Sapphire felt her chest fill with emotion again. Every gesture, every comment was making her heart want to burst.

She knew that this time was precious and she did not want to ruin it by being sad. They finished the food and sat back to enjoy the last of the wine. "So, Saf, I was thinking … Tomorrow we could go and do some shopping, get some more clothes – and I desperately need some make-up. I just grabbed a few bits today, but a girl has to look her best and you can't do that without some serious beauty products." Sapphire looked a little cagey, but smiled at her. "I'll see how I feel tomorrow, Charlie. I might need to pop into the bank, get some money and stuff sorted." Charlie nodded "OK, sure. Just call me."

Pearl was watching her every move; she was obviously seeing the heavy burden weighing down on Sapphire's shoulders. "Well, as much as I would like to stay longer, I'd best be getting back to Nathan's. I'll text him to pick me up. Can I use your loo before I go, Pearl?" Pearl stood up and started to clear the plates. "Of course, my dear. It's at the top of the stairs; you can't miss it." Charlie beamed at her; she took her mobile out of her new bag and text Nathan before heading up the stairs.

As she left the kitchen Sapphire jumped up and grabbed the envelope with the letter for Charlie; she tucked it into the bottom of her bag and placed it back on the chair so that she would not notice it had been moved. Pearl watched her silently as she ran water to wash up the supper things. Sapphire said nothing. Charlie came back down the stairs; her mobile beeped as she stepped into the kitchen again. Opening it, she read the text and then smiled at Sapphire, a big happy smile. "Right. Nat is on his way. He will be five minutes. I'm going outside for a smoke, if that's OK to wait for him. Pearl, it's been wonderful. Thank you so much for dinner and, of course, for looking after my bestie. I hope she doesn't leave too many wet towels on your bathroom floor while she stays here; she is quite good company, actually, just a bit messy sometimes." She laughed at her own joke.

Sapphire felt her bottom lip tremble. "I'll come out with you, Charlie. See you in a mo, Pearl." Pearl was wrist-deep in water and washing-up liquid. She smiled at them both. "Of course. Well, you have a good rest tonight, Charlie; see you again sometime." Charlie skipped across to her and kissed her on the cheek, which shocked Pearl a little, but she chuckled at her none the less. "Sure. I'll see you soon. Thanks, Pearl."

They headed out to the garden; the sky was clear and the moon was bright, giving everything a wonderful silver haze. Charlie reached into her bag for her tobacco. Sapphire held her breath, afraid she might find the envelope. Luckily she had tucked it right at the bottom and Charlie found her tobacco pouch without discovering the secret in her bag. They walked to the gate and sat on the little wooden bench under a honeysuckle bush. Charlie rolled herself a smoke with the skill of a practised smoker. She lit it and blew the smoke up into the air; Sapphire watched the grey mist swirl in patterns as it hit the cooler night air. They sat quietly looking up at the sky.

Charlie nudged her shoulder playfully. "It's kind of like sitting in *The Secret Garden* here, Saf. I have to say it's an awesome spot; I feel like any minute fairies might pop out from under the bush." Sapphire laughed. If only she knew. "I know it's a wonderful place, full of magic." Charlie giggled. "I think you have had your fair share of magic lately, Saf, what with the magical mysterious Fox. You let me know well in advance before you take off on this road trip, won't you? I need to thank him properly for everything. Maybe we could do a double date night, go to the cinema or something."

Charlie was babbling like she usually did, and it was comforting for Sapphire to know that her friend had seen nothing amiss. She leant into her and laid her head on her shoulder as she smoked her roll-up. Charlie mirrored her and for a moment they sat silently leaning on each other on the bench in the magical garden looking up at the stars. It was the most perfect moment for Sapphire. A moment to remember. Nathan pulled up outside the gate, lighting up the lane. Charlie jumped up, stamping out her dog end. "Right, I'll be off then, Saf. Speak to you tomorrow. Thanks for tonight; it was fun."

Sapphire stood and said nothing for a moment; she was at a loss for words. Charlie leant in for a hug. Sapphire grabbed her and hugged her tightly, not wanting to let go. "Hey, girl. Easy there; everything is cool. I'll see you soon, maybe tomorrow if you fancy a shop." Sapphire let her go reluctantly and stared at her, not wanting to cry and give the game away. "Yeah, sure. Love you, Charlie."

Charlie smiled a big, sweet smile and hugged her again quickly. She opened the gate and waved over her shoulder. "Love you, too. Bye, hon. Sleep well." And then she was gone. Sapphire stood by the gate for a moment watching the car turn around and then head back down the lane, the lights eventually fading as they turned off on to the road. Everything was silent and still. She so desperately wanted to cry, but she did not. She felt cold suddenly and rubbed her bare arms.

Heading back to the cottage, she took in her surroundings one more time and smiled. Opening the cottage door, she found Pearl standing in the hallway. She had her arms out ready for a hug, Sapphire fell into her embrace and the tears finally fell, silent but steady, releasing her from her guilt. Without a word Pearl led her back into the kitchen and sat her at the table; she patted her arm and sat next to her, handing her a tissue. "There, there, Sapphire. You are doing the right thing; you know that, don't you?" Sapphire nodded and blew her nose loudly. She looked up into those kind, wise eyes and smiled. "I'm ready, Pearl." Pearl nodded and took her hand and squeezed it gently. "I know, my dear."

Sapphire stood up and let out a sigh. "Would you be kind enough to post the letter I have written for my mother? I am afraid I forgot to get a stamp." Pearl nodded. "Of course, my dear." She wanted to say so many things, but there was nothing more to say except "Goodnight." "I will see you again, Sapphire. Travel safely, my child, and remember I am always here if you need me." Sapphire bent down to kiss her softly on the cheek. Pearl remained seated as she left the kitchen and headed back up the stairs. She went to the little bathroom and brushed her teeth and took a pee; she washed her hands and splashed cool water on her face, staring at her reflection in the mirror. Sapphire Whittaker looked back at her, eyes wide and deep blue, a new wisdom in their gaze. She nodded at herself and headed into the bedroom. It was lit with candles again and fresh flowers were on the dresser, giving off the scent of lavender and rose. Sapphire slipped off her flip-flops and lay on top of the bedcovers; she placed her hands on her stomach and smoothed down her pretty summer dress. She breathed in deeply and closed her eyes.

In her mind she reached out for Fox and his world; she felt her energy shift as she focused on the silver cord that connected them. Her body felt heavy and warm; she was safe and happy. The obsidian necklace pulsed warmly between her breasts as she called to him. A warm breeze caressed her body and she felt her body start to rise upwards; Fox was smiling at her, his eyes flashing amber and gold. Sapphire sighed softly and smiled. The air around her shifted and rippled with power and just like that she crossed over, leaving her world and the life she had known for a new beginning. A new life.

Epilogue

Friday

Charlie lay in bed and reached out for Nathan, who was asleep next to her. It was daylight and she had woken up suddenly from a weird dream. She had dreamt that she was at a wedding, standing in lush gardens surrounded by trellises covered in ivy and white roses. Sapphire was standing with Fox on a stage covered with willow and honeysuckle. They were dressed in white finery, smiling at each other. It was their wedding. She smiled and stretched. What a lovely dream; she hoped it came true. Pushing herself up, Charlie scratched her head and yawned sleepily. Nathan snored softly beside her. She needed to pee. Heading out of his bedroom, she padded silently across the hallway to the bathroom. She was looking forward to some serious shopping today and wondered if Sapphire would join her. It had been really nice to spend time with her at Pearl's last night; the old lady might be bat shit crazy but she was actually really sweet.

Finishing her business in the bathroom, she headed downstairs to make some coffee and have her morning roll-up. She grabbed her bag and flipped the kettle on. She sat at the kitchen table and pulled her bag up on to her lap, rummaging inside for her tobacco pouch. She frowned as she touched something in the bottom and pulled it out. She held a manila-coloured envelope which had her name written on it in Sapphire's neat handwriting. Intrigued, she opened the envelope to find a letter. She opened it slowly.

"My Dearest Charlie,

First things first, my friend. Don't be pissed at me, but some of the things I have told you are not completely true. You have been the best friend a girl could ever have and you changed my life for the better when you invited me into your home. For that I am truly grateful. There are so many things I would like to tell you right now,

306

but it isn't the right time. I am going away now for quite some time; I am not sure when or if I will be back, but know this. I am safe and I am happy. Fox is taking care of me and I am the happiest I have ever been. I love him, Charlie, with all my heart. He is my life now and we are going to travel to places together that you could never even begin to imagine.

Don't worry about me; I will be fine. Enjoy your new home with Nathan; I know it will be full of fun and happiness. You are truly the most special person I have ever known. I have enclosed a cheque which I want you to have to give you all the things you deserve. Make sure you get yourself some new vintage gear and that holiday you have been thinking about. My father left me money when he died so really, don't stress hon; I have plenty.

I love you, Charlie, my best friend – the person who always pushed me to be more and feel more of this wonderful life. I'm not saying goodbye, honestly, I'm just saying, "See you later".

Have fun. All my love, always, Sapphire xxxx"

Charlie stared at the letter. Her mouth was open slightly. She looked inside the envelope again and found a cheque folded in half; she opened it and gasped, her hand flying to her chest. The kettle pinged off as it boiled.

The cheque was written out to Miss Charlotte Daines to the sum of two hundred and fifty thousand pounds and fifty-four pence. Charlie dropped her bag and stood up. She shouted up the stairs at the top of her lungs "Nathan. Get the fuck up. We are going shopping."

6891452R00173

Printed in Great Britain
by Amazon.co.uk, Ltd.,
Marston Gate.